Squatting behind the sights of his twin-type rocket launcher, the blackcollar permitted himself a moment of mild regret. It had been so long in coming, this last act of defiance, and he wished he could see it through to the end.

The patrol boats were settling into position, hovering on gravs as they sought the rioters. He waited until they were nearly stationary and then gently squeezed the trigger grip. The result was all he could have hoped for.

A blue-white sun burst dead center on one of the boats, which yawed wildly in dying reflex before plummeting to the ground. A second craft, maneuvering frantically to avoid its flaming companion, backed directly into the path of the second missile. A third patrol boat swung dangerously near the ground. . . .

TIMOTHY ZAHN received a B.S. in physics from Michigan State in 1973, and an M.S. from the University of Illinois two years later. He worked summers at the Fermilab, and continued full-time towards a doctorate at Illinois. After the death of his advisor while his thesis project was halfway through, Tim decided not to go back to starting a new project, but to try his hand at full-time writing. With his first sale to *Analog* in 1979, he has been selling short stories and novelettes steadily since then. *The Blackcollar* is his first novel.

THE BLACKCOLLAR

Timothy Zahn

DAW BOOKS, INC.
DONALD A. WOLLHEIM, PUBLISHER
1633 Broadway, New York, NY 10019

Cover art by Vincent DiFate.

FIRST PRINTING, JULY 1983

1 2 3 4 5 6 7 8 9

DAW TRADEMARK REGISTERED
U.S. PAT. OFF. MARCA
REGISTRADA. HECHO EN U.S.A.

PRINTED IN U. S. A.

CHAPTER 1

Blazing down from a clear blue sky, the mid-morning sun seemed to be making only token effort to drive away the cold snap that had interrupted spring for most of central Europe. Tightening his collar against the northerly wind blowing off Lake Geneva, Allen Caine picked up his pace a bit. It would have been nice to ride at least part of the way, but only the uninformed waited for autocabs in eastern New Geneva on Victory Day. Most of the vehicles had been preempted early in the day to take government officials to the stadium for the annual rally celebrating the end of the Terran-Ryqril war. Caine had half expected the cold to keep participation to a minimum—loyalty-conditioning didn't extend to anything as trivial as rallys—but there would be several Ryqril there and New Geneva's officials clearly knew which side of their bread should stay off the carpet. Already Caine had heard the muffled roars of two cheers, and he was a good three kilometers from the stadium. An amazingly unashamed display of hyprocrisy, he thought bitterly; and at this, the twenty-ninth year of such pageantry, one of the longest lived. A visiting stranger would have concluded the Terran Democratic Empire had *won* the war.

The streets at this end of town were bustling with business as usual—the common people treated Victory Day with sullen indifference—and Caine had no trouble blending into the throng. He'd only come to New Geneva two weeks ago—a slightly late twenty-sixth birthday present, he considered the trip—but already he felt like a native. Like every other group of people on Earth, this one had its own characteristic gestures and mannerisms, the learning of which had been Caine's most recent task. Combined with his clean-cut appearance, such preparation would permit him to pass, if necessary, as a student, a rising young executive, or—if he trimmed his beard in the proper fashion—a member of one of the city's semiprofessional guilds. Of course, it wasn't really a question of whether or not he could pass muster on this side of the city, but since he wouldn't be crossing to the government end for some weeks yet, he wasn't especially worried. Presumably he'd be prepared for that by then.

His clothes were a bit on the thin side, but Caine arrived at his destination before he was too badly chilled. Sandwiched between two bars in a lower-middle-class part of town was a small tape-and-book store with faded volumes of Dickens and Heinlein in the front window. Entering, Caine stood just inside the door a moment, letting his eyes adjust to the relative darkness. A few meters away, lounging by his cash register, the store's proprietor eyed him. "Getting any warmer out there?" he asked.

"Not really," Caine replied, glancing around the store. Three or four other men were browsing among the shelves. Looking back at the owner, he raised his eyebrows. The other gave a fractional nod and Caine moved off down one of the two aisles, pretending to study the titles as he did so. Taking his time, he worked his way to the back. There, half hidden behind a wide shelf, was a door with a faded "Employees Only" sign taped to it. Waiting until all the customers were facing away from him, Caine slipped silently through the door and into the cluttered stockroom beyond. He squatted down in the middle of the old tile floor and gave a gentle push on one of the tiles. Clearly, he was expected; the two-meter square of concrete floor pivoted open without resistance. He stepped into the pit, his feet finding the wooden stairs there. Crouching down, he let the concrete block rotate shut above him; and as he did so a metal bar slid sliently across its underside, locking the trap door in place. Turning, Caine headed down the dimly lit stairway.

A short hallway awaited him at the bottom of the stairs; and at the end of the hall was a door. Opening it, Caine stepped through into a dark room. The door closed itself behind him.

And abruptly a blinding light flashed on. He threw an arm up to protect his eyes and took an involuntary step backward. "Who are you?" a voice demanded.

Caine's response was immediate. "I'm Alain Rienzi,

aide to Senator Auriol," he snapped. "Get that damn light out of my face!"

The spotlight winked out and other, more muted lights came on. Through the purple blob floating before his eyes Caine could dimly see three men and a woman seated around a low table. "Excellent," one of the men said, fiddling with a shoebox-sized gadget. "No hesitation, no recognizable 'liar's stress,' and just the right amount of arrogance. He's ready, Morris."

Another man nodded and gestured to Caine. "Sit down, Allen," he said in a gravelly voice.

Caine took the indicated chair and looked around at the others, and as his eyes recovered, his heart began to beat faster. This was no routine meeting; the four people facing him were probably the top Resistance leaders in all of Europe. The man with the box was Bruno Hurlimann, a former captain in the Terran Star Force; the second man was Raul Marinos, who'd been planning and executing sabotage operations against the government and even the Ryqril's own military bases for most of the past twenty-nine years; the woman was Jayne Gibbs, a former member of the long-since dissolved Parliament; and "Morris" was General Morris Kratochvil himself, the last commander of Earth's final defense efforts. None of them looked their proper ages, of course; despite government controls, enough bootlegged Idunine was getting to the Resistance via the black market to keep even the ninety-two-year-old Kratochvil at the biological equivalent of forty. Caine had met all four of them at one time or another, but he'd never seen them together in one place. Something important must be happening.

General Kratochvil might have been reading Caine's mind. "I'm afraid your orientation has come to an abrupt end, Allen," he said. "We're moving things up drastically. All the cards have unexpectedly fallen into place, and you're going to be leaving for Plinry in just under twenty hours."

Caine's mouth felt a little dry. "I thought I was going to have to replace Alain Rienzi first for a few weeks."

"So did we," the general said, "but it turns out that's not going to be necessary. Rienzi left yesterday on a private vacation and doesn't seem to have told anyone where he was going. It was the perfect opportunity, and we decided to take it."

So much for the rest of his training . . . but if he wasn't going to be spending much time with government people he could probably get by without it. "You've got Rienzi tucked away?"

Marinos nodded. "Picked him up this morning. No problems." He gestured to an envelope on the table. "There's his ID—suitably altered, of course—and the rest of your stuff."

Caine picked up the package, careful not to bump the mushroom-shaped "bug stomper" which sat in the table's center, electronically blanking out any nearby monitoring devices. Opening the envelope, he withdrew a blue ID, a wallet containing both government and personal credit plates and several hundred marks in crisp TDE banknotes, and an unconfirmed ticket for the distant world of Plinry. "The ticket is basically just a reservation," Marinos explained. "You'll need to have your ID checked at the 'port before you can board."

The face on the ID was long and a bit thin, framed by a carefully coiffured mass of brown hair—a clean-shaven replica of Caine's own. But there were also a set of thumbprints and retinal patterns sealed under the supposedly tamper-proof plastic—and those patterns were duplicated in a heavily guarded computer system not ten kilometers away. "You're sure my prints and patterns have made it into the government's records?" he asked Marinos.

"It's all been taken care of," the other said, his offhand tone belying the difficulty of what must have been one hell of a job. Broaching Ryqril security was no joke.

"We don't yet have authorization for you to examine the Plinry archives," Kratochvil said, "but it'll be here by six this evening. If you're lucky all you'll have to do is walk in, spin your yarn about a book, pull the proper record, and cut out." He gave Caine a tight smile. "In practice it's never that easy, of course. But I expect you'll be able to handle most problems they throw at you."

Caine nodded. Though he'd never been on any actual missions, he'd had the best combat and psycho-mental training the Resistance could offer. "What's the latest military situation, and how is it likely to affect conditions on Plinry? The Ryqril will probably have a base there, right?"

"We expect so, but it shouldn't bother you any." Kratochvil turned to Hurlimann. "Captain?"

"The reports of a big Ryqril victory over the Chryselli near Regulus appear to be true," Hurlimann said, his manner reminding Caine of a college lecturer. "However, it seems to have cost more than they admit. Already they've pulled two Elephant-class troop carriers and a full wing of Corsairs from various bases on Earth and sent them off, presumably to the Chryselli front. If there's a base on Plinry the same sort of mobilization may be going on there. But that shouldn't be a problem; as long as you've got the proper papers any extra confusion will be to your advantage." He smiled. "And for our purposes, the more the Ryqril are tied up in Chryselli territory, the better."

"As I said, the cards are falling right," Kratochvil said. "By the time you get back with the information we hope to have crews ready to leave." He glanced around at the others. "Was there anything else?"

"Assistance on Plinry," Jayne Gibbs murmured.

"Oh, yes. Allen, we haven't had any contact with Plinry since it was captured thirty-five years ago, so we don't know what you're going to be walking into. We expect a political structure like Earth's—a group of Ryqril ruling through a loyalty-conditioned human government—but we have no way of confirming that. If you have any problems you should try to contact whatever underground has been put together there and enlist their aid."

"Assuming there *is* one," Caine pointed out.

"True," Kratochvil admitted. "Still, I have hopes that General Avril Lepkowski survived the planet's capture. Mark that name, Allen; if Plinry has an underground, Lepkowski will probably be the man in charge of it. There were also nearly three hundred blackcollars there at the end—some of them may also still be alive."

Blackcollars. Caine straightened a bit at the word. He'd never met any of those superbly trained guerrilla warriors, but their wartime exploits were legendary. Only a few still existed on Earth, and most of those had destroyed their uniforms and disappeared into the general population. The handful who remained in active service were reportedly harassing the hell out of the Ryqril in North America.

Kratochvil was still speaking. "I'll try to get a few more names of people who may be on Plinry before tonight. I'll also make up a micro-letter of introduction for you in case you find General Lepkowski. It'll be a bit risky to carry, I'm afraid, but I think it'll be worth having. Of course, that decision's up to you." He stood up, Caine and the others following suit. "I think that's all we can do right now. Be here at six tonight for the rest of your papers and any final instructions we can think up. You might as well keep the beard until then; it's unlikely you'll run into any of Rienzi's acquaintances out here but there's no point in taking chances. Also, starting at noon today we'll be on a two-hour security cycle in the bookstore upstairs. Watch for that."

"I understand."

"Good." The general reached over the table and grasped Caine's hand. "I may not be here tonight when you arrive, so I'll say my farewells now. You're very valuable to us, Allen, and of course we want you to be careful and protect yourself. But at the same time, this is probably the most important mission we've undertaken in twenty years, and I'm not exaggerating when I say that any chances for a free Earth depend on you. We may never again be able to send a person off-planet on this kind of quiet probe, and you know the impossibility of getting the information by force. Don't let us down."

Caine looked the general straight in the eye as he shook the other's hand. Kratochvil's brown eyes were clear, alert, and—thanks to Idunine—relatively young. But there was something else there, too, something no youth drug could touch. Ninety-two years of life, thirteen of them spent in a losing war and another twenty-nine endured under enemy rule, had aged those eyes in a way that suddenly made Caine feel like a child again, and the confident statement he'd been about to make evaporated from his lips. "I'll do my best, sir," he murmured instead.

It was five to six as Caine, buffeted by the usual throngs of homeward-bound workers, once again approached the bookstore. The Victory Day festivities had long since ended, and the streets were once again buzzing with autocabs and the occasional private car. The pedestrian traffic wouldn't clear out for at least another hour, he knew; plenty of time to slip in, get his remaining papers, and still have a crowd to lose himself in when he left.

He was almost there, and was starting to work his way through the press so he could cross the street, when something in the window froze the breath in his lungs. With a two-hour cycle, the window display would have changed three times since his morning visit. By now the Heinlein should have been rotated ninety degrees and a tape cassette should be resting against the Dickens. But the cassette wasn't there; the display was still in its two o'clock position. *Someone forgot,* was his first hopeful thought; but it emerged stillborn. There was only one explanation, and he knew it.

Sometime in the past four hours, the bookstore had been raided.

The possibility of such a thing had always been there, of course, but it had never before happened this close to him and the shock was numbing. In the absence of conscious control his training took over, walking him past the bookstore without any visible hesitation, and by the time his brain began to clear he was two blocks away and safe.

Safe. But for how long? If the government had been watching the bookstore they knew he'd been there four times in the past two weeks. Even if they didn't yet attach any significance to that they would eventually find out about him. Surely at least one of the four Resistance leaders had been there when the Security forces came, and was probably even now undergoing verifin or neurotrace interrogation. Caine had to escape . . . but to where? The Resistance had established numerous boltholes, but none of them could be trusted now. Kratochvil and the others had had the best psychor training available, but even that wouldn't hold against a neurotrace reader for very long. Eventually, they would break . . . and when they did the government would be able to hunt him down anywhere on Earth.

It took a second for that to sink in; and as it did so Caine became aware of the thick packet in his inside coat pocket. Rienzi's ID, a small supply of money . . . and a round-trip ticket to Plinry. Clearly, if Kratochvil had been captured, the Resistance in this area was probably doomed—but that didn't necessarily mean his mission was. If he could enlist the aid of General Lepkowski and the Plinry underground, there was still a slight chance of pulling this off. Slight, hell—microscopic. But what other choices were left? And if it fell apart anyway, he would at least have the minor satisfaction of making the Ryqril chase him down over eight parsecs of space.

It took him just under an hour to return to his apartment, shave off his beard, change his clothes, and destroy all documents pertaining to Allen Caine. Then, carrying the more expensive luggage suitable to a minor government official, he took an autocab to the western end of the city. Rienzi's ID got him through the fence with no trouble, and for the first time in his life Caine entered New Geneva's government sector.

The first hurdle—the guard at the gate—had been passed; but now Caine faced an unexpected problem. He had eleven hours till his ship's six a.m. liftoff—far too long to spend at the 'port. But if he checked in at a hotel, he would have to show Rienzi's ID, and the less he waved that around the better.

The solution was obvious. Redirecting his autocab, he went to the 'port and dropped his luggage into a locker. Then, using the cash Rienzi had so thoughtfully provided, he launched himself on a one-man tour of western New Geneva. Between the bars, restaurants, and pleasure spas, he got through the night without being recognized. Finally, as the first hint of dawn touched the eastern sky, he returned to the 'port.

Even at that hour the 'port was reasonably busy. New Geneva hadn't been made Earth's capital until after the war and the field had been designed to handle passenger air traffic as well as spacecraft. In pre-war days such an arrangement would have swamped the 'port beyond hope; but now, with only government officials and accredited business personnel allowed to fly, the setup was manageable. Retrieving his luggage, Caine headed down a long corridor toward the off-planet terminal, his heart pounding painfully.

The check-in station was visible now, and he could see a half-dozen people milling around or waiting quietly in the chairs near the boarding gate. Off to one side a bored-looking guard leaned against a wall. Caine grimaced. The whole thing looked like a classic sucker-trap, where everyone within two hundred meters was a plainclothes Security man. But it was too late to back out. If it *was* a trap, he'd certainly already been spotted and identified, and turning tail now would only spring it a bit prematurely. Clenching his teeth, he kept walking.

The clerk smiled as he approached. "Yes, sir?"

"Alain Rienzi, traveling to Plinry," Caine said through stiff lips. He fished out his ticket/reservation and Rienzi's ID, watching the clerk's face as closely as he dared.

There was no visible reaction. "Yes, sir," the other said, sliding the ID through a slot on his console. "If you'll just put your thumbs against the plates and look over here. . . ."

This was it. Unlike the simple visual check the Security man at the outer fence had done a few hours earlier, Caine was now in for the complete thing. His retina patterns and thumbprints would be compared to those on Rienzi's ID, and also checked against the main computer records. If Marinos hadn't performed the miracle of changing those files, it was all going to end right here.

A flicker of light, almost too fast to see, touched his eyes and the plates felt warm against his thumbs. The clerk touched a button and Caine held his breath . . . and on the console a green light winked on. "All set, Mr. Rienzi. Now, which account is this to be charged to?"

It was an anticlimax, though a welcome one, and Caine began to breathe again. Keeping his expression neutral, he handed over Rienzi's personal charge plate. The clerk inserted it in another slot, and in a few seconds the machine disgorged an official ticket, his ID and charge plate, and a small magnecoded card. "What's this?" Caine asked, frowning at the letter.

"Medical form, sir," the clerk told him. "Apparently there's something in Plinry's environment that may give you some trouble. You can have the prescription filled at that window over there."

Caine was about to ask how in hell anyone knew what kind of pills he might need on Plinry, but caught himself in time. Clearly, government personnel had their medical records on file, and the computer must have compared Rienzi's profile to Plinry's conditions and made a fast diagnosis. "Okay," he said. "Thanks."

"You're welcome, sir. Boarding will begin in ten minutes."

It took nearly fifteen for the druggist to fill the prescription, and so Caine was able to go immediately from there into the boarding tunnel, bypassing the bored guard who would probably never know how close he'd come to a promotion. The little vial of pills rattled uncomfortably in his pocket and Caine wondered what he should do with them. It was unlikely that his own medical quirks were close enough to Rienzi's for the drug to be worth anything to him. On the other hand, it was conceivable that Marinos had replaced *all* of Rienzi's records—in which case the pills might be all that would keep him alive on Plinry. He would just have to hang onto them and hope that whatever it was wouldn't kill him without lots of obvious symptoms first.

Disease, however, was likely to be the least of his troubles. So far his attention had been concentrated on getting out of New Geneva and onto a spaceship before the Resistance came apart like a house of cards. Now, with that much nearly accomplished, he was able to focus on the staggering problems still facing him. Without the forged authorization papers Kratochvil had planned to give him, it was unlikely the government officials on Plinry would let him near the records he needed. And without a letter of introduction it could be equally difficult to get any cooperation from Plinry's underground. His only hope lay in the chance that General Lepkowski was indeed in charge of the underground. If he could convince Lepkowski he was a colleague of Kratochvil's, he might get some help. And once he got the information . . . Caine shook his head to clear it. There was no point in looking that far ahead; there were too many impossibles facing him as it was. He was just going to have to take things one at a time.

He emerged from the boarding tunnel onto the pad where the passenger ship—a converted pre-war freighter, from its appearance—was waiting. Shifting his grip on his suitcases, he paused and looked around him. The pad was built up from ground level, and large parts of the city, the lake, and the surrounding mountains could be seen. But even as Caine glanced around at the scenery, his eyes turned almost magnetically to the southwest. There, seven kilometers away, was the blackened region where old Geneva had been. Caine shuddered, once, and headed again for the ship.

The Ryqril, he knew, played this game to win.

CHAPTER 2

First contact had occurred in early 2370 when a TDE exploration ship stumbled on a Ryqril outpost some two parsecs from the Terran colony world Llano. Within ten years there was regular communication between humans and the tall, leathery-skinned bipeds, and various trade agreements were being planned. The Ryqril seemed strangely reticent in matters concerning themselves or details of their empire, but this was generally chalked up to normal shyness; and the rumors that the aliens were fighting a war of conquest on their far frontier were never checked out.

Forty years later, the situation abruptly changed. Efforts at "normalization of relations" between the two races—efforts the Ryqril had been dragging their paws on—were suddenly abandoned, and new intelligence probes finally uncovered the truth. The Ryqril had indeed been fighting a war, and had won it nearly twenty years previously. All indications were that their post-war rearmament was nearly complete, and that their next target was to be the Terran Democratic Empire.

Preparations were started immediately, but it was largely an exercise in futility. The TDE controlled twenty-eight planets; the Ryqril one hundred forty. Nevertheless, there was no question but that the TDE would go down fighting.

And fight it did. Eight years passed from the revelation of its sitting-duck status to the outbreak of all-out war, and in that period mankind designed, built, and tested an impressive array of new weaponry; everything from handguns to huge Supernova-class warships. Though it had never fought with an alien race, the TDE had had enough internal squabbles in its history to have learned something of space warfare, and countless pre-war skirmishes with the Ryqril gave human forces the chance to hone their skills. But the situation was still hopeless, and in its desperation mankind was forced to rethink accepted military theory, including such basic concepts as what exactly defined a weapon.

The blackcollars were the result.

Caine had always been interested in the blackcollars, but there had been little information available to non-government citizens on Earth. Now, locked for ten days into a spaceship with a good collection of history tapes, he had the time to satisfy his curiosity.

The tapes were a disappointment, however, telling him little he didn't already know. The blackcollar program, he was informed, had begun in 2416, two years before the war, and had continued up until Earth's surrender. Besides the heavy combat training, which was strongly rooted in the ancient Oriental martial arts, blackcollars received a version of the same psychor mental conditioning Caine himself had had. Strangely enough—or so he thought at first—the tapes made no mention of the various drugs used in the training, which he understood had been the crux of the project. At least three had been used: ordinary Idunine, which in small quantities kept muscles, bones, and joints youthful while allowing the warrior's appearance to age normally; an RNA derivative to aid memory development, enabling training time to be cut drastically, and a special drug code-named "Backlash" which was reputed to double a blackcollar's speed and reflexes. The result was a soldier who could fit into any crowd, who could not be identified except by a complete physical and biochemical exam, and who could theoretically even hold his own in an unarmed fight with a Ryq. Dangerous opponents . . . and perhaps, Caine decided, that was why the tapes were incomplete. The information was clearly aimed at the lower-ranking government members, and the upper echelons had apparently decided to play down any danger the surviving blackcollars might pose. The conclusion was not a heartening one: if the blackcollars were still considered a threat, it was likely that any still left on Plinry would be so well hidden he might never find them.

Caine was the only passenger getting off at Plinry, which turned out to be the third stop of a seven-planet loop. But Plinry was a fueling 'port, and so Caine was spared the experience of a shuttle landing. Instead, he remained strapped down in his cabin while ship gravity was slowly withdrawn and replaced by the genuine thing. Finally, with little more than a gentle bump, the liner was down.

It took only a few minutes for Caine to make his way to the exit ramp, where the captain and cabin attendant were waiting to see him off. Perfunctory good-byes were said; and then Caine was walking down the ramp, eyes darting in an effort to see everything at once.

He was at one end of a large glazed-surface field, clearly designed for a great deal of traffic. Off to his right were a half dozen spaceships, most of them medium-sized freighter types, and a few official-looking VTOL aircraft. To his left, farther away and separated from the rest of the 'port by a wire-mesh fence, was a sight that made his stomach turn. Squatting in neat rows were at least thirty Corsairs, the long-range scout/fighters that formed the shock front of the Ryqril war machine. At one to three crew and four support personnel per craft, that meant the aliens had a garrison of two hundred in this one part of Plinry alone. A hundred meters past the Corsairs was another fence, a sturdier-looking one, which encircled the entire 'port, forming a barrier between the glaze-surface and the sparsely wooded grassland beyond. Directly ahead of him was a complex of several buildings, clearly the 'port's administrative and maintenance center. One of the buildings appeared to be a hangar; another—near the Corsairs—looked like a barracks.

And waiting at the foot of the ramp were two men in gray-green uniforms.

Caine's heart skipped a beat, but he continued down without pausing. A Corsair could have made the trip from Earth in a little over four days, he knew, and if the government had succeeded in breaking the Resistance leaders quickly enough all of Plinry could know about him by now. But once again there was nothing to do but keep walking.

The taller of the two men took a step forward as Caine approached. "Mr. Rienzi?" he asked. When Caine nodded, he went on, "I'm Prefect Jamus Galway, head of Planetary Security; this is Officer Ragusin, my aide. Welcome to Plinry, sir."

"Thank you. Do you always come out to the 'port to greet tourists?"

Galway gave a smile that was well on its way to becoming a simper, and that smile told Caine more than anything the prefect could have said. It was not the kind of smile given by a Security head to a suspected rebel, but rather the kind given by a rank-conscious politician to an official whose influence was likely greater than his own. Caine's cover was still intact.

"Actually, Mr. Rienzi," Galway said, "I *do* make a practice of welcoming first-time visitors and explaining some of the services we have here. It saves time for everyone involved." He gestured toward the buildings. "If you're ready, I'll escort you through customs. After that, perhaps you'll ride into Capstone with us for a routine identity check."

Caine nodded easily. He'd passed Earth's scrutiny without trouble; Plinry's wasn't likely to be more thorough. "Certainly, Prefect. Lead on."

The customs check was little more than a formality. Besides his clothing, Caine had brought only a pocket videocorder, a few spare cassettes, and the pills he'd been given at the New Geneva 'port. Everything was quickly cleared, and minutes later Caine and Galway were riding in the back seat of a Security patrol car toward the city of Capstone. Ragusin, who seemed to be the strong silent type, was driving.

Preoccupied with other matters, Caine hadn't yet paid any attention to the planet itself, and as he gazed out the window he was surprised by both the differences from and the similarities to his own world. As on Earth, the predominant color of vegetation was green; but Plinry's green was shaded more toward blue, and there were also an unusual number of plants that favored yellow, purple, and even orange. The smaller, ground-hugging flora was impossible to see clearly from a moving car, but looked too broad-leaved to be grass; the trees and shrubbery, in contrast, tended to look like tan stag horns liberally draped with Spanish moss. Winging their way among the trees were several small creatures which looked too streamlined to be birds. "Nice planet you have here," Caine commented. "Very colorful."

Galway nodded. "It wasn't always that way. When I was a boy most of the plants were shades of green and blue. The more wildly colored ones didn't show up until after the war—mutations from something in the Ryqril Groundfire attack, I'm told. Most of them will probably die out eventually."

Caine turned back to his window, a shiver running up his back. There had been no regret or hostility in Galway's voice as he spoke of the Ryqril's devastation of his world. As if he were on their side . . . which he was, of course. No one worked in the TDE government without first undergoing loyalty-conditioning. Whether the conditioning actually changed the subject's attitudes or merely rendered them powerless was an open question among the uninitiated, but the basic fact remained: in neither word nor action could a conditioned person go against the authority of the Ryqril. They couldn't be blackmailed or bribed—only outsmarted or outgunned. And Caine didn't have any guns.

They were into the outer parts of the city now, a region which seemed to be middle class or a bit higher. Residential and business districts were mixed together indiscriminately, unlike the pattern Caine had often seen on Earth, and he asked about it.

"Vehicles are fairly rare on Plinry," Galway explained. "Even the more well-off among the common people need to live within walking distance of their work and shops. Actually, out here in the newer areas home and work are relatively well separated. Farther in, in the poorer parts of the city, people often live and work in the same building. Of course, things are different in the Hub. We have a fair number of autocabs, so you should have no problem getting around."

"The Hub, I take it, is the government center?"

"Yes, and most government families live there, as well." He pointed out the front of the car. "You can see some of the main buildings from here."

The structures were no more than a few kilometers away, Caine estimated, which made the tallest only a dozen or so stories high. Not exactly skyscraper class, but they still towered over the two- and three-floor buildings Caine could see around him. Capstone, it appeared, was a very flat town.

As Galway had indicated, the city was becoming progressively more lower class as they traveled inward. Houses became scarcer as nearly all business buildings included a floor or two of apartments. There were more people on the walkways than had been visible farther out, too, and they looked shabbier. It was hard to read expressions at the speed they were making, but Caine thought he saw unfriendliness and even hostility in the occasional glances sent at the Security car. That was a good sign—if the people had come to respect the government his chances of finding a useful underground would have been negligible.

The car turned a corner, and a block ahead Caine saw a gray wall cutting across their path. A metal-mesh gate sat across the road, flanked by two guards in the same gray-green uniforms Galway and the driver were wearing. One of them approached the car as it rolled to a stop. "IDs, gentlemen?" he said briskly.

All three, including Galway, handed over their cards. After a quick perusal he returned them and gestured to a third guard behind the mesh, who promptly disappeared behind the wall to his left. The gate slid open, closing again once the car had passed through. "New recruit?" Caine asked, nodding back toward the gate.

"Not at all," Galway answered. "Our security checks are done by the book here." There was a touch of pride in his voice.

It was only a short drive to the five-story building labeled *Plinry Department of Planetary Security*. Galway and Caine got out at the main entrance and went inside, leaving Caine's luggage in the car with Ragusin. Two floors up they entered a small room equipped with two chairs, a table and phone, and a device Caine remembered from the New Geneva 'port. "If I may have your ID, Mr. Rienzi . . . thank you. Would you please sit here and put your thumbs on the plate?"

Again the brief flicker of light touched Caine's eyes.

Galway tapped a switch and nodded at Caine. "You can relax now, sir. I'm afraid it'll be another few minutes—one of the city's computers broke down yesterday and the other two are under a heavy load." He remained standing by the machine, as if his presence might encourage the computer to work faster.

"No problem," Caine said easily. "No reason why routine security checks should have a high priority."

Galway seemed to relax a bit. "I'm glad you understand. Tell me, are you staying on Plinry long?"

"Just ten days, until the next flight heading back to Earth. I have to get back to work then."

"Ah, yes—the captain radioed that you were from the Senate. Aide to Senator Auriand, or something equally important."

"Auriol," Caine corrected automatically. "Yes, I'm one of his aides. It's really a minor post, but Dad thought this would be a good way to get some experience in politics."

"Your father's in government work too?"

"Yes. In fact, he's been in politics since the end of the war. Started out as Councilor in Milan and is now Third Minister for Education."

"So you were prepared at an early age, I gather?"

Prepared—a euphemism for *loyalty-conditioned.* The conversation was taking an uncomfortable direction. "When I was five," he replied curtly, dropping the temperature in his tone a few degrees. A senatorial aide shouldn't have to put up with questions like that.

Galway got the message and back-pedaled rapidly. "I'm sorry, Mr. Rienzi—I didn't mean to get personal. I was just curious." He stopped abruptly, and Caine could almost hear him casting around for a safer topic of conversation. "Are you here on business or just for a vacation?"

This was safer territory for Caine, too. "Both, actually. I'm here on my own time and charge plate, but I'm going to be working, too." He paused, radiating a combination of shyness and pride. "I'm going to write a book."

Galway's eyebrows arched in polite surprise. "Really! About Plinry?"

"About the war, actually. I know a lot of books have been written, but most of them focus on Earth or the Centauri worlds. I want to write one from the point of view of people in the more distant parts of the TDE. Since Plinry was a sector capital and major military base, I figure it should have all the background records I'll need."

"Our archives are quite extensive," Galway nodded. "I trust you have the proper authorization papers?"

Here was where the bite of the government's eleventh-hour raid was going to catch up with him, Caine knew. "What, you need permission to write books here?" he said, smiling.

"Oh, no—I meant your permit to look in the records. You've got that, don't you?"

Caine let his grin vanish. "What permit is this?"

Galway frowned in turn. "The standard TDE Record Search form. You need one any time you want to look at official documents."

"Damn! Nobody told me I'd need anything like that here." Caine let indignation slip into the embarrassed anger in his voice. "Hell. Look, I'm a member of the TDE government, and nothing I want to see is classified. Can I maybe look at them with a guard watching over my shoulder?"

Galway shrugged. "You can ask at the Records Building, but I don't think they'll let you. Sorry."

"Damn." Caine glowered at the floor for a moment, then looked up at the verification machine. "Isn't that damn computer done yet?" he muttered irritably.

"I'll see if I can hurry it up." Galway touched a switch; seconds later a green light came on and Rienzi's ID appeared. "Ah. All set," he said, handing back the card.

Such convenient timing, Caine thought. He doubted it was coincidence, but had no intention of challenging Galway on it. Belatedly, he was beginning to wonder if the prefect really was the eager-to-please lightweight he seemed. Fortunately, grinning idiocy was a game for any number of players. If Galway had, in fact, deliberately kept the verification machine from finishing its job Caine had every right to be angry; but it would be more to his advantage to let the prefect think he was stupid. So he took the card without comment and stood up. "Is that all?"

"Yes. I'll get you an information packet on the way out. It lists restaurants and entertainment, gives autocab and air travel information, maps of the city and surrounding area—that sort of thing." He hesitated. "I'm sorry, but I won't be able to offer you a full-time guide. I'm afraid we're a little short-handed."

"That's okay," Caine said magnanimously. The last thing he wanted was an official baby-sitter. "Doesn't look like I'll have much use for one, anyway."

"What are you going to do?" Galway asked as they left the room and walked down the hallway toward the elevators.

Caine spoke slowly, as if he hadn't already thought it all out. "I hate for the trip to be a complete waste—you wouldn't believe what the ticket cost. Maybe I can talk to some of the people in Capstone who lived through the war. I wasn't going to do that until I had the background researched, but. . . ." He shrugged, then frowned. "I seem to remember that there was some hotshot general or admiral on Plinry when the war ended, but I don't recall his name. You know who I mean?"

Galway frowned back. "Umm. Maybe you mean General Lepkowski? He was in command of this sector when it fell."

"Could be. I remember thinking the name was Vladimirian sounding."

"Seems to me Lepkowski *was* from Vladimir, come to think of it. But I'm afraid you're out of luck again—he died during the war."

Caine's stomach knotted. "You sure?" he asked as casually as possible.

"Yes. He was caught in his command center when the Groundfire attack demolished it, or so the story goes." Galway paused, as if thinking. "I don't know anyone else off hand who might have the kind of information you're looking for. A lot of people here lived through the war—I did, myself—but none of them knew much about the big picture."

"Well, maybe I'll look some of them up anyway." For the first time Caine noticed a slight tightness in his chest and a faint rasping in his voice. "I should be able to get *something* out of it—the little guy's point of view, maybe."

"What's wrong with your voice?" Galway asked abruptly. His hand, which had been reaching for the elevator call button, moved instead to a supportive grip on Caine's arm, and he frowned into the other's face.

"I don't know." The rasp was getting louder, and the first stabs of pain were beginning to intrude on Caine's breathing.

"I do." Still holding Caine's arm, the prefect half led, half dragged him to a refreshment station at the end of the corridor. With one hand he dialed for a cup of water; with the other he deftly reached into Caine's jacket pocket and pulled out the vial of pills. Handing Caine the water, he glanced at the vial's label and tapped two of the capsules into his hand. "Take these," he ordered.

Caine did so. He very much wanted to sit down, but there were no chairs or benches in the hallway and Galway didn't seem inclined to help him into one of the nearby offices. Fortunately, though, the medicine worked fast, and within a few minutes he was able to let go of Galway's arm. "I'm okay now," he nodded, taking an experimental breath. The pain was gone, the rasping nearly so. "Thanks."

"My pleasure." He handed Caine the vial. "I'd assumed you'd taken your medicine before landing, or I would've had you do it when you went through customs. I presume you'll be less forgetful in the future."

"You bet," Caine assured him. "What the hell *was* that, anyway?"

"Tormatyse asthma. Affects about three percent of the offworlders that come here. It's caused by something in the air—I'm not sure what—but it's pretty harmless as long as you take a daily dose of histrophyne. You feel ready to travel yet?"

"Sure."

Galway led the way back to the elevators, and minutes later Caine was standing by the building's main entrance, a thick packet in his hand. "Your luggage should already be in your hotel room," Galway told him. "We only have one guest hotel in the Hub—the Coronet—so I took the liberty of sending your things there."

"Fine." They'd no doubt searched his things en route, but there wasn't anything incriminating for them to find. As far as Caine was concerned, the sooner Security came to the conclusion that Alain Rienzi was an honest—if not overly bright—member of the government, the better.

"Thanks for all your help, Prefect. I expect I'll be seeing you again."

Galway smiled. "Very likely. Enjoy your stay, Mr. Rienzi."

The Coronet, while probably run-of-the-mill as government hotels went, was the most luxurious Caine had ever seen. His room boasted a full-sized bed with sleepset and fantistim attachments, a private bathroom, room service conveyor, and an entertainment center that even included a computer terminal.

He unpacked carefully, storing his clothing in the walk-in closet and the drawers built into the bed frame. As he worked he kept an eye out for hidden cameras or bugs, but didn't spot any. Not that it mattered—he knew the bugs were there somewhere, but he wouldn't be doing any important work in the room, anyway.

His unpacking finished, he looked over the menu list by the phone and called down an order. Then, kicking off his half-boots, he sprawled face-down across the bed, a wave of fatigue rolling over him. Outside, Plinry's sun was only halfway from zenith to horizon; mid-afternoon of a thirty-hour day. But Caine's biological clock was still set on ship's time, and for him it was already approaching midnight. He could run another hour or two on nervous energy, if necessary, but there seemed no point to that. Morning would be early enough to get to work.

Rolling over, he propped up his head with the pillow and reviewed his situation. His identity as Alain Rienzi, at least, should be rock-solid now, especially after that asthma attack. The pills had been clearly issued on Rienzi's medical profile, something Prefect Galway was bound to have noticed. How Marinos back on Earth had managed to switch those records—or how he'd had the foresight to do so in the first place—Caine couldn't imagine. But it had worked out well, and it should have allayed any suspicions Galway might have had.

Galway. Caine shifted uncomfortably as he tried to form a coherent picture of the man. The slightly pompous, slightly fawning, slightly bumbling image that had been Caine's first impression was sharply inconsistent with the prefect's actions during the asthma attack. He'd made a fast, correct diagnosis and had followed up on it without a single wasted motion—even to remembering exactly where Caine had put his pills. A competent, confident man . . . who had tried very hard to give the wrong impression of himself. Why? Did he normally play this game with visitors, or was Caine a special case? At this point there was no telling, but it made Caine uneasy. Perhaps, he thought, it was supposed to.

A soft chime made him start, and it took a second for him to realize the sound was just the herald of his dinner tray. Getting up, he retrieved it from the conveyor and took it across the room to where a table and chair were automatically folding down from the wall, presumably keyed by the chime.

The food was foreign to him but good nonetheless, and as he ate his spirits revived somewhat. The mission had hardly started, true; but then, he'd already come farther than he'd expected to. He'd reached Plinry, had safely penetrated enemy territory, and had established an excuse to go wandering around asking questions of Capstone's citizens. From his fourth-floor window, he could just see the top of the gray wall that separated the Hub from the rest of the city, and raising his glass to his lips he silently gave a toast to those on the far side. Even if General Lepkowski were truly dead, the common people had surely organized an underground against the Ryqril and the Hub.

Tomorrow he would go out and find it.

CHAPTER 3

The director of the Archives Division was a young-looking woman whose eyes nonetheless showed the evidence of great age. She was severe, unsmiling, and as protective of her records as a mother bear. "There are no exceptions, Mr. Rienzi," she told Caine firmly. "I really can't make it any clearer. I'm sorry."

She didn't look sorry, and Caine wasn't especially surprised he'd lost his bid. But he'd had to make the effort. "Okay. I understand, I guess. Thanks anyway."

He headed out again into the early morning sunlight. Already the Hub was bustling with activity; Plinrians seemed to take their work seriously. Finding a bench near the Records Building, Caine sat down and consulted the map of Capstone that Galway had given him. He was itching to go outside the wall and start looking for the underground, but first he had to spend a few hours researching his "book" with various government officials in the Hub. A waste of time, of course, but it would look strange if he didn't start his research at the top before moving down to the bottom of society. If someone was actually watching him, that is—and someone probably was.

The interviews proved almost disconcertingly easy. All but the busiest officials seemed willing to juggle their schedules furiously to accommodate the visitor from Earth. It was amusing, in a way, to have such influence over his enemies, but Caine knew full well that it was a two-edged sword. Too much attention and publicity could be dangerous.

He taped nearly four hours of wartime reminiscences from seven officials before calling it quits. It was mid-afternoon, and he couldn't afford to waste any more time in the Hub. Finding the underground could take days; and he didn't have very many of those. Summoning an autocab, he headed toward the gray wall.

The machine let him out at the wall's northern gate, the one they'd entered by the previous day. "I'd like to go out," he announced to one of the guards on duty there.

"Yes, sir," the young Security man said briskly. "Just get back in your autocab and I'll open the gate."

Caine shook his head. "I'm walking."

The guard blinked his surprise. "Uh . . . that's not recommended, sir."

"Why not?"

"The common people aren't all that friendly sometimes. You might have some trouble."

Caine waved the implied warning away. "Oh, I'll be all right. Come on, open up."

"Yes, sir." The guard still looked doubtful, but he stepped to a small control panel and the mesh slid open a meter or so. Nodding his thanks, Caine went through.

He walked slowly, all his senses wide open as he tried to absorb everything around him. The city was like no other he'd ever been in, at least on the surface. But underneath were the same bitter tastes the Ryqril had also left on Earth. The dusty buildings, each two or three stories high, were boxlike and coldly functional, with even less ornamentation than their Terran counterparts. The "architecture of the vanquished," Caine had heard it called; and it was clear that Plinry had suffered considerably more than Earth from the war. The people shuffling through the streets were in little better shape. Poorly dressed, their expressions ranged from resigned to hopeless to merely blank. Most of them looked middle-aged or older; clearly, little Idunine made its way to this side of the wall. Still, young men and women had to exist *somewhere,* and Caine wondered where they were hiding.

He found a partial answer two blocks later. Half a block down on a side street was what seemed to be an open-air café of sorts, from which emanated the sound of conversation and occasional laughter. Curious, Caine headed over.

It was, it seemed, a bar. Caine stood for a moment, looking the place over. About twenty small tables were scattered around under the open sky near the walkway; another fifty or so sat farther back from the street in a sheltered area that had been created by knocking out the front wall of a one-story building. About a quarter of the tables were occupied, by older men drinking alone or in twos, or by youths in groups of half a dozen or more. It was from this latter age group that most of the noise was coming.

Just under the overhang, against one wall, was a horseshoe-shaped table behind which a middle-aged man stood watching the teen-agers. Caine hesitated, then walked over, trying to ignore the eyes that followed him.

The barman shifted his gaze as Caine came up. "Afternoon, friend. What'll you guz?"

Caine caught his meaning. "Beer. Any brand."

The other nodded and pulled a bottle from under the counter. "Haven't seen you around, have I?" he asked casually as he poured the drink into a chipped glass mug. "You new in town?"

"Just visiting," Caine told him, sipping cautiously. The

beer had a strange taste, and he wondered what it had been brewed from. "Name's Rienzi."

"I'm John, Mr. Rienzi," the barman said. "Where you from?"

"Earth."

John's eyes widened momentarily, and he seemed to withdraw slightly into himself. "I see," he said, his tone suddenly neutral. "Slumming?"

Caine ignored the insult and shook his head. "I'm writing a book about the war, from the point of view of the outer worlds. I thought I'd be able to find some old soldiers or starmen here to talk to."

The other was silent for a moment. "There are some still around," he said at last. "But I doubt that what they'd say would make it into any collie book."

" 'Collie'?"

John flushed. "It's slang for government people," he muttered. "Short for 'collaborator.' "

"Oh. So their views wouldn't be very complimentary?"

"You can hardly blame them." He stopped abruptly, as if afraid he'd said too much. Picking up a mug and towel, he began rubbing vigorously.

Caine let the silence hang for a few more seconds before speaking. "I'm only a very minor government official, but I *do* have access to a TDE senator. If there are problems on Plinry something can be done about it."

"There's nothing you can do to help, unless you've got a million jobs in your pocket." John sighed and put down the mug he was polishing. "Look. We were stomped by the Ryqril here. That multi-damned Groundfire technique wiped out three-quarters of our population and made seven-eighths of our land uninhabitable. Most of our industry went, and a hell of a lot of farmland. A million more people starved or froze to death the first winter—" He took a ragged breath. "I won't bore you with the details. Things are improving, but we still don't have enough jobs to go around. Why else would *they* be here at this time of day?" He jerked a thumb toward the teen-agers.

Caine sipped his beer and studied the youths. Now that he was paying attention he could see the frustration in their faces and hands, the thinly suppressed bitterness in the clusters of empty and half-empty bottles in front of them. "I see what you mean," he said. "But I'm sure something can be done to help. I'll bring this to Senator Auriol's attention as soon as I get back. In the meantime, perhaps you could suggest other people I could talk to, both about Plinry's problems and about the war."

John's mouth tightened, and Caine could read the barman's mind: *doesn't care about anything but his damn book*. "Well, if you're looking for honest opinions, you could try Damon Lathe. He's right over there," he added, pointing past Caine's ear.

Caine turned and saw a grizzled old man with a bushy beard sitting alone at a table in the open-air section. He was of average height and build, and Caine judged his age to be early sixties or older. "Thanks," he said. "What branch of service was he in?"

John snorted. "He *was* a blackcollar."

"Really!" Caine said, not trying to keep the interest out of his voice. Laying a two-mark note on the bar, he picked up his mug and headed toward the old man's table.

Lathe, lost in contemplation of his mug, didn't look up as Caine approached; didn't look up, in fact, until Caine cleared his throat. "Mr. Lathe?" he asked cautiously. "My name's Alain Rienzi. I wonder if I might talk to you for a moment."

Lathe shrugged and waved toward one of the other chairs. "Why not? Don't get much else to do. Don't know you, do I?"

Caine sat down across the table from him, feeling the clash of experience with cherished belief. Lathe was nothing like the youthful, keenly alert blackcollar he had always envisioned. Too late, he realized he'd forgotten what thirty-five years without Idunine would do to a man. "No, I've just arrived here. I'm from Earth."

"A collie, huh?" Lathe nodded. "So how's things back home?"

Caine had expected a negative reaction similar to the barman's. The lack of one caught him somewhat by surprise. "All right. You were from Earth?"

"Yup. Born and raised in Odense—that's in Denmark. Lived there till I joined up with the blackcollars in 2420. Haven't been back for a few years—the war, you know. I'm a blackcollar—did you know that?" He spread open the neck of his faded shirt and tapped the snug-fitting black turtleneck he wore underneath. "It's real flexarmor—the sort of stuff we all used to wear." Letting his hand drop back to the table, he sighed, watery eyes gazing backwards in time. "Yes, those were the days," he murmured. "They're gone now. All gone."

Caine nodded silently, feeling as awkward as if he'd stumbled into a private wake. Whatever Lathe might have once had the Ryqril and the passing years had stripped from him, leaving a useless wreck behind. Gathering his feet under him, Caine was preparing to make a graceful exit when Lathe's eyes came back to focus. "What'd you want to talk to me about, Mr.—?"

"Rienzi," Caine supplied. "I've been looking for some of the old military men on Plinry, to talk about a book I'm writing. Would you know where any of them might be?"

"Oh, sure. We blackcollars get together and talk all the time. About the war," he added in a thoughtful voice, fingering the ring he wore on the middle finger of his right hand.

Caine had already noticed the ring. Made of a heavy-looking silvery metal, it was shaped like the head of a reptile of some sort. A wide, batwing-like crest rose from the back of the head, curving smoothly over Lathe's knuckle. For eyes the reptile sported two bright red gems.

"Like it?" Lathe asked, raising his hand so Caine could see it better. The hand itself, Caine noted, looked strong, despite its wrinkled skin.

"Yes, I do. I've never seen a ring like it."

"Not surprised," Lathe mused. "The Carno fan-dragon was our symbol. Fast little devils; good hunters, too. Only blackcollars were allowed to wear these dragonheads." He snorted. "No one wears them any more. The collies don't like to see them, and the Ryqril hate them. But I wear mine." He looked up suddenly, gazing intently at Caine. "All the way from Earth, eh? Must be an important book."

"Well . . . it's important to me."

Lathe nodded as if he found that perfectly reasonable. "Yep. Well, I'd be happy to help you, son—Mr. Rienzi. But . . . my memory isn't as good as it once was." He touched the red eyes on his dragonhead gently. "I used to be a comsquare—commando commander, to you. Did you know that? Yep. Comsquare Lathe, in charge of eleven other blackcollars—best damn fighting squad in the galaxy." He shook his head and sighed. "Now it's just me."

"Your men are all dead?" Caine asked after a moment.

Lathe nodded. He stroked the ring once more, then looked up again. "But that's the past. What can I do for you—oh, that's right, you wanted to talk to the other blackcollars. Shouldn't be too hard—" He broke off and craned his neck. "Matter of fact, here comes one now. Hey, Skyler! Come here a sec!"

Caine turned to see a tall, generously built man striding down the walkway toward them. He seemed to hesitate when he saw Lathe wasn't alone, but with a slight pursing of lips he came over to the table. "Hello, Lathe," he said. His voice was firm and steady, with just a hint of good humor hidden underneath. "Who's your friend?"

"Fellow from Earth—name's Rienzi. This is Rafe Skyler, son—good pal of mine."

Caine nodded. "Pleased to meet you."

"Earth, huh?" Skyler studied Caine coolly. "Aren't you a bit out of your environment on this side of the wall?"

Caine shrugged. "I'm looking for people to talk to about the war."

"Uh-huh." Deliberately, Skyler turned back to face Lathe. "I've been thinking, Lathe. How about us getting together out at the lodge day after tomorrow? It's time we got out of this rat hill for a while."

"Sure, why not? *I* haven't got much to do." Abruptly, he slapped the table top. "Say! That would be a great chance for Rienzi to talk to everyone about his book. How about it, Rienzi? You want to come to the lodge with us for a couple of days?"

"Lathe!" Skyler exclaimed, aghast. "*He* can't come."

"Why not?" Lathe's jaw jutted out defiantly.

"He's an outsider. *And* a collie."

Lathe held up his right fist in front of Skyler's face and tapped his ring. "I'm a comsquare, remember? The red eyes say so. If *I* say he can come, he can come."

"But—" Skyler ran a hand through his thinning hair. "Oh, hell, all right. *If* he wants to. But the others won't like it."

Both blackcollars turned to Caine. "Well?" Skyler said.

Caine thought quickly. Clearly, the mental deterioration which had affected Lathe wasn't universal—Skyler looked only slightly younger than Lathe, and his mind seemed still intact. The blackcollars were natural rallying points for any underground movement, and the chances were good that some of those coming to the lodge would have the proper connections. He couldn't afford to pass up this chance. "If it won't cause too much trouble," he said carefully. "I'd very much like to come. It would mean a great deal to my project."

"There you go." Lathe nodded at Skyler. "I knew he'd want to go with us." To Caine he said, "The lodge is mainly east of Capstone, up in the Greenheart Mountains. You have a car?"

"I could probably get one."

"Never mind," Skyler cut in. "We'll have someone pick you up. Be at the east gate of the Hub at six-thirty in the morning, day after tomorrow."

"Fine. Thanks a lot for—" Caine broke off as a Security patrol car turned the corner and glided to a stop in front of the bar. Three men got out and headed toward them.

Run! Caine's Resistance-bred reflexes screamed, and it took a supreme act of will to hold his muscles still until the impulse passed. Prefect Galway himself headed the Security team; he spotted Caine immediately and came over, his men remaining on the walkway.

"Ah! Our Security prefect, visiting his inmates." Lathe's tone was light, but there was an edge to it that Caine hadn't heard in the old man's voice before. He clearly didn't like Galway, and just as clearly didn't care whether the other knew it or not.

Galway nodded to the two blackcollars. "Good afternoon, Comsquare Lathe; Commando Skyler." Skyler nodded in return but remained silent. Galway shifted his attention to Caine. "Mr. Rienzi, I was greatly concerned to discover you'd left the Hub alone. I guess I didn't mention that this part of town can be dangerous."

"Oh?" Caine pretended surprise. "Sorry, I didn't mean to cause trouble for you. I was just looking for people to talk to about my book. And guess what? I've been invited to talk with a whole group of blackcollars!"

Skyler's eyes flashed something like disgust at that, and Caine knew he hadn't gained any points with the big man. But odds were Galway would know about the invitation soon anyway and Caine wanted to volunteer the information before he was asked about it. He couldn't afford even a hint of intrigue around him at this point.

"I'm not sure that's wise," Galway said slowly. "But we can talk about that later. If you're done out here, I can give you a lift back to the Hub; otherwise, I'll leave you one of my men as an escort."

"I'm ready to go now." Caine got to his feet and nodded to the seated blackcollars. "It was nice meeting you," he said. "I'll see you in a couple of days."

"Bye, now," Lathe said with a wave of his hand. Skyler stared at the table and said nothing.

"I don't think you should go out there with them," Galway told Caine as the Security car started back toward the gray wall.

"Why not? It sounds like just a sort of army reunion; old comrades getting together to play soldier again."

"These aren't ordinary soldiers, though. They're blackcollars."

Caine shrugged. "That was a third of a century ago. They surely can't be dangerous anymore. Otherwise, you would've locked them up long ago, right?"

Galway scowled. Caine realized he had pushed his point a shade too hard and backed off. "Look, I've already messed up my chance to use the archives here. This may be my only chance to salvage something from this trip. I'll be okay—really."

Galway stared straight ahead for a long moment. Then he gave a single sharp nod. "All right. I guess I have no authority to stop you, anyway."

Caine leaned back into the seat cushions, suppressing a smile. "Thank you, Prefect," he said humbly.

A dozen reports sat on Galway's desk, mute evidence that he was getting behind in his work. Leaning back in his chair, he toyed impatiently with a stylus, glaring at and through the backlog. Where the hell was Ragusin with that report?

There was a knock at the door. "Enter," he called.

The door opened and the young Security officer stepped in. In his hand was a cassette and a sheaf of papers. "I've got the stuff you wanted, Prefect," he said.

Galway nodded. "Let's have it."

Ragusin placed the cassette and half the papers on the desk and sat down facing Galway. "So far as we can tell, everything seems aboveboard. The suggestion of a black-collar retreat came from Skyler, not Lathe, though it was Lathe's idea to invite Rienzi along. There was no chance for consultation between the two of them."

"Unless they already knew Rienzi was here and had everything planned out."

"That seems a little far-fetched," Ragusin argued.

"True," Galway admitted. He thought for a moment. "What about hand signals? Any chance Lathe could have cued Skyler to mention a retreat?"

"Uh . . ." Ragusin frowned. "I don't know."

"Let's find out." Galway picked up the cassette and plugged it into his intercom. Ragusin had tagged the appropriate section, beginning with Rienzi's entrance into the bar. Galway played it twice, watching carefully. "Nice," he growled. "You see how Lathe's left hand just happens to be under the table when Skyler walks up? The camera can't see it, but I'll bet you Skyler can."

Ragusin shrugged. "With all due respect, sir, I think you're making too much of this. The blackcollars have been getting together two or three times a year at that run-down lodge ever since their war ended. We watched them for fifteen years straight without catching them at anything. What's bothering you so much this time?"

Galway shook his head. He couldn't explain his gut-level feelings about the blackcollars to his aide, any more than he could explain why everything about Alain Rienzi smelled wrong to him. "It's the fact that they're breaking their pattern," he said, choosing the most easily verbalized of his concerns. "They've never before invited outsiders to the lodge; certainly not a government man."

"Excuse me, Prefect, but that's not strictly correct. You remember about six years ago when Skyler and a couple of the others tried to get the unemployed teenagers interested in martial arts classes? About twenty of their top students went up to the lodge that fall."

"Oh, yes. I'd forgotten that." Galway frowned. "As I recall, those classes petered out shortly afterwards for lack of interest, didn't they?"

Ragusin nodded. "So it's not entirely without precedent. And it *was* Lathe who invited Rienzi. Who knows how Lathe's mind works these days?"

"Lathe. Yes." Galway leaned back, fiddling with his stylus again. "What do we really know about him?"

Ragusin shuffled through his papers. "I've got his file here. Born in Odense, Denmark, on Earth, July 27, 2403. Blackcollar training began—"

"Not that stuff," Galway interrupted. "Lathe told us all that himself, after the surrender. I want to know what we have independently."

"Uh . . . precious little, I'm afraid. All military records on the blackcollars were destroyed back on Earth. Lathe just basically came out of the woodwork when the amnesty was offered and told us who he was. All of them did that. They could be just about anybody, as far as we really know—in fact, I don't think we've ever even seen any of them fight."

"Yes, we have," Galway said absently. "Ten years ago, when Mordecai was jumped by six toughs."

"If you really consider that mauling a fight," Ragusin said, shrugging. "I guess even blackcollar skills deteriorate without proper discipline."

"Um." Galway tapped the stylus gently on his palm. "I want a close eye kept on that retreat. You have enough bugs planted?"

Ragusin nodded. "We've got micros sewn into all of Rienzi's outer clothing, except what he's currently wearing. We'll get those tonight when they're cleaned. The bugs in the lodge are still operating, of course."

"Good. Now, any word on my request for a courier to check on Rienzi's identity?"

"Afraid so, sir," Ragusin said apologetically. "The Ryqril vetoed it. No reason given, but I got the impression they thought it would be a waste of time." He shrugged. "I can't say that I blame them. Rienzi's ID checked out, and they're supposed to be tamper-proof."

"I know," Galway growled. "But he still bothers me."

"You think maybe he's a Ryqril spy?"

Galway snorted. If there was one thing he truly hated about the Ryqril occupation, it was the aliens' practice of maintaining their own private spies in conquered territories. As Security prefect, Galway needed to know who was operating where to do his job properly, and he didn't like having wild cards running around loose. But in this case . . . "I doubt Rienzi's one of theirs. If he was supposed to spy on *us,* they would have made him a new official assigned here; if he was supposed to work among the common people they would have landed him secretly somewhere. No, it's his story about forgetting his authorization papers that bothers me. That and his personality in general." For a moment Galway glowered at the cassette in his intercom. "Hell," he said finally, tossing his stylus back onto the desk, "we can't do anything for now except wait." He glanced at his watch. "You might as well go home. On your way out assign someone to watch the east gate day after tomorrow—I want to know who Skyler sends to pick up Rienzi. And leave those files here, too."

"Yes, sir." Ragusin set his sheaf of papers down on a corner of the desk and stood up. "Good night, Prefect."

Galway waited until his aide was gone before picking up the pile of dossiers. So damn little information—and none of it worth betting money on. He wished, not for the first time, that he'd been in charge of Security thirty years ago when the blackcollars had finally given up their guerrilla war in exchange for amnesty. Promises or no, he would have insisted on full verifin questioning then and there. Now, he couldn't do so without evidence that they were violating their parole. Gut-level feelings didn't count.

Abruptly, Galway slapped the files back on his desk and shoved them to one side. Picking up one of the reports on his desk, he forced himself back to work.

CHAPTER 4

The Hub was just beginning to awaken behind him as Caine stepped through the east gate at precisely six-twenty in the morning, and he was faintly surprised to find that the non-government section of Capstone was already up and running. Lunchbox-carrying men dressed in well-worn laborers' coveralls strode briskly down the streets, their shadows stretching long in the sliver of sun poking above the mountains to the east. Other men and women prepared small shops for opening: washing windows, sweeping walkways, and adjusting awnings and window displays.

Fifty meters from the wall sat the only vehicle in sight: a battered box-shaped van with the partially obscured name of a butcher shop on sides and back. Leaning against the door on the driver's side, his arms folded across his chest, was a small, wiry-looking man with dark skin and hair and a prominent nose. A bit hesitantly, Caine walked over to him.

The other got in the first word. "You Rienzi?" he asked gruffly, eyes boring into Caine's face. When Caine nodded, he said, "I'm Mordecai; Skyler sent me. Get in."

Caine obeyed, and was surprised to find the space behind the twin seats filled with blankets and hiking gear. "You seem well equipped," he commented as Mordecai guided the vehicle down the street.

"The van belongs to all of us; we bought it from the shop where I work," Mordecai said, his tone stiffly formal. "Most of the others are walking or cycling to the lodge, so I'm bringing all the gear."

"The lodge itself doesn't have much in the way of facilities?"

"Hasn't for years." He glanced over at Caine. "Look, Rienzi, I don't know what Lathe thought he was doing inviting you along. We humor him, so I'll try to be polite to you. But I don't have to *like* you—and I don't. So keep the chatter down, okay?"

Caine swallowed hard. The undertone of anger in that voice. . . . Would most of the blackcollars feel that strongly about him? Stealing sideways glances, Caine studied the lined face that gazed stonily ahead. A thin scar he hadn't noticed curved along the blackcollar's right cheek. There were no humor or laugh lines anywhere that Caine could see; Mordecai's grim expression had been a part of the man for a long time.

Sighing inwardly, Caine settled back and prepared himself for a long, awkward drive.

* * *

Hamner Lodge lay nestled in the western slopes of the Greenheart Mountain Range sixteen kilometers northeast of Capstone. Once a prestigious hunting lodge, it had been a favorite retreat of Plinry's rich and influential, even having its own station on the underground tube that linked Capstone with the city of New Karachi on the far side of the mountains.

The war had changed all that. New Karachi was now a shallow depression in the blackened ground, the tube was out of use and in disrepair, and the lodge was abandoned . . . most of the time.

"We've been coming up here two to four times a year since about 2440," a spry oldster named Frank Dodds explained to Caine as they walked through the wooded area surrounding the lodge. Dodds had taken over as tour guide for Caine shortly after the latter's arrival with Mordecai and was filling him in on history as well as geography. Caine was grateful for the change in babysitters; while Dodds wasn't welcoming Caine with open arms, he at least was marginally friendly.

"I'm surprised the owners didn't repair the place after the war," he commented to the blackcollar, shivering slightly in the chilly mountain air. "It's not in bad shape."

"As I recall, the owners lived in New Karachi," Dodds said quietly.

"Oh." Caine felt foolish.

Dodds looked at him. "Those clothes aren't really suited for the temperature up here, are they?"

"I'm okay."

"Yeah. Well, Skyler brought some extra clothing for you in case you didn't have anything proper. You ought to go and change."

"That was very kind of him. I think I will." A motion through the trees to his left caught Caine's attention. "Who's that over there?"

"Hunting party, probably," Dodds said, craning his neck. "Let's go see."

They walked through the undergrowth and dead leaves for about twenty meters to a small clearing where three men were waiting for them. "Heard you coming," one of them, a lanky man with pure white hair, commented. Under their jackets, Caine noted, all three wore the same black turtleneck shirt that he'd seen on Lathe at their first meeting; and each wore a dragonhead ring with slitted metal eyes. Brave enough to wear the hated rings, Caine thought cynically, as long as no one else was around.

Dodds made the introductions. "Alain Rienzi, this is Dawis Hawking; that's Kelly O'Hara, and this is Charles Kwon."

"Pleased to meet you," Caine said. With their large arms and shoulders, O'Hara and Kwon both looked like former wrestlers, despite their age. Kwon's eyes held just a touch of Oriental slant.

Hawking nodded with cool politeness. "Heard about you," he said. "Writing a book about the war."

"That's right."

"Maybe Rienzi would like to see how we hunt," Dodds suggested.

Hawking shrugged. "Just keep him out of the way." Reaching into a pouch attached to his belt, the blackcollar pulled out a larger silvery object. "Ever seen one of these, boy?" he asked.

Caine stepped forward, curious. It was an eight-pointed metal star about fifteen centimeters across. Though tarnished in places, the star's points were still sharp.

"It's called a throwing star, or *shuriken*," Hawking explained. "It's used like—well, like this. Watch that squirk over there."

Caine glanced in the indicated direction in time to see a gray, flat-tailed creature the size of a small monkey hop up onto a dead log. Planting his feet carefully, Hawking gripped the star in its center and cocked his arm inward, toward his chest. For just a second he held the pose; then, leaning forward, he whipped his arm, sending the star spinning through the air. The squirk's reflexes were fast, though, and the animal leaped for a nearby tree even as the star flew past it. With an outraged *yip*, the squirk scampered up the trunk and vanished from sight.

"Damn," Hawking muttered. He retrieved the star and returned to the group. "Doesn't always work," he shrugged. "But I'll nail one in a couple more tries, if you want to come along and watch."

"Uh, no thanks." Caine shivered again, and not entirely from the cold. Just playing soldier, all of them;

reliving past glories that were long gone. "I'm going to need warmer clothes, I think."

"Yeah, don't want you catching pneumonia or something—the collies would probably take it out of our pensions," O'Hara commented dryly.

"Come on, Rienzi, we'll go see Skyler," Dodds said. "You guys better hustle—we'll need some meat by thirteen o'clock if we're going to eat by noon."

"Don't worry about it," Hawking growled.

Unbidden, tears came to Caine's eyes as he and Dodds headed back toward the lodge. He did not look back.

The three hunters remained silent until they heard the distant sound of the lodge door closing behind Dodds and Caine. Then Hawking returned the big silvery star to his belt pouch. "Seemed a bit dejected, didn't he?" he remarked to the others.

Kwon nodded. "It could be an act, of course."

"Pretty good acting, in my book," O'Hara said.

Hawking shrugged. "Well, we'll find out this afternoon. Let's wrap this up while Dodds has him out of the way, shall we?"

All three men froze, listening. From the multitude of chirps, buzzes, and clicks coming from the leafy canopy overhead, Hawking picked out the faint noise of squirk claws on tree bark. Locating it by the sound, he was watching the proper spot when the creature cautiously moved into sight.

Hawking reached to his belt—but not to the pouch holding the silvery stars. His fingers dipped instead into a smaller pouch, hidden behind the first, and emerged with another throwing star. It, too, had eight points—but there the resemblance ended. This star was half the diameter of the other; heavier, sharper, and colored a jet black. A wolf, to the silvery star's Saint Bernard. His eyes on the squirk, Hawking permitted himself a smile at Caine's naïveté—imagine thinking blackcollars used demonstration *shuriken* for hunting!

The star flashed across the clearing, burying itself deeply into the squirk's body before the animal could react. The squirk dropped like a stone; and its noisy passage through the branches triggered sudden activity above the clearing. In a single smooth motion O'Hara snatched a star from his own pouch and snapped it skyward. A second squirk, killed in mid-leap, slammed into its target tree and slid to the ground.

"Show-off," Hawking muttered as he moved off to retrieve his star and squirk. O'Hara just grinned and went to get his own.

"I'll take them in," Kwon volunteered. "Better get at least four more; we've got a full house today."

"No problem," Hawking assured him. Gesturing to O'Hara, he set off deeper into the woods.

Considering the trouble Hawking and the others had been having, Caine was mildly surprised when dinner was indeed ready by noon. The food was good enough—roast squirk reminded him of very tough shrimp, somehow—but he paid only token attention to the meal. His real interest lay in the group of men gathered around the large wooden table. What he saw wasn't encouraging.

There were thirty-one blackcollars present, all proudly wearing black turtlenecks and dragonhead rings. Only one other man had the red-eyed ring that signified a comsquare: Trevor Dhonau, the wizened old man at the head of the table. Lathe, sitting next to Caine, identified Dhonau as the doyen, or senior member, of the Plinry blackcollars. Whether the title held any real power Caine didn't know; but it almost didn't matter anymore. Looking at the faces around him and listening to the conversations, he knew there was no help here for him. The blackcollars hated the Ryqril and their domination; that much he was sure of. But equally clear was the fact that all of them had resigned themselves to it. In hindsight, Caine knew he should have expected nothing more—the Ryqril would hardly have allowed them to live had they been otherwise. But it was still a crushing disappointment.

Blackcollars, even old ones, were evidently not the kind to linger over their meals, and soon the plates were empty. At the head of the table Trevor Dhonau got awkwardly to his feet, favoring a game right leg. Tapping his knife on his plate until conversation ceased, he raised his glass. "Blackcollar commandos, once more we are met together," he said, his voice slightly slurred. "Let us dedicate our time here to those our comrades who have gone before us, and pledge that their sacrifice should not be in vain."

The others picked up their glasses and drank. Caine, conscious of his role as a collie, left his untouched. Lathe nudged him. "It's good stuff," he said. "Tardy Spadafora makes it himself. Aren't you going to try it?"

Caine shook his head. "Sorry. I shouldn't have come—I don't belong here." He looked across the table, where Mordecai was sitting. "I heard you mention you were going back to Capstone tonight. Could I possibly ride with you?"

Mordecai's eyes burned into him. "I suppose so."

Lathe plucked at Caine's sleeve. "Hear, you can't leave today. You'll miss the *shuriken* and *nunchaku* contests and—"

"I'm sorry." Caine got to his feet, abruptly sickened by the whole pathetic farce. "Excuse me, please."

Back in the room Skyler had assigned him Caine began pulling together the clothes and other things he had brought. But he had barely started when a sudden dizziness swept over him, sending him to a sitting position on the floor. For several seconds he tried to fight it as strength flowed out of him like sweat. By the time he realized what was happening, it was too late to call out.

He was asleep before his head hit the floor.

CHAPTER 5

Caine was floating in a dark mist shot through with firefly bursts of light. He had no idea where he was, but lacked the alertness to wonder about it: He got the impression that something had awakened him, but he didn't really know what. It was sort of—ah, there it came again: a voice.

"Who are you?" it said, with a tone of insistence impossible to resist.

Allen Caine, his mind said promptly, pleased that he

had remembered it so well. But his tongue had other ideas. "Al-Alain Rienzi."

"Who are you?" the voice asked again.

"Alain Rienzi," his tongue repeated. Caine watched its performance with interest, as he would any other magic act.

"Who do you work for?"

That was a tricky one. Technically, Caine was a free agent, far away from those people whose names he couldn't remember. While he was mulling it over his tongue gave its own answer. "Senator Auriol of the TDE."

This was becoming boring. Caine decided to go back to sleep. "Wake up!" the voice demanded. Resentfully, Caine did so.

It went on and on. . . .

"Well?" Trevor Dhonau asked.

Freeman Vale turned off the microphone link to the next room before answering. "He's definitely not Alain Rienzi—that much I'm sure of. There's just a little too much hesitation before his answers. I'd guess the rest of his story is phony, too, which implies either thorough conditioning or some very excellent psychor training."

Dhonau nodded and looked around the windowless room at the silent group of blackcollars. "Comments?"

"How about increasing the verifin dose?" Kelly O'Hara suggested.

Vale shook his head. "Won't help. We're already at the maximum level. More than this and he just goes to sleep faster."

"His fingerprints match the ones on his ID," another blackcollar reported. "If he's a collie spy why didn't they at least set him up with his real name? It's not like we can fly to Earth and check him out."

"Good point," Dhonau agreed. "On the other hand, if he's an agent for some sort of underground—on who knows what mission—how did he get here? He would have had to get by both Earth's security setup and Galway; and Galway, at least, is nobody's fool."

"Let's ask him," Lathe's cool voice broke the short silence. "We're not getting anywhere this way."

Dhonau pursed his lips. "I suppose you're right. Vale, Haven—bring him here."

* * *

Caine's head was aching fiercely and his legs were none too steady as the two blackcollars who'd awakened him half led, half carried him into the room where the silent group of old men waited. It was not a total surprise—he already knew he'd been drugged—but he hadn't expected so many of the blackcollars to be involved. Fourteen of them—almost half the total—were crowded into the cramped space, including Dhonau, Skyler, Mordecai, and Lathe. Why Lathe had been included he couldn't guess.

"Sit down," Dhonau said, and Caine found that a chair had been moved into position behind him. He sank into it gratefully as his two escorts stepped back to stand by the room's only visible exit.

"Let's start with your name," Dhonau suggested. "We know you're not Alain Rienzi; we also know you've had some pretty esoteric psychological training. I don't know whether or not that training would protect your secrets under physical torture, but if necessary we can find out."

A chill went up Caine's spine. He looked around the room, wondering what would happen if he made a break for the door. Two old men were all that blocked his way, and his own combat training was considerably fresher than theirs. But he was still weak from the aftereffects of the drugs they'd used on him. Besides, these men were theoretically on his side . . . and there was something in Dhonau's voice he hadn't heard there before.

"All right," he said slowly. "But I must have your word of secrecy. My life's on the line here."

Someone off to the side snorted. "Ours aren't?"

"I only meant—"

"We're well aware of the danger," Dhonau said. "There's a bug stomper going behind you."

Caine turned his head. Sure enough, off in the corner sat the squat mushroom shape he'd seen so often at furtive Resistance meetings on Earth. Turning back to face Dhonau, he steeled himself. "All right. My name is Allen Caine. I'm a member of Earth's Resistance . . . and I need your help."

No excited murmur ran through the group; only here and there was there so much as a thoughtful nod. Dhonau's face remained impassive. "Can you prove it?"

"I don't know. I was hoping to find General Avril Lepkowski here—one of our leaders, General Morris Kratochvil, was going to give me a letter of introduction for him. I don't suppose Galway lied about his being dead?"

Dhonau shook his head. "Sorry. Lepkowski fried with his senior staff under New Karachi during the Groundfire attack. Do you have that letter with you?"

"Unfortunately, things went sour." Caine described the raid on the Resistance hideaway and his own escape to Plinry. "Without the proper papers I can't get into the Plinry archives. I was hoping the underground here could help me."

"Uh-huh." Dhonau looked thoughtful. "I notice you've carefully avoided mentioning *why* you want in the archives. What's in there that's so important?"

Caine took a deep breath. The culmination of years of preparation, the knife-edge on which the freedom of Earth blanced—he'd been told often enough how important the secret was. But he had no choice now but to tell them. "Out there, somewhere," he said, nodding skyward, "there's a great treasure hidden. Five Nova-class starships. Fueled, armed, and ready to fly."

Again there were no murmurs; but this time the silence was due to shock. Dhonau recovered first. "You must be joking," he said, his voice strangely tight.

Caine shook his head. "I agree, it sounds impossible. Here's what happened.

"The TDE was turning out vast numbers of warships in the early years of the war. In early 2424 someone in the High Command had the bright idea of hiding some fully armed and crewed warships in one of the systems near the battle front. The plan was to let the Ryqril sweep past—they were going to, anyway—and then suddenly pop up with this assault force right in the middle of their supply vectors."

"Wouldn't have helped much," someone muttered.

"Nothing would have," Dodds, sitting next to Lathe, countered.

"Well, we'll never know for sure," Caine said. "The five ships were delivered on schedule by special skeleton crews, who hid them and then returned to Earth. The convoy that was carrying the regular crews ran into a Ryqril ambush and was completely destroyed, though we're sure the Ryqril never knew just what they'd done. Anyway, with the incredibly tight secrecy around the project the report of the incident didn't get to the right people until it was too late. The Ryqril had already passed and it would have been nearly impossible to get crews through the front. All records on Earth were destroyed before the Ryqril victory, and everybody who knew where the ships were hidden is dead now, so the handful of officers who knew about the project gave up on it . . . until about seven years ago."

"Duplicate records exist on Plinry?" Skyler asked.

Caine nodded. "General Kratochvil located a former Rear Admiral who'd been based on Plinry. The ships' location is hidden in one of the mundane, non-military records in the archives. It's in a special code, overlaid on the wording of the record."

"Go on," Dhonau prompted.

"No. The rest has to remain secret."

"I see." Dhonau scratched his chin. "What were your plans once you had the information?"

"The original plan was for me to return to Earth, still as Alain Rienzi. The Resistance was supposed to recruit all the old starmen that they could find, steal some ships, and try to get to the Novas before the Ryqril figured out what they were doing. Now—" he shrugged uncomfortably— "I'm not sure what I'll do."

"Speaking of Alain Rienzi," Dhonau said, abruptly changing the subject, "how come you're able to masquerade as him?"

"Oh, he really exists—aide to a TDE Senator, son of a well-connected government family—all of that's true. I apparently look enough like him to pass. The Resistance kidnapped him and changed his ID and the computer banks to fit my fingerprints and retinal patterns."

"That's impossible."

Hawking's flat tone left no room for argument. Caine tried anyway. "I don't know how it was done, but—"

"Look, Caine, you can't tamper with the plastic on a collie ID. I've seen yours, and I've tried it on others. And as for getting into an ID computer file unnoticed, that's even worse nonsense."

"Well, it obviously *was* done." Caine felt anger rising within him and forced it down. "If it was impossible I wouldn't *be* here. They would've nabbed me right at the New Geneva 'port."

"All right, at ease, everyone," Dhonau's voice cut in. "Vale, Haven—escort Caine back to the other room. We need time to discuss this," he added to Caine. "We'll let you know our decision shortly."

Caine stood up, but his muscles were strangely tense, and he didn't trust himself to speak. So he simply nodded and left. The door closed solidly behind him.

For a few moments the room was silent as the assembled blackcollars considered Caine's words. Stroking his dragonhead ring gently, Lathe glanced surreptitiously around him, trying to judge the others' thoughts. His own mind was racing with possibilities.

Dhonau spoke first. "Comments?"

"I think," Skyler said slowly, "the first order of business is Caine's credentials. Hawking, were you overstating your case?"

"Nope. It's probably possible to get into a collie ID computer, but not without someone finding out."

"Before he got off the planet?"

"Easily. The most likely explanation is that the Ryqril had broken the Resistance leaders by then and let Caine go, hoping he'd lead them to the ships."

"But if they're on to him, why didn't Galway let him into the Records Building?" O'Hara objected. "The collies should've been falling all over themselves giving him what he wanted."

Beside Lathe, Dodds shifted slightly in his seat. "There's one other possibility," he said. "The Resistance may have pulled a very sophisticated trick with Caine. It's possible he's a clone of Rienzi."

Dhonau's eyes narrowed. "Explain."

"Within a couple of years after the war's end it should have been possible to guess which of the collies were likely to hold onto position and power. The Rienzi family sounds like a prime choice. All that would be needed would be to obtain a scratch sample of skin from a newborn Rienzi baby, make a clone from it, and raise the resulting child under Resistance supervision. He'd have the same fingerprints and retinal patterns, and the few months' age difference would be undetectable."

"Where was Security while the sample was being taken?"

"Bound to be loose in the first couple of years," Lathe pointed out. "It was on Plinry, certainly."

"Maybe," Dhonau grunted. "Anyone know whether cloning techniques had advanced that far by the end of the war? Dodds?"

"They were working on it a lot, I'd heard," Dodds said. "I know they'd finally broken the instability problem, but whether the method was ready to use I don't know. But I'd say the chances are good that it was."

"Let's let that pass for now," a big black man named James Novak said. "Even if the Ryqril are on to this, we can stay a jump ahead of them. What *I* want to know is whether five Novas are really worth going after."

"Good point," O'Hara agreed. "After all, the Ryqril fleets must have a good two hundred comparable ships, plus an unholy number of smaller craft."

"True, but those are probably all off fighting the Chryselli," Hawking said. "Not much left in the TDE except Corsairs, I'd imagine."

"We're way behind their shock fronts, too," Kwon mused. "Thirty years late, but we could follow the original script and hit their materiel shipments."

"Hmm. The Chryselli." Dhonau looked thoughtful. "What does anybody know about them?"

There was a short silence. "The TDE sent a mission to talk with them a couple of years into the war," Lathe offered at last. "General Lepkowski was in charge of it, before he took over the war theater here. I had a brother aboard his ship." He said this last with complete confidence; only Dodds knew it wasn't true, and Lathe could trust him to control his face.

"What are they like?" Novak asked.

"Short, dumpy things—like giant hairballs on legs, Paul described them. Warm-blooded, oxygen-breathers—I forget the rest. Anyway, Lepkowski was supposed to talk them into coming into the war on our side."

"Obviously, he failed," O'Hara said dryly.

"Yes, but not because they didn't see the danger. They just weren't ready for war yet and figured they would do better to build up their defenses while the Ryqril were busy stomping us."

"Helpful types."

Lathe shrugged. "You can hardly blame them. Even now, after forty years' head start, they're barely holding their own against the Ryqril, if news reports are to be believed."

"If things really are balanced out there, five Novas *would* be a force worth taking seriously," Kwon commented.

"Agreed," Dhonau said. "Alternatively, if we decide the Chryselli aren't worth helping directly, we could pull the ships into Earth orbit, say, blast as much Ryqril hardware as possible, and try to precipitate a revolt. Just having the ability to break the isolation they've put our worlds into would be a big help."

"Just remember that they'll have hunters on our tail from day one," Chelsey Jensen cautioned, running his fingers through his mop of gray-blond hair. "So don't get any ideas about massed assaults—five Novas together would leave a wake-trail six parsecs long."

"That's no problem," Skyler said, "unless you're partial to big space battles. Even skulking around individually the ships would be well worth having. I say we go with it."

The discussion trailed off into silence. "Other comments?" Dhonau said. "No? All right, then, who's in favor of taking the mission?"

Technically, Lathe knew, the vote was unnecessary. If he and Dhonau, the two comsquares, agreed on a course of action, the others were duty-bound to obey their orders. Nonetheless, he was pleased to see the vote was unanimous. Pleased, but not surprised. They'd all been waiting for something like this for a long time.

Dhonau nodded to Vale and Haven, who went into the next room and brought Caine in. Lathe watched the youth's face carefully. It was under good control, letting only a hint of his tension show through. Dhonau waited until he was seated before speaking.

"We've talked things over, Caine, and have decided to give you whatever help we can."

"Great. Thank you very much." Caine leaned forward

in his chair. "Then if you can just get me in touch with the underground here, I'll—"

"Whoa! Hold on!" Dhonau held out a wrinkled hand. "There isn't any underground on Plinry. There's just us."

Caine's jaw dropped fractionally. "No underground? But that's impossible. I mean, your people are discontented, especially the youth. Don't they hate the Ryqril enough to fight back?"

"Probably. But resistance movements form around natural spark points. If those points don't make any moves, the populace usually won't, either." Dhonau glanced around the room. "I'm afraid that's what's happened here. Our one effort to hold martial arts classes was too little too late, and nothing came of it."

"I see." Caine's voice was coldly polite. "May I ask how you intended to help me, then?"

"I thought we'd ask the collies to let us go in to study our old military records. Legally, we're allowed to do that."

Caine shook his head. "That hasn't got a chance," he said harshly. "Galway knows we've been together today. He'd know you were asking that on my behalf, and he'd wonder why. And the minute he gets suspicious it's all over."

Dhonau scratched an ear. "Well . . . I wasn't sure myself it would work. But don't worry—we've got a few more days to figure out something. Look, why don't you and Mordecai go on back to Capstone now, instead of waiting till later. I've had your bag packed, so you can leave right away. We'll kick ideas around another day or two out here. Let's see . . . why don't you plan to meet Skyler at that bar three days from today. Say, two-thirty?"

Caine hesitated, then shrugged and nodded heavily. "All right." He stood up and glanced around the room, and it seemed to Lathe that pity was the predominant emotion in his half smile. "Whatever happens, I appreciate your help."

Mordecai rose from his place on the floor and went forward. Caine nodded again and the two of them left the room.

"I think we've disillusioned the poor boy for life," O'Hara murmured.

"He'll get over it," Dhonau said grimly. "If the Ryqril

are on to him we'll have to hit while they're not expecting it. We move tonight—full alert; modified plan Delta."

Lathe sat up a bit straighter, muscles tightening briefly before he consciously relaxed them. Around the room the others were reacting similarly, with amazing results. Years seemed to fall from their faces; their eyes were locked on Dhonau in anticipation. Lathe had the sudden mental image of a jungle cat the instant before its attack.

"Vale, you'll go to Capstone immediately and play Paul Revere." Dhonau's voice had taken on a whiplash texture; no longer a decrepit old man, but a blackcollar comsquare giving orders. "O'Hara, you're Bait leader; Skyler, you're Liberator; Kwon, Haven, and Novak, you're handling Assault. I'll take Swatter duty myself. Lathe, you'll go into the Hub with Caine. Questions? Jump-off's in—" he consulted his watch—"four hours, at twenty-five hundred exactly. Collect your teams and get moving."

Dodds was standing by the window of his room when Lathe slid silently through the door and closed it behind him. "I rather expected you to show up," Dodds said, without turning.

"I'm not surprised. You probably also know what I'm about to ask you to do."

Dodds glanced once at the humming bug stomper and then turned to face Lathe. "You can explain it anyway, if you'd like."

Lathe did so. "Well?"

Dodds smiled crookedly. "If I refuse, who else would you get? Of course I'll go."

"Good. Be sure to hang back until all the shooting's stopped. I'll set you up in a non-combat position with Haven—spotter or something. Can you fly a Corsair?"

"Yes. But I'll need to know the system before I lift."

"Don't worry about it," Lathe assured him, stroking his dragonhead ring gently. "You'll have it."

CHAPTER 6

Closing the hotel door behind him, Caine tossed his bag the length of the room to land on the bed. All the anger, frustration, and—*yes, admit it*—the contempt had drained out of him on the ride back to Capstone. Mordecai had been no more talkative than he had been earlier in the day, and if he was friendlier it would have taken a micrometer to measure it. Maybe that had been for the benefit of hidden microphones, but Caine doubted it. The smaller man just didn't like him. In all fairness, Caine couldn't blame him. Dhonau's rash pledge of cooperation, inefficacious though it was, would still get the blackcollars in trouble if Galway found out about it. If, hell—*when*.

Sighing, Caine went to the bed and began to unpack his bag. Dusk was falling outside; there wasn't much else he could do today except try to think up a new approach. Probably a waste of—

The thought coasted to a halt, and he stared down at the clothes he had dumped onto the bed.

His pills were missing.

"Damn," he muttered, searching in vain through folds and sleeves. How had he forgotten—? Then he remembered: the blackcollars had packed for him. Swallowing another curse, he went over to the phone and dialed for the directory.

Mordecai, it turned out, was one of the thirty percent of non-government Capstonians who had private phones. The blackcollar answered on the sixth ring. "Yes?" he said, and his face immediately went neutral. "Oh. What is it, Rienzi?"

Caine explained the problem, feeling obscurely gallant for not mentioning whose fault it was. "I can't find any phone listed for the lodge. Do you know any way to get in touch with them?"

"Yeah—by car or by foot." Mordecai exhaled noisily.

"Meet me at the east gate in thirty minutes; I'll drive you back up there."

"No, that's all right," Caine said hastily. "Look, I can probably get a refill in town somewhere—"

"It's no trouble. Wouldn't want you put out on our account. East gate, thirty minutes." The screen blanked.

Scowling, Caine scooped up his coat and left.

The drive into the mountains was quiet agony. Mordecai never actually used the word "stupid," but Caine knew he was thinking it. It was a relief when they finally pulled up at the lodge.

Lights were blazing through the curtains from the main hall, and as they walked to the door Caine could hear loud, slightly raucous voices. The homemade liquor was flowing freely tonight.

Reaching for the door handle, Mordecai turned to Caine and put a forefinger to his lips. Frowning, Caine nodded. Mordecai pushed open the door and they stepped into the babble of voices.

The room was deserted.

Caine looked at Mordecai, swallowing his questions, to find the blackcollar studying his face. Whatever he saw seemed satisfactory, and he nodded to the long table they'd eaten dinner at. Moving silently to its edge, Caine glanced over its top and then squatted and peered at its underside. Five cassette players were fastened there, playing their hearts out.

He stood up. From a door across the room Mordecai beckoned. Caine joined him, and the voices faded away as the blackcollar led them through a maze of darkened halls and down long stairways. They were, Caine judged, a good fifty meters underground when they reached a dim passage. At the far end, lit by two small lights, was a double door.

"Welcome back," a voice behind them said suddenly. Instantly, Caine spun around, arms snapping into a karate defense stance as he tried to pierce the gloom.

The voice chuckled. "Nice reflexes," it said, and a big, black-clad figure slid noiselessly from a darker alcove into the dim light. Pushing back his non-reflective goggles with one gloved hand, Skyler grinned at Caine and shifted his attention to Mordecai.

"Good." Mordecai nodded toward the double door. "Let's go, Caine."

They walked through into a large, well-lit room . . . and Caine stopped short in astonishment.

The room was full of blackcollars!

Blinking as his pupils adjusted to the light, Caine gave the room a fast scan. No mistake—there were at least a hundred men, maybe more, all dressed in tight-fitting black outfits like Skyler's. Most were checking their equipment or carrying boxes to the far end of the room, where two large monorail cars waited; others were in the final stages of dressing. Caine was still staring when someone stepped to his side. "Sorry we had to pull that stunt with your medicine to get you back here on the sly. But the collies have ears everywhere."

Caine turned to face him, noting in passing that Mordecai had vanished. He almost didn't recognize the newcomer, even though he wasn't yet wearing headgear and goggles. "Lathe?" he asked in disbelief.

Lathe smiled wryly. "So I'm told."

Caine could hardly believe the change in the man. His beard had been trimmed down to a neat fringe; it and his hair had been dyed back to their original dark brown. Even more striking, though, was the new determination in his face. For the first time Caine could see past the lined skin to the blackcollar spirit underneath. An involuntary shiver went down his back. "You've changed since this afternoon," he managed. "About fifteen years' worth."

Lathe smiled again, his eyes not leaving Caine's face. "Most of those years were superficial. Idunine in small doses does wonders for muscle and bone."

"So you *did* get Idunine. I hoped you had, but I had doubts . . ."

"My senility?"

Caine nodded. "It was a good act." He looked around the room. "*All* of it was. I can't believe you managed to fool everyone for so long."

"Thirty years." Lathe glanced around, then turned back, all business again. "Come over here and get suited. We've got a flexarmor outfit that should fit you."

He led the way toward a bank of lockers. "Where are we?" Caine asked as they passed a humming bug stomper, one of five or six he could see spaced around the room.

"The old tube station under Hamner Lodge," Lathe told him. "Been unused since the end of the war. We started uncaching our equipment and moving it here about five years ago, after the collies got tired of dogging our every move. The track between here and Capstone is still good, and we've put our own power supplies into those two monorail cars. Here we are."

They had stopped before an open locker, and on Lathe's order Caine began to strip. "I hope that stuff's all it's cracked up to be," he commented, eyeing Lathe's own flexarmor dubiously.

"It is," Lathe assured him as Caine put on a soft one-piece suit of underwear. "It'll stop most non-explosive handgun projectiles, including some that'll throw you a meter backward from the impact alone. It goes rigid under that kind of punch, by the way, spreading the impact around. A clean hit with an antiarmor laser will get through, but the usual antipersonnel settings will just take off the top layer."

"So the *second* shot gets through?"

"The average gunner only gets one," Lathe said calmly.

Caine swallowed. "Oh."

"Understand, though, that this isn't medieval plate armor," the other continued. "For hand-to-hand combat you're on your own. Punches and kicks are too slow to make it go rigid."

Great. "Thanks for the warning."

Lathe apparently heard something in his tone. "You should consider yourself lucky we even had an outfit you could wear," he said, a bit tartly. "A lot of the boys going into combat tonight won't have anything but plain black cloth and maybe a flexarmor vest."

"How come?"

"Because most of the kids are just that: kids. We recruited them during martial arts classes a few years back—right under Galway's nose, as a matter of fact. They've been training with us ever since."

There was something in the old blackcollar's voice that made Caine pause in the act of fastening on a short-sleeved bodysuit. "It was pretty rough, wasn't it?" he asked. "All the ridicule and disrespect . . . I don't think I could've taken it."

"A lot of us couldn't," Lathe muttered. "That's what

kept the guerrilla war going so long. They wouldn't give up the fighting."

"Whereas you knew when to quit?"

For a second Caine thought he'd overstepped a fine line. But the anger only flickered across Lathe's face without staying there. "We didn't give in, we just changed tactics. Those of us who could." He made a sound that was half sigh, half snort. "Let me tell you a story.

"About seven hundred years ago, back in Old Japan on Earth, there was a lord named Kira who tricked an enemy into shaming himself. The enemy, Asano, committed suicide, the customary response for shame in that culture. Asano's forty-seven samurai warriors were supposed to follow suit, but instead they disbanded and dropped out of polite society. They lost their wives, families, and friends, and were treated with contempt by everyone. Naturally, Kira decided they were harmless.

"And then, one winter morning, all forty-seven suddenly appeared at Kira's palace. They overpowered the guards, captured Kira and killed him. Only then did they fulfill their duty and commit suicide themselves."

He fell silent. Caine, not knowing what to say, concentrated on his dressing. Aside from its exotic material, the suit was standard commando design, with built-in knife sheaths on forearms and calves and square pouches on the front of each thigh and behind the belt buckle. All were empty, a fact he found a bit curious. "How does it feel?" Lathe asked.

Caine took a few steps and tried a series of karate punches and kicks. The flexarmor was remarkably supple. "Feels fine," he reported.

"Good. Grab the gloves, battle-hood, goggles, and also the coat and pants you wore here, and we'll get going."

"What about weapons?"

"You don't get any," Lathe told him, cutting off his protests with a raised hand. "I know, I know, you're combat trained to the hilt and can use any weapon this side of Chaparral. But to us, you're a dangerous amateur who'd do more damage to himself with our kind of weaponry than to the enemy."

Caine felt a flash of anger. "Look, Lathe—"

"No, *you* look." Lathe jumped back and from a long sheath on his hip withdrew two thirty-centimeter-long wooden sticks connected at one end by a few centimeters of black plastic chain. Gripping one stick, Lathe proceeded to whirl the other around his head and body in a bewildering pattern, occasionally snapping the sticks so that one whipped out and back in a barely visible blur. Caine swallowed—he'd never before seen a *nunchaku* handled with such lethal skill. "Okay, I'm convinced—for close-range work. But for long-range you'll need guns, and I hold a marksman rating."

Lathe brought the sticks together and slid them back into their sheath. "Jensen!" he called across the room. "Give me a target!"

A blond-haired man nodded and broke a piece of plastic board off the crate he'd just opened. Glancing around, he tossed it toward a relatively empty section of floor.

His attention on the board, Caine saw only a flicker of motion from the corner of his eye—but there was no missing the sharp *thwok* as the board jumped in midair like a scorched bat. Jensen retrieved the board and spun it in a lazy arc back to Lathe. "We seldom use guns," the comsquare said quietly, extracting the deadly looking black throwing star from the plastic and slipping it back into one of his thigh pouches. "They're too easy to track."

Caine got his tongue working. "All right. I'm convinced."

"Good. Then there's just one other thing I want to say." He turned and locked eyes with Caine. "I still don't know whether you're really who you claim to be or a spy sent to betray us . . . but if you do, I swear your friends won't be able to stop me from killing you. Understand?"

Caine forced himself to return Lathe's gaze. "Yes. And I won't betray you."

Lathe held his eyes another second, then nodded curtly and stepped back. "All right. Let's get moving."

CHAPTER 7

The last few wispy clouds had been blown away by the time they left the lodge, and the stars were blazing down with a brilliance Caine had never seen from Earth. He hardly noticed them, though; there were more important things on his mind.

The van was crowded. Along with Lathe and Caine were Mordecai, Dawis Hawking, and a wizened old blackcollar Lathe identified as Tardy Spadafora. The latter, who was driving, followed Mordecai's earlier route into the city. But as they approached the Hub, he made a slight detour, stopping near the gray wall. When he started up again, he and Caine were alone.

Minutes later, they coasted to a halt twenty meters from the brightly lit east gate. Setting his teeth, Caine took the heavy briefcase by Spadafora's seat and got out, striving for nonchalance as he walked toward the floodlights. His coat and pants concealed all of his flexarmor outfit except his boots—which looked enough like current styles to go unnoticed—but it still took an eternity to reach the nearest of the two outside guards. Handing over his ID, he waited another eternity for the Security man to look it over and give the signal. Seconds later, Caine was inside the Hub.

Autocabs were routinely kept at the Hub's gates during low-demand hours, so Caine had no trouble with transportation. Following his instructions, he arrived a few minutes later at a cul-de-sac ending by the wall. The apartment buildings lining the street were dark, most of the tenants apparently having turned in for the night. A missing light by one of the outside stairways was creating a large wedge of shadow, and Caine stepped into it to await developments.

"Any trouble?" a voice murmured from the darkness, and Caine nearly wrenched his neck spinning around. Lathe crouched a bare meter away; behind him, Mordecai and Hawking were rising to their feet.

"No—none," Caine said. "I left my outerwear under the seat, okay?"

"Fine. I'll take that," Lathe said, pointing to the briefcase. "Call an autocab, will you?"

Caine handed over the case and triggered his hailer, wondering only briefly why he hadn't simply been told to keep the cab he'd arrived in. Clearly, Lathe didn't want to leave too clear a trail through tonight's events. Looking back down the street, he could see approaching headlights.

"We're not taking the briefcase?" he whispered as Lathe joined him at the edge of the shadow.

The blackcollar shook his head. "It's for Skyler's team—their *shuriken,* knives, and other metal equipment. We couldn't bring them over the wall; there's an induction field along the top and outer face that would have triggered an alarm."

Caine glanced back at the imposing gray barrier with some surprise. "You went *over* the wall? I thought there were sensors built into the surface to prevent that."

"There are," Lathe agreed. "But the wall was built by forced labor—and we were among the workers. Certain patches of the surface were specially treated to age faster than the rest. They've since flaked off, taking their sensors with them."

"Why didn't the Ryqril replace them?"

Lathe shrugged. "Why should they? It looks like random decay, and the remaining sensors would detect any ladder or lifter. But if you follow the proper path you *can* climb the thing without setting off its defenses."

The autocab arrived and the four men piled in. "Where to?" Caine asked, hand poised over the map.

"A hundred meters past the Records Building," Lathe said. "I want to get a look at the place."

Caine touched the appropriate spot on the map. Silently, the autocab headed down the empty street.

The air in the Apex Club was thick with the dank smoke of hasta sticks mixed with the odor of beer and cheap hot-pots. Sitting alone at a table near the low stage, Samm Durbin gazed around the room and tried to gauge the mood of the two-hundred-odd teen-agers crammed into the club. Angry, he decided. A rumor about a new government jobs scheme had been officially quashed less than an hour ago, and the loss of even this flicker of hope was sitting poorly with the mostly unemployed young patrons. The lighting manager had sensed the mood, and the flashing light patterns were leaning heavily toward reds, their frequency nervous and slightly irritating. When the crowd was like this, Durbin knew, it followed a standard pattern: lots of beer would flow as the teens tried to get drunk; the music would give them a chance to dance away their frustration; and finally, numbed and broke, they would trudge home. Occasionally a fist fight would break out, but that was the worst things ever got. High sales, minimal risk—few businesses this close to the hated wall could do so well. No wonder the management encouraged angry crowds.

Tonight, though, was going to be different.

On the stage the group struck their first chord, a harsh dissonance that told Durbin they'd picked up on the crowd's mood, too. Sipping his steaming hot-pot, Durbin stole a glance at his watch. Four songs, maybe five, and it would be time to move.

Even in the middle of the night several of the Records Building's windows showed lights. Hugging the building across the street, Caine gazed at the four-floor brick edifice, wondering how many people were in there. It hadn't really registered at the time, but Lathe's comment during the autocab ride that this place was guarded by another induction field alarm meant they would be going in practically unarmed. The three blackcollars had their *nunchakus* and Hawking also sported a wooden slingshot with stones for ammunition. And that was it. A single guard with a laser could take all four of them. Sweating under his flexarmor, Caine wondered if there was still time to call the whole thing off.

The three blackcollars finished their whispered consultation and Lathe pointed Caine to the rear corner of the Records Building. "That looks about the best spot; out of the way and no lights showing. We'll cross one at a time—you're third. You'll feel a tingling near the wall, but ignore it."

Without waiting for an acknowledgment, Lathe glanced both directions down the street and set off in a deceptively fast lope. Hawking was next; and then it was Caine's turn. He ran as fast as he could without sacrificing silence, but it still seemed to take him twice as long as it had the others. He reached the target corner to find Lathe already two meters up the wall, gripping the bricks with the aid of plastic crampons. By the time Mordecai arrived, Lathe was gently testing the latch on the nearest second-floor window.

That particular latch was apparently a good one; Lathe abandoned it and inched his way across the wall to the next window. He had better luck there, and within seconds had it open. Disappearing inside, he reappeared almost immediately and gave the others a hand signal. Tapping Caine's shoulder, Hawking braced himself against the bricks and cupped his hands. Stepping up, Caine pushed off the ground with his other foot, walking his hands up the wall as Hawking pushed upward. The tingling was strongest right next to the building, and Caine's hands were a bit numb as he reached for the sill. Lathe grabbed his arm and gave him an assist through the window into a small office. Scrambling back to his feet, Caine turned to offer a hand to the next one up. Two hands—Mordecai's—were already gripping the sill; poking his head out, Caine saw that Hawking was literally climbing up the smaller man, finding handholds on boots, belt, and shoulder. He reached the window and entered unassisted. Mordecai followed, closing the window behind him.

Lathe was across the room, listening at the door. As Caine and the others joined him, he cracked the panel open. Muted light poured in as Lathe looked both directions and then opened the door just enough to sidle out. The others followed into a dim hallway lined with doors.

"One floor up, right?" Lathe whispered.

Caine nodded. "Right. Stairway's that direction."

They reached the stairs without seeing anyone. One flight up, Lathe stealthily opened the stairwell door and looked out. Just as stealthily, he closed it again.

"Guards?" Caine whispered.

"A Ryq," Lathe whispered back, sliding his *nunchaku* from its sheath.

Caine's heart skipped a beat. What was an alien doing *here*, especially at this time of night?"

"Out late, isn't he?" Mordecai suggested softly. He didn't seem overly concerned.

"Yes, but I'm not worried," Lathe told him. "He wasn't armed more than usual and was talking amicably enough with one of the night staff."

"Think they suspect anything?" Hawking asked. "Or is this just a spot inspection?"

"The latter, I'd say."

"Shouldn't we be doing something?" Caine broke in nervously. *Not armed more than usual* meant the alien was wearing both a wide-bladed short sword and a very lethal hand laser. "What if he comes in here?"

"Relax," Hawking advised him. "He's not going to bother with any stairwells. We just have to wait here until he leaves. There's enough slack in our timing to accommodate him."

"Unless you'd rather attack," Lathe suggested mildly.

Caine shivered. The thought of fighting even an unarmed Ryq would have made his stomach tighten, and he felt a flash of anger at Lathe for making light of a very real danger.

In the distance an elevator motor began whining. Lathe waited until the sound stopped and then peeked out the door again. This time he continued on into the hall.

Unlike the floor below, there were only two doors opening off this hallway. One, on the right-hand side, had a glass panel set into it, through which bright light was streaming. Lathe gestured toward it, eyebrows raised questioningly. "The main records computer," Caine whispered. "The archive tapes are stored across the hall, if the lobby floor plan was correct."

Lathe nodded and motioned to Hawking. Together they moved down the hall, Lathe taking a careful look through the computer room window as Hawking crouched low and tested the doorknob opposite. After a moment they both returned.

"Door's locked," Hawking reported.

"Mine, too," Lathe said. "Four operator types inside."

"Straight frontal?" Mordecai murmured.

Lathe shook his head. "They're too far away. However, the room's two stories high and there's a wide cable tray spanning it about three meters up, with a service hatch at each end. Take a look."

Mordecai went to the door and glanced inside. Returning, he gestured back and all four men retreated again to the stairwell. "No problem," Mordecai said. Without further comment he headed up the stairs.

"Where's he going?" Caine asked.

"To clear out the computer room," Lathe told him in an abstracted tone.

"Alone?"

Lathe gave him a patient look. "Caine, Mordecai just happens to be the best hand-to-hand fighter I've ever seen—possibly the best that's ever lived. He won't have any trouble in there."

"Time to go," Hawking murmured a moment later.

Lathe nodded and—after checking the hall—led the way back to the computer room. Glancing cautiously through the window, he motioned for Caine to look.

The room was indeed large, with much of the central area taken up by a "pillar computer" of pre-war human design. Lining the walls were peripheral units of various sorts, and the hum of cooling fans could be heard even through the door. Next to the pillar was a control station; grouped around it were the four operators Lathe had mentioned. Almost directly above them, crawling carefully along the overhead cable tray, was Mordecai.

Caine's heart was pounding painfully, and he licked his dry lips without obvious effect. No matter how good Mordecai might have once been, the odds here were lousy. All one of them had to do was look up and it was all over. And even if he took them by surprise, it was still four to one. Hands itching for a weapon, Caine watched helplessly as Mordecai reached position above the control station—and, down the hall, the elevator opened.

Caine spun as a sharp *whap* sounded, and he caught just a glimpse of the startled guard's expression as he collapsed in a heap, blocking the elevator door. Slingshot ready for a second shot, Hawking glided over and pulled the crumpled form free. As the elevator closed, Caine glanced back into the computer room, wondering if the noise had alerted the operators. What he saw made him look again.

All four men were unconscious, either stretched out on the floor or slumped over their console. Mordecai, a set of keys in hand, was striding toward the door.

He reached it and opened up as Hawking arrived with the guard he'd stunned. Without comment, Mordecai handed Lathe the keys and helped Hawking drag his burden into the computer room.

"Caine!" Lathe called from the other door. "Come here and get your tape."

Numbly, Caine stepped across the hall. Four men, dropped where they stood or sat . . . and it didn't look like Mordecai had even drawn his *nunchaku.*

Lathe found the right key and he and Caine entered the room. Flicking on the light, Caine found himself facing several rows of floor-to-ceiling-length shelves holding hundreds of tape containers. "A lot of records," Lathe grunted.

"Everything for this sector since the TDE began," Caine said, scanning the shelf labels. "The one I want is in this direction. Why don't you go to that side and grab three tapes at random?"

"Good idea."

A minute later they were back at the door with three boxes apiece. Mordecai had taken up a guard post by the computer room door; inside, Hawking was seated at the computer console, studying the controls.

"Ever run a collie computer?" Hawking asked Caine as they joined him.

"No, but I've been pretty well trained in computers generally."

"Fine." Hawking stood up and reached for the tapes. "You run it. I'll load these for you."

The procedure took less than three minutes. Once the six tapes were mounted, Caine read two records from each onto a blank cassette. Eleven red herrings, drawn at random, and that one very special record. He found his hands trembling slightly as he withdrew the cassette and rewound the tapes. "Done."

Hawking looked at Lathe. "Do we return the tapes?"

"No, we'd better get moving. Mordecai, did you pick up a hailer? Good—I don't want to use Caine's any more than necessary. We'll leave by the front door; the induction field control's probably there."

They trooped down the hall together. As they entered the elevator, Caine sneaked a glance at Lathe. The old blackcollar's expression—what Caine could see of it under the battle-hood and goggles—was not that of a man whose task is nearly done. Caine shivered, but kept his questions to himself. Whatever else Lathe had planned, he would learn about it soon enough.

The briefcase was right where Lathe had said he would leave it. Crouching in the relative darkness, Skyler quickly emptied it, keeping an eye on the street. Hopefully, the faint whine of a car he could hear approaching was evidence that Braune and Pittman had been successful. Even as he closed the briefcase the vehicle rounded the corner, turned down the steeet, and then U-turned to face the cul-de-sac's entrance. Seconds later it was rolling again, with Skyler inside.

"Any trouble?" the blackcollar asked as he passed out knives, throwing stars, and short-range radio gear.

Woody Pittman, who was driving, shook his head. "None," he said. "Braune had it unlocked in half a minute."

Skyler nodded. He wasn't exactly thrilled with the idea of taking two novice trainees on a raid into the collies' stronghold—but as long as he had to do so, Pittman and Stef Braune were the best possible choices for the job. Pittman, especially: twenty-two years old, with five years of secret combat training under his belt, he had shed the rashness of youth and was beginning to develop the calculating mentality that made for a good fighter. Braune, three years younger, had the same characteristics at a more undeveloped stage. For the umpteenth time Skyler wished they'd had some of the Backlash drug when the planet went under. Without it none of Plinry's youthful fighters would ever have a blackcollar's superfast reflexes. Still . . . Skyler studied Pittman's face out of the corner of his eye. Alert, determined, with that trace of fear that made for caution. Backlash or no, the kid was going to be a good fighter someday.

Most of the lights that blazed from the Department of Planetary Security were on the first floor: the night shift of those guardians of Ryqril interests. The most dangerous place in the whole city for a blackcollar to be, but at least he'd have the use of his throwing knives and other weapons. With armed Security men going in and out at all hours, an induction field alarm was impractical. Lathe's mission was potentially a lot riskier, and Skyler wondered briefly how his friend was doing.

Pittman stopped the car across from the Security building, and he and Skyler slid out opposite sides as Braune took the wheel and continued down the street. Pittman vanished into a shadowy doorway to stand guard as Skyler, loosening his knives in their forearm and belt sheathes, headed across the street.

The main doors were large and imposing and, providentially, inset with lots of windows. Standing off to one side, Skyler peered inside. A short, glassed-in foyer led directly into a larger room dominated by a reception desk. One Security man lounged at the desk, fiddling with a pocket knife; two others leaned against the wall facing him, apparently just chatting. The standees were armed; Skyler could assume the desk man was, too. First target would be the latter, the only one within reach of the various alarm buttons. The others would have to be taken before they could draw. *Nunchaku* in his left hand, knife in his right, Skyler pulled open the outer door, crossed the foyer in two strides, and emerged into the reception area.

They had turned when he opened the outer door, but astonishment had frozen their muscles—frozen them long enough, in fact, that Skyler decided to risk an act of mercy. "All right; no one move," he ordered in his most authoritative voice . . . and the spell holding them vanished like a soap bubble.

The desk man lunged toward his control buttons and was knocked backward by the impact of Skyler's knife hilt between his eyes. The other two, still standing together like amateurs, were clawing at their holsters as the *nunchaku* spun through the air to catch them both across the forehead. One went down instantly; the other, dazed, nevertheless kept his feet until Skyler finished the job with a backfist punch behind the ear.

Ears cocked for sounds of an alarm, Skyler retrieved his weapons, checking the fallen guards as he did so. Two of them would be out for the duration of his stay. The third—the desk man—was out forever.

Skyler gazed at the dead man for a moment, his stomach tightening painfully. It had been a long time since he'd had to kill anyone. . . . Sheathing his knife almost viciously, he turned to the room directory on the desk.

The list was short and Skyler found the Hostage Holding Room without trouble. It was off to his left, through double doors and down the hall. *Nunchaku* at the ready, he crossed the reception area, opened one of the doors a crack and slid through.

An open door twenty meters ahead of him spilled light and cheerful conversation into the hall. The holding room, undoubtedly; only hostages would be that noisy. Skyler glided forward, conscious of the ironic twist this particular collie gambit had taken. Shortly after conquering Plinry the occupying Ryqril had required civic leaders to be held as hostages, on a rotating schedule, to insure cooperation from the populace. That order had never been revoked, but in the years following the blackcollar surrender the perception of it had shifted. It was now considered a mark of status to be chosen for one of the four-day stints as hostage—a mark of success, as it were. Luxuries had been added to the holding room, and the hostages treated their stay like the expense-paid vacation it essentially was. In many ways the ten men and women in there were as guilty of collaboration with the enemy as were the loyalty-conditioned collies, and it was a little galling to Skyler to have to get them out. But they *were* hostages—and when the balloon went up, their private club would turn nasty very quickly.

He was at the open door now and, without hesitation, strode in. Directly in front of him were the hostages, as yet oblivious to his presence. Flanking the doorway were two Security men: one lounging against the wall; the other, a youngster, standing at a conscientious parade rest. Skyler took the kid first, with a backfist to the solar plexus and another to the side of the neck. The older guard, grabbing for his gun, went down with a jab in the stomach and two head punches for his trouble.

The room had gone deathly still by the time Skyler looked up from the unconscious Security men. The hostages stared at him with wide eyes, their cards, drinks, and conversations forgotten. "Ladies and gentlemen," Skyler began—and suddenly the tingler on his right wrist came to life, tapping dots and dashes into two sections of skin. In the economical blackcollar combat code the message took only twelve letters—but its meaning was a heart-stopping mouthful! *Ryq coming in the main entrance—will attack—request aid.*

Skyler was out the door and running down the hall almost before the message ended, but even so he knew he would be too late to get there first. A muffled *thud* just as he reached the double doors confirmed that fear, and he flung open the door to find the battle already joined.

The Ryq, looking from the rear like a tall upright Doberman covered with brown rubber, was striding across the reception area, his short sword slashing viciously at Woody Pittman. The trainee was doing his best to dodge the blows or to deflect them with his—now—badly splintered *nunchaku,* but he was giving ground rapidly and within seconds would have his back to the wall. Shifting his *nunchaku* to his left hand, Skyler snatched a knife from his belt, wondering briefly at his chances of missing the rapidly moving Ryq and striking Pittman instead. But there was no choice. Raising the knife, he took aim—and Pittman stumbled and fell on his back. With a thin wail of triumph, the Ryq raised his sword high.

And Skyler's knife flashed across the room, burying itself in the alien's back.

The Ryq jerked as if with an electric shock, his sword clattering harmlessly to the floor behind him. Some trick of balance and locked joints kept him upright long enough for Skyler to put two more knives into the tough hide. Then, almost gracefully, he toppled over.

Pittman was getting to his feet as Skyler reached him. "You okay?" the blackcollar rumbled, noticing for the first time the handful of bloodstained cuts in the youth's non-flexarmor sleeves and gloves.

"Yeah. His laser's over by the desk."

"Your sneak attack was a bit off-center, huh? Well, at least you disarmed him. Get the gun; I'll be back in a minute."

Retrieving his knives, Skyler hurried back to the holding room. The hostages were still seated where he had left them, but they'd gotten over their surprise, and a burly man at a gaming table spoke up indignantly as Skyler entered. "Look here, you—what do you think you're doing?"

"Getting you out," Skyler told him. "We're about to launch an attack on the Ryqril."

The burly man's face turned pasty white. "Are you *insane?*" he gasped. "You'll kill us all! Haven't you fools learned yet that you can't fight the Ryqril?"

Skyler ignored him. "On your feet, everyone. Let's go."

"No!" The burly man's hand came up from under the table, clutching one of the fallen guards' lasers. "Call it off!"

Skyler reacted instantly, leaping to his left faster than the other's weapon could track. His knife was in the air before he landed, and an instant later the laser was flying across the room as its erstwhile owner hugged his hand where the hilt had most likely broken a bone or two.

"I said *let's go,* damn it," Skyler said to the group, putting steel into his voice.

Moving with terrified jerkiness, the hostages scrambled to their feet. Feeling like a glorified sheepdog, Skyler herded them down the hallway to the reception area.

Pittman was crouched by the desk, watching the front door. "Braune just pulled up with a van," he reported.

"Good. I'll see them off, then we'll follow in the other car."

"But we can't leave the Hub," one of the hostages objected mechanically, her horrified eyes glued to the dead Ryq. "The gate guards—"

"Will be out of the way soon," Skyler told her. "Looks clear—let's go."

Braune had clearly lifted the van from Security's own parking area; though unmarked, its sealed-off driver's section was designed with prisoner transport in mind. Skyler got the hostages aboard, gave Braune some final instructions, and headed down the street to their original vehicle as the van rolled off toward the Hub's south gate.

Pittman was climbing in the driver's side when Skyler reached the car. "Shove over, Pittman; I'm driving."

"I can drive, sir."

"Tricky to do while you're bandaging your own hands, isn't it? Move over."

The youth complied, and Skyler soon had them heading south. He glanced occasionally at Pittman as he drove, noted that the trainee was having a bit of trouble manipulating his medkit's bandages. It didn't matter how realistic the training simulations were, Skyler told himself silently—genuine combat always was different. "You did a good job tonight," he said, breaking the silence.

"Thank you, sir. I'm sorry I missed the Ryq's head with my *nunchaku.*"

"Forget it. It's hard to believe how fast they can move." He paused. "By the way, that was a damn fool stunt you pulled, faking that fall. By all rights you should've died there."

Pittman shrugged. "I saw you come in with your knife ready. It seemed to me you'd have a better target if I could get the Ryq to stand still a second. I figured it was worth the risk."

"And besides, you didn't want to be in my line of fire?"

"I thought you might be worried about hitting me."

"I appreciate your consideration. But don't *ever* do that again. Duck, go left or right, jump *over* the son of a cockroach if you have to, but *never* go down on your back in front of a Ryq. Understand?"

"Yes, sir."

Skyler clapped the boy on the shoulder. "After all," he said in a milder tone, "I'd hate to lose you now after all those hours of training."

Under his hand, he felt some of the tension go out of Pittman's muscles. "Yes, sir. I'll try to watch out for your investment."

In the darkness, Skyler smiled to himself. Yes, this kid was for sure going to be one hell of a fighter someday.

The insistent buzz of his bedside phone dragged Prefect Galway from a deep sleep. Reaching over, he turned off the visual and picked up the handset. "Galway," he yawned.

"Prefect, this is Sergeant Grazian, monitoring Alain Rienzi. Sorry to wake you, but I just noticed something that might be important."

"Go ahead," Galway said, rubbing his eyes.

"Well, sir, Rienzi left his pills at the lodge and had to be driven back up there to get them. I've got the East Gate reports on his departure and arrival and—well, I'm puzzled by the extra briefcase he came back with."

Galway came wide awake. "An extra briefcase? Was it searched?"

"No, sir. And something else: Rienzi came through the

East Gate almost fifty minutes ago, but there's no report of him arriving at his hotel. And nothing's coming in over the bugs in his clothing except what sounds like street noises."

"Call the main desk and have him pull autocab records for the last hour."

"Yes, sir." A long pause. "That's funny. No one's answering."

An unnamed fear curled itself onto the back of Galway's neck. "Go out there and find out what's wrong. Take a couple of men with you."

"Sir, he's probably just—"

"Do it, Sergeant. Call me right back—I'll be getting dressed."

He hung up and rolled out of bed, thankful that Marga-rite was a sound sleeper. His clothes hung neatly on a nearby chair, and he got dressed as fast as he could. He was just putting on his boots when Grazian called back with the news. "Beta Alert," the prefect ordered. "Get extra men to the gates; I want the Hub sealed off. See if they've done anything else in the building—" a memory clicked with a hunch—"and get some men to the Records Building right away."

The other acknowledged and signed off. Scooping up his gunbelt, Galway fastened it securely around his waist. It had finally come, he thought grimly, checking his laser's power level: the explosion he'd feared for so many years had finally started.

With one final look at his sleeping wife, he hurried from the apartment.

CHAPTER 8

It was time.

The music in the Apex Club had reached a thundering climax; the echoes of it still reverberated through the room. Together, the music, lights, and alcohol had turned the crowd into a seething cauldron of anger and frustration. The teen-agers were ready to explode.

And the necessary catalyst was also ready. From the other side of the stage Denis Henrikson was looking across at Durbin, his eyebrows raised questioningly. Durbin nodded agreement. Smiling grimly, Henrikson got to his feet and stepped onto the stage, picking up a mike. For his part, Durbin pushed his chair back and prepared for action.

"Friends!" Henrikson's amplified voice boomed into the room, and a few of the teen-agers paused in their conversations to look back at the stage. "What are we sitting here for? What are we letting the damn collies *do* this to us for? Don't we *care* any more?"

More and more heads were turning, and the buzz of conversation was fading as Henrikson launched into a scathing indictment of the government. It wasn't so much the words themselves, Durbin knew—everyone had heard all this before—but the *way* Henrikson said them. He had that undefinable aura of authority, that charisma that made for a born leader. To his natural abilities had been added three years of secret training in psychology and sociology, until Henrikson had become a master manipulator of human emotion.

And the crowd was responding. The background noise was growing again—but it was no longer composed of frustrated conversation. The sounds were animalistic, full of hate and violence. In one corner a chant had started: "Burn it down! Burn it down! Burn it down!" More and more people took it up, and within seconds the building was shaking with the angry stamping of feet.

At the table in front of Durbin's a dark-haired youth reached furtively into his pocket. Unnoticed by the mesmerized chanters around him, Durbin moved up behind him; and as the teen-ager's hand emerged, Durbin struck the back of his neck a short, carefully placed blow. The youth sprawled unconscious across the table, and Durbin stooped to retrieve the object the other had dropped. It was a tiny communicator.

Durbin replaced it in the youth's pocket, smiling in satisfaction. He'd long suspected this one of being a Security informer—it was the main reason he'd chosen the table he'd been sitting at. The collies couldn't be allowed even a hint of what was about to happen.

Suddenly, without warning, the crowd was on the move, streaming past Durbin toward a side exit like a gale-force wind. Jumping to the lee side of a table, he looked over in time to see Henrikson leave the building at the head of his mob. Joining the flow, Durbin moved toward the exit, realizing he'd been concentrating so hard on the collie stooge that he'd missed the final punch of Henrikson's speech. That was a shame; he'd wanted to hear it.

Outside, the mob made a sharp right turn. Ahead, two blocks away, loomed the Hub's south gate. Running along the crowd's edge, Durbin worked his way up to the middle of the group, where he'd be able to function as secondary leader if necessary.

"Halt!" a voice boomed from in front of them—one of the gate guards with an amp. "You are ordered to disperse."

In answer, Henrikson half turned, roared something Durbin didn't catch, and doubled his speed. A flash of light lanced out from each of the outside guards, slashing across the front rank. The weapons were apparently set low—to burn instead of kill—and for a second the crowd faltered as screams of pain mixed with the rage. But Henrikson didn't even slow down. His clear voice called and the mob surged forward once again. Ahead, Durbin could see both guards resetting their lasers even as they began to retreat. The gate was opening behind them as they raised their weapons for a second shot—a killing one, probably, which even Henrikson's hidden flexarmor shirt might not be able to stop.

The shot never came. Simultaneously, both guards' heads snapped back, and the two men collapsed into heaps on the ground. The inside man gaped at them for a heartbeat, all the time he had before he too was dropped by O'Hara's hidden blackcollar marksmen. And the gate was still open.

With a shout of triumph Henrikson led the way through the barrier. Some of the teen-agers stopped to strip the downed guards of weapons; and when a carload of Security men whipped around a corner seconds later it was caught completely off-guard, riddled with laser burns before its occupants could react. That gained them eight more weapons, and soon the air was filled with laser fire as the rioters vented their rage on the surrounding buildings. Again Henrikson shouted and gestured, and the mob once more began to move forward, striking out for the Hub's business and governmental center.

Because he was watching for a Security attack on their rear, Durbin saw the three vehicles—an autocab, a private car, and a van—that slipped out the abandoned gate behind them. *Phase one completed,* he thought, ticking off an imaginary checklist. Now came phase two, the mission that gave them the title of Bait: to draw down upon their own heads the worst the collies could offer. Shivering slightly, one eye still on their rear, he hurried to keep up with the mob.

The report reached Galway while still en route to the Security building. "How many got in, Sergeant?" he asked tersely.

"A couple hundred at least, sir," Grazian, who had taken over the main desk duties, said. His voice quavered despite obvious efforts to control it. "I don't know how. All three guards just collapsed suddenly while the gate was open, but the power and metal detectors didn't show anything that could be a weapon."

"Slingshots," Galway muttered.

"Sir?"

"Blackcollar sniper's weapon," the prefect amplified. "Put out an M-Seven; I want everyone in riot gear immediately."

"Yes, sir," Grazian said. Simultaneously, a large red *M-7* appeared on Galway's car display screen. "Done, Prefect."

Galway pressed the reset and the *M-7* vanished. "All right, now what about the other men we lost?"

"They were the four backups you'd ordered to that gate. They'd just called in that they heard the rioters when they were hit. I guess they thought the mob was still outside the wall."

"Why?" Galway pounced. "You were monitoring it, weren't you? Why didn't you warn them?"

"Sir—I—" Grazian sounded miserable. "It all happened so fast. . . ."

"So you froze, and four men are dead." Galway's words were harsh, but his anger was quickly changing to apprehension. The blackcollars had the initiative now—as the attacker always did—and his Security forces weren't responding nearly fast enough. They'd trained for this sort of thing, of course, but no one had taken it seriously for years. Could they get organized in the heat of battle? Galway wasn't sure.

One thing he *was* sure of, though: allowing his men to be tied down defending the Hub was an invitation to disaster. He had to stop the riot, and fast, before the blackcollars pulled whatever else they had planned. "Sergeant, what do we have in the air?"

"All eight spotters are up, coordinating the ground action. The mob's pretty well fragmented now, and each group has at least one stolen weapon. Mobs are starting to form outside the other gates, too, but so far we're holding them back."

And coordination was about all the spotters could do; they lacked the sophisticated firepower for pinpoint attacks that could hit the rioters without tearing up the surrounding neighborhoods. But there *were* ships on Plinry that could accomplish that. "Call the 'port. I want their patrol boats immediately."

"All six of them?" Grazian sounded doubtful. "That'll leave the 'port undefended."

"They've got their fence, don't they? Besides, clearing out the rioters with those boats won't take long. If they get nervous they can always ask the Ryqril to take a couple of Corsairs up."

"Yes, sir." A pause. "I have the 'port duty officer now; channel three."

Switching his phone, Galway gave the orders.

They came in low over the city: six sleek aircraft, heading in from the north and displacing the stubby Security spotters that moved up to give them room. From his lonely tree-crowned hill two klicks east of the city Trevor Dhonau counted them as they appeared, nodding in satisfaction. Galway had called the 'port patrol boats into the fray a bit sooner than he had expected, but that was all right: Dhonau and Terris Shen, the other Swatter, had been in position for nearly an hour.

Squatting behind the sights of his twin-tube rocket launcher, his game leg stretched awkwardly to the side, the old blackcollar permitted himself a moment of mild regret. It had been so long in coming, this last act of defiance, and he wished he could see it through to the end. But *someone* had to take Swatter duty, and better him than someone with two good legs. Idunine could keep you alive a long time, but for damaged tissue other treatment was needed—and the collies' refusal to supply that was just one more score that needed settling.

The moment passed, and Dhonau actually smiled as he picked up the trigger grip and thumbed off its safety. All of them had had a price to pay, and if his was to be heavier than the average that was merely a comsquare's duty. Certainly Lathe had done his share without flinching. Dhonau winced inside as he thought of Lathe's lonely vigil as their contact man, the patient wait in that highly visible role for the long-shot contact that had finally happened. He would be a good successor, Dhonau knew. He just hoped there would be enough pieces left after tonight for Lathe to pick up.

Almost time. The patrol boats were settling into position over Capstone, hovering on gravs as they sought the rioters. Dhonau waited until they were nearly stationary, and then gently squeezed the trigger grip.

With a burst of sparks and the sizzle of water dropped on a hot griddle, the tiny surface-to-air missile shot from the leftmost firing tube. Shifting aim, Dhonau fired again.

The result was all Dhonau could have hoped for. A blue-white sun burst dead center on one of the boats, which yawed wildly in dying reflex before plummeting to the ground. A second craft, maneuvering frantically to avoid its flaming companion, backed directly into the path of the second missile. It didn't even have time to fall, but disintegrated instead in midair as a secondary explosion of its fuel and armament momentarily lit up the sky. A third patrol boat swung dangerously near the ground, impelled by the force of the explosion, and was just regaining equilibrium when a missile rose from Shen's position to the southwest, bringing it down for good. It had all happened so quickly that only then did the thunderclaps from the explosions finally reach Dhonau's hill.

The old blackcollar grinned as the sound washed over him. Three down in the first salvo—better than he'd expected. The other three boats were buzzing around like hornets now, seeking their attackers, but Dhonau wasn't particularly worried yet. The boats, though of Ryqril manufacture, were copies of pre-war Terran design, and Dhonau knew that their sensors couldn't simultaneously handle both narrow- and wide-angle detection. Concentrating on the rioters in Capstone, they couldn't possibly have tracked the missile trajectories. A basic problem with stealing someone else's technology, Dhonau reminded himself dryly: the original owner always knew too much about it.

Two of the boats had shifted to a standard search pattern now, the third rising to a high-altitude position where it could watch the whole area. An unimaginative approach, and potentially expensive: it could cost them one of their low-flying boats to locate each Swatter position. Dhonau reloaded his tubes, waiting for the searchers to move closer. But as he watched, one of them broke sharply from its path, swinging in a tight circle off to Dhonau's left. Shen had been spotted.

The other Swatter knew it, too, and two missiles flashed out in quick succession. Both exploded harmlessly in midair, caught by bursts of laser fire.

Dhonau cursed under his breath even as he swung his firing tube around and squeezed the trigger. It would give his position away, but he had no other choice. With both tubes empty, Shen would be a sitting duck for several seconds before he could reload.

The missile arced toward its target—and Dhonau's gut-feeling that the collie crew were essentially rookies was confirmed. Concentrating on Shen's defenseless position, they completely missed the arrow climbing up their exhaust until it was too late. Even then, the pilot tried to escape the inevitable, scooting maybe a hundred meters before the missile caught up with him and ended his flight. Dhonau grimaced with contempt even as he searched the sky for the remaining boats. A blackcollar pilot, seeing death was certain, would have held position and crashed on his enemy.

Suddenly, with a roar, the hilltop erupted with blue flame, and he just managed to snap his eyelids shut before the concentrated laser fire could blind him. The light winked out as fast as it had come, leaving the gentler flame of burning vegetation in its wake. Dhonau lay on the ground where his reflexes had thrown him, feeling his inner flexarmor layer grow hot enough to scorch skin. Opening his eyes, he tried to see around the purple afterimage in front of him. He'd been lucky, he knew; if the attacking boat had stayed overhead instead of making a fast strafing run he'd be dead by now. Even so, his flexarmor wouldn't survive another attack. Rolling over, he gave the sky a quick scan and turned to his rocket launcher.

Not good. The missiles seemed intact, but the thinner metal of the firing tubes had warped slightly in the intense heat. Gritting his teeth, Dhonau opened the breech of the nearest tube and began removing the firing mechanism.

He was flat on the ground a second later as an explosion ripped through the air, and he turned his head just in time to see a crippled patrol boat spin helplessly to the ground. One more for Shen. But the triumph was short-lived; seconds later the last patrol boat dropped from the stars and Shen's position was abruptly awash with laser fire. Another second and Shen's remaining missiles blew, sending a fireball high into the sky. Still the boat swept the area with its lasers, making sure their enemy was dead. With one final tug, Dhonau got the firing mechanism loose. Picking up one of the missiles, he stumbled down the hill, working on the connection as he traveled.

The jury-rig was ready by the time the boat swung around and headed toward him. Lying back against the hill, the old blackcollar froze, the missile tucked firmly under one arm. There was no hope of escaping detection; the light from the burning trees above him would reflect clearly from his half-vaporized flexarmor. His only hope was to play possum and lure them close enough for one last shot.

The boat moved toward him; not slowly, but not with the crushing acceleration of a strafing run, either. Dhonau waited, holding his breath . . . and finally he judged the boat near enough. His left hand squeezed convulsively on the trigger grip, and the missile blasted away from him, its exhaust burning his right arm and side. He gasped with pain and shock as his vision wavered. But before he passed out he had the satisfaction of seeing the patrol craft's tail shattered by blue-white flame.

He was already dead when the crippled boat crashed to the ground where he lay.

The mud outside the 'port was cold, and the scrubby trees did nothing to break the light wind coming in from the north. James Novak hardly noticed the elements, though; spread-eagled five meters from the outer fence, his full attention was on the sparse lights of the buildings across the field. He'd been watching them for the past half-hour, waiting tensely for signs that the blackcollar force had been spotted. But apparently the deliberate slowness of their crawl had left the collies' motion detectors untriggered. Now only the fence and its associated defenses stood between them and the shadowy Corsairs.

For a moment Novak focused on the fence itself. Unlike the Hub's protective wall, this barrier had been built by the Ryqril, to Ryqril military specs. Besides the motion sensors implanted in the nearly unbreakable mesh, there were metal and radiation detectors designed to watch for heavy equipment and to help aim the antiaircraft lasers mounted on the 'port tower. For antipersonnel defense, there were strips of needle mines on both sides of the fence, triggered either by pressure or by the fence's sensors. It was small wonder that the fence had never even been attacked, let alone breached.

Any minute now, though, and that would be ancient history. Just minutes ago the 'port patrol boat crews had rushed out to their aircraft and headed out like big brother out to settle some bully's hash. They should have arrived over Capstone by now. . . .

He saw the first flash from the corner of his eye, and glanced over in time to see the second and third. Looking back at the 'port buildings, Novak fidgeted as he tried to judge the timing. The patrol boats had to be sufficiently engaged that they couldn't easily break off and return, but he couldn't give the Ryqril any head start toward their Corsairs, either.

In the barracks, a light suddenly came on.

Novak didn't wait any longer. Reaching to his left he

flipped the switch on the short mortarlike gadget he'd carefully anchored in the mud twenty minutes ago. Regular ladders were useless near the fence; either they were large enough to trigger the motion sensors, or they took too long to set up. However. . . .

With a hiss of compressed air a telescoping, semirigid tube snaked out of the mortar barrel, clearing the top of the fence by two meters. Even before the arch was completely formed, a white fluid began flowing through it, spilling into a pool on the ground across the fence and squirting generously through perforations in the hose itself. The liquid solidified rapidly as it hit air, and within seconds a solid, half-meter-diameter bridge was in place. Shutting off the flow, Novak began to climb, using the natural hand and footholds that eddies had frozen into the surface.

Three mines went off in sequence as he passed over them, the needles doing only minor damage to the bridge as the tough foam in turn slowed them down to energies his flexarmor could easily handle. Off to his left, he could hear similar explosions as Kwon and Haven led their teams over.

The tower lasers were apparently not set to automatically fire on a ground-level intrusion—a system, Novak decided, that the collies would probably regret very soon—and he reached the far side without being shot at. His twenty-man team was right behind him, the twelve trainees climbing almost as well as the eight blackcollars. Crouching near the foot of the bridge, Novak waited until the others were across.

"Everyone ready?" he whispered.

"Ryqril!" someone hissed, pointing.

Novak had already seen the alien figures pouring from their barracks. "No problem," he said confidently, though his mouth seemed unusually dry. "Let's move."

They fanned out into the darkness, the blackcollars heading to intercept the approaching aliens as the trainees scattered among the parked Corsairs. By now the Ryqril would have discovered the emergency floodlights were gone—Haven's sharpshooters had taken care of that earlier—and would realize a major assault was in progress. Novak swallowed hard as he slipped between the rows of parked fighters, feeling out of practice and very vulnerable.

Ahead, in the starlit area between the Corsairs and the Ryqril barracks, a one-sided battle was already in progress as hidden blackcollars picked off the approaching aliens with slingshot and throwing star. Occasional flashes of laser light briefly illuminated the scene, but the aliens seemed understandably reluctant to risk damaging their Corsairs.

That phase ended quickly, though, as the surviving Ryqril reached the shadows around the Corsairs. Crouching near the front landing skid of one of the fighters, Novak realized he had a macabre game of hide-and-seek on his hands. The aliens had realized that firing a laser invited a quick death and had adopted the blackcollars' skulking technique, relying on their short swords and superhuman speed. It was a risky game for both sides: the Ryqril had a numerical edge, but the longer they delayed the obvious gambit of putting one or more Corsairs in the air, the better the blackcollars' chances. Sliding a gloved finger under his right sleeve, Novak tapped out a message on his tingler: *Ryqril gone to ground; hurry with main objective.*

His answer was a short flurry of combat-coded orders as Kwon and Haven shifted some of their forces to his aid. With luck, the Ryqril would be effectively encircled before they realized it—

A faint rustle of cloth was Novak's only warning. He half leaped, half rolled to the side, not quite fast enough, as a short sword whistled through the air and caught his left forearm. He twisted the limb as fast as he could, letting the blade skitter off along the flexarmor sleeve, but it still felt like being hit with a brick. He continued his roll, yanking out his *nunchaku* and lashing out blindly in an effort to keep his assailant away until he could regain his balance. The counterattack was clumsy, and the Ryq avoided it easily, swinging under it at Novak's neck. But the alien apparently underestimated blackcollar reflexes. Novak evaded the blade by a whisker, took a couple of steps back, and drew a long knife from his left forearm sheath.

The Ryq was on him immediately, slashing silently with speed and skill. Sweating under his flexarmor, Novak continued to back up, fending off the attacks with knife and *nunchaku*. His left arm ached fiercely, a mute reminder of his danger. Theoretically, the sword couldn't penetrate his flexarmor, but the blows were easily hard enough to break bones if they landed right. And once disabled . . . well, the Ryq could always strangle him.

Novak swallowed involuntarily. He was between two rows of Corsairs now, exposed to the faint backwash of light from the distant buildings. It was a lousy position to be in—not only was he wide open to attack, but the Ryq could easily be forcing him toward a second alien's hiding place. Desperately, he tried to take the offensive . . . but the alien was a trained warrior, too. Slowly but steadily, Novak lost ground.

And then, like a gift from heaven, a terse signal tingled into his wrist: *stand clear; two seconds.*

Novak's heart leaped. Wielding his knife with new vigor, he got ready . . . and with a roar, a flash of flame erupted simultaneously from the tail of every Corsair around them.

For a brief instant the Ryq froze, startled by the unexpected explosions. But Novak was ready, and in that instant he hurled his knife at the alien's face. Breaking his paralysis, the Ryq ducked, raising his swordarm reflexively—and Novak swung his *nunchaku* with all his strength into the other's side.

There was the dull crack of bone breaking and the alien stumbled, off-balance. Novak pressed his attack, flailing the Ryq's head and torso with all the power he could muster. Again and again he struck; and even when the Ryq lay unmoving on the ground he kept up the assault for several seconds before it occurred to him to stop.

Kneeling beside the body, he drew a shuddering breath. That had been close—far too close. And yet, strangely, he felt a sudden new confidence in himself. It had been a long time since he'd fought for real, but he'd done all right—and against a Ryq, too.

A flash of laser light erupted off to his side, and even as he snatched out a throwing star he knew what was happening. The Ryqril, startled back into the open by the blasts, had reverted to the use of their superior firepower in an effort to regain the upper hand.

The laser flashed again. Someone screamed, but even as the Ryq swung his weapon at a new target, he fell,

Novak's star buried in his neck. Farther ahead, Novak could see reflected light from other lasers. Sheathing his *nunchaku*, he drew two throwing stars and, keeping to the shadows, moved silently forward. Firepower, the Ryqril would learn, was of only limited use against blackcollars.

Twenty minutes later, it was all over.

The 'port had been quiet for half an hour before Lathe let Hawking guide the autocab through its main gate. Gazing out the window, Caine spotted two or three blackcollars loitering in various shadows; none of the usual Security uniforms were visible anywhere. "You took the whole *'port*?" he asked unbelievingly.

"That's what we're going to find out," Lathe told him. "Over there, Hawking—looks like Kwon."

It was indeed the husky blackcollar, sporting a captured laser. He stepped forward as the autocab rolled up.

"Report," Lathe said.

"The tower and most of the 'port are ours. There are still some Ryqril in the barracks, but they're pinned down. If necessary we could fry them with the antiaircraft lasers, or even drop the whole building on top of them—Novak looked it over and says it could be done with five modest-sized bombs thrown in at key sites."

"I'll take his word for it," Lathe said. "We'll hold off on that for now—there might be something in there we'd rather have in an undemolished condition. What about the Corsairs?"

"All but one are effectively disabled, at least for anything involving the rear grav stabilizer. We left one intact, as per your instructions. Dodds is out there looking it over."

"Casualties?"

"Here at the 'port, nineteen: three blackcollars and sixteen trainees. Durbin reported two trainees killed among the rioters in Capstone—that number could go higher. And both Shen and Dhonau were killed."

Lathe nodded heavily. "Victory's expensive these days."

"As always."

Rubbing his chin thoughtfully, Lathe gazed across the landing field. "Those freighters look pretty small. Any idea what size they are?"

Kwon squinted into the darkness. "Not sure. F-class,

I'd guess. Jensen could tell you better—he's around here somewhere, probably within tingler range. Shall I ask him?"

"Please. If he confirms they're big enough, call the trucks in and start loading; I want to get off before daybreak. And let me borrow your long-range—I need to call the tower."

Kwon unclipped a small lens-shaped object from his belt and handed it over. "Tower can probably be reached by tingler, if you'd rather use code."

"I need to call Dodds out on the field, too." Lathe fingered the communicator. "Hawking, go over and help Jensen pick the freighter we're going to take. Mordecai, start rounding up the expedition—you know who's going? Good. And if you find Dayle Greene, ask him to step over. He's going to be in charge here while we're gone."

Kwon drifted back to his shadow as Hawking and Mordecai left the autocab. Alone with Lathe, Caine suddenly felt a bit uncomfortable. "Where are we going?" he asked.

"To get your starships, of course."

"Right *now*?"

Lathe fixed him with a curious gaze. "Certainly. Surely you didn't expect to climb aboard a passenger ship and fly back to Earth as if nothing had happened." He gestured at the cassette reader in Caine's lap. "How's the decoding coming?"

"Slowly. It's a tricky code."

"You know which system yet?"

There was something in Lathe's eyes that Caine didn't like. "Why?" he asked cautiously.

"Because I need to know where we're going before we lift off."

"But we have to go to Earth first and organize a crew."

"Earth is the first place they'll look for us," Lathe explained patiently. "We'll just have to try and pick up a crew in the other system instead. Now which is it?"

Caine pursed his lips. "System M-4. Orion Sector."

"Hmm. Argent's system." Lathe nodded, frowning slightly.

"Is that good or bad?"

"A little of both. A thriving planet—I assume Argent's still thriving—will make it easier to find a crew. On the other hand, Orion Sector runs up to the TDE-Chryselli border, which probably implies a strong Ryqril presence."

"Uh-oh. That doesn't sound good."

"It could be better," Lathe agreed. Raising the communicator, he flipped it on. "Lathe to Dodds. Lathe to Dodds."

A moment later a response came. "Dodds here."

"How's flight prep coming?"

"I just finished. You have the information?"

"Yes—number thirteen on our list. Got that?"

"One-three, right. If you'll clear me with the tower I'll be off. Safe flight to you."

"You too." Lathe tapped a couple more switches. "Lathe to whoever's in the tower."

"Novak here," the answer came promptly. "We were eavesdropping on your last call. What's Dodds doing?"

"Special assignment," Lathe said curtly. "I want you to shut down the lasers until he's cleared atmosphere."

There was a short silence. "I don't recall Dhonau mentioning this," Novak said.

"He didn't; this is on my authority," Lathe told him.

"I see." A moment passed. "Antiaircraft lasers shut down."

"Good. Call Dodds and tell him we can lift when ready." Shutting off the communicator, Lathe fastened it to his belt and turned to look at the rows of Corsairs.

Caine cleared his throat. "Just what *is* this mission, Lathe?"

"Later." He nodded at the field. "There he goes."

A diffuse glow was visible now, reflecting faintly from other fighters and the glaze-surface. As Caine watched, a dark bulk rose from the far end of the field, the blue-violet light from its gravs casting strangely colored shadows. Rotating to point eastward, it shot upward with surprising speed until it was almost invisible against the starry background. Then, abruptly, a white star erupted as the main drive kicked in. Arcing across the sky, it was lost to sight within seconds.

Lathe stirred, his left hand seeking his right wrist. "Someone's approaching the 'port," he told Caine. "Security car, the tower says. Mordecai's on his way; I want you to go to the ship with him, where you'll be safe."

"What about you?" Caine asked.

"I'm going to meet the car." He saw the look on Caine's face and added, "I'll be in no danger—this isn't an attack force coming. But your safety's too vital to take even small risks with. Go on."

Reluctantly, Caine got out, watching as Lathe circled back toward the 'port gate. Mordecai appeared at his side and together they set off across the field.

Lathe was waiting by the gate when the Security car rolled to a stop. The driver stepped out, his hands empty and held slightly away from his body. Spotting Lathe, he walked toward him.

It was Prefect Galway.

"I'm alone and unarmed," were his first words. "I'm here for a parley."

"What makes you think we've got anything to talk about?" Lathe asked, quietly putting away the throwing star he'd been palming.

Galway frowned as he studied what he could see of Lathe's face. "Comsquare Lathe, isn't it?" He shook his head ruefully. "Damn, but you had us fooled. I still can't believe what you've done to us."

"It wasn't all that easy, actually," Lathe told him. "You, particularly, have an unceasingly suspicious mind. But you didn't come here just to exchange compliments. What do you want?"

Galway glanced through the gate into the 'port. "Basically, I'm here to offer some advice." He turned back to face the blackcollar. "As a diversion and a lure, the riot you started was brilliant. But don't overdo it."

"What do you mean?" Lathe asked evenly.

"I mean you've got the population at flash point. Everyone in Capstone knows what's happening by now. They're looking at the trouble a few hundred teen-agers are giving us and probably wondering what an uprising by the whole population would do."

"What *would* it do?"

"Destroy Plinry," Galway said, and Lathe was struck by the intensity in the prefect's voice. "The Ryqril section of the Hub can't be taken—I'm sure you know that. Even if a revolt succeeded in boxing them in, it would last only until the next Ryqril courier showed up. A week after that the Corsairs would come." Galway waved toward the south, where the lights of Capstone were visible. "We haven't even recovered from the last war. How much punitive action do you think we could take?"

"Not much," Lathe admitted. "So what do you want from me?"

"I'd like you to stop the revolt. I'd settle for slowing it down, since you probably aren't interested in stopping it. We can negotiate a deal, if necessary, but bear in mind the kinds of concessions I can make are limited."

Lathe remained silent for a moment, then slowly shook his head. "No negotiations needed, Galway. We're not out to liberate Plinry—not this time, anyway. Our people will be going underground for a while, but if you don't push them or retaliate against Capstone's people they won't give you any more trouble."

Galway's eyes burned into his. "Your word?"

"I'll give the orders. That's all I can guarantee."

A slight twitch which might have been a smile. "All right. I'll try to keep my people in check, as well. Otherwise, there might not be a world here when you come back." Once more his eyes flicked toward the landing field and the dark ships there. "I'd give my last dose of Idunine to know what you're up to."

"You'll find out some day."

"I'm sure I will," Galway said dryly. Turning, he returned to his car and drove off.

From his vantage point near the lumpy freighter, Caine watched Galway drive away, his mind a tangle of conflicting thoughts. The meeting had been peaceful, even friendly, and the two men had talked for a long time. Why? More importantly, why had Lathe made so sure that there weren't any witnesses to the conversation?

He shook his head, feeling a little silly. Suspicions like that were highly unfair—the meeting had probably been a perfectly aboveboard parley. Still. . . . Caine became aware of the cassette reader in his hand and, almost unconsciously, gripped it a little tighter. Practically since his arrival the blackcollars had been calling the shots, and even now he was being treated rather like a piece of valuable cargo. But when the final crunch came, it would be Allen Caine who held the ace. And it wasn't a card he would give away lightly . . . nor to just anyone.

Lathe was coming toward the freighter now. Shifting the reader to his other hand, Caine headed for the ship's cargo hatch. Perhaps the blackcollars would let him help with the loading.

CHAPTER 9

The freighter's navigational computer put the distance to Argent as six parsecs. A Corsair would make the trip in three days; Caine's old passenger liner could have done it in seven. The freighter, designed for fuel efficiency rather than speed, took almost twelve.

There were twelve exceptionally busy days, however. While most of the eleven blackcollars aboard worked at organizing the equipment they'd brought along, Lathe detailed Skyler and Novak to give Caine a condensed version of blackcollar training. It was an intensive course, straining Caine's mnemonic and fighting skills to the limit. He learned the blackcollar combat codes, both tingler and hand signal forms; was given new unarmed fighting techniques and drilled in their use; and acquired at least a modest proficiency with *nunchaku*, slingshot, and *shuriken*. In between lessons he spent his time getting to know his fellow travelers . . . and asking carefully worded questions.

"Oh, yeah, me and Tardy go back to before the war. He knew every still on Plinry, and we used to steal the whiskey from 'em and use it as a primer in our bombs. Lathe? No, I didn't meet him till after the amnesty. . . ."

". . . Seems to me Lathe and Dodds had adjacent units—somewhere in the New Karachi area, I think. I didn't know either of them until I started coming to the lodge get-togethers. . . ."

". . . Dodds was always a quiet sort; never worked out with us at the lodge. I hear a nerve gas attack laid him out during the war and sort of scrambled his fighting reflexes. Smart guy, though, and he and Lathe get along pretty well. Sure, I've known Lathe a long time—we were standing in line together for the collie interrogation. . . ."

And so it went, until Caine was forced to the inescapable conclusion that no one aboard had ever heard of Lathe or Dodds until after the war.

The revelation wasn't all that remarkable, of course. Plinry had started with three hundred blackcollars—twenty-five of the standard twelve-man guerrilla teams—and with only thirty-one left it was reasonable that several of them would be the sole survivors of their units. Still, combined with Lathe's steadfast refusal to discuss Dodds's special mission, this new bit of information made Caine uneasy.

Three days out from Argent, when he finally finished decoding the Plinry record, he put the eight critical numbers—six spatial, two temporal—into a special mental file. Six hours of self-hypnosis later, it was ringed by a series of psycho-mental blocks that no drug or neurotrace could break before killing him.

No one—neither Lathe nor anyone else—would get those numbers until Caine was good and ready to give them up.

Argent was a bright speck with a clearly discernible disk when the freighter reentered normal space. Chelsey Jensen, at the helm, set the computer to working out an approach curve, and then punched for a schematic of the system. "That one's Argent," he told Caine, tapping the second planet. "Third or fourth most Earthlike world in the TDE and a real goldmine of minerals. The place was filthy rich before the war."

"Hmm." The schematic showed twelve more planets plus a strangely shaped haze. "What's that?" Caine asked, pointing to the latter.

"It's an asteroid belt, called the Diamond Ring for obvious reasons."

"What makes it bunch like that instead of distributing itself more evenly?"

"No idea. Made mining a lot easier, though, with so much of the stuff concentrated in one place. Ten to one it's where your Novas are hidden, too."

"Maybe. A good place to run guerrilla raids from, too."

In his mind's eye Caine could see tiny fighters appearing from nowhere to strike at the Ryqril forces—

"Not really. Asteroid belts aren't *that* dense; even the Diamond there is mostly empty space, and a ship moving with any decent drive trail would be trivial to track You'd do better hiding in a swamp or forest down on Argent."

The heroic vision vanished. "Oh. Is that what we're going to do, then?"

"Yes and no," a new voice said, and Caine turned as Lathe came up the tight spiral staircase. "We'll hide someplace like that for a day or so until we can contact the local underground."

Caine blinked. "You've been in touch with Argent's underground?"

Lathe gave him an odd look. "Of course not. We've been isolated on Plinry; you know that."

"But you just said—" Caine snapped his fingers. "Oh, of course. Dodds. He's already here, isn't he?"

"Caine, you have a bad habit of jumping to conclusions." Lathe turned to Jensen. "Situation?"

"The autopilot's taking us in," Jensen said, studying the readouts. "ETA of fifteen hours. Of course, we'll be challenged long before then."

"All right. Go get some rest and finish your preparations; I'll have Spadafora watch things here. Be back in nine hours."

"Right." With one last glance at the instruments Jensen crossed the room and vanished down the stairway.

"You, too," Lathe told Caine. "Go to the cargo bay and help get the drop pods ready."

"I want to be here when you talk to the planet," Caine said.

Lathe shrugged. "Okay. Just make sure you're in your flexarmor, ready to go."

Thirty minutes out of Argent's main traffic orbits, the call finally came. "Unidentified freighter on vector two-eight-zero, plus four-mark-nine, this is Argent Space Control. Identify yourselves."

Jensen gestured to the hand mike clamped to the control board. Picking it up, Lathe glanced at Caine and thumbed it on. "This is Trader First Class Donovan;

special cargo from Magna Graecia. Request priority orbit insertion away from major lanes."

"Your landing ID code?"

"I have none. This is a special cargo, as I said. I was given a code number and told to repeat it only to the Security Prefect's office."

Caine could almost hear the traffic controller sit up straighter. "Understood. Ringing Security now," he said. A minute passed and a new voice came on the speaker. "Security Prefect's office; Lieutenant Peron. What's this about a special cargo?"

"That's right," Lathe said. "Special *and* hazardous. The code *gamma-twelve* should identify it to you."

"Who gave you that code?"

"A Graecian Security officer—called himself Hydra. Look, he's down there somewhere; just get him over there and he'll confirm it."

There was a short pause. "We have no agent with that code name," he said, suspicion creeping into his voice. "Are you sure he was a genuine Security agent?"

"Positive, but I told you he works out of Magna Graecia, not Argent. He said he'd fly on ahead to get all the paperwork done so I could get rid of this stuff."

Another pause. "One moment."

Lathe turned off his mike. "Jensen, call down and order everyone into the pods. I don't know how long I can keep them running in circles down there, and we may need to break fast."

Jensen nodded and began speaking softly into the intercom. Glancing out the viewport, Caine could see the edge of Argent's blue-and-white disk, now less than a hundred thousand kilometers distant. A big, dangerous world—and the fact that he would be with eleven blackcollars didn't seem nearly as reassuring as it had a few days ago.

At the control board, the speaker again came to life. "This is Colonel Eakins, Assistant Security Prefect for Argent. Can you tell me anything more about this Hydra?"

"I can describe him for you," Lathe offered, launching into a three-minute description which seemed, to Caine, to be that of Plinry's Prefect Galway. Perhaps, he thought, Lathe *did* have a sense of humor. "But if he's not already down there I don't know what's happened."

"It's possible he works directly under the Ryqril military governor," Eakins rumbled. "We'll send a message there right away. In the meantime, you're cleared for deep polar orbit; we'll feed course data to your computer."

A two-tone signal acknowledged receipt. "Thank you," Lathe said. "And make sure everyone else stays clear of me. This stuff is damn touchy and I don't want a drive backwash anywhere near it."

There was a short silence. "I think I understand," Eakins said. "Very well. Argent out."

Lathe shut off the mike and replaced it in its clamps.

"Just about in orbit," Jensen reported. "When do you want to head in?"

Lathe rubbed his dragonhead ring thoughtfully. "Let's hold off as long as possible," he suggested. "If we can study the territory we'll have a better chance of finding a good landing spot."

"Right." Jensen hit some switches and four display screens came to life.

Lathe glanced at Caine before turning to the screens. "Caine, go to the bay and get into your pod. I don't want you hanging around here until the last minute and then rushing to get strapped in."

Caine nodded. "Okay. See you below." He hesitated. "Good luck, Jensen," he added.

The drop pods were shaped like truncated cones, each about three meters tall with a two-meter-diameter base. There were five of them crowded by the cargo hatch: two four-passenger models and three which would be carrying cargo plus one passenger. Jensen, who would still be flying when the others left, had a smaller pod stashed in the bridge's emergency lock.

The others were already in their places, and from the open pod doors came rustlings as straps and buckles were adjusted and double-checked. Crossing the floor, Caine peered into the narrow door of his pod. "There room for me in there yet?" he called.

From the shadows inside, Skyler waved an arm. "Sure; come on up."

Stepping up over the pod's thick ceramic heat shield, Caine squeezed through the opening and sidled a step to his right, twisting and ducking to avoid the three-dimensional maze of cables, straps, and bars hanging from the ceiling. Wedging himself between Vale and Novak, he strapped into his harness.

And then came the waiting.

Listening to the quiet conversation in the pod, studying the blackcollars' faces, Caine was struck as never before by the underlying similarity between these men. Underneath their differences in style and manner was a deep feeling of . . . what? Strength, he decided, combined perhaps with a casual confidence—qualities hard to reconcile with the raging warriors of the legends. A bit disappointing, he had to admit; and yet, the quietness was somehow reassuring.

They had been waiting nearly an hour when the pod abruptly jerked to the side as Jensen threw the freighter into a maneuver too fast for the artificial gravity to quite compensate. Conversation cut off instantly, and Caine could hear the muted whine of straining engines.

"This is it," Novak, by the pod door, announced grimly. He seemed unusually tense; but Caine knew it had nothing to do with the upcoming ride. He'd noted earlier in the trip that a special friendship existed between Jensen and Novak . . . and for several minutes after the others were gone Jensen was going to be a hellishly big target. "Shall I seal up?"

"Wait'll Lathe gets here," Skyler told him.

Seconds later the bay door slid open. "Button up, everyone," Lathe called, loping to his pod. "Jensen will blow the hatch in less than a minute. When you pop, head due west."

Novak reached out and pulled the door closed, plunging the pod into darkness. In his imagination Caine could see patrol ships diving toward them, threatening to open fire. Jensen would be stalling for time, claiming mechanical trouble, trying to get them in as close as possible—

And with a dull blast the pod gave a spine-wrenching lurch. An instant later they were tumbling through space, twisting violently as the freighter's turbulence caught them.

Fortunately, it was only a few seconds before the pod settled into a relatively stable vertical position, with air resistance providing a small but noticeable effective weight. Outside, Caine could hear the faint hiss of air whipping by, and it was all he could do to keep from reminding Skyler to watch the altitude gauge.

The minutes dragged by. Caine's weight increased steadily as the pod slowed, and he could feel the floor heating up beneath him. The air around them was getting warm, too, and the scream of their passage made conversation impossible. Gripping the straps of his harness, Caine tried to relax.

"Stand by chute!" Skyler had to shout to be heard. "Three, two, one—"

The first tug, as the drogue popped, was fairly gentle; the second, as the main chute snapped open, jammed Caine hard into his harness. Almost instantly the scream outside dropped to a whisper as full gravity returned. Getting his slightly trembling legs under him again, Caine took a careful breath. "Some ride," he commented.

"You think so?" Skyler said. His face, visible in the faint light of the luminous gauges, showed no more strain than his voice did. "We're thinking of selling it to an amusement center. Okay. We're two klicks up; break-out's at one-five. Forty seconds—everyone set?"

There were three affirmatives, and for a moment the pod was silent. "Five seconds; brace yourselves."

Caine tightened his grip on his harness . . . and with a jerk the pod's walls split from floor to ceiling. The floor disintegrated, and the sudden inflow of air snapped the walls up like a broken umbrella. Still fastened by the harness to his section of wall, Caine was thrown outwards as the pod fell apart in midair.

He had time only to notice that they had come in on Argent's night side before something snapped in the wall section which now hung over his head; and, with a loud hissing of compressed air and the clicking of spring-loaded connectors, a shadowy wing unrolled and stiffened above him. Within seconds, Caine found himself lying horizontally in his harness, gliding swiftly through the cold night air.

"Caine, you're pointed the wrong way," Skyler's voice said in his ear. "Turn about twenty degrees left."

The plastic control bar hung just in front of him, and Caine felt a touch of trepidation as he grasped it with both hands. He'd trained with grav belts back on Earth, but they were a far cry from hang gliders. Gingerly, he pulled on the bar—

The glider turned sharply left, and Caine got a glimpse of other dark wing shapes as he swung past the indicated direction. "Easy, easy," Skyler said. "The steering is very sensitive."

"Read that 'touchy,'" Caine muttered. He tried again and this time came around more smoothly.

"Good. One more tap and you should be on course."

Caine did so and then took a moment to search the sky. "I only see two other gliders," he said. "Where is everyone?"

"Well, *I'm* above and behind you," Skyler told him. "You can't expect all the pods to come down within eye-shot of each other. That's why someone always pops early, to act as spotter."

A new voice cut in. "Skyler, this is Kwon. Hit your UV, will you? Okay, turn it off. Your group together?"

"Affirmative," Skyler answered.

"Okay. Shift south; you're about half a klick north of O'Hara. Lathe? Okay; you're ahead of O'Hara, so just hold course. Haven?" Pause. "Yo, Haven? Your UV?"

"Must be broken," Haven's voice came back. "It's okay, though; I can see Skyler ahead and left of me."

"All right," Lathe said. "Our target is a wooded area about two klicks north of a medium-sized town. It's about thirty klicks away—a bit of a stretch—but we spotted some hotspots from the ship, so hopefully we'll get some assist from thermals. Kwon'll signal via tingler if the IR shows anything promising. Strict radio silence once we're back in tight formation."

The two gliders ahead of Caine had turned about fifteen degrees; carefully, he matched the maneuver. "Good turn," Skyler commented. "Not hard to pick up, is it?"

"No. Uh, Skyler, what exactly are we going to do once we get to this town?"

"Contact the local underground, of course."

"Fine, but how do we *do* that? Just walk up to a local and ask for directions?"

The blackcollar chuckled. "Not at all. It's simpler to let ourselves get captured."

And with that the radio went silent. "Great," Caine muttered to himself, and then settled down to concentrate on his flying.

Like black-winged wraiths the eleven gliders slid silently along between the stars and the dark landscape.

CHAPTER 10

The tingler on Caine's wrist gave notice that the five-hour wait was over: *bait returning; plus six and two vehicles*. "They're coming," he said unnecessarily, scrambling to his feet and glancing south, as if in the pre-dawn light his eyes could penetrate the forest around them.

"Yeah, I heard," Hawking said dryly, standing up more leisurely. "You sound surprised they got out."

"Little town or not, a jail's still a jail," Caine said. In the clearing, the other four were already collecting backpacks and moving to the shelter of the trees. Spotting Skyler, he walked over to him. "I've been wondering about something," he said quietly. "What if the guys who sprung Lathe and the others *aren't* the underground?"

"Who else would they be?" Haven, walking by with two packs, put in.

"Security forces," Caine suggested. "It would be an ideal way to infiltrate us and find out what we're up to."

Skyler shook his head. "Interesting idea, but too devious for this stage of things—loyalty-conditioning tends to make people think in straight lines. They may try something that convoluted later, but not now."

Caine still had his doubts, but just then his tingler came to life, signaling the party's arrival. Four of the six Argentians were accompanying Lathe's group into the woods, while the other two stayed with the vehicles. Silently, the blackcollars faded into the perimeter of the clearing. Caine chose a position behind a thick bole, where he would have a good view. Heart pounding, he settled down to wait.

He heard them shuffling through the dead leaves underfoot a good thirty seconds before they came into sight. Peering around his tree, Caine studied the four Argentians walking in a rough semicircle behind Lathe, Valen, Kwon, and Spadafora. They were dressed identically, in loose brown jumpsuits and military-style boots, with snug mesh-masks that reduced their facial features to vague shadows. Their weapons, pellet rifles of some kind, looked well cared for and were being held in a casually ready way that indicated good training.

Lathe, in the lead, walked to the center of the clearing and stopped by a half-rotted tree trunk. The others stopped, too, and it seemed to Caine that the rifle barrels rose just a fraction.

"Well? Where are the guns?" one of the Argentians demanded, and Caine blinked with surprise—it was a *woman's* voice!

"There aren't any, I'm afraid," Lathe said apologetically. "The gunsmuggler hints we dropped in town were really just to get your attention."

The guns definitely rose this time. "Cute," the woman said, her voice icy. "Well, you have it. You'd better have a damn good explanation or you may wish you didn't."

"It's quite reasonable, actually," Lathe told her. "We've just arrived on a special military mission and needed to link up with the underground. Letting ourselves be captured in a suitably out-of-the-way place where you could rescue us seemed the easiest way to do it."

"Uh-huh. Easy, but stupid. Suppose we *hadn't* gotten you out?"

"Oh, we could have escaped by ourselves," Lathe shrugged. "Can you get us in touch with whoever's in charge of your organization?"

"Not so fast," another Argentian—a man—growled. "Li, they've got to be spies. Let's burn 'em and get the hell out of here."

"Sit on it, Rom," the woman said. To Lathe: "He's got a good case, you know, even though this sounds stupider than some of the things they've tried to suck us in on. Let's start with your name and go on from there, shall we?"

Lathe shrugged. "All right. I'm Comsquare Damon Lathe; Blackcollar Forces. We're on a special mission from Plinry with the authority of General Kratochvil of Earth. For now that's all I can say."

There was a murmur of surprise from the other three Argentians, but neither the woman nor her weapon so much as twitched. "Offworld blackcollar, eh? Well, it's original—I'll give it that. Can you prove it?"

"I can try," Lathe said. His hand curved—

And three *shuriken* thudded into the dead tree trunk.

Instantly, the Argentians spun around . . . or, rather, they tried to. But before Caine even realized they'd moved, Lathe and his companions had their rescuers' weapons. And their rescuers.

"Excuse the rough handling," Lathe said mildly. He held the woman's rifle in one hand; with the other he maintained a negligent-looking grip on her wrist which was somehow holding her motionless. "But we don't carry ID cards."

"Doesn't prove a thing," one of the Argentians bit out, struggling unsuccessfully against Kwon and the wrist lock that had him on his knees. "Their rads threw those things to startle us—they jumped us when our backs were turned."

"Maybe yours was turned." Surprisingly, the woman didn't sound angry. "Mine wasn't. And those 'things' are *shuriken*—genuine blackcollar weapons." She nodded back toward the woods. "I'm convinced. You want to ask your rads in to join the party?"

"Certainly," Lathe said, releasing her arm and handing back her rifle. "What are rads?"

"Your friends," she said, accepting the weapon. Touching what was probably the safety, she slung it over her shoulder. "The guys who provided your handy little diversion."

"Oh." Lathe gave the all-clear, and with a crunch of dead leaves Caine and the five hidden blackcollars stepped into the clearing. Caine wished he could see the expressions under those mesh-masks; combat-garbed blackcollars were an impressive sight—

"You sure brought a mob with you," she said, eyeing them. "Is this it?"

"We also have a spotter at the edge of the woods," Skyler said.

"All right. The cars won't carry everyone; some of

you'll have to walk." She nodded to her three companions who, unlike her, still held their rifles uncertainly at the ready. "You can take these four directly through the woods to the house. We'll take the others and their baggage in the cars."

"But, Li, we still don't know who they are," one of the Argentians objected, gesturing toward Vale with his weapon.

"They're *blackcollars*—which means they're on our side," she explained patiently. "So get moving. And I suggest you sling your rifle before he takes it away from you again."

The man snorted, but started off into the woods, the other six men close behind. The woman nodded to Skyler. "Let's go."

The "house" they were driven to was actually more like a woodland estate. Nestled into the far edge of the woods were a three-floor stone house, a large garage, and three or four shedlike buildings at various distances from the main building. A concealed trap door in one of the latter led to a tunnel heading in the direction of the main house. Following it, they emerged into a well-furnished subbasement. Two threadbare couches and several chairs lined the walls, and there was even a microwave cooker and a stack of sterile-pack food. Less domestic looking was the humming bug stomper sitting next to the phone. Two other tunnels and a door headed off from various walls.

"Make yourselves at home, gentlemen," the woman said. She had pulled off the mesh-mask and Caine got his first look at her face.

It was a great disappointment. From her voice Caine had rather expected her to be beautiful; the lovely, stormy-eyed patriot of youthful fantasies. Instead, she was about as plain-featured as she could possibly be. Her light-brown hair, cut short in a style which was easy to care for, did nothing to soften the squareness of her face, and her violet eyes seemed more tired than stormy. He felt vaguely cheated—and was instantly ashamed of his reaction.

"I suppose we should introduce ourselves somewhere

along in here," Skyler said. "I'm Rafe Skyler; this is Mordecai; Allen Caine; Kelly O'Hara. . . ."

She nodded to each as Skyler went down the list. "My name's Lianna Rhodes," she said when he had finished. "I'm more or less in charge of the Radix cell in this region."

"Does this Radix have a central leadership?" Hawking asked.

"Yes—the main HQ is in Calarand, Argent's capital. We've got a supposedly secure phone link to them, but I don't like to use it. If you'll write up something about this mission of yours, I'll encode it for you and we can send it by runner."

"Fine." Skyler nodded.

The two drivers, who'd been hiding the cars, came in as Skyler and Hawking were composing a suitable note, and Lianna pulled one aside for a brief conversation. He nodded and headed across the room, disappearing through the door there. Caine caught Lianna's eye and nodded questioningly toward it. "Leads to a storeroom," she explained. "That was Jason Ho; he'll be running your note to Calarand and needs to change clothes first. We'll get all of you some normal clothes, too," she added, eyeing his black flexarmor.

"Perhaps we could take a look outside and upstairs first," Novak suggested. "Nothing against your security, but we like to check things out ourselves."

"Look outside all you want," Lianna said. "But the main house is off-limits. It's owned by the local Commerce Subaltern and is loaded with anti-intruder systems."

The air was suddenly electric. "Explain, please," Skyler said softly.

"Oh, don't worry, nobody's up there—Navare and his people only come here during vacations. We don't come near the place then, naturally, but at other times it's safe enough as long as you avoid the main house."

"Debatable," O'Hara rumbled. "Don't they ever wonder what happened to their subbasement?"

"They don't know it's here—the connection was sealed off and the official blueprints altered before the war ended. Besides, who would even look for a Radix cell under a quizler's own nose?"

"Practically no one," Skyler admitted. "Your idea?"

For the first time Lianna dropped her eyes. "No, it was my father's. He headed this cell until . . . recently."

The awkward silence was broken by the sound of footsteps, and from one of the tunnels Lathe and his group appeared, along with their Argentian escort. "Any trouble?" Lianna asked the latter.

One of the men shook his head. "No, but we'd better get them out of here soon," he said as he and the others pulled off their mesh-masks. "A Security flier just came in from the direction of Calarand—they're not going to be happy to find their prisoners gone."

"Pretty fast reaction," Lianna said thoughtfully. "Okay, we'll take them to the Harmon house—that should be far enough away from Janus to be outside any cordon they throw up. Jason's going to Calarand, see if HQ wants them. You about ready with that?" she added to Skyler.

Lathe had moved to Skyler's side and was reading the note over his shoulder. "There's one other thing," the comsquare spoke up. "One of our people didn't jump with us, but rode the ship farther in. If he made it out he'll be alone and probably gone to ground. Can you get a search party out to try and find him?"

"Put it in your note," Lianna said shortly. "We can't handle something like that from here."

The safe house was a couple of hours' drive away, and they reached it without incident. They stayed there most of the day, catching up on food and sleep and being fitted with Argentian clothing. Hawking discovered that the cell's spare bug stomper was broken and spent most of the afternoon fixing it. For the rest of them, though, it was mostly waiting.

Finally, around sunset, word came from Calarand via secure line that the Radix chief would meet with them. Half an hour later they were rolling down a dusty road in a loose convoy of five vehicles. Sitting in the back seat of the middle car, wedged between Mordecai and Kwon, Caine tried to doze through the long trip. He wasn't very successful. Calarand, a small voice kept whispering, was a complete unknown, full of Security forces and untested allies.

And very likely lots of Ryqril, too.

CHAPTER 11

Argent's yellow-orange sun was peeking over the horizon as the convoy came in sight of Calarand. After the relative flatness of Capstone, Calarand's thirty- and forty-story buildings gave Caine a flash of déjà vu back to New Geneva. But as they drove through the outskirts of the city, he saw that, like Capstone, Calarand had seen its share of war. There were no blast holes or piles of rubble, of course, but the buildings were liberally dotted with slightly mismatched patching, a few of them showing glazed areas where laser cannon had been used. Even in the relatively dim light the sight was depressing, and it sharpened Caine's already guilty awareness of how little Earth itself had suffered.

"This section is mainly low-skill laborers and light industry," Lianna, sitting next to the driver, was saying when Caine tuned back in to the conversation in the car.

"What sort of industry?" Kwon asked, gazing out the side window.

"Around here, mostly textiles and small appliances. Farther in, in the Strip, there's weapon-component manufacture. The Strip's a sort of buffer zone between the government center and the outer city," she added. "You go through metal and power source detectors and usually soniscopes to get in or out, but you don't need a quizler ID card."

"Odd setup," Kwon commented.

She shrugged. "The weapons work fluctuates a lot, depending on Ryqril war needs. I guess they didn't want to condition a whole crowd of workers that they'd only occasionally need."

Kwon glanced at Mordecai, and Caine could read the thought that passed between the blackcollars: a weapons plant that was only semi-restricted was practically a hand-lettered invitation for havoc.

Pedestrians and a fair number of vehicles were on the

move by the time they pulled up in front of a blocky four-floor apartment house. A hundred meters ahead, Caine caught a glimpse of Hawking's white hair disappearing into a different building. "Hey!" he said, pointing.

"Relax, Caine; they're just using a different entrance," Lianna told him. "Come on, let's go."

They went inside and Lianna took them down a flight of stairs to a basement apartment. The middle-aged occupant let them in and, after exchanging sign and countersign with Lianna, ushered them into a tunnel hidden behind the bedroom wardrobe. Lianna, penlight in hand, went first, and Caine counted a hundred thirty steps before they arrived at a narrow spiral staircase and started up. He estimated they were three floors above street level when Lianna pushed open a panel and led them, blinking, into a brightly lit room.

Squinting in the glare, Caine looked around. The room was windowless and respectively sized, sort of a cross between a large private office and a small company boardroom. A dozen young, hard-looking men stood against the walls; from an open door across the room the remaining blackcollars and Argentian escort were filing in. And in the center, seated on one side of a large bug stomper-equipped table, were four men.

They were the leaders of Radix; Caine knew it instantly. The cool, speculative looks they wore as they studied their visitors, the age and experience that even periodic Idunine use couldn't erase from their eyes—all of it merely reinforced that undefinable air of authority and responsibility that he'd seen in the Resistance leaders on Earth. Casually, Caine studied each of the four in turn, trying to gauge their reaction to the newcomers. It was a futile exercise—necessity had long ago made masks of their faces.

The door closed, and one of the seated men stood up. "Janus team, please step off to the side there."

Lianna's group complied, leaving Caine and the ten blackcollars standing in front of the table. The man raised his eyebrows questioningly, and Lathe took a half step forward. "I'm Comsquare Damon Lathe, in command of this squad, acting under the authority of General Kratochvil of Earth," he said in a clipped, military tone. "And you?"

"Ral Tremayne," the other said. "In charge of the organization Radix. Can you prove your identity or authorization?"

"If you mean with signature tapes or papers, no. However, given that we're blackcollars, our loyalties should be obvious."

"A lot of you blackcollars just gave up after the war," the olive-skinned man at Tremayne's left said coolly.

"A lot of us *died* in it, too," Lathe said.

"All too many," agreed the slender man sitting on Tremayne's right. His eyes were on Lathe's face as he rose to his feet. "Serle Bakshi; Comsquare," he introduced himself, his hand forming a fistlike salute. The red eyes in his dragonhead ring flickered briefly in the light.

Lathe smiled with clear surprise and repeated the gesture. "Greatly pleased, Comsquare. I'd hoped to find other blackcollars on Argent, but I hadn't really expected—"

The faint sound behind them had barely registered on Caine's consciousness when the room abruptly exploded with activity. Twisting around, he was just in time to see Haven's thrown *nunchaku* wrap itself around the outstretched gun arm of one of the Radix guards standing there. The arm swiveled against the wall with the impact, the clatter of the *nunchaku* sticks drowning out the youth's exclamation. The pistol he'd been holding skittered across the floor and into the wall; another guard, reaching to retrieve it, jerked back as a black star buried three centimeters of itself in the wall directly above the weapon.

And then there was silence . . . the silence of a tautly coiled spring. From the karate stance he'd automatically dropped into, Caine saw that the blackcollars were similarly poised for combat. Crouched low, they faced outward from their central position, waiting with throwing stars at the ready.

All except Lathe. As far as Caine could tell the old comsquare hadn't moved a single muscle during the incident. Now, in the brittle stillness, he stepped to the edge of the table, his eyes blazing with anger. Shifting his gaze between Tremayne and Bakshi, he jabbed a finger at the phone sitting by the bug stomper. "Call them up here," he said, biting out each word. "Everyone; all your guards and soldiers. We'll take them hand to hand, maybe kill a dozen or so. Will *that* convince you we're really blackcollars?"

"My sincerest apologies," Tremayne said in a low voice. Strangely enough, he didn't seem particularly frightened. "I know it wasn't fair, but we had to make sure."

"Fair? We might have killed him. We might have killed *all* of you."

A faint smile brushed Tremayne's lips. "I have perhaps more faith in your self-control than you do, Comsquare."

"And *I* have better knowledge of blackcollar reflexes than you do," Lathe countered, cooling down some. "Okay, you've had your fun. Next time, we assume it's a real attack and aim to kill. Make sure your people know it." He gave the all-clear and stepped back as the blackcollars straightened up, *shuriken* and *nunchakus* vanishing once more.

Tremayne glanced around at the guards. "All right, you can go now. Make sure everything's secure." He gestured at Lianna's group. "And see that Janus team gets breakfast and a place to sleep."

When the door was again closed, Tremayne gestured to the other chairs around the table. "Comsquare; gentlemen . . .?" he said as he and Bakshi seated themselves.

Lathe, Skyler, and Hawking took him up on the offer and sat down facing the Radix leaders. Caine and the others remained on their feet, either standing nearby or drifting around the room.

"Now, what exactly is it you want here?" Tremayne asked, leaning forward and clasping his hands atop the table like a horizontal victory salute.

"First of all, answers to a few questions. Number one: have you had any word about Jensen yet?"

Tremayne gestured to the scholarly looking man at Bakshi's right. "My aide, Jeremiah Dan, is handling that. Jer?"

Dan steepled his fingers. "Your ship—I assume it was yours—crashed on the eastern slope of the Rumelian Mountains some thirty hours ago. We know approximately where; the problem at the moment is that Security has closed off the whole area. We have a small cell already in the region and they've been alerted, but that's the best we can do right now."

Lathe's jaw tightened momentarily. "Well, keep us

informed. If you hear he's been found—by either side—let me know immediately." He looked back at Tremayne. "That leads into my second question. I'd like to know something about your organization; specifically, its size and distribution and how well you've done against the Ryqril."

"Seems to me it would be simpler for you to tell us first exactly what you want," Bakshi suggested mildly. "Then we can tell you if we can supply it."

"Simpler, maybe, but not as interesting," Skyler spoke up. "Besides, knowing what size team you've got often determines which game you're going to play."

Bakshi started to reply, but Tremayne laid a restraining hand on the blackcollar's arm. "No, he's right, Serle. Well, let's see. Radix currently has something like half a million members and active support personnel, out of a planetary population of one and a quarter billion. We're distributed pretty well around the world, though we tend to be concentrated in large cities like Calarand."

"What about your security?" Lathe asked. "I'd think with cells as big as this one you'd have a large infiltration problem."

Tremayne shrugged. "Actually, I think we have less of one this way, since everyone in a cell has to agree on accepting a new member. The quizlers occasionally try and slip in ringers, but we catch them quickly enough."

Lathe nodded. "All right. Now tell us about your notch record."

"Well, we're still here, despite quizler efforts to the contrary," Tremayne said with a humorless smile. "Other than that, it's not as good as we'd like. We harass them here and there—hijacking goods shipments, for example—but the really big targets are essentially invulnerable."

"You know this from experience?" Skyler asked politely.

"Very painful experience. Usually we recognize the inevitable early enough to pull back and cut our losses."

"You have some specific target in mind?" Jeremiah Dan asked.

"Eventually, yes," Lathe said. "First of all, though, we'll need you to locate all the old Star Force veterans you can find. I presume there were a number trapped on the ground when the defense folded?"

"Yes," Tremayne said, forehead corrugating. "But the war was a long time ago."

"That won't be a problem if they've been getting Idunine regularly," Vale put in quietly from somewhere behind Caine.

"They *have* been getting Idunine, haven't they?" Skyler asked, eyeing the Argentians' youthful faces.

"Now *look*—" the olive-skinned man began.

"At ease, Uri," Tremayne said. "As it happens, Commando, we've been very successful at intercepting Idunine shipments. And war veterans are high on our priority list."

"Good." Lathe nodded. "Then I'd like your people to start rounding them up as soon as possible."

"I'm afraid the rounding up's already been done," Dan spoke up. "Word came last night, Ral; I didn't get a chance to tell you."

"Oh, hell," Bakshi growled. "Again?"

Dan nodded.

Tremayne looked like he had a bad taste in his mouth. "I guess you're out of luck, Comsquare. All three hundred fifty of the old starmen have been locked away, probably for a couple of months."

"What?" For the first time since Caine had known him Lathe looked completely taken by surprise. "Why?"

"Happens every time the Ryqril launch a major thrust against the Chryselli in this theater," Bakshi explained. "The front's only a parsec or so away at this point. I guess they're afraid that someone will grab a ship while their forces are busy and can't give chase."

"That's ridiculous," Lathe snorted. "Where could he go?"

"Practically anywhere," Bakshi shrugged. "A single ship could penetrate almost any picket screen, even near a battle front."

"I know *that*," Lathe snapped. "What I meant was where would he *land*? Everything within thirty parsecs is owned, occupied, or under attack by the Ryqril."

"Look, *we* don't make up these rules," Bakshi pointed out with some heat. "The quizlers don't ask our permission before putting people in jail."

"You're right." Lathe rubbed a hand across his face. "Sorry. Any idea where they're being held?"

"Same place as always: Henslowe Prison, on the southern edge of the Strip," Dan said. "It's about twelve kilometers from here."

"Well guarded, I suppose."

"Very much so." Tremayne was looking more and more curious. "What exactly do you need these vets for?"

"For the moment that's still confidential," Lathe told him.

"Look, Comsquare—"

"You've had a long night," Bakshi interrupted his chief. "Why don't we let you rest for a while, and continue our talk later?"

"That would probably be a good idea," Lathe agreed.

Tremayne looked less than happy, but he nodded. "All right. Jer, did you arrange space for them?"

Dan nodded. "The man just outside will show you to your rooms."

"Thank you for your hospitality," Lathe said, getting to his feet.

"It's no problem. Rest well."

The door closed behind the blackcollars and Tremayne pushed his chair back. "Thanks for short-circuiting the argument, Serle," he said to Bakshi. "Comments?" he added, glancing to both sides.

"I still think it was a bad idea to bring them here," Uri Greenstein, the olive-skinned man to his left, said. "We still don't know quizler spit about either them or this wild-duck run of theirs, and meanwhile they're stirring up Security like crazy. Even if they're on our side—"

"If?" Bakshi cut in mildly.

"Yes, *if*. Blackcollars are human, too, Comsquare, and I don't believe all of you can be as noble as you'd like us to think. As I was saying, even if they're really on our side the extra Security activity they've precipitated could be a real problem."

"That's a good point," Jer Dan agreed. "If reports from the Rumelian district are indicative, the quizlers are preparing to turn the whole planet over."

"What do you suggest?" Tremayne asked.

"Isolate them," was the prompt reply. "Break off contact with all other cells so that only the Calarand group is at risk."

"Will that leave us enough manpower?" Bakshi wondered.

"What, with a dozen new blackcollars at your disposal?" Greenstein snorted.

"We can keep the Janus people here," Tremayne told Bakshi. "That's no extra risk, since Lathe's men already know them. Other comments? All right, then. Jer, I want you to start alerting the other cells to stay clear of us. Uri, you'd better get back to Millaire and pass the word to the southern division."

"Right," Greenstein noded. "Also, since Calarand is going silent, you won't be able to monitor the search for the missing blackcollar, Jensen. I'll handle that."

"Thanks." Tremayne paused. "Speaking of blackcollars, did anyone else notice something unusual during the mock attack earlier?"

There was a moment of silence. "I did," Bakshi said. "One of them fell into a slightly different combat stance than the others."

Tremayne nodded slowly. "That's what I thought, too, The Janus report said they were from Plinry but were operating under Earth auspices. I wonder. . . ."

"You think the odd man's an Earther?" Dan asked.

"Could be," Tremayne said. "Which raises the question of how he got out past Earth Security."

"Maybe there isn't any," Bakshi suggested. "Depending on how hard Earth was hit, there may not be much there to guard."

"Well, there's no profit in speculation." Tremayne shrugged. "We'll give them four or five hours to sleep, but after that I'll want to nail Comsquare Lathe down as to exactly what his credentials are."

"And exactly what his business here is," Bakshi added.

Tremayne nodded grimly. "Especially that."

CHAPTER 12

"I know I saw something," one of the five Security men puffed as the group came through the narrow gap and onto the bluff. "Like a reflection from metal or glass." He gestured about midway up the rugged, tree-covered slope ahead.

"Keep watching," another advised him, shifting his snub-nosed laser rifle uncomfortably as he looked around. "And don't forget he's had half an hour to move since you first saw it."

Hidden behind a tree a bare ten meters behind them, Jensen raised his assessment of the group a notch or two. Inexpert though they seemed to be at this sort of outdoor work, they *were* observant; and their leader, at least, was no fool. He had no way of knowing, after all, that Jensen had hung that spare binocular lens on the tree branch over an hour ago, when he'd first spotted the group moving up the mountain toward him. The intent had been to lure them into dashing gleefully upslope toward his supposed position, hopefully without leaving a guard by this key route off of the bluff. He was beginning to have his doubts whether this was the right kind of group to fall for that trick, though.

"There!" the first man exclaimed, pointing.

"I saw it, too," one of the others seconded. "About ten degrees to the left of that dead redthorn."

"Okay, let's go," the leader said. "Remember that this guy is dangerous, so if things get hot go ahead and shoot to kill. Dennie, get some other teams moving across into our sector and alert air support. Warn 'em to hang back, though—we don't want to spook him. Cham, you'll stay here in case he gets past us. Okay, move out."

Secure behind his tree, Jensen watched as four of the five disappeared into the brush. The trick had still been worth a try, he decided. Possibly he'd even gained on the exchange: though Security now had a fair idea of his location, Jensen had learned in turn that they were so eager to get him that they were including inexperienced city men in their patrols. Interesting, too, was the fact that they knew he was alone.

The guard, Cham, found some mossy-looking stuff next to a large boulder and sat down stiffly, giving Jensen a good profile view as he rested his snub-nosed rifle butt-down on the ground between his knees. Moving aside the thin wire-mike that extended from his helmet, he turned a knob near its connection point all the way over. Leaning his head against the boulder, he closed his eyes.

Jensen eyed him thoughtfully, wondering what he had just done. Had he turned his intrasquad radio down, so he could sleep without the others hearing any snoring, or had he turned the radio *up* so that they would hear the sound of a weapon if he was ambushed? Probably the latter, Jensen decided—which implied, in turn, a very cautious soldier, since Jensen was supposedly a good distance away. Grimacing, Jensen settled down to watch for an opening.

The minutes ticked by slowly. The guard's eyes remained closed, but his breathing indicated he wasn't asleep. Around them the mountainside was silent except for various insectean sounds; nothing but occasional birds crossed the sky above them. But Jensen knew the isolation was largely illusory, and that if the alarm went off the sky and landscape would fill up with remarkable speed. *Patience is a virtue*, he told himself, and continued watching.

But finally he could wait no longer. The rest of the patrol should be halfway to the hanging lens, and he would need at least a few minutes to get through the gap before they discovered the trick and whistled for reinforcements. To make his own opening was dangerous, but he had no other choice. Picking up a stone, he fitted it into his slingshot and lobbed it into a patch of reedy-looking grass fifteen meters upslope. It landed with a completely satisfactory *chunksh*.

The guard came alert instantly, swinging his rifle to the direction of the sound with one hand while adjusting the position and volume of his mike with the other. "Cham here," he said softly. "I heard something in the hill-rushes near me. I'm going to investigate."

Warily, he stood up, rifle held waist-high and swinging in a gentle arc. Jensen watched as he approached the knee-high grass cautiously, head moving slightly as he scanned the area. At the edge he stood for a moment, then suddenly fired three shots into different parts of the patch. Nothing happened, and after a moment he turned back. "Must've been an animal," Jensen heard him say as he headed back to his boulder. The response wasn't audible, but Cham smiled tightly. "Sure, but who knows how fast these blackcollars can travel? . . . You too."

With one last look around, Cham sat back down on his moss. Pushing his mike to the side again, he reached for the volume control—

And the stone from Jensen's slingshot caught him full force in the side of his throat.

He slumped, his hand falling limply to his side, and in seconds Jensen was beside him. Carefully removing the helmet, he held it like a sea shell to his ear. Faintly, he could hear grunts and occasional comments from the others as they worked their way up the mountain. There was no indication they'd heard anything unusual; or if they had, that they'd attached any significance to it. Jensen's gamble had paid off.

Quickly, he searched the dead man, coming up with a field medkit and ration package which he added to his own supplies. The laser rifle was tempting, but its power pack could be sensed at an uncomfortably great distance, especially here on the back side of nowhere. The helmet, unfortunately, was almost as bad, even with the transmitter off, its electronics and battery would show up like a large Scotch tartan. Picking up both the helmet and rifle, he tossed them a few meters into the forest. They would be found, of course, but he might as well cause the enemy as much trouble as was practical.

And then it was down into the gap. Jensen moved as quickly as he could without making too much noise, driven by a sense of urgency he hadn't felt earlier. Being chased by Security forces was nothing particularly unexpected—but when they knew both that he was alone *and* that he was a blackcollar, something was very wrong. Wherever Lathe and his team were, the enemy was on to them.

He was a good fifteen minutes past the bottom of the

gap and into heavy brush again when the dull crack of a blast grenade drifted down from upslope. Apparently the Security team had found the booby-trap he'd left for them. Very soon now the whole face of the mountain would be crawling with enemies.

From here on, things would start getting sticky.

CHAPTER 13

Caine wakened at the soft mention of his name. Eyes closed, he remained motionless for another few seconds. All seemed peaceful; across the room, near the door, Lathe was speaking softly: ". . . still asleep, and there's no point in waking him."

"Sorry," a new voice said, "but Ral said specifically to bring Caine along."

Caine opened his eyes. "I'm awake, Lathe," he said softly, trying not to wake anyone else. "What is it?"

Both Lathe and the other speaker—it was Jeremiah Dan—looked over at him; Lathe, he noted, with mild annoyance. "Ral Tremayne wants you and Lathe to meet with our tactical group," Dan explained.

"It's not necessary that you go," Lathe interjected. "I can handle any tactical discussions."

The first step toward freezing him out? Getting to his feet, Caine threaded his way through the rows of cots the Radix people had set up for them. "No problem. Sounds interesting, actually."

"All right." Lathe shifted his gaze from Caine and nodded an invitation across the room. Haven and Novak, seated on opposite sides of a chessboard, stood up and came forward. "I'd like you there, too," Lathe told them. "If we wind up assaulting this Henslowe Prison you'll each be leading a squad."

Dan's eyes widened. "Comsquare, uh . . . we really don't have the manpower for anything that big."

"Why not? Tremayne said you had half a million people.

You could storm the place with rocks with numbers like that."

"But then we wouldn't have half a million people anymore, would we?" Dan said icily. Turning on his heel, he strode out into the hall.

Caine felt an acute sense of embarrassment as he and the three blackcollars followed. Hoping to smooth relations, he caught up with Dan and gestured at the long, high-ceilinged hallway. "Just what *is* this place. Mr. Dan?" he asked. "It doesn't look like any building I've ever seen."

Some of the stiffness went out of Dan's back. "It was once a government building, back about sixty years ago, housing the Mining Department. When a new place was built for them this one was sold and made into private offices. Since then the takeover parts have been further converted into apartments. We own the whole building through various business and private fronts."

Dan took them to the same small boardroom they'd been in earlier. This time, though, the central table was considerably more crowded: along with Tremayne and Bakshi were six other men and two women. For Caine, the most unexpected—and welcome—sight were the four men seated next to Bakshi. They looked young, tough, and alert . . . and they wore black turtlenecks and dragon-head rings.

Tremayne was sitting at the head of the table this time, with Bakshi at his right. Lathe took the chair at the other end of the table; Caine took the empty seat next to him.

"I'm sorry," Tremayne said, glancing at Novak and Haven as Dan slid into the last chair, "I wasn't expecting anyone else. I'll send for two more chairs."

"No need," Lathe told him. "They can stand."

"It's not necessary—"

"I said they can stand."

A faint shuffle of people shifting in their seats went around the table, and Caine saw one or two brief frowns. Tremayne's lip twitched, but he nodded. "As you wish. Let me introduce our tactical group." He gestured to the left side of the table. "Next to Jer is Salli Quinlan, in charge of military intelligence; Miles Cameron, intelligence chief; and Stuart York, supply chief. On my right, Comsquare Bakshi is overall tactician and field operations chief; Commandos McKitterick, Valentine, Fuess, and Couturie lead our raiding parties; Faye Picciano is another tactician."

There were nods all around. "I'm looking forward to hearing about conditions on Plinry from you," Faye said, shifting her gaze between Lathe and Caine. Looking across the table at her, Caine decided she was much closer to his mental image of the female Resistance fighter than Lianna Rhodes had been—more attractive, but still with the necessary toughness hovering behind her eyes. And unlike the matronly Salli Quinlan, she wasn't wearing a wedding band.

"Certainly," Lathe said. "But later. Right now conditions on Argent are more important." He looked down the table at the other woman. "Mrs. Quinlan, is there any way to estimate how long the current Ryqril campaign will last?"

"Just a minute, Comsquare," Tremayne cut in before Salli could speak. "Before we go any further we'd like to know exactly what your mission here is."

"As I explained before, that's confidential," Lathe said. "You'll be told what you need when you need it; not before. It's safer for everyone that way."

"And what gives you the right to make that decision?" Valentine, one of the blackcollars, objected. "This is *our* world, not yours."

"Really?" Lathe said dryly. "I thought the Ryqril held title to Argent at the moment."

Valentine scowled. "Look, Lathe, the occupation stopped being funny about thirty years ago."

"Sorry. But *you*, of all people, shouldn't be questioning me. As long as you call yourself a blackcollar, *this*—" he held up his red-eyed dragonhead ring—"gives me all the authority I need."

"Unless we're under command already," Fuess, a big blond man with sunken cheeks, put in. "And we are."

Lathe stared coolly at him for a second, then turned to Bakshi. "Comsquare, do *you* accept my authority?"

"To give non-contradicting orders, yes," Bakshi replied. "But the line of command here is anything but clear. For instance, you claimed to have authority from General Kratochvil of Earth. Did you swing by there on your way from Plinry, or what?"

Lathe shook his head. "Kratochvil's message was brought by one of his agents—Caine here. As there was no one left on Plinry of comparable rank to either endorse or reject the orders, we accepted them on Caine's word."

Tremayne nodded slowly. "We wondered about Caine. . . . But what about General Lepkowski? He was supposed to be on Plinry."

"Lepkowski stopped endorsing orders thirty-five years ago," Lathe said grimly. "He died in the Ryqril Groundfire attack."

"I see." For a long moment Tremayne sat silently, frowning as his eyes searched Lathe's face. "Very well," he said at last. "We'll trust you—for now. But you're to confer with Comsquare Bakshi or myself before doing anything that may put my people in danger." He nodded to Salli Quinlan. "All right, Salli; go ahead."

Glancing once at Lathe, she dropped her eyes to the papers in front of her. "As near as we can tell, the Ryqril are committing a *lot* of forces to this assault. We've tracked four Elephant-class troop carriers and three Corsair wings through the fueling bases in the past week, and we're pretty sure two wings normally based here have also gone. I'd guess at least fifty days before the Star Force vets are let out."

Lathe shook his head. "That's too long. Bakshi, what size force can you field?"

"Not enough to take Henslowe by storm, if that's what you're getting at. About forty men, plus your own blackcollars."

"*Forty* men? What happened to your half-million rabid patriots?"

Tremayne kept his temper. "We've isolated the Calarand group from the rest of Radix, in case something goes wrong."

"Great. What do we do if we need more—take out ads?"

"We're keeping the Janus group here for the duration. That's another ten people available in emergencies."

"Somehow, I get the impression you don't really trust us," Haven spoke up from somewhere behind Caine. "We really *aren't* here to betray you, you know."

"But you might do just that—accidentally, of course,"

Miles Cameron said. "Argent Security is very sharp, and some of their techniques are probably different from what you're used to. We can't risk everything for some scheme we know nothing about."

"That happens all the time in a war," Lathe pointed out. "That's why you have a general staff and chain of command instead of deciding things at a mass meeting of the troops."

"You can't expect military precision from us, Comsquare," Faye spoke up as Cameron's face darkened. "The war was a long time ago, and most of us weren't very deep in the military system."

Lathe gave her an appraising look. "Were you?"

She shrugged modestly. "A bit. I was on the tactical staff of General Cordwainer's Sector Command."

"I'm impressed. Also surprised the Ryqril let you run around loose."

"Actually, they don't know about me," she admitted. "The records got destroyed—these things happen."

Lathe smiled and looked back at Bakshi. "Miss Picciano's point is well taken. I withdraw any and all unkind remarks. Perhaps an assault won't be necessary. Do you have any data on the prison itself?"

"Quite a lot," Tremayne said, sounding relieved. "Miles?"

Cameron reached down to a case by his chair and extracted a thick file. Opening it, he chose several papers and photos and slid them across the table to Lathe. "Henslowe Prison," he announced.

Caine craned his neck to see. The prison was an unimaginative fifteen-story rectangle made of a stony-looking material and sitting squarely in the center of an otherwise empty block. Narrow windows lined the walls from the third floor to the thirteenth, with larger windows on the top two floors. Armed guards patrolled the four-meter-high perimeter mesh fence, and the massive gate was flanked by guardhouses. A street map showed the prison to be about a hundred meters inside the wall marking the edge of the Strip. "Where are the veterans being held?" Caine asked.

"Eighth floor, south side, if the quizlers are playing things as usual," Cameron said. "They can see over the wall from there; I expect that's done on purpose to make them homesick."

"Security here does things like that?" Lathe asked.

Fuess growled deep in his throat, grinding his dragonhead ring almost savagely into his palm. "Security Prefect Apostoleris was hatched from a Ryq and a tarlegan lizard," he said with disgust. "If he wasn't so canny with his own skin we would have killed him long ago. But we'll get him yet."

Caine looked at the glowering blackcollar, something stirring within him. *This*, finally, was the fire he'd expected of the legendary blackcollar warriors, the anger and drive whose absence on Plinry had been such a disappointment. Looking at the relatively youthful faces across the table, he wondered suddenly if the difference could lie in the extra Idunine the Argentians had clearly received over the years. Could the quiet calmness he'd seen in Lathe's men actually be more a sign of weakness than of strength? That wasn't a very pleasant thought.

Tremayne was speaking again. "Fortunately, most Security operations in Calarand are headed by the Assistant Prefect, Colonel Eakins. He's dangerous enough but generally pretty restrained—he doesn't overreact and execute innocent people after one of our raids, for instance, like Apostoleris occasionally does. But the prison system is directly under the prefect's command."

"Hmm." Lathe studied the diagrams, rubbing his dragonhead gently. "What sort of weapons do the guards carry?"

"The outside men and those in the administrative areas have laser rifles and paral-dart pistols," Cameron said. "Cell-block guards just carry the dart guns."

Caine felt his cheek twitch. Several different paral drugs were in use back on Earth, none of which was much fun. "Which drug do they use?" he asked.

"It's called Paralyte-IX, if that helps," Cameron told him. "It causes instantaneous muscle relaxation at the point of entry and spreads to the rest of the system in under a minute. The guns use scatter-shell loadings, so you usually catch a dozen or more of the darts when you're shot."

"Dissolving darts, I presume?" Lathe asked.

Cameron nodded. "It takes a few minutes for them to disappear completely into the bloodstream, though, and since the sensory nerves are only partially paralyzed you can usually feel them that whole time."

Lathe nodded. "Is there an antidote, or does it just have to wear off?"

"Oh, there's an antidote, all right, and we've got a fair supply of it. Unfortunately, it happens to be a poison unless Paralyte-IX is already in your system."

"No big surprise," Novak put in from across the room, where he seemed to be examining the woodwork. "Obviously, any drug you could immunize yourself against would be pretty useless."

Cameron bristled. "Forgive me if I'm boring you, Commando—"

"Not boring at all, Mr. Cameron," Lathe soothed. "We haven't had much experience with paral-guns since the war ended."

"Plinry Security doesn't use them?" Faye asked.

"Not very often," Lathe said. "Tremayne, I'd like to spend a couple of days getting acquainted with the city. Can we get some maps and vehicles?"

Stuart York made a note on a pad in front of him. "I'll have some cars assigned to you," he said.

Tremayne gestured at the Henslowe file. "Any ideas yet?"

Lathe shook his head. "For now I'd like to borrow the packet and look it over some more."

Silently, Cameron replaced the papers in the file and handed it over. Lathe nodded his thanks and looked back at Tremayne. "Any late word on Jensen?"

"Or any other ships that may have landed?" Caine added.

"Other ships?" Tremayne frowned, glancing at Bakshi and Cameron. "Are you expecting someone else?"

"Someone will eventually come from Plinry with the news of our rather abrupt leave-taking," Lathe spoke up quickly. "We'll need to be well-hidden by then, since they'll be bringing ID data on us."

Caine turned to the old blackcollar, but before he could explain that that wasn't what he meant a foot came down on top of his—not hard, exactly, but with clear warning. Swallowing, he kept his mouth shut.

The frown was still on Tremayne's face. "I see. Well, you can either stay here or move to one of our other safe houses. As to Commando Jensen, there's still no word on him." He shifted his glance to the right. "Fuess, you'll act as guide to Lathe's team while they learn their way around."

Fuess gave the closed-fist salute Caine had seen Bakshi use earlier. "Yes, sir."

"All right, then. Unless there's anything else . . .?"

"I've got one question," Caine said.

All eyes turned to him. "Yes?" Tremayne asked.

"Coming in to Argent we heard a Ryqril military governor mentioned. How actively are the Ryqril involved in things here?"

Salli shifted her matronly bulk uncomfortably. "More than we'd like," she admitted. "Besides their six bases, they also maintain private areas in many of the main cities, Calarand included. Chances are you won't run into them, though."

"Of course, whatever you do at Henslowe could change things," Faye pointed out. "Perhaps we should talk about Ryqril tactics sometime; this close to a war zone their methods might be different than what you're used to."

"Good idea," Lathe agreed. "I'll let you know when a good time would be."

She smiled. "I'll look forward to it."

"Other questions?" Tremayne asked. "All right, then, that's all for now."

Chairs squeaked as people began to get up. York, sitting next to Caine, tapped the younger man's arm. "About those vehicles: you have a preference for either open—that's with full wraparound windows—or enclosed style?"

"Enclosed," Lathe said before Caine could answer. "Haven here can go down with you if you'd like and show you what we'll need."

York nodded. "Fine. Commando?"

"Let's get back," Lathe said to Caine as Haven and York headed for the door.

Caine glared at the comsquare. "What are you, my private wet nurse? I can answer my own questions."

Lathe had Caine's arm and was steering him gently but inexorably toward the door. "I know you can," he said. "We'll talk about that when we're back in our rooms."

"Lathe—"

Novak materialized on Caine's other side. "Never argue with your comsquare in public, Caine," he advised quietly. "Especially an unknown public."

Fuess was waiting at the door. "Anything I can do for you, Comsquare?" he asked.

"Why don't you get some maps of Calarand and meet us back at our quarters," Lathe suggested. "I'd like to go over them with you if you have time."

"Certainly."

Fuess headed off in another direction as Caine and the two blackcollars made their way to their rooms. Inside, Caine turned to Lathe; but the old blackcollar got in the first word.

"From now on, Caine, the less you talk to the Argentians the better," he said. "Pretend you're the strong, silent type who thinks deep thoughts, okay?"

"*Not* okay," Caine said. "Why am I suddenly incapable of speaking for myself?"

"The speaking isn't the problem; it's the knowing when to stop. Specifically, you were all set to tell them Dodds was out there with a stolen Corsair."

"What's wrong with that?"

"Number one: I'm telling you not to. And number two: never, *never* tell people more than you need to. At best, it's stupid; at worst, it's suicidal."

Caine snorted. "A fine ally you are. Those people are on *our* side."

"Most of them are, sure. They're not the ones I'm worried about."

"What, you think there might be a spy in that group? That's crazy—the government would have crushed them long ago."

"Not necessarily. It's often more profitable to leave the structure in place and simply neutralize it. Don't forget Tremayne himself admitted their raids weren't very successful."

Caine pursed his lips. He still felt resentful, but Lathe was making uncomfortable sense. "Going to be hard for them to help, though, when they don't know what we're doing."

"They'll know what they have to, when they have to—and *I'll* make those decisions."

"Yeah." Taking a half step closer to Lathe, Caine lowered his voice to a whisper. "Lathe, what exactly is Dodds up to?"

Lathe returned the gaze steadily. "I'm sorry, but I can't tell you. Or anyone else, for that matter."

"Your secrecy rule applies to friends, too? Or do you still think I'm a spy?"

"No, I think I can trust you. But knowing Dodds's mission won't do you any good, and *could* do us harm."

"It would help my peace of mind."

Lathe gave him a look of strained patience. "What do you want me to do—make something up? I said I can't tell you." Turning on his heel, the comsquare left, walking over to the table where Hawking had some of his electronic gear laid out. A few soft words and Hawking nodded and began clearing off some space.

Caine didn't watch anymore, but went over to his bunk and lay down, trying not to be too angry. What the hell, he wondered, was Dodds up to that was so all-fired important? Lathe's point about secrecy was reasonable enough, but Caine's interest wasn't exactly idle curiosity. His life and mission were on the line here, and Lathe had no right to keep *any* knowledge to himself that might affect either of those.

There was a knock at the door, and Caine turned his head as Kwon let Fuess in. The Argentian carried a stack of papers and, at Kwon's direction, took them to the newly cleared table. Lathe and Skyler were seated there, and the other blackcollars were drifting in that direction. Rolling out of his bunk, Caine went over to join them. At least, he thought firmly, Lathe wouldn't keep him from learning how to get around the city.

His map of Calarand in hand, Lathe strolled over to Skyler's bunk, glanced around to make sure no one was within easy earshot. "Make some room," he said.

Still studying his own map, Skyler moved his feet over. Lathe sat down and nodded toward the door. "What did you think of him?" the comsquare asked.

"Fuess?" Skyler shrugged. "A real fireball. Ryq-hatred oozing from every pore. Novak told me all four of them are like that."

"Yeah. Strikes me as odd that they've stayed alive this long, given how half-cocked that type usually is."

"Says a lot for Bakshi's leadership and discipline, obviously."

"Maybe." Lathe surveyed the room. "We're going to have to split up as soon as possible—we're too centralized here, too vulnerable to attack."

"Or surveillance," Skyler nodded. "Though most of that should be aimed at you or Caine. Did your excuse for hauling Novak and Haven to that meeting fool anyone, by the way?"

"I doubt it," Lathe admitted. "Bodyguards look like bodyguards no matter how they're packaged. Odds are somebody's figured out by now that he's more important than we're letting on."

"Well, it was a nice try, anyway," Skyler said. "I'll take O'Hara and Spadafora out later and find a good hideout or two. I wouldn't count on getting anything more secure than this place, though." He cocked an eyebrow. "From the questions you were asking Fuess I'd say you've already got an attack plan in mind for the prison. Care to let me in on it?"

"Not yet. I need to work out more of the details. Tell me, who would you say has the toughest constitution of all of us?"

Skyler glanced around the room. One of his best attributes, Lathe thought: he didn't ask unnecessary questions. "I'd say O'Hara, Mordecai, and Haven, in that order. Vale would know—he's practically got our medical histories memorized."

Lathe nodded. "I'll talk to him, but your opinion jibes with mine. While you're out later look for a separate, out-of-the-way place where three men could stay, all right?"

"Okay. When will we be moving against the prison? A day or two?"

Lathe hesitated. "More like a week."

Skyler's eyebrows rose fractionally. "I would have thought you'd want to finish up before the collies got their balance back."

"Some delays are unavoidable. But we'll save all the time I thought it would take to gather the vets together, so we should come out about even. Talk to you later."

He stood up and looked around. Vale was lying on a bunk across the room, apparently asleep. Lathe hesitated, decided his questions and orders would keep, and went over to his own cot to lie down. He was more fatigued than he cared to admit—he'd forgotten how much of a strain leadership could be, especially under conditions like these. Bad enough to be fighting on a foreign world, let alone one where your allies weren't fully on your side. He could work around that . . . but the growing discontent in Caine's eyes was something else entirely. Caine still held the key to this mission, and if his questions about Dodds sprouted into full-fledged suspicions, it could mean disaster.

The faces of Lathe's old blackcollar squad rose unbidden behind the comsquare's eyelids. He blinked once, to drive them away. His new squad would *not* die like his first had, he told himself firmly. He was too old to go through that again.

Rolling onto his side, he set his mental alarm for two hours and went to sleep.

CHAPTER 14

Glinting brightly in the noonday sun, the needle-shaped patrol boat hovered in place for a second before settling into the clearing near the winding dirt road and parked vehicles at the edge of the Security base camp. A half-dozen men emerged almost immediately and walked into the rough semicircle of tents, disappearing into a square tent near one end of the ring. The main command post, Jensen decided. A few minutes later another six men left the tent, walking with the bounce of fresh troops. Climbing into the boat, they took off and headed west.

Lowering his binoculars, Jensen rubbed his eyes. He'd been sitting above the camp for the past hour, observing events below and deciding on the best way to get in and out again. It was a risky proposition, to be sure; even with nearly everyone out chasing around the mountains, he estimated there were between ten and twenty men still in camp. The odds weren't good, but by their very nature they provided him the advantage of surprise. No fugitive in his right mind—in which category Jensen included himself—would normally go anywhere near an enemy stronghold, let alone consider sneaking in. But in enemy territory food and transportation were vital, and both of those were to be had below. Stowing his binoculars in his pack, he got to his feet and edged his way down the slope.

There were no trip wires or other intruder-detection devices at the edge of camp that Jensen could detect. Moving like a gentle breeze, he worked his way around to a point opposite the road and landing area. Once, he had to freeze among the trees as the patrol boat crew came out of the command tent and crossed over to a long structure that seemed to be a barracks. Cautiously, trying to watch every direction at once, Jensen slipped to the front of the nearest tent and looked inside.

It was someone's quarters, currently unoccupied. Officers' quarters, most likely—and where there were officers there were spare officers' uniforms. With one final glance around, Jensen went inside.

Moments later he was back in the tent's entrance, attired in the distinctive gray-green he'd fought against for so long on Plinry. There was a time, he remembered wryly, when he would have felt defiled to be wearing a collie uniform. Now, he merely felt a little safer.

A little, but not much. The uniform wasn't a bad fit, but it didn't go with his graying hair and wrinkled skin, and the blackcollar field pack dangling from his left hand was emphatically not standard collie equipment. Staying in the shadow of the tent, he considered his next move.

To his left was the barracks and three tents of unknown purpose; to his right were two more unknown tents, the command post, and a third unknown tent. Wishing the sun were lower, Jensen studied the middle of the compound. The plants there seemed particularly resilient and didn't show wheel tracks well, but it seemed to him the heaviest marks went to the tent just left of the command post. Taking a deep breath, Jensen headed off to his right, trying to walk as if he owned the place. Passing the first tent, he stepped into the second.

Pay dirt. Stacks of white plastic crates filled the interior, and inside the open ones Jensen could see packages of field rations. Dropping to one knee, he began to fill his pack.

There was still no one in sight in the compound when he again looked outside. Not sure he believed the kind of luck he was having, he stepped out quickly, went behind the command post tent—and came face to face with two Security men emerging from the woods not thirty meters away.

Jensen was caught flatfooted. There was no place to hide, even if the others hadn't already been looking straight at him. But his training was equal to the shock, and he kept walking without the guilty stop that would have caught their attention.

The Security men didn't have the benefit of his training, and had the further disadvantage of seeing a familiar uniform. They continued toward Jensen for several steps before one of them suddenly focused on the blackcollar's face. A puzzled look flickered across his eyes, and suddenly he jolted to a stop. His left hand slapped his companion's arm as his right clawed at his holster—but he hadn't even closed on the pistol's grip when Jensen's throwing star knocked him backwards into oblivion. The other soldier, startled into belated awareness, had no chance at all. His scream of terror had hardly begun before it was cut off by a second star.

Cursing under his breath, Jensen dropped to one knee beside the bodies and retrieved his stars. Too slow, too damn slow—and the sloppiness was going to cost him dearly. The whole camp must have heard that yell, and his chance of sneaking out unnoticed was gone forever. Glancing over his shoulder, he saw seven men come boiling out of the barracks, weapons at the ready.

Jensen didn't hesitate. They would spot him anyway, and the longer he could maintain his camouflage the better. Waving one arm, he shouted, "Over here, quick!" He turned back to the dead men, watching the other group from the corner of his eye.

He would have been surprised if they hadn't fallen for it; and fall they did, five of them running toward him while the other two headed in another direction, presumably to get a medkit. Jensen's pack was on the ground at his side; keeping his movements to a minimum, he pulled the *nunchaku* out with his left hand, sliding it along the ground to where he could lift it without it being seen. There was no time to get to his other weapons; he would have to hope the *nunchaku* and six throwing stars in his belt pouch would be enough. Averting his face, he pressed the *nunchaku* to his chest and waited.

The footsteps arrived behind him. "Oh, God," a shocked voice panted. "What happened?"

"Don't know," Jensen grunted. The others were coming up now; half standing up, Jensen stepped backwards as he rose. "I heard a scream and saw him fall."

"Are they—?" the first man began as he dropped to one knee.

He never finished the question. Shock had dulled whatever combat reflexes he and his men had ever had: they were clumped together, their weapons pointing the wrong way as they scanned the woods nervously—and Jensen's back-and-rise maneuver had put him into the center of the group.

He took out the soldier behind him, first with an elbow in the solar plexus and a backfist to the side of the face. Simultaneously, his other hand swung the two *nunchaku* sticks like a club into the throat of the man to his right. A short kick caught the kneeling man in the back of the head, and the last two had barely time to turn before the *nunchaku*, flailing at full length now, broke both their necks.

Scooping up his pack, Jensen ran for the front of the command tent. The fight had taken place barely fifteen meters from the tent, and it was impossible for those inside not to be aware that something was wrong. He had to stop them before they sent out an emergency call that would bring the scattered patrol boats down on top of him.

He nearly ran down two men as he rounded the corner. "What—?" one of them managed to say before the *nunchaku* caught him across the face. With a yelp the other jumped to the side, firing a dart pistol wildly in Jensen's direction. The blackcollar felt a cluster of needles ricochet from his hidden flexarmor as he dived for the ground, his leg sweeping horizontally to knock the legs out from under his opponent. The other fell heavily, his pistol flying from his hand. Two more quick blows with the flail and Jensen was again racing for the tent entrance, jamming the *nunchaku* into his belt as he scooped a handful of throwing stars from their pouch. The flap which was the entrance was wide open; hoping fervently that there were no obstructions to the side of it, he dived through the opening.

They were waiting for him, of course: three men standing well back from the entrance with weapons ready. But they'd clearly expected him to come straight in, and his sideways dive took them by surprise. Clusters of darts hit the tent wall and nipped at Jensen's legs as he hit the ground and somersaulted, sending two stars spinning toward his attackers halfway through his roll. The stars missed, but accomplished their intended goal of forcing the Security men to dodge. The second fusillade was completely off target; and then Jensen was back on his feet, his stars flashing on their way. Within seconds it was over.

Panting, Jensen gave the tent a quick once-over. A huge map, covered with colored markers, dominated the center of the floor. On one side of the tent sat a mass of communications equipment; on the other was a rack holding six snub-nosed laser rifles. He eyed the latter, wondering why the Security men hadn't used those instead of dart pistols. It looked like Security had decided to try and take him alive, a policy he certainly couldn't argue with. Leaning over the map, he tried to figure out where he was.

A sudden crackle from the communications gear made him turn his head—and probably saved his life. Framed in the doorway, at the edge of his peripheral vision, were two figures.

Jensen dropped and rolled even as the first laser blast sizzled the space he'd just vacated. The second man's shot was closer, and Jensen felt the heat on his face as he came up on one knee and scrabbled for his throwing stars.

There was only one left.

He deserved to die, Jensen thought bitterly, his mind working with a clarity and speed which seemed to freeze the scene before him. He'd completely forgotten the two men who'd left the main pack earlier, and that act of stupidity was now demanding its price. The two men were standing together, one to the left and slightly behind the other, their laser rifles tracking him—close enough together to be taken out by a thrown *nunchaku* if the weapon had been in its usual holster. But it was still stuck in the Security uniform belt, and he knew he couldn't free it in time. Another half second and the lasers would be lined up on him . . . and with all his strength Jensen hurled his last star at the rear man's right leg.

It hit just above the ankle, with the result Jensen had hoped for. Knocked off balance, the soldier fell heavily into his companion's side, tumbling them both to the floor as their shots went wild. Long before they could untangle themselves Jensen was on them, *nunchaku* swinging with the savage intensity of someone who has squeezed one last chance from a hostile universe.

He was trembling with reaction when he finally straightened up, so drained emotionally that the voice bursting abruptly from the speaker didn't even make him jump. "Base Five, this is Spotter Sixteen. Are you all right there?"

For a moment Jensen hesitated. Then, picking up one of the laser rifles, he stepped over to the communications equipment, a vague plan forming in his mind. The controls didn't seem complicated; tentatively, he touched a button. "Spotter Sixteen, this is Base Five," he gasped. "We're under attack!"

"By the blackcollar?" the voice asked, suddenly crisp.

"Oh, God, I don't know," Jensen said, putting a frightened whine into his voice. "They're shooting at us from upslope. We're mostly pinned down, and the captain's been hit—"

"Get ahold of yourself!" the other snapped. "We'll be there in fifteen minutes. How many snipers are there? There's only supposed to be one man out there."

"Maybe he just moves around a lot—I don't know." Jensen fired twice near the antenna, knowing the other's radio would pick up a slight but distinctive crackle. "God, they're firing in here again," he groaned. "Look, sir, I'm going to try and get the captain out—he's hit bad."

"Nega—" The voice cut off as Jensen sent two shots into the equipment. With luck, he thought as he ran for the tent entrance, they would assume the camp radio had been shot out before he heard their order.

Nothing was visible overhead when he emerged, but that would soon change, and Jensen needed to give the approaching patrol boats at least a little of what they would expect to see. Flipping his rifle to full power, he began sending shots into the slopes above the camp as he retrieved his pack and ran to one of the open-roofed vehicles parked by the dirt road. They were standard military-looking models, little changed from those he'd used in the war. Climbing in, he checked the power gauge and drove back into camp, where he picked one of the dead men at random and loaded him aboard. The patrol boat would expect to see him bravely rescuing his wounded captain and he couldn't disappoint them. Turning onto the dirt road, he headed downhill.

He wasn't any too soon. He was only two minutes out of the camp when, sweeping in from the west like Phaëthon's chariot, a patrol boat thundered by overhead. Hunching over the steering wheel, Jensen concentrated on his driving. It would be at least a while, he hoped, before the forces that were gathering grew tired of trying to draw fire from the hills and finally landed. When they discovered how the men at the base had died . . . well, Jensen planned to be far from his stolen vehicle before it was found.

But whether they knew it or not, Security had won this round. Jensen had hoped to be several hours on his way before anyone even knew he'd been in camp. Now, the alarm would be out within a fraction of that time.

There was really only one alternative that offered any hope of success. They would expect him to head east, for the flatlands and a populace he could hope to vanish into—and therefore he had to make the less obvious move back into the mountains. It seemed crazy, but with a week's worth of new rations and most of the enemy's activity to the east it was a gamble worth taking. If he could work his way far enough south, he had a chance of slipping out of the net completely unnoticed. At that point. . . .

He frowned. His original plan had been to link up with Argent's underground as soon as possible, but that might turn out to be no better than walking into Security HQ. It was painfully clear that the organization leaked information like a string bag—the searchers here knew far too much about him. Unless one of the others had been captured and made to talk . . . but they wouldn't be so interested in taking him alive if they already knew about Caine's starships. No, Lathe must be playing it cautious in an unsafe position—and in that case Jensen's best plan might simply be to go to ground for the duration. It was a thought worth serious consideration.

From far behind came the faint multiple-*crack* of a strafe-charge attack. Grimacing, Jensen increased his speed slightly. Very soon now it would be time to abandon the car.

CHAPTER 15

The hallway was deserted as Lathe strode along it; which was just as well, since he wasn't feeling much like company. His lust was starting to fade now, but Faye Picciano's face hovered like a succubus before his eyes and he could still smell her perfume. He wanted to go back to her; wanted her more than he cared to admit. And surely he could handle it. . . . Gritting his teeth, he kept walking.

He was still feeling irritable when he reached the blackcollar room, throwing the door open suddenly enough to make Skyler, Novak, and Mordecai reach reflexively for their weapons. Lathe didn't like startling his men like that—even blackcollar combat reflexes could be blunted—but at least they'd know now to leave him alone for a while.

Caine, unfortunately, either missed the hint or simply ignored it. He'd been pacing near the door when Lathe entered, and almost before it was closed he'd planted himself in the comsquare's path. "Lathe, we need to talk."

"Later," Lathe growled, moving to go around him.

Caine stuck out an arm. "No, *now*," he snapped. "I've had too much 'later' already."

Clenching his teeth firmly, Lathe held onto the shards

of his temper. Caine was the last person on Argent he could afford to blow up at. "All right. What's on your mind?"

"Finishing up our mission before the government finds us." Caine waved his arm, the gesture encompassing the other blackcollars as well as the room around them. "We've been cooped up in this place for six straight days now—I've hardly even been outside this *room* in that time. About all you've done is move everybody except us out of the building and hold lots of meetings. When's something going to happen?"

"You know the military," Skyler spoke up from the table where he'd been reading a tape. "Double-time it, then wait at parade rest."

"Don't give me that. You guys move fast enough when you want to—what's left of Plinry could attest to that."

"This isn't Plinry," Lathe reminded him. "We're in unknown territory, forced to rely on an organization that's probably riddled with collie spies. We need to get as much information as possible before we move."

"Is *that* why you've been monopolizing Faye Picciano lately," Caine snorted. "I should have known it was business."

For some reason Caine's words suddenly put things in perspective; and rather than boil over, Lathe's anger drained away. "It was, on both sides—and her business is also information. Be thankful I deflected her away from you—you wouldn't have lasted an hour once she got started."

"What do you mean?"

"I mean the complete temptress routine, all the way down to the pheromone-based perfume she was wearing. And she's damn good at it, too."

Caine suddenly looked wary, as the source of Lathe's mood must have dawned on him. "Did she—ah—?"

"No, she didn't succeed," the comsquare said. "The sexual ploy's the oldest in the book, but no less potent for all that. I know better than to risk emotional entanglement on a mission; I'm not sure you do. Chances are you'd be in bed with her right now, telling her anything she wanted to know."

"Ridiculous," Caine said . . . but he didn't sound entirely sure of himself. "You think she's a government spy?"

"Not necessarily." Lathe stepped past Caine and sat down across from Skyler. "Whichever side she's on she'd want to pump us for all she could. Tacticians *always* want all the information they can get."

"Is that why you sent the others away from here?" Caine asked, coming over to stand beside the table. "So she couldn't get to them?"

"She or other potential spies. Also, it's a good general policy not to load all your torpedoes into the same tube. Actually, *you're* the only one we absolutely have to keep the collies from getting hold of."

"Hence the bodyguards?"

"We just like your company," Novak assured him from his bunk.

Caine's response was a snort.

"But you've got a point," Lathe said, thinking quickly. The timing was critical here. . . . "If we sit around too long the collies may try something. Okay. Tomorrow, Mordecai and I will go take a close-up look at Henslowe Prison, try to find the best approach for getting the vets out."

Across the room Mordecai raised his eyebrows, but remained silent. Caine said. "Well, that's something. I'll come, too."

Lathe shook his head. "Sorry. We're keeping you out of collie reach, remember? You'll stay here where it's safe."

Caine's lip twisted, but something in Lathe's face must have warned him not to argue the point. Turning on his heel, he strode over to the window and stared out.

The impatience of youth, Lathe thought, stroking his dragonhead ring as he looked at Caine's stiff back. A wave of weariness swept abruptly over him. Why was he going through all this torture again, especially for a mission with such a poor chance of success? Sighing, he turned his eyes away from Caine.

Skyler was still sitting across the table from him. "You all right?" he asked softly.

Lathe managed a lopsided smile. "Sure."

"He'll learn. You serious about tomorrow?"

"Yes. Have you talked to Vale lately?"

"Novak saw him this morning. O'Hara and Haven seem to be coming along okay. Still pretty weak, though—high-dose Idunine treatment's no fun."

"None of us are in this for the fun of it," Lathe said dryly. "When will they be able to fight?"

"Vale guessed a couple of days—maybe three or four before they're back to full strength."

"Okay." Lathe glanced at his watch. "The tactical group's meeting in an hour; I'll tell them about the trip then. Not about your part, of course."

Skyler rubbed his fingertips thoughtfully on the table-top. "You have to tell them anything at all? If there's a collie spy in the group, you'll be inviting a trap."

"Possibly. But if we *don't* say anything they'll never trust us again—Tremayne already thinks we ask too much on blind faith. Besides, we might prove this way whether or not there *is* a spy in the group."

"Um. Just you and Mordecai going, then?"

"Plus one of the Argentians, probably—I expect Tremayne will insist on that. Our loyal guide Fuess would be a good choice. If it comes to a fight an extra blackcollar would be handy to have around." Lathe cocked his head slightly to one side. "I see an objection in there that still hasn't been answered."

Skyler nodded fractionally in Caine's direction. "You're going to leave him alone with Novak? If *I* wanted to capture him alive, that's when I'd pull *my* raid."

Lathe was silent a long moment. "You think Security's that desperate yet? If they miss they risk driving us out of range of their spies."

"Granted. But I don't think we should count on the opposition having good sense."

"In that case maybe we'd better send him over to stay with Hawking, Kwon, and Spadafora."

"Or else take him with you in the morning. Seriously. They'll be trying to keep you alive anyway, and if they realize who they've got they'll be doubly anxious to do so. It'll make your odds that much better."

"True. Means they'll be using those Paralyte-IX darts. Have we got a supply of the antidote?"

"Yes—and Vale's already prepared the hypos you're going to ask for next."

Lathe grinned. "I wonder sometimes why I bother to give orders. . . . All right, I'll think about taking Caine in tomorrow. But don't mention that to him or anyone else yet."

"Right." Skyler pushed back his chair. "I'd better start organizing my equipment."

He walked over to Novak, conferred for a few seconds, and then went to the corner where the blackcollar's equipment was piled. Lathe watched him thoughtfully, noting the bounce in the big man's step and the sure, quick movements of his hands. Skyler was happy—happier, in fact, than Lathe had seen him since the end of the war.

Smiling to himself, the comsquare glanced at Caine's still-angry back. Yes, it was worth it. For a long time the blackcollars had been dying in degrees from the inside out as their hope of doing something meaningful faded with the years. But no matter what happened now, they would at least have had the chance to live as blackcollars again, the chance for one last shot at the collies and their Ryqril overlords. And if the price was death on a foreign world . . . well, they'd been prepared for that forty years ago, on Plinry. It wouldn't be harder now.

The thought of death brought a new frown to Lathe's face, and his eyes defocused to stare past Caine at the cloudless sky.

Where *was* Jensen, anyway?

CHAPTER 16

The Radix garage was located at the end of another of the long underground tunnels Caine had come to expect of the Argentian resistance. Sweating under three layers of flexarmor and local clothing, he walked through the narrow passageway between Lathe and Mordecai, wondering why the comsquare was allowing him to come along. It *was* what he'd wanted, of course, but after that business about how valuable he was, he hadn't expected Lathe to back down so easily.

The "garage"—a large abandoned store—was heavily boarded up, but after the gloom of the tunnel the bits of morning sunlight filtering in gave adequate light for them to thread their way through the parked vehicles to the exit doors where their own waited. Three figures also waited there: Fuess, Tremayne, and Bakshi.

"Good morning, Tremayne; Comsquare," Lathe said as they approached. "I wasn't expecting to see you two here."

"Morning," Tremayne nodded. "We wanted to make sure you had the latest information on quizler movements."

"I picked it up from Mrs. Quinlan's people on the way down," Mordecai told him. "Seems quiet out there."

"Yeah, well, take it easy anyway," Bakshi warned, a slight frown creasing his forehead as he shifted his gaze between Caine and the others. "Are all three of you going?"

"All four, if you count Fuess," Lathe said, looking at the latter. "Everything ready?"

The tall blond nodded. "All set, Comsquare."

"Okay, let's go." He nodded at Tremayne and Bakshi. "See you later."

The vehicle was a dented van similar to the one Caine had ridden in back on Plinry. This time, though, he was obliged to sit on the floor in the storage area as Fuess and Lathe took the driver's and passenger's seats. Mordecai, sitting down against the side opposite Caine, wedged himself between the wheel well and one of the vertical wraparound support struts. Caine tried that position on his own side, found it comfortable.

The doors opened and the van lurched out into the street. Three turns later, they entered the mainstream of Calarand traffic.

It didn't take much longer for Caine to become completely lost. Seated as low as he was, he could see virtually nothing through either the front windshield or the van's small rear windows, and his efforts to correlate the van's turns with the maps he'd memorized proved useless. The quiet conversation between Fuess and Lathe was less than useful, too. "That's the Security Headquarters—that white building with the dish antennas all over the roof."

"For just Calarand or all of Argent?"

"For everything." Long pause; one turn. "This is Victory Avenue—renamed *after* the war, of course. It runs through one of the western entrances into the Strip and then into the government center. We'll have to get off before then—we haven't yet figured out how to make passable quizler IDs."

"We'll be getting off even earlier," Lathe said. "I don't want to go into the Strip this trip. Just parallel it and drive past the prison."

Fuess sent a brief glance sideways. "You won't see much that way."

"True, but we won't be scanned, either."

"You're armed?" The Argentian sounded irritated. "I *told* you you can't take weapons into the Strip."

"That's why we're not going there," Lathe said patiently.

"Forgot to tell me, huh? Like you forgot to mention Caine would be coming along?"

"What are you getting all hot about? You're just here to assist, remember?"

"Sorry," Fuess muttered, barely audible over the hum of the van's wheels. He looked at Lathe, and Caine caught a glimpse of a wry smile. "I guess I'm used to being in charge of these missions."

Lathe dismissed the matter with a wave of his hand. "Is that the Strip wall ahead?" he asked.

"Yes. We'll have to swing parallel to it for a ways to get to Henslowe."

"Turn down the next street—we'll keep our distance for a while," Lathe ordered. "There's a gate in the wall just this side of the prison, isn't there?"

"Yes—Avis Street runs through it, crossing Parlertin just outside the wall. I could give you a look at the gate from Avis, then turn down Parlertin and drive past Henslowe."

"Good. Do it."

Caine pushed himself into a kneeling position and got a glimpse of the wall as Fuess made his turn. It was a dirty-white slab rising three or four meters above street level and topped by a meter of metal-mesh fence. The gate was like the ones in Capstone's wall, but with what looked like two pedestrian turnstiles flanking it. Four guards were visible; there may have been others out of sight. Settling back to the floor, Caine wondered how Lathe was going to handle this one without the stacked deck the blackcollars had given themselves with the Capstone wall.

The van continued on. Still unable to see anything worthwhile, Caine drifted into his own thoughts—and was jolted out of them as Fuess abruptly made a sharp right-hand turn. Looking up, Caine saw that Lathe was staring back through the rear windows, his expression tight.

"Is he following?" Fuess asked.

"Not yet," Lathe replied, still looking back.

"Who?" Caine asked, stretching to try to see.

"Keep your head down," Lathe ordered. "I think we've picked up a tail." He turned back to face front, pointed ahead. "Fuess, turn left there and get us back to the wall."

"You think that's wise?" Mordecai asked.

Lathe shrugged without turning. "If it's a collie trap, we're already inside it. Might as well keep going and watch for a place to punch our way out."

A cold knot settled into Caine's stomach. He'd expected Security to move against them eventually, but had assumed the attack would be aimed at Radix HQ. Lathe's suggestion that Faye Picciano might be a spy flashed through his mind. She'd known the blackcollars would be making this trip today.

"Hell!" Fuess snarled and hit the brakes. Caine grabbed for the support strut and hung on as the van made a hard right and accelerated, sending him sliding along the floor. Scrambling back, he had barely gotten himself wedged in again when Fuess braked once more. With a prolonged screech of tires, the van came to a stop.

"Roadblock," Lathe said quietly before Caine could form a coherent question. "We're bottled into an alley; car crossways in front, second car pulled in behind us. Looks like five collies in each. Four coming in, one staying back with each car in backup position."

"Shall I take them?" Mordecai asked with a calmness that made Caine shiver.

"Not yet. Let's get in the open first. Watch for my signal."

The words were barely out of Lathe's mouth when the rear van doors were abruptly wrenched open and a pair of pistol muzzles were pointed in. "Everyone out," an authoritative voice snapped. *"Move!"*

Silently, Mordecai slid out, keeping his hands visible. Caine took his cue and did likewise. A heavy hand grabbed his arm and pulled him to one side of the alley. Mordecai was shoved against the other wall; and a moment later

Lathe and Fuess came back to join them. The four Security men from the front car were close behind, and their appearance quashed any thoughts Caine had had of waiting until they were herded into vehicles before overpowering the guards. Lathe hadn't mentioned that one of the Security men was lugging four sets of heavy-duty maglock forearm shackles. Once secured, Caine knew, that type of restraint could only be removed by special equipment. If they were going to make a break for it, it would have to be right away.

Clearly, Lathe had followed the same line of reasoning. "Hey, what's going on?" he asked the guard holding him, his free arm gesturing with just the right degree of nervousness. It was his other hand, though, which gave the subtle signal: *attack!*

"Shut up—" was all the guard got out before Lathe's knee snapped sideways to catch him in the abdomen.

The guard's pistol fired reflexively as he doubled over, but Caine didn't wait to see which way the darts went. Twisting his right arm against his own guard's grip, he broke free, simultaneously sweeping the gun away with his left hand. He wasn't as fast as Lathe; one shot at point-blank range tore into his shirt and ricocheted from the flexarmor beneath. There was no second shot; Caine's elbow smashed hard into the guard's face and two more punches sent him sprawling to the ground.

He never got a chance to do more. Even as he assessed the general situation—Fuess just finishing off his guard, Lathe's crumpled at his feet, Mordecai lashing out at the rest with three already down to his credit—there was a sharp report behind him, and his hands and scalp erupted with white-hot lances of pain. He gasped and tried to turn, his arm coming up to protect his face; but a second later it fell numbly to his side and his legs turned to rubber beneath him. The world tilted crazily and exploded into a shower of sparks.

The sparks cleared away slowly, and he found he was facing the alley wall from a distance of perhaps thirty centimeters. Between him and the wall was a hand with three slender needles sticking out; gradually, he realized it was his own. From behind him came cautious footsteps, and then a voice: "Okay, Garth, they're all down."

"You sure?" came a more distant voice. "They may be wearing body armor."

"Sure I'm sure," the first said impatiently. "I can see needles in skin on all of them. Get over here and help me cuff 'em."

More footsteps as the front backup man came around the van. "What happened? I couldn't see much up there."

"You wouldn't have seen much more back here," the first retorted. "They just exploded. I'm lucky I was behind the car—there's something with lots of points stuck into the fender and I didn't even see who threw it. C'mon, get those cuffs loose."

Straining with all his might, Caine tried to clench the hand lying in front of him. It made no move he could detect, but the effort sent waves of pain along the dimly felt arm. He tried it again, and again, desperation fueling his efforts.

And suddenly there was an exclamation from one of the Security men, cut off by a flurry of thumps. Clothing rustled, and a metallic clank was followed by the sound of two bodies hitting the ground.

For a moment there was silence, as Caine tried once more to move. Then a gnarled hand came into view and lifted his limp hand. A second hand injected his wrist with a small hypodermic. Even before it was withdrawn he felt a prickly tingle coursing down his arm, and seconds later he had enough control to turn his head and look up.

Lathe was kneeling beside him. "How do you feel?" the old blackcollar asked.

Caine's tongue was still somewhat numb. "Better," he managed. "How—?"

"Later. Can you sit up?"

With Lathe's help, Caine forced himself into a sitting position. The ends of the needles fell away as he did so, their tips already partially dissolved, though still solid enough to hurt. The tingling was fading, and aside from some trembling in his arm and leg muscles he felt nearly recovered. "I'm okay, I think, if I don't have to fight right away," he said. "The others okay?"

Lathe's mouth twitched in a slight smile and he glanced over Caine's shoulder. "Mordecai?"

"We're about ready," the blackcollar's voice said, the words slightly slurred.

Gripping Lathe's arm, Caine got to his feet and turned around. Mordecai was just helping Fuess to a standing position; sprawled in the middle of the alley were the two backup Security men.

"We'd better get moving," Mordecai said, looking at Lathe.

Lathe nodded and stooped to pick up two of the paral-dart pistols. "The front car's closer. Let's go."

They moved around the van, Caine and Fuess still a little wobbly. The patrol car was old but well-equipped, carrying communications and electronic locator equipment as well as what looked like a paral-dart rifle. Sliding into the driver's seat, Lathe pulled the rifle from its clips and handed it to Caine as the latter climbed into the back seat with Mordecai.

"I can drive," Fuess objected as Lathe waved him to the front passenger door.

"Maybe later," the comsquare said, eyes and hands exploring the instrument panels. "For now, just get in."

Fuess complied, clearly unhappy with what he probably considered a demotion. Reaching across the seat, Lathe handed Mordecai the two dart pistols he'd picked up. "Check the magazines, will you?" he said. Gripping the wheel, the comsquare gave the instruments a final once-over. "Here we go."

They hadn't quite reached the corner when a voice abruptly came from the car speaker. "Station Topper Fifteen, report. Are prisoners secured?"

"What do we tell them?" Fuess stage-whispered.

"Nothing." With one hand Lathe activated the locator screen, bringing a section of Calarand's street plan into view. "Maybe they'll assume the car's occupants are still busy. See if they've got the rest of their cars programmed into this thing."

As Fuess fiddled with the controls, Mordecai spoke up. "Whatever you wind up doing, don't count on these guns. They've only got three rounds between them."

"The rifle's only got two," Caine reported. "Looks like someone was playing things safe."

"Sure does," Lathe agreed. "Two shots per gun, just in case we somehow managed to get hold of one. Clever."

"Speaking of clever," Caine said, "what did you and Mordecai pull back there with those darts?"

"Mordecai didn't pull anything," Lathe said. "He was paralyzed with everyone else. So was I . . . for a few seconds."

"Station Topper Fifteen, respond!" the speaker snapped abruptly. "We track you moving west on Maris; do you need assistance?"

"Ignore it," Lathe ordered as Fuess reached for the microphone. "Let them keep guessing."

"They'll figure it out soon enough," Fuess argued. "If I can fool them into thinking we're Security men, we may gain some time."

"Too late." Mordecai pointed at the locator screen. "There were a lot of other blips on the screen a minute ago—Security car positions, probably. They just vanished."

"We've been cut out of the information net," Lathe amplified. He glanced both ways as they entered an intersection, turned right. "Did you get their setup?"

"A double semicircle with its base against the wall," Mordecai said.

"They'll be shifting, though, won't they?" Caine asked.

"Yes, but it'll take time," Lathe pointed out. "As I was saying, the trick I used was very simple. When the darts hit me I made sure to fall on my left arm, breaking the subcutaneous capsule of antidote I planted there this morning. The rest follows easily, of course."

"Of course." Caine had wondered why Lathe had seemed to leave most of the fighting to Mordecai. Now he understood. "Lucky it didn't break early."

"Life's full of calculated risks."

"Hey!" Fuess said suddenly. "That's Parlertin Street and the wall up ahead—you've gotten us turned around!"

"Not really." Reaching forward, Lathe touched the switch that activated the car's warning lights. The traffic ahead of them swerved to get out of the way, and Lathe made a smooth turn onto Parlertin. "The way they're set up implies the Strip wall is part of their enclosure," the comsquare continued. "They won't be expecting us to go that direction."

"Into the Strip?" Fuess yelped. "That's crazy!"

"Another calculated risk," Lathe corrected mildly. "They'll have to scramble to cover all the Strip's exits, and in the confusion we'll have a better chance of slipping out."

"We'd do better to run for it directly," Fuess ground out.

Lathe glanced at the Argentian. "Recommendation noted, Commando," he said with a coldness that surprised Caine. "Now strap in."

"Yes, sir," Fuess muttered.

Ahead, through breaks in the traffic, Caine caught a glimpse of more warning lights. "Someone coming," he said, pointing.

"I see it," Lathe said. "You strapped in? Good. Hang on, everybody." Tapping the brakes, he turned right and once more accelerated. Barely twenty meters ahead was the wall's Avis Street gate.

The Security guards behind the mesh, caught completely by surprise, had no chance to offer resistance. Both froze for a second, then scrambled madly to get out of the way. Caine never saw whether they made it; his eyes closed automatically as he braced for the impact.

They hit with a spine-wrenching shock that threw Caine hard against his seat belts as the air exploded with the screech of tortured metal. For a long instant he was sure the gate had held . . . and then, abruptly, they were accelerating again and the racket was falling behind them. Opening his eyes, he saw through the badly cracked windshield that the front of the car was still relatively intact. "We made it!" he said, not quite believing it.

Beside him, Mordecai exhaled quietly. "I wasn't at all sure that would work," he said.

Lathe seemed to be fighting the wheel. "Security cars are usually built pretty strong. I wouldn't want to try that on the inner wall's gates, though."

"You were right," Fuess admitted, shaking his head. "I apologize, Comsquare. You pulled it off."

"Save the back-patting for later," Lathe told him shortly. "Look for a car we can commandeer—this one's crabbing to the left."

Glancing down a cross street as they passed, Caine caught a glimpse of warning lights. "Security car approaching from the west," he reported.

"From behind us, too," Mordecai added.

"Okay." Lathe turned left at the next street and immediately braked to a halt. "Mordecai, play backstop. We'll take that car up ahead."

"Right." Wrenching open his door, Mordecai slid out, taking one of the pistols with him.

Starting up again, Lathe drove another half block to the parked car he'd pointed out. "Everyone out," he ordered. "Fuess, get that car unlocked."

Seconds later, the first Security car squealed around the corner behind them. "Caine, take cover," Lathe snapped, snatching the rifle and pistol from him and running across the street to a recessed doorway.

Caine obeyed, jumping in front of their car and crouching low. The chase car had meantime skidded to a crossways stop, blocking the street and providing cover for the six Security men who poured from it. With a glance down the street behind him—where a handful of pedestrians were prudently running away from the confrontation—Caine drew out one of the three throwing stars he had with him. Straightening up, he threw it, ducking down again even as a load of paral darts whispered by overhead. Clutching the other two *shuriken*, he crouched as low as he could, wishing bitterly he'd stayed home. He was nothing but a liability out here, someone to get them all captured or killed.

And then, suddenly, the hail of darts ceased. A motion from the side made him start before he realized it was only Lathe. "Is that car ready yet?" the comsquare called, loping toward him.

"Uh. . . ." Confused, Caine looked cautiously over the top of the car.

Mordecai was running down the street, dart pistol dangling negligently from one hand. Behind him, near the Security car, Caine saw six unmoving forms.

Once again Mordecai had beaten heavy odds . . . and once again Caine had managed to miss the show.

Beside him, there was a click. "Should work now," Fuess reported, sliding out from under the vehicle—just as two more Security cars came tearing around the far corner.

Mordecai and Lathe reacted together, and two stars went streaking down the block. Incredibly, despite the range, at least one of them found a target, and the sound of a tire blowing was audible over the squeal of brakes. "Get in!" Lathe snapped, throwing two more stars as the Security men began firing ineffectively through their car windows.

Fuess had the doors open, and he and Caine scrambled in. Lathe followed, shouldering Fuess from the driver's seat. "I'll drive," he said, checking the controls. Mordecai emptied his dart gun and tumbled into the back seat next to Caine as the car started to roll. Whipping around in a tight semicircle, Lathe sent them hurtling toward the Security car blocking the road. Caine tensed for another crash, but the comsquare took the car up onto the walkway, edging perilously close to the building on that side and just brushing the Security vehicle. Accelerating, Lathe took a left at the next corner.

Caine didn't even try to suppress the sigh of relief that escaped him. Under his flexarmor he was soaked with sweat. "That was too close," he said to no one in particular.

"It's not over yet," Fuess growled from in front of him. "Lathe, this is crazy. The quizlers back there have broadcast our description to every patrol in the city by now. What are we going to do, keep changing cars and hope we lose them?"

"We could do that," Lathe agreed. "But then we'd still have to get out of the Strip. I don't really want to try smashing another gate."

"So what are we going to do?" Fuess persisted.

Lathe took another couple of corners before answering. "Put yourself in their place," he suggested. "We've got the whole Strip and its eleven exits to play with, and we know that a lot of their manpower was concentrated in their trap south of the Strip. We may even have found a new car by now. Given all that, what would you guess we're doing?"

"Heading east or west, I suppose," Fuess shrugged.

"Right. So we're going where they won't expect us." Even as he spoke Lathe turned a final corner and brought the car to a stop.

Caine blinked. "The wall? The *south* wall," he added, noting the direction of the sun.

Fuess craned his neck to see the street signs at the corner. "We're only three blocks west of the Avis Street gate," he said, sounding both alarmed and puzzled.

"Right again," Lathe acknowledged. "Everyone out; from here it's on foot."

"We can't climb over it," Fuess said as they got out.

"The mesh is loaded with detectors and high-voltage antipersonnel wires."

"I know. We're going to walk out the gate. Weapons situation?"

"Low," Mordecai said before Fuess could recover from his surprise. "I've got one *shuriken* left, plus my *nunchaku*."

"Caine?"

"Two stars."

"Give them to Mordecai. Fuess?"

"This is *insane!*" the Argentian exclaimed. "They'll still have left a force there to keep unauthorized people out—"

"Weapons, Commando?" Lathe cut him off.

"None!"

"*None?*" Mordecai was incredulous.

"Of course not—I assumed we'd be going into the Strip. I already told you that."

"Never mind," Lathe cut in. "I've got two stars left; maybe it'll be enough. Let's go. Mordecai, you and Fuess stay a few meters ahead of us for now."

They walked back to the corner and turned right. Other pedestrians were visible far down the street and vehicular traffic was beginning to increase. Walking beside Lathe, trying to imitate the comsquare's slightly indolent gait, Caine felt his heart pounding loudly. This simply could *not* work—and the fact that at one point a Security car barreled by without slowing did nothing to change that opinion. Clearly, the government troops weren't expecting them to be this far south and on foot, though *someone* had to notice them eventually.

But they completed the three-block walk to Avis Street without that hypothetical person coming along. Turning south, they started down the long block toward the ruined gate.

Considering how short a time had elapsed since Lathe had smashed through, the defensive gap had been plugged with remarkable efficiency. A car was lying across the road, filling all but about a meter at each end of the gateway. The two pedestrian turnstiles had survived, and a small stream of people were being passed through by a contingent of Security men. "Look—six guards," Caine murmured, nudging Lathe nervously. "We're one throwing star short."

"Two, actually. See that guardhouse?"

The tiny glassed-in cubicle sat against the wall a couple

of meters from the gate area. One of the six guards sat inside, looking tense and painfully alert. "I counted him," Caine told the comsquare.

"There's a cable leading from its base—disappears underground about a meter away where an older guardhouse must have once been. It probably carries phone and power lines and will have to be cut."

"Oh. Great." Caine hadn't noticed the cable. "So what about the extra guards? Try to get close enough to use Mordecai's *nunchaku*?"

"Doubtful," Mordecai said over his shoulder, he and Fuess having drifted back into conversation range.

"Agreed," Lathe nodded. "We're going the wrong direction for this time of day, and they'll have plenty of time to wonder about that." He paused. "All right, let's try this. That outside stairway across the street, about fifty meters from the gate, should have adequate cover for two. Mordecai, you and Fuess will cross over and move up next to it. Caine and I can duck into the doorway directly opposite on this side. When we're all within jumping distance of cover, we'll open fire."

"Right." Mordecai nudged Fuess and they began angling across the road.

"Lathe!" Caine hissed. "What about the extra guards?"

"Don't worry about it. Just walk casually and be ready to run."

Caine gritted his teeth and kept walking, his eyes flicking between the guards and the recessed doorway Lathe had indicated. Seven or eight pedestrians were between them and the gate now, and Caine wondered belatedly if Lathe had taken their presence into account. The doorway was five steps away now . . . four . . . three. . . .

One of the guards was looking back at them, a slight frown on his face. Suddenly, his eyes widened and his hand dropped to his holster. "Hey!"

"Move!" Lathe snapped at Caine, and even as the younger man lengthened his stride a chunk of black lightning streaked past his ear. He caught a glimpse of Security men toppling backwards before the edge of the doorway blocked off the sight. Before he had time to flatten against the wall Lathe charged in on top of him, slamming him into the door.

"You okay?" Lathe muttered.

"Just winded . . . a bit," Caine managed, trying to get a hand free to rub his ribs. Over Lathe's shoulder he could see Fuess and Mordecai crouched behind their stairway. "You get them?"

"All but the last two. I suspect they know we're out of *shuriken*—they weren't even close to having their guns out before we took cover." Even as he spoke a shower of darts bounced off the far side of the doorway.

"Great," Caine groaned. A doorknob was digging into his kidney; reaching behind him, he tried to turn it. "The door's locked. Can you give me room to try to pick it?"

A second load of needles went by. "I'm already practically exposed," Lathe said.

"You'll be a lot more exposed soon," Caine snapped tensely. "They'll be down here any minute!"

To his surprise, Lathe chuckled. "I'm counting on it," he said. He glanced quickly around the edge. "Yep—here they come."

There was nothing Caine could do, and the sense of helplessness was almost suffocating. Surely the Security men were smart enough to avoid the risk of hand-to-hand combat. All they had to do was come down opposite sides of the street, covering each other, until they could shoot directly into the fugitives' skimpy cover. No risk at all. . . . Hands curled into painful fists, Caine waited for the sting of needles—

And Lathe suddenly lunged half out of concealment, whipping his arm in a throwing motion that Mordecai, across the street, matched to the precise second. A final burst of darts clattered noisily as Lathe ducked back, and Caine heard something large fall to the walkway. Lathe glanced out and was gone; more cautiously, Caine followed.

The Security man was sprawled on the walkway, something shiny glittering in his left temple. Lathe bent briefly over the body and removed the object. It was small and silvery, with a bloodied batwing edge and a sort of loop. . . . With a shock, Caine realized it was the comsquare's dragonhead ring.

Mordecai and Fuess were alongside them now. "We going to walk all the way back?" Fuess asked as they hurried toward the gate.

"No need." Mordecai gestured at the car in the gap. His ring, too, had blood on its crest.

Lathe nodded. "They'll have left it unlocked and ready to go. Fuess, you're driving."

A handful of bystanders still hovered near the gate, showing expressions that ranged from terror to grim approval. Caine watched them warily, but no one made any move toward the weapons lying on the ground. Fuess and Lathe slid into the front seat as Caine and Mordecai climbed into the back, and moments later the car was rolling down the street.

"It's a civilian car," Fuess said, gesturing to the instrument panel. "Commandeered from some passerby, probably. We going home, or haven't you had enough excitement yet?"

"Turn left at the next street; you'll drop me off in a couple of blocks," Lathe said. "Then you can go home."

"What are you staying here for?" Caine asked, frowning.

"I still haven't had my look at Henslowe Prison," the comsquare said mildly.

CHAPTER 17

"Don't bother switching cars; just hurry back and stay put," Lathe said in final instruction as Fuess pulled over to the curb. The comsquare got out quickly and stepped across the walkway toward one of the taller buildings that lined the street. The car pulled back into the traffic flow, and Lathe paused long enough to watch a second vehicle leave its parking space and give leisurely pursuit. Smiling in satisfaction, he went inside.

The building's lobby was reasonably full, most of the occupants grouped around the elevators. Lathe didn't wait, but went directly to the nearby stairway door and started up, emerging on the seventh floor. It took a minute to locate the service stairs leading to the rooftop equipment shed, and a minute after that he opened the shed door and stepped out onto the roof.

Sitting comfortably with his back against the shed wall, a quietly hissing box at his side, Skyler looked up.

"I was wondering if you were going to show," he said in greeting, heaving himself to his feet.

"Damn near didn't," Lathe answered, puffing slightly from his climb. "Ran into a massive collie trap down there."

Skyler nodded. "I figured as much. Was that you who ran down the Avis Street gate?"

"Yes. Did you find me a uniform?"

Skyler pointed. "Behind the door there. A lieutenant was kind enough to donate it. You'll need to get rid of your beard, but I think then you'll be close enough to pass a casual inspection."

Lathe closed the shed door. Resting atop a suitcase was a gray-green Security uniform. "Anyone going to miss its owner?" he asked as he began stripping off his outer clothing.

"Not any time soon." Skyler had a speculative look on his face. "So tell me more about this trap."

"All laid on and waiting for us to walk into." Lathe found the ID card in a tunic pocket, studied the picture briefly, then picked up a tube of depilatory and towel that were lying half under the uniform and set to work on his beard. With an elbow he indicated the hissing box. "You hear any troop movements on your eavesdropper?"

"Not until you escaped," Skyler told him. "Before then there were a few coded signals, but not nearly enough to set up a full-size trap from scratch."

"So that clinches it," Lathe said with a tired sigh. "There's a spy in Tremayne's top echelon."

"Looks that way," Skyler agreed. "Unless someone was hiding in the garage when you left . . . no, they still couldn't have deployed people that fast without using radios."

"Besides which, I had Spadafora hiding there to watch for something like that."

"Um. Did Kwon ever show up, incidentally? I didn't want to use the tingler."

"Yes—he picked up backstop position as they drove off. They shouldn't be in any danger. Mordecai's there, anyway."

Only Skyler's long association with Lathe could have permitted him to properly read that remark. "Something wrong with Fuess?" he asked.

Lathe pursed his lips. "I don't know. Nothing I can put my finger on. He doesn't fight as well as I'd expect, maybe. But the training program may have slipped near the end, so that might not mean anything. Maybe it's just that he's too argumentative."

"He's used to being top kid in this playground," Skyler said. But he looked thoughtful. "He reminds me a lot of Fafnir Riesman; remember him? In fact, all four of them—everyone but Bakshi—would fit Riesman's image of the perfect blackcollar."

"Yeah. On Plinry all of that type got themselves killed taking one stupid chance too many."

"This isn't Plinry," Skyler reminded him. "Maybe exaggerated virility is a survival trait in this war."

"Maybe," Lathe grunted. Sealing the depilatory tube, he tossed it aside and finished fastening his new tunic. "How do I look?" he asked, handing the other the ID card.

Skyler gestured for him to turn around. "Well . . . not too bad. You'll pass, I think." He slid the card back into Lathe's pocket.

"Good enough." Crouching by the suitcase, Lathe opened it and examined the contents. Two-thirds of the space was taken up by a compact rocket launcher and four sleek surface-to-surface missiles; the remainder was filled with flexarmor gloves and battle-hood, an amazingly flat gas filter, and an assortment of weaponry. "Okay," he said, closing the case and straightening up. "Are the window dressing and escape route ready?"

"All set up in a corner of the equipment shed—all I have to do is move the launcher out here and anchor it."

Lathe nodded. Stepping to the edge of the shed, he looked around it. Barely three hundred meters away, across the Strip wall, sat Henslowe Prison. Shifting his gaze slightly, Lathe studied the handful of guards patrolling its perimeter, their gait indicating no special alertness.

Behind him, Skyler said, "Are you sure you want to go through with this?"

"No," Lathe admitted, turning back to face the other. "But I don't see any other way to get the vets out. Do you?"

"Suppose we went ahead and told Radix why we were here," Skyler said slowly. "When the word got back to the collies, wouldn't they release the vets in hopes we would lead them to the ships? We'd have to outmaneuver whatever trap they set, of course, but we'll probably have to do that anyway."

Lathe shook his head. "The problem is that they would hold off any release until they had some of the vets loyalty-conditioned. We're going to have enough trouble with the Radix spies; I don't want to have any in our crew, too."

"They may already be conditioning them," Skyler pointed out.

"Undetectable conditioning can't be done in under fifteen days or so. They've known about us less than half that time. If we get the vets out in the next couple of days we can weed out any plants."

"Unless the collies caught Dodds right after he landed and made him talk," Skyler said, eyeing Lathe speculatively. "That could have given them up to nine extra days."

Lathe kept his face expressionless. "What makes you think Dodds is even *on* Argent, let alone captured?"

Skyler smiled lopsidedly. "Still a military secret, huh? Come on, Lathe—you can tell me what sort of devious chicanery you and he are up to."

Lathe shook his head. "If it doesn't work out it'll be better if no one knew anything about it."

For a moment Skyler studied his face. Then he gave a small shrug. "Okay. It's your show. I just hope none of us accidentally trips over him."

"Dodds knows how to stay out from underfoot," Lathe said shortly, picking up the suitcase. "I'll give you a 'ready-one' when I want to leave. You have a couple of cars ready?"

"Yes—yours is a dark blue one across the street. It's already unlocked." He hesitated, as if about to say something else, then touched Lathe on the shoulder. "Be sure to keep your facial muscles firm—you don't want to look too old."

Lathe gave him a tight smile. "You just worry about your part. I'll be okay."

He waited until he was on the stairs before he let the smile fade. Skyler was Lathe's best friend, and he would never come right out and demand to know what Dodds was doing, even in private. But if he was wondering about it, others probably were too, and it didn't take much uncertainty to interfere with combat abilities. But there was nothing Lathe could do about it.

The car was waiting where Skyler had said it would be, and soon Lathe had arrived back at the mangled Avis Street gate. Again, the opposition had moved quickly: a fresh crop of Security men were already on duty, though the bodies of the previous guardians still lay where they had fallen. One of the new men, a laser rifle clutched across his chest, signaled for Lathe to stop.

"What the hell happened here?" the blackcollar demanded as the other stepped to the side of the car.

The other straightened minutely as he caught sight of the uniform's insignia. "Gate crasher, sir. May I see your ID, please?"

"Someone unauthorized got in?" Lathe asked sharply, handing over the card. The patrol car parked nearby might have the equipment for a full fingerprint and retina scan, and a properly done air of urgency should help discourage its use. "When was this?"

"Half an hour ago, sir," the other replied. "They got out, too. Haven't you been in the comm net?"

"I've been on an assignment outside the city that I couldn't take communications gear on. Damn! I've got to check in right away."

"Yes, sir." Hesitating only an instant, he handed back the ID and waved the blackcollar on.

There were several tall buildings within two blocks of Henslowe Prison, but only one had both the necessary height and a clear view of the prison yard. Leaving the car out in front, Lathe lugged his suitcase into the lobby and rode the elevator all the way to the twenty-second floor. The service stairway was locked, but not seriously, and within another minute he was on the roof. Stepping to the edge nearest Henslowe, he opened the suitcase and got to work.

His first task was to set up the rocket launcher, carefully positioning it for the necessary azimuth range. When it was finally ready, he pulled a large capsule from the suitcase and slammed it down hard near the launcher's base. It split open, releasing a bubbling, foul-smelling brown fluid which pooled around it. Stepping back quickly,

Lathe stripped off his borrowed Security uniform and began arming himself with *nunchaku*, *shuriken*, and throwing knives. The pool stopped bubbling before he finished, and when he checked it a minute later it had hardened into a shiny mass, solidly gluing the launcher to the roof. From the suitcase he pulled a coil of silvery line, tying one end of it to the launcher's take-up reel and the other to a blue-and-white-striped rocket. Adding gloves, battle-hood, goggles, and a radio headset to his flexarmor outfit completed his preparations; and, with one last look at Henslowe, he fitted a rocket into the launcher and sent it on its way.

It hit just in front of the prison's main entrance, and suddenly there was a cloud of thick white smoke expanding in all directions. Lathe reset the launcher's aim as the dull *phuff* of the impact reached him and picked up his second missile. "Spotter one: direct hit," Skyler's voice crackled in his ear. "Correct four degrees for second shot."

"Acknowledged," Vale's voice came back. "Second shot away." Obeying the cue, Lathe fired again, and a second cloud erupted directly between the sentry boxes flanking the gate.

"Leader two: preparing Ram," Kwon's voice said.

Lathe touched his mike control. "Leader one: squad ready."

"Acknowledged."

Smiling tightly, Lathe loaded the blue-and-white missile and carefully adjusted the aim. Kwon and Vale weren't anywhere within ten klicks of Henslowe at the moment, but with a simple disk recording plus Skyler's skillful hand on the playback selector any eavesdropping collies should be convinced a major attack was in progress.

The missile arched from its tube, trailing silver line behind it, and Lathe watched its path with some anxiety. The concern was wasted; the missile smacked cleanly onto the prison roof and he could clearly see the brown fluid leaking from the nosecone. Checking his watch, Lathe loaded his last missile and again adjusted aim. "Leader one: starting our run."

"Acknowledged," said Kwon's voice. "Ram away."

Lathe fired the missile, and was fitting a forearm band with attached pulley onto his left wrist when the roar of the explosion reached him. The blast punched a temporary hole in the white cloud surrounding the fence, and through it Lathe could see that the gate had been apparently undamaged by the high-explosive. "Leader one," he said. "Ram ineffective."

"Spotter one: confirmed," Skyler said. There was a brief pause, and Lathe wondered if the other had prepared for this contingency.

He had. "Leader two: we'll just have to go over, then," Kwon said.

"Acknowledged," Lathe said. "Go when ready." Checking his watch, he touched a switch on the launcher and started reeling in the slack in the line. He had to get over to the prison roof while they were busy watching for a ground-level attack. Chances were good they wouldn't see him come in—smoke screens had been militarily obsolete for centuries, but prison guards usually didn't carry fancy scanners. The line tightened; shutting the reel off, Lathe locked it in place and made sure the flaps of his battle-hood were fastened snugly to the edges of his gas filter, leaving no opening for the paral-darts he would probably be facing. Snapping his forearm pulley over the line, he took a deep breath and rolled over the edge of the roof.

The trip down the line took nearly a minute, and in that time Lathe glimpsed three Security cars racing for the prison from different directions. More evidence of Security's quick reflexes, he thought, hoping he hadn't jumped the gun with this operation. If Security reacted *too* quickly . . . but it was too late to worry about that now.

He hit the roof running, releasing the pulley before the downward angle of the line could pull him off balance. Pausing only long enough to hinge the pulley back out of his way, he headed at a fast jog for the equipment shed in the center of the roof. He was barely ten steps away when the shed door swung open and three laser-armed guards charged out.

They weren't expecting to find anyone—that much was instantly clear from their startled expressions and the mad scramble to bring their rifles to bear. Lathe's *shuriken* took the lead man in the forehead, knocking him down for his comrades to stumble over. Half a second later Lathe was among them, and two seconds after that it was all over. Scooping up one of the rifles, he stepped over the bodies and headed down the shed steps. Chances were good that the guards had come from the two administrative floors at the top of the prison, sent to the roof to try to see past the smokescreen hampering the defenders below—and since the top two floors were where Lathe was headed, the more guards he could quickly put out of action, the safer he would be. Theoretically.

The stairs dead-ended at a heavy door one flight down. Cracking it open, Lathe glimpsed a brightly lit corridor and heard the sound of muted alarms and running feet. He eased the door closed and drew his *nunchaku* . . . and a moment later he'd reduced the threat by four more.

About a dozen civilian men and women were already in the corridor when he entered, their faces frozen with shock at the unexpected invasion. "You!" Lathe called, gesturing to the nearest man. "Where are the records kept?"

The other opened his mouth, but no sound came out. Lathe took a step toward him—and suddenly the alarms doubled in volume. "Intruder on fifteen!" a hidden loudspeaker bawled. "Defensive procedures, all personnel!"

Any action, or so the old rule went, was better than doing nothing. A dozen meters in either direction the hallway hit T-junctions; flipping a mental coin the blackcollar ran to his left. The people in that direction scattered as he approached, prudently offering no resistance.

The far corridor, like the one he was in, was lined with what appeared to be office doors. It was possible, of course, that the records section was off in the other direction; but the quality of the hall carpets suggested this floor was occupied by the prison's top management. The next level down, he decided, was a more likely place to look. To the left he spotted a bank of elevators and a stairway door, and he was turning to go in that direction when a white-hot pain erupted in his left shoulder.

Combat reflexes took over, sending Lathe dividing for the corner, his torso twisting to keep the laser beam from resting too long on a single spot. The burning point slid up toward his neck before it disappeared, and as he hit the floor of the corridor he got just a glimpse of a uniformed figure back at the far T-junction.

His landing and roll weren't too bad, given the circumstances, and as he came back into a crouch he discovered he still had a grip on his captured laser. Gritting his teeth against the pain in his shoulder, he hooked an eye back around the corner, rifle at the ready. His assailant wasn't charging, but had taken up a similar defensive position around the far corner. Either very cautious or expecting reinforcements . . . and Lathe suddenly decided he didn't like having an elevator bank behind him. Firing a long burst down the center hall to make sure the guard stayed put, Lathe turned and hurried toward the elevators.

He reached them, paused a fraction of a second, and headed instead for the stairway door. All three elevator motors were operating, and the implications of *that* were all too obvious. There was a chance that the stairs were still free of enemies, though. Slipping through the door, he discovered the landing itself was empty. Senses alert, he started down.

A faint humming from his captured laser was all the warning he got, but he acted on it instantly. Hurling the weapon away from him, he flattened himself against the wall just as the laser exploded, sending bits of metal ricocheting from the walls and Lathe's flexarmor. He turned around cautiously, scanning the walls for the induction resonators that had blown the laser's powerpack. He should have expected something like that, he berated himself; elevators and stairways were about the only places that that kind of resonance cavity could be set up. Taking a deep breath, he continued down to the next landing and carefully cracked the door.

The hallway, resembling the one he'd just left, was similarly deserted. Stepping from the stairwell, Lathe glanced both directions and headed down the hall to his right, an uneasy feeling seeping into him. Certainly the hall should be clear of civilians—they'd had ample time to lock themselves in their offices by now—but surely *all* the guards hadn't gone chasing upstairs after him. The loudspeaker, which had announced his entry into the stairwell, had gone ominously silent. Almost certainly there was a trap already waiting down here for him, and he had to find and neutralize it before Security could bring up more men from the main prison below.

Reaching the floor's central corridor, he paused to glance around the corner—and barely got his head back before concentrated laser fire struck the wall, the thermal shock blasting chips from the masonry. Snatching a *shuriken*, he flipped it blindly around the corner. But the action was more reflex than anything else; his single glance had been enough to show him his mission had just ended. A minimum of ten guards had been visible, arrayed in standing and kneeling semicircles around a glass door that was almost undoubtedly the computer room. Either they'd guessed his target or the man he'd asked directions from upstairs had finally found his voice. The guards, though heavily armed, had been unarmored, and Lathe knew he could eventually beat them down . . . but he also knew he couldn't single-handedly take on a whole prison. Turning, he sprinted back for the stairway, hoping he wouldn't find the stairs to the roof in enemy hands.

By some miracle the landing was still empty as he charged through the stairway door—but it was instantly clear that that was about to change. The whole stairwell echoed with the sound of running feet, coming from both above and below him. Grimacing, Lathe unlimbered his *nunchaku* and started up.

The stairwell loudspeaker had resumed calling out his movements, but with all the noise perhaps the six Security men charging downstairs never heard that he was coming toward them—either that or they didn't really understand how dangerous a blackcollar could be in close quarters. Whichever, they came clattering down with no attempt at caution or tactical spacing. The front rank began firing as soon as he appeared, their aim understandably erratic. Ignoring the deadly lances of light sweeping through the air around him, Lathe snatched a throwing star and, with all the accuracy he could muster, sent it threading through the mob to strike the last man in line . . . and as those just ahead of the dead guard learned first-hand about the domino effect, the blackcollar hurled his *nunchaku* spinning into the faces of those in front. Seldom before had Lathe seen such a standard uphill attack work so well; within a second the entire group of soldiers was tumbling helplessly down the stairs. Scooping up the *nunchaku*, Lathe grabbed the banister and vaulted over the tangle. The remaining steps he took three at a time.

They'd left two men in the fifteenth floor hallway as backup, but they weren't really ready for him and a pair of throwing stars cleared the path. Hurrying down the corridor, Lathe retraced his earlier route, hoping the man who'd been guarding the entrance to the roof stairway had left.

He hadn't. The muzzle of a laser rifle was still poking around the far corner as the blackcollar turned into the central hallway. Hurling a *shuriken* at the single visible eye, Lathe increased his speed, trying to reach the stairway door before the guard could line up a clean shot.

The attempt was only partially successful. The *shuriken* missed completely, apparently whipping by so quickly the guard didn't even have time to duck back. His first shot grazed Lathe's left thigh; his second went over the blackcollar's head as Lathe launched himself into a flat dive and somersault that took him to within a few meters of the stairway door. Still in a crouch, he threw four more *shuriken* in rapid succession, finally managing to force the gunner back long enough to cover the remaining distance and get the door open. Another burst of fire hit the metal panel as he bounded into the stairway and headed up.

For the past few minutes he'd been ignoring the continuous stream of orders and comments Skyler had been feeding into the air waves; orders, he knew, that should be giving Security's listeners reasons why the blackcollars' ground attack had not yet begun. Now, Lathe boosted power on his own microphone and cut in. "Ready-one, this is leader one," he called. "Abort mission, ready-one; repeat, abort."

"Ready-one received," Skyler's voice crackled, sounding tight. "Exit visa away. Did you get it?"

"Negative. Pull back and disperse."

"Acknowledged. Better hurry; vultures on the rise."

Which meant Skyler had spotted patrol boats approaching. He had to get off the roof quickly or risk having his escape route blocked.

He emerged on the rooftop to find a new blue-and-white-striped missile resting in a bubbling pool, its trailing line disappearing off the roof in the direction of

Skyler's building. Low in the sky beyond, he could see four sleek patrol boats rapidly closing on the city.

The adhesive took thirty seconds to solidify, and in that time four Security men charged out the door directly into Lathe's *nunchaku*. For once, the roles were reversed, with Lathe in the relatively safe defensive position. He only hoped that the rest of the guards that were undoubtedly gathering would hold off long enough for him to get safely to Skyler's building before they attacked.

"Ready," Skyler said, and Lathe left the door at a dead run, adjusting the pulley on his left wrist as he traveled. Barely slowing down as he reached the low parapet, he snapped the pulley onto the line and launched himself into space.

The wind of his passage buffeted him as he slid down the taut line. Beneath him the prison yard and Strip wall swept past, and he caught a glimpse of eight Security cars pulled up by the prison fence, their occupants firing wildly at him. But most of the half-minute trip remained afterwards a blur of agony as the tension on his left arm pulled his flexarmor tightly against his burned shoulder. . . . It was almost a shock when Skyler suddenly loomed ahead of him, arms outstretched to break his momentum.

"You okay?" the big blackcollar asked anxiously as Lathe unfastened his pulley.

"I'll live," Lathe assured him, removing his gas filter. "Nice job, Skyler; my skin is indebted to you. Don't bother with anything except the eavesdropper—the rest can be replaced, and there'll be collies crawling all over this building any minute now."

"Okay by me. Hang on a second, though. . . ." Reaching down, Skyler picked up his launcher's trigger grip and squeezed it, sending one last missile flashing into the sky. Lathe turned, watching as it dropped into the gap where the Avis Street gate had stood earlier that day. Three Security patrol cars, racing from the Strip toward that exit, swerved violently to avoid the explosion. One of them didn't make it.

"That should hold up the pursuit a bit," Skyler said blandly, tossing the trigger grip aside. "Did you get everything done in there that you wanted to?"

Pulling off his goggles and battle-hood, Lathe took a deep breath of fresh air. The gentle breeze felt cold on his sweaty skin. "I think so," he said. "Let's go home; it's been a busy morning."

CHAPTER 18

The radio code used by Argent Security was just different enough from Plinry's system to be incomprehensible to Prefect Jamus Galway as the patrol car maneuvered through the crowded Calarand streets. But that crisp tone of voice and his driver's impotent swearing were all too familiar.

Somewhere, Lathe's blackcollars had struck.

Calarand was larger in both directions than any city Galway had ever seen, and he looked around with interest and some envy as they drove toward its center. Despite occasional war scars the buildings were generally in better shape than those of Capstone; the pedestrians walking along the street were better dressed and fed; and there were a *lot* more vehicles. Apparently Argent had accepted the inevitable early on, surrendering before something like the Groundfire attack became necessary. The moral was obvious. Perhaps Lathe was just a slow learner.

A thin trail of smoke was rising into the air ahead and slightly to their left. "Are we going past that smoke up there?" Galway asked the driver.

The other shook his head. "Too risky. The rebels might still be around."

"I doubt it. Blackcollars tend to hit fast and pull out. I'd like to see what they've done."

The driver gave him a sideways glance. "Well . . . all right." Picking up his phone, he reported the change in route.

The gate area was a mess. The smoke was coming from a burned-out patrol car that had crashed into the dirty-white wall. Crashed *after* it had been hit, he noted; the blast pattern from an airborne missile was evident in the twisted metal. The gate itself was crumpled off to both sides. Galway shivered as the car moved slowly through the Security, fire, and medical people swarming around the area. It was too reminiscent of the aftermath on Plinry.

The driver obviously didn't like the sight, either—or perhaps the white knuckles and hard stares of the guards who passed them through made him nervous. He sped up as soon as they were clear of the bedlam, and the area was soon lost behind them. A few blocks brought them to a second metal-mesh gate, this one stronger looking than the first. The wall it was set into looked like the one enclosing Capstone's Hub; tall and gray, with an induction field sensor system. The outside guards looked as edgy as those back at the ruined gate had, and the four inside men had their lasers raised. The ID check was no simple visual, either—portable equipment was brought out to take both men's finger and retina prints. Gazing down the laser muzzles, it seemed to take forever for the city computer to finish its comparison. But at last it did so, and a few minutes later the car pulled up to an impressive white building.

A dignified-looking man with colonel's insignia was waiting at the curb. "Prefect Galway? I'm Colonel Eakins, head of Security for Calarand. Sorry I couldn't meet you at the spaceport, but we've been busy this morning. Please come along—Perfect Apostoleris is waiting."

"I couldn't understand much of what was coming in over the radio," Galway said as they entered the building. "What was it, a guerrilla raid?"

"We're still trying to figure it out. It was *supposed* to be only a soft probe."

An elevator ride and two short corridors brought them to a conference room. A pile of tapes and papers sat on a reader-equipped table. "I'll get the prefect; you can start reading what we've got so far," Eakins said, pointing him toward the stack before vanishing back out the door. Sitting down at the table, Galway began to skim the papers. He was about a third of the way through when Eakins returned with a short, heavyset man.

Galway stood up as Eakins made the introductions. "Galway," Prefect Apostoleris nodded in greeting, his eyes measuring the other briefly. "Excuse me for dropping your title, but there's only one Security Prefect on Argent and I'm it. Sit, sit; let's see what you've brought us."

Galway sat down slowly as the others took seats across from him. Opening his briefcase, he pulled out the stack of files and handed them over. Apostoleris took the top one off and flipped through its pages. He opened the second briefly, then reached for a tape and slid it into the reader. The screen lit up, and Galway found himself looking at a room containing several cots. Lying on the cots or moving among them were half a dozen black-clad men.

"Recognize any of them?" Apostoleris asked.

Galway leaned forward slightly. "I'd say that, from left to right, you've got Dawis Hawking, Freeman Vale, James Novak, and Mordecai. The big one lying down is probably either Charles Kwon or Kelly O'Hara, and the one at far right is Alain Rienzi, from Earth."

"Very good. Except that Rienzi's going by the name Allen Caine here. That name ring any bells?"

Galway considered, then shook his head. "Where did you get the tape?"

"One of our spies," Apostoleris said shortly, changing tapes. "All right, now, what about these?"

This one was audio, and Galway listened to the four voices in growing fascination as he realized what it was. "Leader One is Comsquare Damon Lathe," he told them. "Leader Two is Kwon, and Spotter One is Rafe Skyler. I'm not sure about the other one." He looked at Eakins. "This the raid they just pulled?"

"Yes and no," the colonel said. "One of them—Leader One, we think—slid down a line to Henslowe Prison, came in the roof door, and damn near got into the records room two floors down before escaping. But the rest of their operation never materialized. We're still not sure whether it was real or just a feint."

Galway was still struggling with the first part. "He got in *and* out? Weren't there guards—?"

"Of course there were," Apostoleris snapped. "He demolished eighteen of them along the way—six of them dead."

"Oh." Galway winced inwardly; but mixed in with the

sympathetic pain was a tiny nugget of personal vindication. At least he wasn't the only one who'd underestimated the blackcollars.

"Never mind that for now." Apostoleris tapped the files. "This everything you've got on them?"

Galway nodded. "I'll warn you that the personal information—"

"Is worthless. I don't care about that. What I really want is whatever old pictures you've got."

Galway understood. "There's a chronological set near the end of each file, taken three years apart."

Apostoleris shuffled through the first file until he located the photos. "Damn. Face covered up by beard on most of these. You should've ordered him to shave."

"On what grounds? They weren't criminals—they'd received a complete amnesty when they surrendered."

Apostoleris's response was a snort. Gathering up the files, he headed for the door. "I guess it's better than nothing. I'll be back in a minute."

The door closed behind him, and Galway looked over at Eakins, wondering what to say. Surprisingly, the colonel chuckled. "Fearsome, isn't he? Don't worry, he'll cool off when things are under control again."

"That's good to know. I thought he was mad at me personally." He nodded toward the door. "I'm not sure how much those photos would have helped even if they *hadn't* been wearing beards. Going back to normal Idunine dosages after so long won't bring them back to *exactly* the same facial structures."

"I know. So does the prefect. But he's worried enough to take anything at this point."

"Are you? Worried, I mean."

Eakins's face was grim. "An hour and a half ago we had three of your blackcollars trapped like lizards in an ice pit. They escaped, broke into the medium-security area called the Strip, broke back *out* of it; and *then*, having gotten completely clear, came back in and tried to get to Henslowe's records before escaping for good. You *bet* I'm worried." He pulled the tape of the raid from the machine and put it on the pile. "Look, Prefect—"

" 'Galway' will do, Colonel. You heard what Prefect Apostoleris said."

A quick smile. "Okay, Galway. Look, we didn't just

bring you here to play escort to those files. Your black-collars went to an incredible amount of trouble to get here—ditto and a half for this Caine. We need to know *why*."

"Can't your spies tell you? I assumed you had the underground fairly well infiltrated."

"Oh, we do. We've got agents from one end of Radix to the other. But so far all we know is that Lathe wants to bring together all the old veterans of the TDE Star Force. At the moment they're all locked in Henslowe, which is probably why he went there today."

"I wondered about that. . . ." Galway pondered. "I don't know what to tell you. They broke into the archives on Plinry and recorded sections of six tapes—we know which parts but not what they needed them for. Everything else they did, I think, was just designed to get them their freighter and Corsair."

Eakins sat up straighter. "They took a Corsair too?"

"Yes. I saw it lift myself. Didn't it arrive?"

"Not to my knowledge." Frowning, the colonel touched a button on the reader. "Get me Data Search."

"Data Search; Vetter."

"Eakins. Pull all records on Corsairs entering Argent system in the past two weeks, including Ryqril military data if you can get it."

"Yes, sir."

Eakins switched off. "This may not do any good. Corsairs have a bundle of sensor shielding gear, and if it came in on low drive with everything running only the Ryqril would have detected it. It's possible they let him land without telling us."

"To interrogate him?"

"Or else he was already one of theirs," Eakins said uncomfortably.

Galway tapped his fingertips idly on the table. He'd had the same thoughts about Rienzi—Caine—once. "I've heard blackcollars can't be loyalty-conditioned, though. And it's hard to believe a fake one could fool the rest that long."

"Oh, it's possible. Believe me." He shook his head. "But it doesn't make sense in this case. Why would the Ryqril play along with them if they could have quashed it back on Plinry?"

"Well, clearly the blackcollars are looking for something. The Plinry archives had part of the puzzle and the Star Force vets must have another." Galway frowned. "Lathe told me before they left that revolt wasn't his immediate goal, and also that I'd find out someday what they were up to. That implies it's something big. Maybe the Ryqril are going to hold off until they find it before moving in."

"Possible," Eakins conceded. "If blackcollars really can't be mind-probed that would be the only way to do it. And the Ryqril *are* interested; they passed some information to us just this morning. Not that it helped much." He shook his head, as if still not believing it.

"You haven't had much experience with blackcollars?" Galway probed gently.

"There are some left on Argent, scattered through Radix. But they've kept to more limited forms of action. Supply shipment hijackings, occasional bombings—harassment, really. This open warfare stuff is new to us."

Galway smiled bitterly. "Tell me about it."

The door opened and Apostoleris strode in. "All right," he said, as if the conversation had never been interrupted, "let's discuss our next move. It seems clear that someone we're holding in Henslowe is vital to whatever Lathe is trying to accomplish. Our reports say he wants all the vets, but his actions today suggest a single man among them might have what he wants. Since we don't yet know who, we'll have to put *all* of them beyond his reach."

"Can we increase the guard at Henslowe?" Eakins asked.

"Not enough." The prefect shook his head. "Henslowe's too vulnerable, too accessible to outsiders. I think this morning adequately proved that. We're going to move them—that much I've already decided. The question is where."

"Why not split them up?" Galway suggested. "Scatter them around the planet in groups of five or ten."

"Because we don't have enough men to guard that many groups," Apostoleris said, with contempt.

"You assume they're looking for a single man *and* that they know who he is," Galway answered, piqued in spite of himself at the prefect's attitude. "For all we know, they could need information from ten of them. And even if it *is* only one, odds are a dispersion would drop him halfway around the planet."

Again Apostoleris shook his head. "Good points, but consider the possibility that this whole thing is an elaborate feint. In that case we'd be committing suicide if we tied up that many men on guard duty. No, we need some place both inaccessible and relatively easy to guard. Aboard an orbiting troop carrier, maybe. *That* would be out of Lathe's reach."

Galway and Eakins exchanged glances. "Possibly not, sir," the colonel said slowly. "A Corsair lifted with them from Plinry. I've got Data Search trying to find out if it's landed here or not."

Apostoleris picked up one of the tapes and fingered it idly, frowning. "Hmm. Well, even with a ship they'd have trouble getting to the prisoners up there . . . but they *could* decide to kill them rather than let us learn their secret." He shook his head decisively. "No, I'm not giving Lathe that option. I suppose that leaves Cerbe Prison."

Galway looked at Eakins and raised his eyebrows questioningly. "It's a converted fortress a hundred kilometers southeast of Calarand," the colonel explained. "High-security place. Not really designed for so many prisoners, though."

"We'll manage," Apostoleris said. "They won't be there very long. We can have them all interrogated in a few weeks, and when we find the one—or ones," he added, nodding at Galway—"the rest can be returned to Henslowe. Comments?"

For a moment there was silence. "All right," the prefect said. "Eakins, get this Corsair business nailed down. I'll call Cerbe and start making arrangements for the transfer. Galway, you might as well keep reading the reports. Maybe you'll come up with something useful. Questions? Fine; get busy."

He was out the door almost before the others could stand up. With a reassuring smile, Eakins followed his boss out, leaving Galway alone with the pile of reports.

Frowning, Galway looked at the stack. It seemed so reasonable . . . and yet, there was something about it he didn't like at all. The prison raid, perhaps. It seemed obvious that Lathe had badly underestimated Henslowe's strength; but somehow Galway couldn't see the blackcollar making mistakes like that. But if the raid hadn't been for information, then what *had* it been for? He had no answer for that. Yet.

Sliding the first tape into the reader, he hunched over and got to work.

For nine of Argent's ten months the riverside community of Split was just one of dozens of small towns dotting the eastern regions of the Rumelian Mountains, its residents maintaining a quiet existence unnoticed by anyone except the loggers working upriver. The tenth month was just the opposite, as for five weeks daredevils from as far away as Calarand descended on the region to ride the spring-swollen Hemoth River. The income that brought in was usually enough to finance the town for the rest of the year. It was an arrangement everyone seemed happy with, and it hadn't changed in years. Until now.

Now, suddenly, the mountains had become a beehive. Patrol boats dotted the skies off to the north, and military-style vehicles were driving through town at least once a day. No one was talking much, but rumor had it someone had broken jail and Security wanted him back.

The latest convoy—two vehicles with maybe four men in each—roared past San's Supplies, headed south. Sandor Gree looked up briefly, then returned to his inventory list and order forms. Business had undergone a boomlet recently, and there were several items he would have to reorder. The trick was in not ordering too much, of course. Swearing genially at the mixed blessings that had fallen upon him, he made a mark on one of the forms.

The front door opened with a squeak and Gree looked up again as a man in Security gray-green walked in. "Afternoon," he nodded. "What can I do for you?"

"I need some low-bulk foods that my team can carry into the mountains," the Security man said.

"Sure thing." Gree came from behind the counter and led the way to one of the shelves. "Thought you folks had your own stuff," he commented, hoping the other would speak again.

"We ran out and are having trouble getting resupplied."

"Ah." He'd been right; the Security man had a slight

accent. One he couldn't place. "Well, here's what we've got. They're all pretty much the same, far as nutrition goes. Just a matter of taste."

The other picked up one of the packages and studied the nutrition listings, and as he did so Gree gave him a surreptitious once-over. The young side of middle age, perhaps, but in excellent physical condition. His uniform was reasonably clean but curiously rumpled, and he noticed a slight odor. The uniform, it appeared, was cleaner than the man wearing it.

"I'll take these," the other said, jostling Gree's train of thought. He held a stack of ten packages.

"Yes, sir." Gree took them and returned to the counter. "Cash or on the plate?"

"Cash."

Gree had expected that. "All right. Ten at two marks each is twenty; plus tax—" Impulsively, almost of its own accord, Gree's finger pushed a button on his register. "Plus tax, twenty-two," he announced through suddenly dry lips.

The Security man had several crumpled bills out already. Extracting two tens and two ones, he handed them over and in the same smooth motion picked up the packages. "Thank you," he said.

"Do you want a sack?" Gree asked as he turned toward the door.

"No, thank you," the other threw back over his shoulder. "I'm being picked up."

And then he was gone. "Sure you are," Gree muttered, his knees beginning to tremble with reaction. A big risk, but it had paid off. A real Security man would have gone through the roof if he'd been charged luxury-item tax on food. The penalty for fraud—but never mind that. He'd been right; that had been the elusive blackcollar Jensen. In full Security uniform, yet, and with the gall to just stroll into town for supplies. No wonder they hadn't caught him yet.

Reaching under the counter, Gree found his phone and began punching numbers. The connection was made, and he let it ring twice before hanging up. Thirty seconds later he repeated the procedure, checking his watch carefully as he disconnected. Exactly two minutes and forty seconds and he would call one final time, and the phone would be answered on the eleventh ring. Presumably.

Involuntarily, he glanced at his front door. He'd had a grace Gree had never before seen, a sort of submerged feline power that almost made the grapevine reports about the man believable. And if his rads were anything like him, maybe the vague rumors coming out of Calarand this morning weren't as exaggerated as he'd thought, either.

Almost time. Gree punched in all but the last number, watching his old Army chrono and waiting for the exact second to complete the connection. As he did so, the half-completed order forms on the counter caught his eye, and he smiled.

He'd best not swell his inventory too much more. He had an idea that the activity around Split would be breaking off very soon.

CHAPTER 19

The tension in the conference room was thick enough to slice up and make into sandwiches. Gazing around the table, Caine saw nothing but hostility; from Bakshi's icy expression to his blackcollars' more open contempt to Jeremiah Dan's steepled fingers with their white nails. Salli Quinlan and Miles Cameron had the look of lions awaiting their turn in the arena, and even Faye Picciano was unnaturally silent as she worked on Lathe's burns. And Ral Tremayne, standing behind his chair, was as mad as Caine had ever seen a man get.

"Soft probe. A look at the prison. Really cute." Tremayne's eyes bored into Lathe like twin antiarmor lasers. "What the *hell* did you expect to accomplish by that half-assed play?"

"I got in and back out alive," Lathe answered, wincing as Faye spread salve on his shoulder.

"Hold still," she chided. "This stuff's expensive—we can't afford to waste it on healthy skin."

"Or on stupid grandstanders. Put it away, Faye," Tremayne ordered. "Save it for Radix people injured in the line of duty. You haven't answered my question, Lathe."

"What are you griping about, Tremayne?" the comsquare said as Faye capped her tube of burn salve and began to bandage the skin already treated. "I don't need your permission to take action as long as it doesn't involve your people or equipment."

"What about the van you lost?" Cameron growled. "*That* was our equipment." He glanced over irritably as Novak passed by along the nearby wall. "*Will* you two sit down, damn it?"

Neither Mordecai nor Novak paid any attention, but continued their quiet wanderings. "They aren't hurting anything," Lathe told the intelligence chief. "And as for the van—"

"I'd rather they sat.

"All right, enough," Tremayne snapped. "Forget the van. The issue—"

"No, let's *not* forget the van," Lathe interrupted. His tone was suddenly hard. "We lost it because we were ambushed. And that means we were betrayed—by one of you."

"I've heard Commando Fuess's report," Tremayne said. "There's no conclusive evidence of that."

Lathe glanced at Fuess, and Caine thought he saw the Argentian squirm a bit. "Did Commando Fuess mention they were on to us ten blocks from the Strip? And that they had their roadblocks all set up—complete with heavy mag-lock shackles, which I'm told are *not* standard patrol car equipment? How much evidence do you want?"

"Someone could have seen you leave this morning," Faye suggested.

"That wouldn't have given them enough time. Besides, I had people in the garage watching for that."

Tremayne slammed his fist on the table. "That does it, damn it." Abruptly, he sat down and leveled a finger across the table at Lathe. "I've had it with taking you on faith and then watching you go off and work behind our backs. You're going to tell us what you're up to, and you're going to tell us *now*."

"I'm sorry," Lathe shook his head.

"You don't have a choice." Tremayne raised his hand.

And in the side wall across from Caine three small sections of the woodwork suddenly swung inward. From the gloom behind the openings three laser rifles appeared.

Caine froze, caught completely off-guard—but Novak was already moving. The blackcollar had been standing against the wall directly between two of the eye-level gunports, a meter and a half from either one; but almost before the rifles had steadied he'd taken a long step toward the one at his right and smashed the muzzle straight back into its port with his *nunchaku*. His back still to the wall, he reversed direction: two quick steps to his left, and his left leg snapped up and back in a hook kick, again jamming the protruding laser back into its owner. His *nunchaku* was spinning through the air before his foot was back on the floor, catching the last muzzle between the two sticks and slamming it against the edge of the port. The laser spat once, cutting a deep groove in the table. By the time the gunner recovered his aim Novak was there. Grabbing the muzzle, he first shoved and then pulled, and a second later was down on one knee with his prize pointing past the table. Caine glanced behind him, realizing only then that Mordecai had similarly taken out the three gunports on *his* side of the room.

In the brittle silence Bakshi's voice carried clearly: "Drop those guns or I'll kill you."

Caine focused on him. The comsquare hadn't moved, hadn't drawn a single weapon; and yet, looking at his expression, Caine had no doubt he could carry out the threat. Suddenly the room felt very cold indeed.

"Everyone just relax," Lathe said calmly. "We're not trying to take over. But I warned you against pulling weapons on us again." He eyed the walls and jerked his head toward the door. "Out, all of you. Tremayne?"

Glowering, the Radix leader gave a hand signal. Splitting neatly along lines in the woodwork, a door swung open around each of the gunports. Six men, nursing cut lips and sore shoulders, stepped from the dark alcoves and headed for the door. Lathe motioned, and the Plinry blackcollars returned the captured lasers to their owners.

"We'll have no more of this eavesdropping," Lathe said as the door closed behind the guards.

"Don't worry," Cameron growled. "Those men are completely trustworthy."

"No one on Argent is completely trustworthy," Lathe said, "and before you get your hackles up I simply mean we're too small a group to take the wrong chance twice. That's why we didn't tell anyone about our plans this morning. I'm sorry if you feel offended, but that's how we have to operate here."

"It's not a matter of wounded pride, Damon," Faye spoke up. "Whatever you were trying to do in Henslowe, chances are Miles could have made things easier for you if you'd consulted with him beforehand. Were you hoping to find where a particular prisoner was being kept? If so, we could probably have gotten that for you from out here."

Lathe shrugged noncommittally. "There'll be other chances."

"Not if I know Apostoleris," Bakshi said. "He's bound to move the vets now—and wherever they're put it'll cost us a lot of lives to get them out. *That's* what your private raid really accomplished."

"Perhaps," Lathe admitted. "If so, I'm sorry. Where would the vets be sent—any ideas?"

"Cerbe Prison's their best bet," Faye said. "It's an old fortress southeast of here, out in the middle of nowhere. Smallish building, four floors up and six down, surrounded by a walled courtyard big enough to land a Corsair in. The wall's got a weapons turret at each corner, controlled either from inside or from the main building."

"If the quizlers put them there you might as well pack up and leave," Dael Valentine interjected, his face stormy above his black turtleneck. "In fact, maybe you ought to leave anyway."

"Easy, Dael," Bakshi murmured.

"Sorry, Comsquare, but I'm getting sick of this. We give them safety and information by the truckload and get absolutely *nothing* in return."

Bakshi cocked an eyebrow at Lathe. "You care to respond?"

"Certainly. If you'd open your eyes and imagination you'd see useful fallout from our work all around you."

"*What* fallout?" Valentine snorted.

"Well, for lack of a more obvious example, we just

demolished a gate into the Strip. Someone's got to rebuild it, and one or two of those someones could build miniature mines into the hinges. You'd then have a one-shot chance later to bring a carload of stolen parts or whatever out of the Strip without having to actually ram the gate."

From the looks and murmurs around the table it was clear no one had thought of that. Tremayne and Bakshi exchanged glances, and Caine saw the blackcollar nod fractionally.

"Do you promise to consult with us—or at least me—before any further actions?" Tremayne asked.

"If it involves Radix personnel, yes," Lathe said promptly. "Assuming there's time, of course. Otherwise, I claim the right to act unilaterally."

"That's not good enough," Valentine shook his head.

Lathe shrugged. "It's the best I can offer."

There was a moment of awkward silence. "All right," Tremayne said at last. "I guess I can see your side of it. *But*—" He leveled a finger at Lathe. "We can play by military rules too. If any Radix member gets killed because you didn't consult with us you'll face a summary court-martial. I mean it."

"Understood. You'll let us know right away about any prisoner transfer?"

Tremayne looked at Cameron. "Yeah, I'll get some people on that," the intelligence chief growled.

"Good. Anything new at the Chryselli front?"

"The fighting's still going on," Salli Quinlan spoke up, somewhat grudgingly. "Argent's not about to be flooded with returning Ryqril, if that's what you're worried about."

"I was," Lathe acknowledged. "Thank you." He started to stand up.

"Just a second," Valentine objected. "Assuming it's not tied up with this precious mission of yours, I want to know how Caine did his vanishing act from Earth." He sent Caine a baleful glance. "Fair is fair—you don't trust *us*, either."

"A government man was kidnapped by our people," Caine said evenly. "His ID was altered, and somehow the computer records were also changed."

" 'Somehow'? You'll have to do better than that."

"I don't know how it was done—"

"Oh, that's helpful. Very convenient, too."

Caine felt his face getting red. "I'm an agent, not one of the leaders. They don't tell me everything."

"That's no better an explanation," Cameron said, getting into the act.

"Just a minute," Lathe interrupted. "I think I may know how they did it." He hesitated, not meeting Caine's puzzled frown.

"Well?" Tremayne prompted.

"Near the end of the war someone apparently broke the old problem of short lifetimes for human clones. . . ."

With a kind of numb horror Caine listened as Lathe outlined his theory. It was a possibility that had never occurred to him. His parents, the Resistance people who'd trained him—none of them had ever hinted that he was anything special. But it made sense . . . and the more he considered it, the more sense it made. There was no other way to explain how Rienzi's medical records had been such a perfect fit for him. No wonder Kratochvil and Marinos had been so casual about the ID records—all the hard work had been done twenty-seven years earlier!

Lathe finished, and for a moment there was silence. "Well, it's an interesting theory," Tremayne said at last. "Unprovable, of course."

"I only offered it as a possibility," Lathe reminded him.

"Yes. I suppose we'll have to settle for that." Tremayne glanced at Valentine, but the blackcollar offered no objection. "All right, then. We'll let you know about the vets; and *you'll* let *us* know your plans for getting them out."

Lathe nodded. "As I said I would."

The meeting broke up, and Caine headed straight for the door. He wanted to be alone, to sort all this out in privacy . . . before he reached the door Novak and Mordecai had fallen into step with him. He ignored them as he strode out into the hall. A clone. A duplicate person—and if one, why not more? He'd assumed the personal tutelage had been a normal part of Resistance agent training. But now he doubted that. Special treatment went with special tools. How many more Allen Caine Specials were there on Earth, being as carefully maneuvered through life as he had been?

A puppet, that's what he was. A clone-puppet, his broken strings picked up by Lathe and Radix.

A clone. *I should feel something*, he told himself dully. *Anger; resentment*. He'd been lied to his whole life; a piece of biological merchandise told he was a human being while everyone else chuckled at his naïveté. *At the very least*, he thought, *I should feel shame*. But all he had was numbness—numbness and the knowledge he still had a job to do. His conditioning was too good to fall apart over even a revelation like this.

"Caine?"

The figure waiting across from the blackcollars' room stepped forward. Stopping, Caine pulled his mind back from its brooding and forced his eyes to focus.

It was Lianna Rhodes, the Radix leader from Janus. "What?" he growled.

"I'd like to talk to you a moment," she said.

The last thing in the universe he wanted at the moment was to talk to an Argentian, and he was opening his mouth to say so when Mordecai butted in. "Probably shouldn't," he muttered.

Something deep within Caine flipped polarity. "Sure," he told Lianna instead. "Come on in."

Just this once, the puppet was going to handle his own strings.

If Mordecai was upset by the decision, he didn't show it, and Novak similarly made no comment as he unlocked the door and slipped inside for a quick check. Once inside, Caine led Lianna to a pair of chairs near the window. The two blackcollars made no effort to follow them, but took up their usual positions near the door.

"What can I do for you?" he asked, motioning the girl to one of the chairs as he sank into the other. Over her shoulder he could see Novak and Mordecai and realized that he'd instinctively seated Lianna with her back to them, allowing the lip-reading blackcollars to confirm he wasn't giving away any secrets and putting her into the worst possible combat position. Even in a rebellious mood, he couldn't shake his training.

So much for handling his own strings.

"Caine—"

"Allen."

"Whatever. Look, we've been stuck here for a week

now, waiting on thin-shelled eggs for something to happen. My men are getting bored and edgy—a combination I hate. We've heard about that crazy raid of yours, and rumors are flying about a massive assault against Henslowe Prison. I need to know whether or not that's true."

"I don't know, but I doubt it. Certainly not any time soon."

"So what *are* you planning?"

Caine shook his head. "Sorry, but the mission's still confidential."

"I'm not asking about your damn mission," she snapped. "I don't really care what you and your hotshots are up to. All I want to know is how my men are going to be involved, because I'm not going to throw them blindly into something unless I know their chances of coming out alive."

Caine looked at her with sudden insight. The slightly sarcastic manner with which she faced the world—it wasn't impatience or ego. It was fear. Fear for herself, perhaps; more likely fear for her people. To lead a resistance cell on a world like Argent was a heavy responsibility. "You must care a lot about your men," he said. "That's the sign of a good leader."

Her lip curled. "Yeah," she said, almost harshly.

"I meant that as a compliment," he told her, frowning.

"I know." She dropped her eyes. "I'm sorry. I'm . . . I don't plan to be a leader much longer. Or a follower, for that matter."

Caine blinked. "You're quitting Radix?"

She nodded. "Just as soon as someone's willing to take over Janus sector. Why? Is that so strange?"

"I thought your father. . . ." He trailed off, not knowing a safe way to end the sentence.

She raised her eyes again, and he was struck by the bitterness there. "Yes, my father *did* raise me to be a good Radix member. It's about all he ever did for me." She shifted her gaze to the window. "Radix was my father's whole life. He never gave my mother and me enough of himself. It hurt Mom terribly. I hated him for a long time because of that." She rubbed a finger across her lips, almost savagely. "I'm not going to make that mistake. I'm getting out *now*, before the damn thing takes over my life."

"Why are you still here, then?" he asked after a moment.

A sardonic smile. "I guess that's something I got from both of them: a sense of duty. I have to stick with it until someone can do my job." She shook her head. "Look, I didn't come here to cry on your shoulder. All I want to know is what kind of risks my men will have to face."

He'd almost forgotten her original question. Meeting her gaze with his own, he tried to think.

What could he say? He didn't have the foggiest idea what Lathe intended to do—and even if he did he couldn't risk telling Lianna. Not that she was particularly untrustworthy; his instincts felt better about her than many others he'd met in Radix. But instinct wasn't enough to go on here. For an instant he saw in her his own demand to know more about Dodds's mysterious mission, and abruptly felt a twinge of sympathetic pain. Her responsibilities were every bit as important to her as Caine's were to him, and she was even more in the dark than he was.

And he had to leave her there. "I'm sorry, but I can't tell you anything that'll help you. All I can do is promise you won't be put into action without *some* kind of information."

Nodding heavily, her lips pressed tightly together, Lianna stood up. "I expected that answer, but it was worth a try," she said as Caine got to his feet as well. For a moment she impaled him with her eyes. "Just remember that this can't stay under your armor forever . . . and if we're being set up for a slaughter you'll have more trouble than you want. Rural Radix cells like mine are pretty tight; we don't take orders well from outsiders when we don't know what's going on. I don't care if I get the explanation five days or five minutes in advance—but I have to have it *some*time. Keep that in mind."

Nodding to him, she turned and walked away. He stayed where he was, watching as she exchanged nods with the blackcollars and left. The door thunked solidly behind her, and Mordecai sent a questioning look at Caine. "Well?"

"Nothing important," Caine muttered, turning his back and sitting down in the chair Lianna had just vacated. If they felt insulted, that was just too bad.

He was a clone. With an effort, he tried to feel anger over what had been done to him.

CHAPTER 20

The rain had been pouring down steadily for the past three hours, and even with the protection of the trees lining the road Jensen was getting soaked. His blackcollar poncho didn't seal tightly enough against the neck of his Security uniform, and every three or four minutes a fresh trickle of water would find its way inside. Jensen had given up swearing at the situation long ago, at about the same time he decided regretfully that he couldn't afford to find a wide-crowned tree and wait out the storm. He was still too close to the mountains and he needed every klick he could get.

A sudden splash came from behind him, and he turned to see a car rolling quietly through the mud toward him. Behind the dim lights he could make out a single occupant.

If he'd heard it coming sooner he could have ducked behind a tree, but it was too late for that now. Standing motionlessly, he waited as the car pulled to a stop beside him.

The side window slid down and Jensen found himself facing a cheerful-faced man. "Hi, there," the driver nodded. "Rotten day to be out. Can I give you a lift?"

Jensen thought quickly, but he really had no choice. Alone, on foot, and apparently unarmed, he couldn't realistically claim to be a Security man on special patrol, and there was no other excuse he could think of that required him to be out in this vertical lake. And to refuse a ride without reason could draw unwelcome attention. "Sure. Thanks," he said. Walking around behind the car, he opened the door and climbed in, spraying water over the seat. Under cover of the movement he drew his *nunchaku*, laying the weapon across his lap. With a slight jerk as its wheels pulled free of the mud, the car started up again.

"Where you headed?" the driver asked pleasantly, apparently oblivious to the water running onto his seats and floor.

"Down the road about twenty kilometers," the blackcollar replied. "I took a bad turn and my car got stuck at a dead end a ways back," he added, to forestall the obvious question.

"Ah."

Jensen studied the other out of the corner of his eye. Short, a little plump, somewhere in his late thirties if he wasn't on Idunine—it wasn't exactly the profile of the Security men he'd seen so far. But he could easily be an informer. "Where are *you* going?" he asked.

"Torrentin, eventually. If this rain floods the bridge I may be stuck on this side of the river awhile. What's at twenty kilometers from here?"

For a second Jensen didn't understand the question. Then he caught on. "I'm meeting with a Security unit there for special duty."

"What, just by the side of the road?"

"There's supposed to be a temporary camp there," Jensen told him, sweating a bit. The line of questioning was beginning to get dangerous. He knew nothing about local geography, and practically any answer he gave could damn him instantly as a foreigner. He was beginning to wish he'd given his destination as five klicks away instead of twenty.

"Bet you're out looking for the blackcollar, huh?" the driver commented, glancing across at Jensen.

Under his poncho, the blackcollar squeezed his *nunchaku* tightly. Had the general population been told of his landing, or was that knowledge limited to the government? "My job is none of your business," he said stiffly. Even to himself it sounded lame.

"Of course." For a moment the driver was silent as he fought the car over a particularly bumpy section of the road. "Most of the searching's still north of here, I understand," he said as the car settled down. "You shouldn't have any trouble."

Jensen stiffened. "What's *that* supposed to mean?" he growled.

The other kept his gaze on the road, a half-smile etched tightly across his face. "Cutter Waldemar at your service, Commando Jensen. Our people have been looking for you for a week now. I'm glad we got to you before Security did."

Jensen had more or less resigned himself to being identified sometime during the ride, but he hadn't expected it to happen quite so soon. But he recovered fast. "What the hell are you talking about?" he snapped.

Waldemar glanced over. "Good try, Commando, but you're wasting your time. We had you identified as far back as Split, and a spot 'twenty kilometers down the road' would more likely be said as being 'near Noma.' And no one knows a blackcollar's loose in the Rumelian Mountains except Security and our organization of Radix. A real Security man would have jumped all over me for that question."

"All right. I concede." Jensen kept his attention on the other. "Now you prove who *you* are."

"Absolute proof I can't give you, but I *can* give you some points in my favor. Number one: if I were a quizler this conversation wouldn't be taking place. I'd have triggered a quiet alarm and talked about the weather while the car filled up with sleep gas. After what your rads did in Calarand yesterday morning there isn't a Security man on Argent who'd confront you alone like this."

"You seem more courageous."

"Not really; I just know you aren't an automatic killing machine, that you'll hear me out. Point two's along that same line: I'm unarmed." He raised his elbows from his sides, inviting inspection.

Jensen shook his head. "I'll take your word for it. You wouldn't be carrying weapons I could identify as such, anyway."

"Point," the other admitted. "Okay, then, here's my final card. Underneath your seat is a paral-dart pistol. Get it out."

Jensen considered. Then, slipping on his flexarmor gloves, he reached under the seat. No booby traps went off as he drew the gun out and examined it. An old compressed-air weapon, it bore the marks of heavy use, as well as those of careful maintenance. "Okay. And?"

"Underneath *my* seat is a set of maps covering everything between here and Calarand, with the most likely places to get through the Security cordon marked. In the trunk are edibles and clothing." Waldemar's voice was steady. "If you don't want to trust me, those darts will keep me out for five or six hours. You can drop me here, take the car, and try to get away on your own. I'll walk home when the drug wears off."

"Your group—Radix—doesn't want to talk to me?"

"Not especially." He sent Jensen a lopsided smile. "Matter of fact, the prevailing opinion down here is that you're all going to get yourselves killed or captured, and the less we're involved with you the better."

Jensen nodded. "Hospitable types, aren't you?"

"It's called self-preservation. Very popular in these parts."

For a long moment no one spoke. Jensen studied Waldemar's face, looking for clues, but in fact he had pretty well made up his mind. The whole thing *could* be an elaborate sucker-trap, but Security was unlikely to go to that much trouble, especially with simpler traps available. And Radix's less than enthusiastic attitude rang uncomfortably true. "All right," he said slowly. "I'm convinced. Where are we going?"

"Millaire." Waldemar's relief was unmistakable; clearly, he hadn't looked forward to taking a long walk in the rain. "That's where the southern HQ is. It's about six hundred kilometers from here, so we should be there tonight. Barring quizler trouble, of course."

"Sounds good." Jensen took a deep breath, feeling some of the tension leave his shoulders as he did so. He hadn't realized how tired he was of being on the defensive. "I'd like to see those maps of yours, too."

"Sure." Reaching under his seat, Waldemar produced a thick sheaf of paper. "Anything you'd like to know about Radix or Argent in general?"

"Sure—everything," Jensen said agreeably. Sorting through the maps he found the one marked "Calarand" and opened it. "Why don't you start by telling me what exactly my friends did to Calarand yesterday?"

*   *   *

The *nunchaku* was a silent blur wrapping itself like half a cocoon around him. Lathe kept his gaze focused beyond the flail, controlling its motion solely through the feel in his muscles. The weapon changed hands once, twice, three times; interrupted its defensive pattern to snap out and back in whiplike motions that could crack skulls; folded itself back along the blackcollar's arm and shoulder, where it could block even a Ryqril-wielded short sword; and resumed its pattern as Lathe snatched and threw three *shuriken* into the targets at the far end of the shooting range.

From the door at his left came a knock. "Come in," Lathe called, breathing a little heavily as he sheathed the *nunchaku.*

The door opened and Bakshi looked in. "Am I interrupting?"

Lathe shook his head. "Come on in."

The Argentian did so, closing the door behind him. "Skyler said I'd find you here. How's the shoulder?"

"Good as new." Lathe stretched his arms forward experimentally. "Just a little tightness where the burn line was. I'd forgotten what good stuff that salve is—we ran out of it on Plinry ages ago." He gestured toward the mats behind them. "If you came to work out I can prove how fit I am."

Bakshi smiled and shook his head. "Perhaps later." He paused. "Speaking of workouts, I've been talking to Fuess about your little foray yesterday. I get the impression you weren't entirely satisfied with his performance."

"Umph." Turning, Lathe set off down the range to retrieve his *shuriken.* "He said that?"

"Not in so many words." Bakshi fell into step beside him. "I'd like to hear your evaluation of him."

"All right. Yes, I was disappointed. His fighting skills aren't up to what I would consider blackcollar level. More importantly, he was a rotten soldier. He wanted to debate every other order, and even when he obeyed me it was only grudgingly. I presume I don't have to explain the need for a smooth command structure to you, do I?"

"No." They'd reached the targets now, heavy wooden boards pockmarked with hundreds of tiny pits that almost obliterated the traditional human-figure outlines painted there. Each of Lathe's *shuriken* had hit one of the outlines directly in the throat. Extracting one of the stars, Bakshi turned it idly in his hand. "You're a good marksman."

Lathe grunted as he retrieved the other two stars. "Not really. Most of my men are at least as good as I am."

"Then your men are extraordinary," Bakshi said, "or else Plinry was lucky. The Ryqril must not have used nerve gases on you."

Lathe gave him a hard look. "No, they didn't do much of that. Most of us didn't arrive until the ground war had begun, when they had too many of their own people down for indiscriminate use of gases. But don't *ever* suggest again that Plinry was lucky because of it."

Bakshi ducked his head briefly. "The groundfire attack; yes. I apologize. I guess they learned their lesson on you; here they pounded us into submission from space so they wouldn't have to use it again. My point was that many of our blackcollars were permanently affected by one of the gases. We don't talk about it much; it's still too painful a memory."

"Affected how? Slowed reflexes?"

"Yes, from light neural damage. You've seen it before?"

"One or two cases." Someone might have mentioned Dodds. "Is that why none of you can fight?"

Bakshi smiled bitterly. "Oh, we can fight, all right. We didn't get your thirty-year vacation, you know. But, yes, that's why Fuess and the others aren't as good at hand-to-hand combat anymore. And as for the other problem—" He hesitated. "I think maybe they resent the fact that you're still as good as you always were. As they were once."

Lathe extended a hand, and Bakshi dropped the last *shuriken* into it. "I suggest you have a talk with them," he told the Argentian. "We're not here to show up anyone. The time for medals and glory ended when the TDE surrendered. If your people can't accept that, then pack them off somewhere where they won't be in our way."

"I'll tell them." Bakshi smiled wryly as the two blackcollars turned and started back toward the door. "We haven't had to fight this kind of war for quite a while. But we'll get the hang of it." He paused abruptly, brow furrowing. "Someone's coming," he murmured.

Lathe had also heard the running footsteps. Speeding up to a fast walk, he headed for the door, automatically reaching for a *shuriken*. Bakshi, he noted peripherally, was matching his pace but drifting to the side with a blackcollar's instinctive aversion to bunching up. They were five paces from the door when someone pounded on the panel and charged in.

It was Jeremiah Dan, clutching a scrawled note. "They've found Jensen!" he announced excitedly, waving the paper.

"Where is he?" Bakshi asked as Lathe snatched the note.

"Millaire," Dan told him, catching his breath and slowly regaining his usual professorial bearing. "They picked him up along the Hemoth River this morning."

Lathe glanced up. "Are the collies still checking traffic in and out of the city?"

"Probably, but there are ways to sneak out, if you want to go down there and get him," Dan said. "Greenstein suggested you might want to do that."

"So his people can stay clear of Calarand, in other words," Bakshi commented.

"Who's Greenstein?" Lathe asked.

"Uri Greenstein's head of our southern division," Dan said. "You saw him at our first meeting, but you weren't introduced."

"This message come in by secure phone?"

"Yes, directly to me. Commando Jensen said to tell you that the moon children agree with your calculations."

Lathe nodded; it was the code phrase they'd set up. "How far is Millaire?"

"About seven hundred klicks southwest of here," Bakshi said. "It should be a relatively safe drive if you want to go."

Lathe hesitated. He definitely wanted Jensen in Calarand . . . and the timing presented unexpected possibilities. "All right," he said. "I'll need two cars—can I get them right away?"

"Now?" Dan glanced at his watch. "It's almost twenty o'clock."

"There's no curfew, is there?"

"No. But it's a long trip and it's supposed to thunderstorm tonight."

"My men don't melt. Two cars, and we could use a guide."

"Take two of my blackcollars," Bakshi offered. "I promise they'll behave this time."

"Well. . . ." Unfortunately, Lathe couldn't think of a good reason to say no. "Okay, but we'll only need one. The second car can follow the first."

"Risky," Dan said doubtfully. "What if they get lost?"

"They won't. Just make sure both cars have lots of maps." He looked at Bakshi. "If you'll excuse me, I have to get my men ready."

"One other thing," Dan called after him. "We've got definite word now that the quizlers are preparing Cerbe Prison for a major influx of new prisoners."

"Good. I'll get the details from you later. Right now, just get me those cars."

He had a workable plan ready by the time he reached the blackcollars' room. Pushing through the door, he gestured to Mordecai—who, as usual, was standing guard—and turned to the three men sitting around the table. "Free time's over," he announced. "Radix found Jensen."

The air was suddenly electric. "Where is he?" Skyler and Novak asked together.

"A place called Millaire." Lathe filled them in on Dan's message. "What's the word on Cerbe?" he asked Skyler. "You and Hawking found a weakness yet?"

"Yes—their secure communications system." The two blackcollars and Caine, Lathe noted, had been looking through Radix's somewhat skimpy file on the old fortress, and Skyler shuffled out a telephoto picture. "Rotating comm laser turret here on the roof of the main building," he said, tapping it with a finger. "Hemispherical, twenty centimeters in diameter. Secure messages from Calarand are relayed through one or more hovering patrol boats. Theoretically, it's a tap-proof system, since the whole thing is up off the ground."

"You have a way to do it?"

"Hawking does. He's making a gadget he says worked perfectly the one time he got to use it on Plinry."

"Can it be ready in an hour?"

Skyler's eyebrows rose fractionally. "Are we in that much of a hurry?"

"Yes, because he's leaving with the group going to Millaire. It's the perfect way to get him out of the city without alerting the local collie spies. Once you're clear of any roadblocks he can fall back and head for Cerbe."

"Was that 'you' singular or plural?" Novak asked, his voice carefully neutral.

Lathe smiled. "Plural, of course. You and Skyler will both be going."

Skyler glanced at Caine, then back at Lathe. "Can you spare both of us?" he asked quietly.

"Mordecai and I can protect Caine," Lathe assured him. "I want you to go to Hawking right away. Tell him what's happening; if he can't be ready in an hour, get his best estimate and I'll do some stalling. Then go to the garage and make sure the cars they assign us aren't bugged or marked. Oh, and Hawking said he was going to put together a portable bug stomper, too—if it's ready you should take it along."

Skyler stood up and began fastening a civilian shirt over his flexarmor. "We traveling alone or with a native guide?"

Lathe grimaced. "The latter—Bakshi's giving us one of his blackcollars."

"Great. I'll warn Hawking." With a cheerful wave at the silent Mordecai, Skyler left the room.

"You don't like Bakshi and the others, do you?" Caine asked quietly. He was seated alone at the table now, Novak having vanished into the corner to begin collecting equipment.

"Bakshi I don't mind," Lathe said, pulling out one of the chairs and sitting down. It felt good; that workout had worn him out. "It's the other four that bother me."

"Why? Because they aren't as phlegmatic toward the Ryqril as you are?"

Lathe declined to take offense. "A good fighting spirit is fine. But so far they haven't shown anything *but* spirit. Tell me, what's your opinion of Lianna Rhodes?"

Caine blinked. "Why, I . . . in what way?"

"How do you think she would do under pressure, for instance? More importantly, what are the chances she's a Security spy?"

Caine frowned. "I don't think she's a spy," he said slowly. "That's only gut instinct, of course. She said she was leaving Radix soon, though, and I can't see a spy doing something like that."

Lathe nodded; Caine's information and instincts meshed with his own. "You think she could face down a group of collies?"

Surprisingly, Caine smiled. "She sure doesn't wilt in front of *us*." The smile faded into curiosity. "Why all the questions?"

"I want her to help us get into Cerbe Prison." Lathe told him.

Caine's expression hardly changed. "I won't waste my breath telling you you're crazy," the younger man said calmly. "Do I get to know anything about this one in advance?"

Lathe hesitated, but only for a second. He'd been cutting Caine out of a lot lately, and the other was clearly beginning to resent it. Telling Caine this part of the plan would be safe enough . . . and it might help divert his mind from Dodds for a while. "Sure," he said, glancing at the quietly humming bug stomper standing sentinel in the middle of the room. "Let's go sit by the stomper and I'll tell you all about it."

CHAPTER 21

The storm clouds had been rolling in from the north for half an hour, replacing the already overcast night sky. Occasional flickers of lightning lit up the landscape, emphasizing the implicit promise of a heavy rain. At the car's wheel, Dael Valentine risked a quick glance behind him. "I told you this would happen," he said. "Driving in convoy at night's just plain stupid."

"Just relax," Skyler advised him from the back seat. "They have maps, and we know they got out of Calarand all right. Maybe they decided to take a different route."

" 'Maybe'?" Valentine snorted. "In other words, they did. And naturally you didn't bother to tell me."

"You were having so much fun complaining about their

incompetence it seemed a shame to enlighten you," Novak, next to Valentine, said tartly.

Valentine didn't reply. Novak was overstating the case a bit, in Skyler's opinion, but not by much. The Argentian had done a lot of bitching during the trip, almost as if he considered a chip on his shoulder to be standard equipment. Skyler had run into that kind before, back on Plinry, and considered the type to be a royal pain in the butt. They were dangerous to be around, too, usually getting themselves killed doing something stupid.

In the front seat a tiny penlight flicked on briefly as Novak checked his map. "Shouldn't we be seeing Millaire by now?" the black man asked.

"It's in a wide valley past these hills," Valentine said, pointing to the shadowy ridge that the car was approaching. "You'll see it in five minutes."

Novak grunted and fell silent. Skyler took a moment to look back along the road, and to study the territory on either side. Only occasional lights could be seen, most of them far back from the road. Not surprising, considering it was way past midnight and all good Argentians were asleep in their beds. Still, the darkness and lack of other traffic made the blackcollar uncomfortable. He'd learned long ago to dislike being conspicuous.

The car topped the ridge—and suddenly Millaire was in front of them, spreading across the valley like a two-dimensional star cluster. "Quite a town," Novak commented. "How's it compare to Calarand?"

"Larger in area; smaller in population," Valentine said. Half of Millaire's lights disappeared as they curved behind a hill, reappearing a moment later.

"Find a place where you can pull over," Skyler spoke up suddenly. "I want a clear view of the city."

"Why?" Valentine asked. "We're getting in late enough as it is."

"Just do it." Skyler's danger sense was tingling, and he was in no mood to argue.

"Yes, *sir*." Valentine ran the car onto the shoulder, raising clouds of dust as they bounced to a halt.

"Novak, give me that map," Skyler said, frowning out at Millaire. Novak handed over both the map and his penlight, and Skyler took a moment to refold the paper to the large-scale map of the city. "Valentine, show me again exactly where Radix HQ is," he ordered, cupping the penlight to block all but a faint glow.

The Argentian reached back over the seat. "It's right here," he said, tapping a spot a kilometer from the center of town. "Why?"

Skyler studied the map another moment, then flipped off the light. "You see it, Novak?"

"Yeah," the other said slowly. "I do now."

"What?" Valentine asked suspiciously, peering out the window.

"You see that patch of darkness, next to the big white building?" Skyler pointed it out. "Radix HQ is inside it."

Valentine shrugged. "So? Probably just a power substation crash."

"Maybe. But doesn't it strike you as odd that there should just happen to be an outage *now*, and at the same place Jensen happens to be?"

"Coincidence," Valentine growled. But he didn't sound entirely convinced.

"Possibly. I doubt it." Skyler handed the map and light back to Novak. "Let's go. We're under battle conditions now—you understand, Valentine?"

"Perfectly, sir," the Argentian said grimly. The car was already back on the road and picking up speed.

Opening the front of his coat, Skyler pulled his flexarmor gloves and battle-hood from beneath his belt and began checking his weapons. In the front seat, he could see movements that indicated Novak was doing likewise.

Outside, it was beginning to rain.

"Your rads won't be here for at least another hour," Uri Greenstein said, handing Jensen one of the two steaming mugs he'd just poured and sitting down behind his plain metal desk. "You're welcome to a bed until then if you'd like to rest."

"Thanks, but no," Jensen said, sipping cautiously. It was some sort of herbal coffee, delicately seasoned. "I napped some in the car. All I really needed was a shower and a hot meal, and your people have been most generous in providing those."

Greenstein shrugged, and Jensen let his eyes drift around the room. The coffee and automatic blend-maker seemed to be Greenstein's only luxuries; the rest of the fifth-floor office was Spartan in the extreme, from the simple furniture to the plain Venetian blind covering the window. He looked back at Greenstein, to find the other's gaze on him. "I take it, Mr. Greenstein," he said, "that you had some reason for asking me up here? Besides the coffee, of course, which is excellent."

The Radix leader smiled thinly. "Not really, Commando. Frankly, I just wanted to see what you were like."

Jensen shrugged. "I hope you're not disappointed."

"Not at all. Intrigued is more like it." Greenstein waved toward the west. "You escaped a crashing spaceship, evaded a massive manhunt for eight days, apparently killed quite a few heavily armed Security men—and yet you don't have a trace of the usual blackcollar bluster."

"Well, you know how jungle animals calm down after they're fed."

"You're joking. I'm not."

"I know." Jensen sobered, sipped again from his mug. "We all started with a little of that, I suppose—being a freshly graduated blackcollar is heady stuff. I think most of us lost our conceit after our first few weeks of actual warfare. When enough of your comrades have been killed beside you the word 'elite' pretty well loses all meaning."

Greenstein nodded heavily. "Yes," he agreed. "I've seen a fair number of friends die like that." He fixed Jensen with a hard eye. "And I don't want to add to that list because of you and your rads."

Jensen understood. "I expect most of Security's fire will be directed at us alone."

"All right." Greenstein stood up. "Understand, please, that I have nothing against all of you personally. It's just that I've seen too many battles where the blackcollars have survived and a lot of other people haven't."

"It's not always like that," Jensen said, also rising, "but we'll do our best to get out of your way quickly."

The words were barely out of his mouth when a box on Greenstein's desk suddenly buzzed and a red light flicked on. "What's that?" Jensen asked.

Greenstein frowned slightly. "Someone coming in through the west—"

Abruptly, five more lights came on; simultaneously, the whole building shook with a muffled roar beneath them. "Sonic grenade!" Jensen snapped, already halfway into his flexarmor gloves.

Greenstein didn't hesitate. Yanking open a drawer, he scooped out a bulky gas mask and a dart pistol and ran to the door. He opened it, looked out quickly, and disappeared. Jensen, in full battle gear now with his pack back on his shoulders, was right behind him.

The hall was only dimly lit. Ahead of Greenstein Jensen could see two figures disappearing through what appeared to be a hidden door; behind the blackcollar three or four others were stumbling out of other rooms. "Where are we going?" Jensen asked Greenstein.

"We're being raided," the other answered tightly, already beginning to breathe heavily through his mask. "We'll help with the fighting and then make for the tunnels."

"Hold it. How secure is this exit?"

He was too late; Greenstein was already through the door and clattering down a spiral stairway. Gritting his teeth, the blackcollar followed.

They didn't get far, Greenstein was barely half a flight down when he suddenly jerked back, his gun arm waving wildly as he spun and collapsed against the railing. Below him on the stairs three or four body-armored figures could be seen coming up.

Jensen reacted instantly, reversing direction and heading back to the floor they'd just left. Two bursts of darts slapped at his legs before he made it through the door—and as he emerged into the hall another burst caught him full in the chest. He leaped to one side, *nunchaku* swinging, and just barely managed to deflect the flail in time to keep from breaking Cutter Waldemar's skull.

"Jensen!" the plump man exclaimed, hastily lowering his pistol. "I'm sorry; I thought you were a quizler."

"You're not far wrong—they're right behind me. Get back."

Waldemar nodded and moved off down the hall. Jensen stepped to one side of the hidden door and had just raised his *nunchaku* when the first of the invaders came charging through.

Jensen didn't even bother with the *nunchaku*, but simply swept the Security man's legs out from under him, sending him crashing to the floor. The second man, too close on his partner's heels, fought to keep his feet under him; Jensen's *nunchaku* smashing into his neck ended the battle. The third man never made it into the hall as Jensen stepped into the doorway and threw a kick to his torso that sent him reeling back into at least one more invader. The sounds of bodies crashing down the stairs were cut off as Jensen slammed the door shut.

"What do we do now?" Waldermar asked tensely, coming up behind him.

"We get the hell out of here," Jensen told him. "Have you been here often enough to know how to get out?"

"I know the standard boltholes," the other said, "But this stairway was one of them."

"Then we can forget the others. How tall is this building?"

"Five floors; nothing above us but the roof. I think this stairway goes all the way up."

"It does. First, though. . . ." Jensen glanced around, located an electrical outlet, then turned back to the fallen Security men. In addition to dart guns and assorted grenades, they were carrying the familiar snub-nosed laser rifles. Scooping one up, the blackcollar flicked it to medium power and fired a shot into the outlet. There was a blue-white flash, and the hallway abruptly went dark.

"That may slow them down," Jensen explained, cracking the stairway door. Nothing was audible; grabbing Waldemar's arm, he guided the Argentian onto the stairs. "They'll have to use infrareds or light-amps this way—and they'll wonder what we're up to. Get moving; I'll stay behind you in case someone below us starts shooting."

They reached the top of the stairs without incident. There, Jensen squeezed past the Argentian and stepped cautiously out. The stairwall exit was as carefully disguised as the rest of it, opening through the back of the shed housing the building's regular stairwell door. For a wonder Security had missed a bet; the roof was deserted.

"Now what?" Waldemar asked, fingering his pistol nervously.

"Watch the stairs while I check out the streets."

The survey was a quick one; Millaire's excellent streetlight system showed all too clearly the forces skulking in the alleys and doorways around the Radix building. Jensen checked all four sides and then trotted back to the center of the roof, where Waldemar was gesturing frantically to him.

"People moving on the stairs," he hissed as the blackcollar slid his pack off and rummaged around inside it. "They'll be here any minute!"

"Here." Jensen handed him the pack, the coil of rope he'd withdrawn from it, and the laser rifle he was still carrying. "Get over to the edge—that side—but stay low. The ground is swarming with collies, and I don't want you spotted."

Waldemar nodded and headed away in a crouching run. Unlimbering his *nunchaku* and checking his *shuriken* pouch, Jensen stepped to the main stairwell door and put his ear to the panel. There were footsteps coming, all right; five to ten pairs of them, probably. Stepping to one side, Jensen waited for them to emerge.

They had, at any rate, learned caution. There was no mad charge onto the roof; instead, the door was kicked open and a grenade tossed out.

Jensen reacted instantly, throwing himself into a flat dive that took him to the side of the shed, rolling as noiselessly as possible. The blast was a small one, and he was back up on one knee by the time the Security men charged out onto the roof. There were seven of them in all, from the sound; four breaking to Jensen's side of the shed, the others going the opposite direction.

It was shooting the proverbial swamp lizard in an ice pit. At such close range Jensen's *shuriken* hit all four with pinpoint accuracy, sliding between helmet and torso armor plates. Jensen didn't wait to see the invaders collapse, but jumped to his feet and slipped around the back of the shed. The Security men on that side of the roof had heard the sounds of Jensen's attack and were heading back to investigate. All three spotted Jensen; one even got a wild shot off before they died. From the sprawled bodies Jensen snatched eight grenades and threw two down each of the two stairways. Slamming the doors on the explosions, he hurried back to the edge of the roof.

Waldemar was crouched by the low parapet, his laser held ready, a stunned look on his face. "Give me the laser," Jensen whispered, "and make a slipknot in that rope."

The words were barely out of his mouth when a sudden hail of darts clattered into the parapet from below. The sound broke Waldemar's awe-struck trance; crouching lower, he shoved the rifle into Jensen's hands and got busy with the rope.

Smiling to himself at the other's reaction, Jensen rolled along the roof to a new spot and hooked an eye over the parapet. More darts hissed through the air and ricocheted from his battle-hood; ignoring them, he flipped the laser to full antiarmor and fired a long burst into the base of the nearest streetlight. Through the whine of darts he could hear the crackle of unevenly heated metal.

And suddenly, the lights all went out.

Lowering the laser, Jensen looked around him. A solid twenty- or thirty-block region had been blacked out, and the nearest light was a good two blocks away. Not perfect, but there were ways of setting up power substations that wouldn't have let him get even this much.

"Did you do that?" Waldemar whispered as Jensen rejoined him.

"Yes. Is the rope ready?"

The Argentian pressed it into his hands, and Jensen confirmed by touch that the knot was properly done. "Good. When I give the word toss one of those grenades off the roof."

Rising to a crouch, Jensen took the loop in one hand, making sure the rope's other end was securely held under one foot. His eyes were adjusting to the faint wash of light from elsewhere in the city, and he'd mentally fixed his target's location before shooting out the lights, anyway. Twirling the loop, he aimed. . . . "Now!" he stage-whispered to Waldemar, and threw the rope.

Jensen had hated lasso practice back in his trainee days. It had been taught by plainsriders from Hedgehog, and being inferior in *anything* to a Hoggy had been particularly galling. But despite that—or perhaps because of it—he'd become the best roper in his unit; and as Waldemar's grenade flashed, momentarily knocking out all nearby light-amps, he saw his loop land neatly over the sturdy-looking chimney vent sticking up from the building across the street.

"Okay," he whispered, pulling in the slack, "we've got a bridge down to that four-floor place. I'll tie this end down and we'll get going." From his pack he produced a wristband attached to a small pulley. "Put this on your left wrist, pulley side up," he ordered, and headed back to the stairway shed with the coil of rope.

No sounds were audible from either stairway as Jensen swiftly lashed the rope to a vertical support at one of the main stairwell's inner corners. That was ominous; either the Radix people were putting up a better fight than Security had expected or else something special was being planned for those on the roof. Tightening the rope, he gave the sky a quick scan and hurried back to the parapet.

Waldemar was kneeling tensely by the low wall when Jensen returned. "Any reaction from below?" the blackcollar asked as he checked the wristband and locked the pulley over the line.

Waldemar's silhouette shook its head. "But they've *got* to have seen the rope," he hissed.

"Not necessarily." Jensen relieved him of the laser and picked up a grenade, arming the latter. "It's thin and dark against a black sky, and the grenade you threw at the same time should have temporarily blinded them." Rising halfway to his feet, he hurled his grenade back over the opposite side of the roof. "To keep them guessing," he explained as the blast echoed dully. "Slide up here onto the parapet and get ready."

Waldemar obeyed. Slinging his pack back on, Jensen picked up the last two grenades and lofted them into the street below. The laser went back into his right hand as he gripped the strap joining the wristband to the pulley with his left . . . and as the grenades flashed he leaped, pulling both men off the roof. Swaying like a twin-bob pendulum gone berserk, they slid down the rope.

Four seconds, Jensen estimated the trip would take; four dangerous, make-or-break seconds. Fighting the swinging motion by pure reflex, he held the laser ready, waiting tautly for the blast of darts that would show they'd been spotted. But no such attack came . . . and then they were over the roof, dragging their feet to kill their speed. Waldemar was new to the technique and promptly flipped over so that he was traveling backwards, bending double as the rope dipped toward the roof. Jensen let go while he still had his balance, braking to a halt in a half dozen quick steps. The gamble had paid off; and if he could now retrieve enough of his rope to try it again on the next building over, they might get out of this yet. Digging out a *shuriken*, he turned back toward the Radix building and took aim.

And from behind him came a flash of laser light, stabbing past his arm to slice the rope a bare meter away. Simultaneously, there were a handful of flat cracks, and the roof erupted in thick white smoke.

There was no time to curse, much as Jensen felt like doing so. Twisting to his right, he dropped the laser and snatched out his gas filter, jamming it tightly over his nose and mouth. They'd been waiting for him, obviously, probably out of sight behind the building's stairway shed. A trap only a blackcollar was likely to wander into—and like a professionally trained idiot, he'd done just that.

Ahead of him another laser flashed, lighting up the smoke like the inside of a light tube. Jensen hurled the *shuriken* he was holding, heard a metallic clank as it ricocheted. Dropping into a crouch, he made himself as inconspicuous as possible and tried to figure out what the hell he was going to do.

Obviously, they still had some hope of taking him alive—otherwise they would have shot him down as he dangled helplessly from the rope. And that might prove to be a bigger mistake than they knew, because by laying down a sleep-fog they had effectively blinded everyone on the roof. Even infrareds and light-amps would be of limited use, especially if they kept overloading their scanners with reflected laser fire. If he could just figure out a way to use that to his advantage.

The soft hum of a flyer interrupted his thoughts. Looking up, he could make out just a hint of blue-violet grav light approaching from the west. Coming in very low. . . .

There were times when stupid chances were the only ones available. Standing upright again, Jensen ran for the stairway shed.

His movement didn't go unnoticed. Before he had taken two steps three lasers had opened fire, two of the beams brushing his chest and arm. But here again the thick fog worked in his favor, scattering away much of the light and leaving something his flexarmor could handle without much trouble. For an instant the heat of the beams burned a path of clear air, and Jensen caught a glimpse of bulky helmets and armor. Doubling his speed, he kept moving, trying to take advantage of his attackers' momentary blindness.

It was a short reprieve. Within a second or two the smoke again exploded with light as laser fire crisscrossed his chest. Gritting his teeth, Jensen twisted aside, hoping he was still going the right direction. Above, the flyer's hum was getting louder.

He almost missed the shed completely, his outstretched hand brushing it as he ran past. Skidding to a halt, he felt around, located the door. It was locked.

Behind him came the faint sound of something moving swiftly toward his head. Spinning around, he threw his left arm upward in a block and countered with a kick to his attacker's midsection. The other went down with a crash; and, as heavy footsteps converged on him, Jensen snatched out his *nunchaku*. Blinking sweat from his eyes, more acutely conscious of his blindness than ever, he shrugged off his pack and began swinging.

The battle was short but furious. Jensen caught at least two of the attackers with what were probably disabling blows, despite their armor, and took nothing worse than a few bruises in return. Swinging his *nunchaku* in a wide arc to keep any others at bay, he stepped back to the stairwell door and snapped a kick at the lock.

The panel shattered, and behind Jensen pandemonium suddenly erupted. At least five laser beams caught him squarely in the back, feeling like a giant welding torch beneath the flexarmor. Jensen gasped . . . but his body was already moving, his legs bending and straightening convulsively, his hands finding purchase on the edge of the shed roof, his arms pulling him up and over to sprawl atop the structure as the lasers continued to blast at the doorway below.

For a moment he lay on his side on the shed roof, breathing as hard as he could through the gas filter and waiting for the pain in his back to ease. He had only seconds before his dazzled opponents discovered he had not, in fact, gone into the stairway and reached the obvious conclusion. Pushing himself up into a crouch, he looked upward. The flyer's gravs were more visible now, and Jensen was able to make out the craft's landing skids and lower fuselage. It was drifting slowly toward him, and for the first time he noticed a quiet spraying sound. His *nunchaku* was still in his right hand; shifting his grip, he took one of the sticks in each hand, the chain stretched taut between them. Distances were impossible to judge accurately in the fog, and the extra twenty centimeters of reach the *nunchaku* provided might be crucial. Bracing himself, Jensen watched the light move closer. A few more seconds—

Abruptly, the flyer twitched. Simultaneously, two laser beams shot at Jensen from below. He'd been spotted.

The blackcollar didn't hesitate, but jumped upward with all his strength, hoping fervently the flyer was still where it had been when the scattered laser light cut it off from his view. For a long moment he floated in glowing mist . . . then, abruptly, he was above the fog, and hovering squarely above him was the flyer. Almost out of reach . . . and at the top of his arc Jensen's arms whipped up, catching the flyer's left landing skid with the *nunchaku* chain.

For a second he dangled there, taking stock of the situation. The flyer was like the ones used as spotters by the collies on Plinry; the underside loading hatch and one of the side doors would be accessible from his skid. Behind the hatch a wide nozzle was directing a rain of heavy-looking droplets to the roof below. An adhesive spray, probably, designed to immobilize all combatants. Twisting up, the blackcollar hooked his legs around the skid, and a moment later was crouching under the boat's left-side door. The crew was undoubtedly aware of his presence, and Jensen had to move fast before they figured out what to do about it. Reaching up, he got a firm grip on the recessed door handle, and with all the speed and strength he could muster began smashing his *nunchaku* into the window at the door's right.

Boats of this size had never been meant for heavy combat, and their windows weren't designed to take that sort of punishment. His third blow sent hairline cracks through the thick plastic, and his seventh smashed it completely. Standing upright on the skid, his left hand still on the outer handle, he reached in through the broken window and groped for the lock mechanism.

Abruptly, the craft bucked under his feet, twisting and

bouncing as the pilot finally reacted. But the maneuver was just a little too late. Jensen had a solid grip now, and all the bouncing would do would be to keep the boat's crew from interfering with him. The boat twisted right, then left as he found the inside handle, strained to release it; and then, as the boat dipped sideways and his feet slid off to dangle in midair, he popped the catch. The door flew open, and as the boat leveled off again the blackcollar swung himself inside.

They were on him instantly—three of them, unarmored, apparently trying to overwhelm him by sheer numbers. Under normal circumstances an easy fight—but Jensen was tired and hurt, and it took ten or fifteen seconds to beat them into unconsciousness. Ten or fifteen seconds too long . . . for as he turned toward the pilot, he saw the wild, white eyes staring at him out of a face of sheer terror. And beyond the pilot the distant city lights tilted crazily in the windscreen. . . .

They hit the side of the building with a cacophony of grinding metal and a shock that sent Jensen hurtling through space toward the broken nose of the boat. He never felt the impact of his landing.

A hundred kilometers south of Calarand, the storm had broken with full force. Lightning flashed almost continuously across the black sky, accompanied by solid sheets of rain and hail that ranged from droplet-size to as big as a fist. None of the latter had hit Kwon yet, but he knew it would just be a matter of time.

Sprawled on his stomach at Kwon's feet, Hawking gave no indication he was even aware of the storm. His face glued to the telescope in front of him, his hand resting lightly on its focusing knob, he hadn't moved for at least ten minutes, ignoring completely the water that was undoubtedly pouring in under his poncho. Kwon admired the other's calmness under such rotten conditions; though he himself was perfectly willing to die for his comrades, some of these preliminaries drove him crazy.

"It's averaging about two meters too far north," Hawking's voice came faintly between thunderclaps.

Peering into the lightning-wracked sky, Kwon located the tiny dot fluttering at the other end of his kilometer-long molecular filament. Directly below the kite the top of Cerbe Prison was visible, the rest of it hidden behind an intervening hill. That the prison staff was unaware of the intruder overhead was practically a given; with no metal in either the kite or the device dangling from it, the prison's radar would show virtually nothing, and the rain and hail effectively neutralized sonic and pulsed-laser sensors. A good thing, too, because this could take a while. . . . Experimentally, Kwon took a step to his right and let half a meter of filament run from his reel. The wind at ground level was generally blowing due east, but the kite had found a layer of air with a slight northern component mixed in. The random thunderstorm-sized gusts didn't help, either. "How's that?" he asked Hawking.

"Whatever you just did, reverse it," the other answered. "It's going farther north."

"Right." Blowing a drop of water from the end of his nose, Kwon touched the proper control on his reel and brought a meter of filament back in. He was just preparing to move back to his left when a snapped command stopped him in mid-step.

"Hold it! You're right on target!"

Kwon froze, carefully bringing his weight back onto both feet. "All right," Hawking murmured, "we're almost there. It's swinging right over the turret. Countdown: three . . . two . . . one . . . *drop!*"

And Kwon touched the release, letting the spool spin freely on its nearly frictionless bearings. Deprived suddenly of the line's tension, the kite should fall pretty nearly straight down—

"Bull's-eye!" Hawking crowed. "Okay; reel in slowly."

Kwon eased off on the release, letting the wind give the kite some lift again. If Hawking's gadget had hit the prison roof solidly enough, the four catches on its underside should have released, freeing it from the kite. "Kite's rising," he informed Hawking, watching the distant dot carefully.

"Beautiful." Hawking backed away from his telescope and scrambled to his feet. "Take a look; I'll bring in the kite."

Handing over the reel, Kwon gingerly got down in the muddy grass and eased up to the eyepiece. Dead center in the field of view was a hemispherical knob sticking up from the prison's main building—the comm laser turret for Cerbe's secure link to the outside world. Now, sitting directly over it, was another roughly hemispherical shape, this one wispy and insubstantial in the lightning flashes. Its bubblelike appearance was not illusion; the device consisted solely of a thousand hair-thin optical fibers arranged with their inner ends pointing radially toward and away from the turret and their outer ends gathered into a horizontal bundle at the base. "This thing really going to work?" he asked, looking up just in time to catch a large drop in his eye.

"Sure." Hawking was reeling in the filament at about half speed and studying the hills to their right. "Comm lasers always have wide apertures, to minimize dispersion over long distances. No matter what direction they point it, some of the fibers will intercept a little of the beam and funnel it to our receiver—ditto for incoming beams. Absolutely trivial and nearly undetectable."

"Unless they spot the receiver."

"They won't." Shifting his grip on the reel, Hawking pointed to the right. "The pirated beam should hit somewhere on one of those two hills. Once the receiver's in place, we can put the actual listening post ten klicks away if we need to."

"If you say so." Kwon got to his feet, brushed the worst of the mud off his pants, and glanced westward. "Looks like the storm's easing up—most of the lightning's already passed over. Let's get the receiver planted before their sensors start working again, eh?"

"Right. Here, you bring the kite in the rest of the way; I'll handle the scope."

Kwon grinned in the darkness as he accepted the reel back again. Hawking's nervousness where his equipment was concerned was legendary. "Not a bad night's work," he commented. "Vale says Haven and O'Hara are finally ready, you and I have a tap into the collies' gossip line, and Skyler and Novak will have Jensen back by breakfast."

"Things are finally moving our way," Hawking agreed, his telescope cradled like a baby in his arms. "About time, too."

Off to the east, the thunder rumbled restlessly.

CHAPTER 22

Caine glanced up as Lathe entered the blackcollars' room, then returned his gaze to the map he was studying. Something about the way Lathe closed the door made him look up again, and this time he saw the comsquare's expression. "What's wrong?" he asked.

"They got Jensen," Lathe said quietly.

"Dead?" Mordecai, sitting near the door, looked as relaxed as always; but his voice made Caine shiver.

"I don't know." Lathe mopped at his forehead with the towel draped across his shoulders. "Skyler called about five minutes ago, and Dan caught me as Bakshi and I were leaving the range. The collies apparently raided the Millaire HQ a short time before they arrived. The Security cordon was just being taken down, and they had to sneak into the area on foot. No indication anywhere as to whether Jensen was dead or just captured."

"Could he have gotten away?" Caine asked.

Mordecai shook his head. "The Security cordon would've still been up."

"Right," Lathe agreed heavily. "The timing's too good for coincidence. They wanted Jensen and they got him." Dropping into the chair across from Caine, he stared off across the room.

"What's Skyler going to do?" Mordecai asked after a short pause.

"He wants to stay and try to find him. I told him yes."

It was Mordecai's turn to stare into space. "We'll have to pull someone back here from Hawking's house to help with guard duty, you know."

"True. But after tomorrow O'Hara and Haven will be available again."

"Or they'll be dead," Caine muttered.

"In which case we'll have lost, anyway." Mordecai shrugged. "All right. I suppose it won't hurt to let Skyler operate down there a day or two. Might even take some of Security's attention off us here." He cocked an eyebrow. "How'd the workout go?"

Lathe had discarded his towel and the weapons on his belt and was worming out of his skintight shirt. "No question—Bakshi's a genuine blackcollar. Speed and reflexes are too good for him to be otherwise."

Caine frowned. "You were testing Bakshi? Why?"

"I want to know what we've got to work with," Lathe said. "Or had you forgotten Fuess's mediocre performance in the Strip?"

"That wasn't really his fault," Caine said. "I understand they were permanently affected by nerve gas during the war."

"I heard that, too," Mordecai said. "It's a convenient excuse, anyway."

"For something no one talks about much, the story sure gets around," Lathe said dryly. "How was your talk with Cameron?"

"Fine," Mordecai said. "Lianna Rhodes will be here in fifteen minutes; then we start a short list of local group leaders that should take us past noon."

"Good. Just enough time to shower." Lathe disappeared into the bathroom, taking his *shuriken* with him.

Caine shifted in his seat, still uncomfortable with this farce. Since early dawn Lathe and Mordecai had been calling in Radix officials one by one and giving them detailed instructions on "their" part in the upcoming raid on Cerbe Prison. The overall battle plan was perfectly believable and halfway practical—and had been concocted by Lathe for the sole purpose of keeping Security's spies too busy to pay undue attention to the upcoming meeting with Lianna Rhodes. Caine wondered what Tremayne would say when he learned how Lathe had been wasting Radix's time and energy.

The map of Cerbe was still in front of him, but Caine found himself unable to concentrate on it. The news from Millaire was heartbreaking—and the worst part was that Caine couldn't decide whether or not he hoped Jensen had been taken alive. The government clearly was desperate for information on the blackcollars' mission, and if Jensen was alive Caine knew what they'd do to get that information out of him.

"It's not over yet," a quiet voice said. Startled, Caine

looked up to see Mordecai studying him, an understanding expression on his face. "Skyler and Novak are down there. If he's alive they'll get him out."

"Yeah," Caine muttered aloud. *Maybe,* he said to himself. *And maybe all three of them will die.*

"Alive." Galway could hardly believe his ears.

Security Prefect Apostoleris nodded, grimly satisfied with himself. "Yes. It cost fifteen men and an expensive aircraft, but it was worth it."

Colonel Eakins hung up the phone he's been talking on. "The hospital says he's stable enough to move to Security confinement," he reported.

The prefect nodded. "Good. Galway, you and I are going to Millaire right away to begin his interrogation."

"Now?" Galway frowned. "But I thought you wanted me at Cerbe by noon to help with preparations there."

Apostoleris waved a hand negligently. "No need. Our spies tell me Lathe's grand assault can't possibly be ready to launch for another twenty-five hours. I've moved the prisoner transfer up to this afternoon, so by the time they're ready to move we'll be solidly dug in at Cerbe, with the prisoners locked away sixty meters underground."

It sounded reasonable enough. And yet. . . . "Prefect, your spies have been wrong about Lathe's intentions at least once before. I really think I'd be more useful at Cerbe than—"

"You know Jensen." Apostoleris's voice was quietly insistent, and one or two degrees chillier. "You know the culture he's lived in for the past thirty-five years. I presume you know how important that can be in an interrogation."

"Yes, sir." Galway felt acutely uncomfortable in Apostoleris's gaze. "May I suggest instead that you have Jensen brought up here to Calarand? That way I could assist in both his interrogation and the Cerbe arrangements."

Apostoleris shook his head. "I'd rather have him where Lathe has to split his forces if he wants him back. There are a couple of blackcollars in Millaire already, and while they're there Lathe can't use them."

"That doesn't sound very good," Galway said carefully. He'd seen what a pair of blackcollars could do.

"It's perfectly safe. One of our people is right there

with them." He turned to the colonel. "Eakins, you're in charge of the prisoner transfer. Make sure Henslowe's ready for anything Lathe might try at the last minute." Standing up, the prefect beckoned to Galway. "Let's go. Can't keep Commando Jensen waiting."

Wordlessly, Galway got to his feet. The sense of foreboding was still with him as he followed Apostoleris out of the room.

CHAPTER 23

Cerbe Prison was ready.

Commandant Kurz Ehrhardt's eyes swept the prison's control center with justifiable pride. The word had come down only an hour ago that the transfer would be taking place a day ahead of schedule; but Ehrhardt's team had risen to the challenge. The weapons turrents were manned and ready, the prisoners' cells had been cleared out to receive them, and an entire extra guard shift had been laid on in case of trouble. The two armed troop transports which had lifted off from Calarand a few minutes ago would arrive in about half an hour; and once in *his* prison those starmen weren't going *anywhere*. Anyone who didn't believe that was going to get a rude surprise, blackcollar or not.

"Commandant?" the Security man at the comm board interrupted his thoughts. "Aircar approaching. No insignia, but the pilot claims to be on urgent Security business and requests landing permission."

A trick? If so, they'd picked a poor target to try it on. Pulling his mike from its belt clip, Ehrhardt keyed it to the outside frequency. "This is Commandant Ehrhardt. State the nature of your business."

"Confidential Security matters; for your ears only," the pilot said promptly. The comm man had a picture now, and Ehrhardt studied the image carefully. A youngish man, in plain clothes, his face serious as he concentrated on his flying.

"Do you have an ID code?" Ehrhardt asked, trying to sound casual. Around him the room was unnaturally still, and Ehrhardt could see fingers hovering over alarm buttons.

The pilot's face disappeared, replaced by that of a woman in one of the aircar's passenger seats. "Commandant, this is Special Agent Renee Lucas, working directly under Security Prefect Apostoleris. Pre-code verbal: January, suborbital, denomination, Alistair. Main code follows."

Ehrhardt let out the breath he'd been holding as the tension throughout the room vanished, and he realized he'd actually hoped the aircar *was* a Radix trick. *Spoiling for a fight, at your age!* he chided himself. But the verbal pre-code and the electronic holocode now being received through the roof comm laser matched perfectly the code Apostoleris had personally set up not six hours ago. Still, if Agent Lucas was genuine, then something important must have happened. Giving orders for the aircar to be passed, Ehrhardt headed out to meet it. Perhaps he'd be seeing some action soon, after all.

Cerbe's central control area was on the lowest underground level, and by the time he reached the main gate the aircar had put down near one end of the enclosed courtyard. Agent Lucas, followed by the pilot and another young plain-clothes man, was walking swiftly toward the building.

Ehrhardt watched them approach, eyes narrowing with sudden uneasiness. It *was* impossible to tap into a secure laser system, and Lucas's companions had obviously been on normal Idunine dosage for longer than the Plinry blackcollars had been here. But there was something disturbing about them just the same. Perhaps the way they walked. . . .

The commandant stepped over to the guard captain standing by the massive gate. "Full scan as they enter; check for weapons of any sort. If they're clean I want the men taken to the guardroom and their IDs run through the reader."

"They may not have IDs," the captain pointed out.

Ehrhardt frowned. Yes; if they were all on special duty they probably wouldn't. "In that case . . . layer-scan them and have the computer do facial-structure comparisons against the Plinry photos. And have six armed men around them at all times—dart guns, no lasers. Clear?"

"Yes, sir." The captain reached for his belt mike. A moment later, the visitors arrived.

The usual pleasantries of greeting were drastically abridged; Agent Lucas was clearly in a hurry and refused to say anything with others present. Ehrhardt complied with her wishes, leading her and a four-man escort to his office in silence.

"Please sit down," he told her, stepping to the far side of his desk. Out of her sight, one of the displays informed him the scans had revealed no weapons; glancing at the escort, he signaled them to wait in the anteroom. "Your men are being checked out down the hall," he added as the door closed behind the guards. "Purely routine, of course—"

"Never mind that." She was still standing by the chair. "I'm here to warn you that an attack on Cerbe may be imminent."

He frowned. "All right—we're ready."

"No, you're not. They've added a new twist." She nodded at the command room monitors. "You'll need to shift weapons control down here immediately and have the turrets vacated. The courtyard guards will have to come in, too, and you should probably put up a sensor drone."

Ehrhardt frowned more deeply. "You sound like you're expecting an air strike."

"Very perceptive. We think the rebels have a Corsair available to attack you with."

Another desk display flashed. The hallway facial scans indicated only a twenty-one percent chance that either of Lucas's companions was a Plinry blackcollar; the computer was still waiting for the more complete guardroom scans. "I'm aware of that, Miss Lucas, but I understand the blackcollars' Corsair never landed on Argent. Even if it was somehow hiding in close orbit it couldn't possibly launch an attack without giving us adequate warning."

"Of course not. But that's not the one we're worried about. Half an hour ago the Ryqril told us that one of their Corsairs has disappeared."

"I hadn't heard that," Ehrhardt said cautiously. What she was implying was supposed to be impossible.

"No one else has, either. If the rebels have tapped the

comm net we'd rather they not know we've discovered the theft." She gestured impatiently. "If you don't believe me, call Brocken spaceport and ask for confirmation of Datum LL-18."

"No that's all right," he said, thinking hard. This changed Cerbe's defense needs completely—a Corsair lurking just over the horizon could be overhead and attacking in ten seconds or less. If it knocked the tops off all four turrets before the gunners could switch control back underground, he'd have only the prison's internal anti-escape weaponry to work with. The setup, designed to keep the perimeter defenses from prisoner control in the unlikely event of a control center takeover, was suddenly looking very vulnerable. "All right," he said slowly, reaching for his mike. "I usually prefer live gun controllers to automatics and remotes, but I can't see how the rebels could use that to their advantage." He hesitated. "Unless they've also stolen a ramtank?"

Lucas frowned slightly. "Good point. I haven't heard anything, but it should be checked. I suppose it's possible the Corsair theft was some kind of crazy feint."

Ehrhardt nodded, pleased he'd come up with a good idea. Punching for the control center, he gave orders to recall the gunners and outside guards; a second call started a search of the Security comm net for possible military thefts. There shouldn't really be anything to worry about; potent though a ramtank's ECM were, live gunners could be put back in the turrets before the vehicle got too close. "Any other suggestions?" he asked as he finished the call.

"No. I think that'll be adequate. Thank you for your prompt cooperation, Commandant; I hope these precautions will prove unnecessary." She glanced at her watch. "The prisoners are due to land in about five minutes. Shall we go to the control center?"

"Yes, I should be there," Ehrhardt said hesitantly. "I'm sorry, though—I didn't think about it before—but the doorway won't pass you without a confirmed ID. Since you didn't show me one . . .?"

"Correct," she nodded. "I don't carry one. I'd forgotten how your system worked, too. Perhaps I can wait somewhere near a monitor."

"Certainly," Ehrhardt said through suddenly stiff lips.

A Special Agent shouldn't forget how top-level security systems worked!

His first impulse was to hit one of the alarm buttons on his desk, to have Lucas and her cohorts surrounded as fast as possible by a ring of lasers. But he resisted the urge. Better to give them a little more rope—and if they *were* Radix spies, he might then be able to find out what their plan was. As to her request, he had the perfect answer. "Certainly," he repeated, rising to his feet. "You can watch the proceedings with your companions on the guardroom monitors."

She nodded agreeably, and he led her out into the anteroom. To his surprise only two of the four guards he'd left there were present. "Where are the others?" he snapped, his right hand curling into the prison's private "danger—enemy present" signal.

"I'm afraid they're no longer available," one of them said coolly . . . and Ehrhardt's hand froze in mid-sign as he focused on the faces above the uniforms.

"My God!" he breathed. His eyes darted involuntarily to the monitor on his secretary's desk, as if he had somehow missed the flashing red "escaped prisoner" signal that must surely be there. But the screen showed only the routine messages of normal prison business. "You can't *be* here," he insisted, turning back to the two men. "There are video and audio monitors all over this floor."

"Sure are," the man who had piloted Lucas's aircar agreed mildly, relieving Ehrhardt of his belt mike. He was a large, strongly built man whose borrowed Security uniform was being gently stretched out of shape. "And you have a man who sits around watching those monitors with his fingers half a meter from an alarm button."

"That's right," Ehrhardt said mechanically. The sight of that wrestler's body belatedly linked up with a bit of data from the intelligence reports. "You're Kelly O'Hara, aren't you? And you—" he shifted his gaze—"must be Taurus Haven. The two who've been out of sight lately. Taking heavy-duty Idunine treatments, right?"

Haven nodded. "A simple method of disguise, but remarkably effective for all that. Now, shall we all take a quiet walk to the control center?"

"It won't do any good," Ehrhardt said, hands grinding

into fists at his sides. "I just explained to your rad that you can't get in there without a Security ID."

"No problem." O'Hara shrugged. "We simply let you and your ID unlock the door and then one of us goes in instead."

Ehrhardt frowned. It would work, he realized suddenly; the man in the monitor booth was supposed to guard against that sort of thing, and if they'd already eliminated him. . . . A chill went up his spine, and Ehrhardt knew he was about to die. "I can't do that," he said with unexpected calmness. "My loyalty-conditioning won't allow it, even if you threaten to kill me. Holding me hostage won't do any good, either—my people can't give in to blackmail." He felt a tic start in his cheek. "But I suppose you'll have to kill me to prove that to yourselves."

"Maybe; maybe not," Haven said. "Tell me, does loyalty-conditioning require you to throw away your life for nothing?"

Ehrhardt frowned. "I don't understand."

"Sacrificing your life won't keep us out of the control center," the blackcollar went on. "We've got your ID, and we can take your thumbprints and retinal pattern along with us to show the scanners."

"How—by dragging me screaming down the hall?" Ehrhardt scoffed.

"Not all of you, no," Haven said calmly. "And what we had wouldn't be screaming."

Ehrhardt stared at him, his blood turning to ice water as he suddenly understood. "You wouldn't!" he whispered.

"We would," O'Hara assured him, his voice as glacial as his rad's. "Severed hands and head can be used for several hours before the retinal pattern decays enough for the machine to notice. I know; I've seen it done. It's your decision, Commandant."

Ehrhardt's throat felt very dry. "One question first," he said. "You left the gate area with six guards. What happened to them?"

"There's a section of the hall just outside the guardroom that's not covered by any of the cameras," O'Hara said. "Your men have a bad habit of bunching up; we just took them all out and then went down the hall to the monitor booth."

"But even if he couldn't see you, the noise of the fight—"

"There wasn't any noise," O'Hara told him. "We made sure of that."

Three to one odds . . . and no noise. They were unstoppable, Ehrhardt realized at last. One way or another they would get into the control center . . . and they were right: without specific orders the conditioning did *not* require him to throw his life away uselessly. "All right," he said, "I'll get you in. But even with full control of the defenses you won't be able to hold Cerbe for long. There are over a hundred armed guards roaming the various levels, and assault units can be sent from Calarand in under two hours."

"Let us worry about that," O'Hara suggested. "Let's go."

Ehrhardt didn't see what happened after Haven disappeared through the control center door; all he knew for certain was that no one inside got to an alarm button in time. "Who's next?" he growled, readying his ID again.

"No one." O'Hara consulted his watch and gestured down the hall. "Come on, we're heading upstairs."

They reached the elevators without incident. For a brief moment, as they entered an empty car, Ehrhardt considered hitting the emergency alarm button to alert the guards on the other floors. But with the control center in enemy hands it would be a futile gesture. Probably suicidal, too. . . . Punching for ground level, he stepped away from the controls.

"Now listen carefully," O'Hara said as the car started up. "Those troop carriers from Calarand should be down by now; my friend will have ordered the pilots and guards to come to the gate for consultation with you. We're going to lock them—and you—into the gate guard station. That's if you cooperate. If you don't, they'll have to be killed."

"With the turret weapons, of course," Ehrhardt said bitterly.

"Or the ones in the entrance hall. I'd rather do it without bloodshed, but it's basically up to you."

Ehrhardt swallowed heavily. The elevator doors opened and the three of them stepped out into the hall. Ahead was the main gate; through the hullmetal bars he could see men moving in the courtyard. The four gate guards were watching the arrival, too, and a half dozen wild plans tripped through the commandant's mind: plans for warning them, or of allowing their lives to be sacrificed to warn those outside. But it was all just a mental game, and he knew it. He couldn't stop the blackcollars now, and throwing good lives away would be stupidity, not loyalty. Better now to observe passively and to be alert for clues regarding their next move.

Fifteen minutes later the troop carriers lifted smoothly from the prison courtyard, their passengers still aboard, the two blackcollars at the controls. Jammed against one wall of the guard station by the crowd of swearing Security men, Ehrhardt watched them disappear over the hills to the west. The emotional reaction was starting to hit him now, the realization that he'd been defeated and would soon be facing the consequences of his failure. And yet, he couldn't help but feel a twinge of admiration for the skill and courage with which the operation had been carried out.

Though somehow he doubted Prefect Apostoleris would see that side of it.

CHAPTER 24

The first thing Jensen noticed on his long climb back to consciousness was the pain.

Not the aches in his arms or chest, the results of the crash and the battle preceding it; those were fairly easy to control. The real pain came from the front of his skull, as if a giant had been resting his thumbs on the blackcollar's eyes. It wasn't an unknown feeling, and even before he was fully awake he knew what they'd tried to do.

The room was likewise no surprise. Small, drab, and solid-looking, it would have been recognizable as an interrogation cell anywhere in the TDE. His naked body was strapped into an unpadded chair, his arms held out, crucifix-fashion, for easy access to veins. Wires and tubes dangled from various parts of his body, and two men in

Security uniforms stood facing him. "He's awake," murmured an unexpected voice. With an effort, Jensen focused on their faces.

"Why, Prefect Galway," he croaked hoarsely. Forcing moisture into his mouth, he tried again, with better results. "What brings you to Argent?"

Galway gazed at him coolly, "Hello, Jensen. How much would you like to live?"

Jensen grinned, even though that made the throbbing pain worse. "Not *that* much, thanks. The verifin didn't work, I take it?"

Galway's expression didn't change, but that of the man beside him darkened considerably. Jensen nodded to him. "I didn't catch the name."

"Security Prefect Apostoleris," the other bit out. "And I'd watch my mouth if I were you. I am *this* close to wiping the whole bunch of you off the planet and to hell with my losses."

A rather strong reaction, Jensen thought. Looking back at Galway, he asked, "What's Lathe done now?"

Galway glanced at Apostoleris, who waved his hand impatiently. "He dosed two of his men with Idunine—O'Hara and Haven, we think—and sent them to Cerbe Prison with a Radix team leader. They took over weapons control and flew two transports of Star Force vets out before anyone knew what was happening."

"Interesting," Jensen murmured.

"Yes, *interesting*," Apostoleris mimicked. "And not the sort of thing you pull off just for fun. What do those men know that's *that* important to you?"

Jensen shrugged, not an easy task with the restraints on him.

"Look, Jensen," Galway put in, "I don't think you appreciate the lengths the prefect's prepared to go to. There are drugs available that would wear you down physically, there are things like extended isolation-tank treatment, and there's always straight physical torture. Psychor pain-block techniques may be good, but I doubt they'd hold up under a slow dismembering of your body."

"Perhaps." The calmness Jensen forced into his voice was a waste of effort—they undoubtedly knew how blackcollars viewed death under a torturer's knife. "Of course, torture takes a great deal of time."

"Are you implying your mission's almost completed?" Apostoleris countered smoothly.

"Not necessarily. I might simply be rescued before you're finished." It was a safe suggestion to make—Lathe wouldn't risk anyone at this stage on something that quixotic. But Apostoleris wouldn't know that, and any extra men Jensen could tie up on guard duty would be that many fewer for the others to contend with.

"Of course," Apostoleris said, "though I wouldn't count on that if I were you. So. Contacting the starmen is likely one of the final steps. Interesting. You're not planning to steal some ships and head off to join the Chryselli, are you? That would be extremely difficult—the Ryqril here won't be taken by surprise like the ones on Plinry were, and you don't have that mob of half-trained children to hide behind. And even if you made it, what then? It's not like the Chryselli are trustworthy allies. They turned their hairy backs on us once before, you know, back when General Lepkowski went to Meelach to ask for help."

Jensen said nothing. Apostoleris's shots were hitting uncomfortably close to the mark.

The prefect interpreted his silence correctly. "So," he almost purred. "We're not so cocky now, are we. You don't like the direction this conversation is taking?"

"Talk all you like. And don't expect to get anything of value from me."

"We'll see." Apostoleris glanced upwards. Prepare number one," he called to some unseen ear.

"Not wasting any time, are you?" Jensen said as calmly as possible. "Not even going to give me the traditional hour to consider how much this is going to hurt?"

"As you said, we're short on time," the prefect said icily. "We'll start with the non-destructive forms at first, in case you decide to be reasonable. After that . . . well, there are some very painful things that can be done directly to the nervous system. Those have permanent effects, of course." He paused. "Anything you'd like to say before we begin?"

"How about 'go to hell'?"

Apostoleris shrugged. "When you change your mind, just shout. If you still can."

Turning on his heel, he strode out of the door behind

them. Galway lingered just long enough to lock eyes with the blackcollar; then he, too, was gone and the door was slammed shut. Its reverberations were still audible when the lights went out, plunging Jensen into total darkness.

Blindness—standard psychological gambit, he thought grimly, even as his deeper mental processes began to trace the familiar pain-block pattern. *Like nakedness. Depressants to civilized man.* But he could handle anything they could throw at him, at least long enough for Lathe to finish the mission. After that—

But it was no use thinking that far ahead. Right now the only goal in the universe was to survive the first battle.

Without warning, a heavy electric shock ran up his left side. Gritting his teeth firmly to avoid biting his tongue, Jensen settled himself for the long fight ahead.

"A frontal assault is out of the question," Dael Valentine said as he eased the car up to a stoplight. "The building's got doubled guard stations inside the main door, antipersonnel defenses in the courtyard, and detection gear in the outer wall. We'd be cut to ribbons before we even got in. Surely your little reconnoiter showed you *that* much."

"What do you suggest, then?" Novak said quietly, and Skyler shifted uneasily in the back seat as he thought of the simmering volcano beneath that veneer of self-control.

"A soft penetration," Valentine said. "Lathe and O'Hara have already shown what an ID or ID code can do. Loyalty-conditioned minds just aren't flexible; you give them what they expect to see and they'll probably let you in."

"Fine," Skyler said, a bit tartly. "And how do we go about getting IDs? Caine's trick isn't likely to be practical here."

"True—but they can't be doing a complete computer check on everyone who enters. If we have IDs that accurately show our thumbprints and retinal patterns it'll probably do the trick."

Skyler frowned, considering. It was an interesting point. Unlike the setup in Calarand, all of Millaire's governmental functions were located in the same ten-story building. In their two-hour walking survey of the area, he and Novak had seen an astonishing variety of people passing in and out of the main gate, from obvious collie types to ordinary citizens—the latter, they'd noted, getting an armed escort across the courtyard. It might be barely possible. "*If* we had IDs, maybe."

"Good—because we can get them." Valentine made a left turn, sending them back toward Millaire's business district. "I wasn't just collecting gossip while you were out walking around. I also made contact with what's left of organized Radix here."

"And?" Novak prompted.

"*And,* there's an ID forger still loose."

Skyler hunched forward to get a better view of Valentine's face. "How good are these forgeries?" he asked.

"Just this side of perfect."

"But if there's nothing in the computer, why—?" Novak broke off his question as Skyler gently tapped tingler code onto the back of his neck.

"Why did I suggest it?" Valentine asked irritably. "I *told* you that—they won't be checking everyone that closely."

"It might work," Skyler said, thinking fast. "Any chance of getting some explosives, too?"

Valentine glanced back at him. "What do you want explosives for?"

"Diversion. We could set off some explosions in the area, draw as many Security men as possible outside the wall to investigate. If we then blasted a hole in the wall, they'd presumably assume the place was being attacked and rush back in, with or without quick ID checks—and we'd go in with them."

"Yeah . . . that might work," Valentine said after a short pause. "When do we hit—nightfall?"

"Or a few hours later," Skyler said. "Let's find this forger and the explosives before we decide that. The explosives first," he added. "If the forger's place is being watched we'll want something to fight our way out with."

"You're the boss," Valentine agreed, turning right at the next corner. "I know who to talk to; we can be there in five minutes."

Skyler settled back in the seat and threw a look upwards. The rain of the night before had ended, but dark clouds still blanketed the sky. Skyler hoped they would stay put; a heavy cloud cover would hasten the darkness and let them make their attempt a little earlier. Even so, it would be at least six hours before they could go in.

He hoped Jensen could hold on that long.

CHAPTER 25

The big conference room table looked empty with just Tremayne and Bakshi sitting at it. Following Lathe's lead, Caine pulled out a chair across from them and sat down, almost wishing that he'd waited outside the room with Mordecai and Kwon. After what had just happened at Cerbe, this was probably going to be a memorable tongue-lashing.

But he was in for a surprise. "For someone who talks so much about obedience, Lathe, you're pretty lax about it yourself," Tremayne said, his tone almost mild. "What do we have to do to be accepted into your confidence?"

"I gather the vets arrived safely?" Lathe asked.

Tremayne nodded. "Janus Leader Rhodes brought the last of them in about twenty minutes ago."

"Good. I suppose I should mention that we used Lianna Rhodes because she said she was going to resign from Radix."

"Yes, I'd already figured that one out. Cute, even for you—you only promised to consult with me if the operation involved Radix personnel." For a moment Tremayne's eyes flashed sparks. "That's marginal at best, you know—whatever her future plans, Rhodes *is* in Radix right now."

"Marginal, hell." Bakshi's voice was cold; for a change he seemed madder than Tremayne. "You violated our agreement, pure and simple. Can you give me one good reason why we shouldn't dump you out on the streets right now—you *and* that mob of security risks you've brought in?"

"Wait a second; we can't do that," Tremayne cut in.

"The vets have technically broken prison—Apostoleris will slap heavy sentences on them if he catches them again. And as to the blackcollars, they *did* achieve their goal."

Bakshi snorted. "So you're not going to argue with success? Well, I am. It was a half-assed stunt, and it was sheer luck it worked at all."

"There was nothing half-assed about it," Lathe disagreed quietly. "Everything we did was carefully planned, from my trip into Henslowe on. Surely you recognize the impossibility of getting that many men *out* of a prison without tremendous casualties. We had to persuade Security to move them for us, and we did."

"Hindsight is marvelous," Bakshi growled.

"And as to a reason—yes, I can give you a damn good one." Lathe looked at Tremayne. "Have you got a room big enough for me to talk to all the vets at once?"

"I think the garage will do," the Radix leader said, frowning. "A lot of the vehicles are out at the moment."

"Good. Assemble both them and your tactical group there, please. We'll be down in a minute."

Slowly, Tremayne nodded. "All right. And this better be good." He gestured to Bakshi, and together they left the room.

"What're you going to tell them?" Caine asked.

"The truth," Lathe said. "Everything except that you're the only one who can locate the ships; though they'll probably figure that out on their own, anyway."

"Do you think that's wise? If you're right about a spy being in Tremayne's team you might as well call Security up and give it to them directly."

"Which is fine with me. I *want* Security in on it now."

Caine felt his eyes narrowing. "I don't understand."

Lathe sighed. "Look. Whatever we're planning, Security must have suspected by now that we intend to go off-planet. Now that we've gotten the vets away from them, the simplest way to stop us is to lock away all the spacecraft."

"Okay," Caine agreed. "But you broke into the 'port on Plinry easily enough."

"It only looked easy because we'd been planning it for thirty years and because we caught Galway off guard," the blackcollar countered. "Here we have neither advantage."

"So how do we gain by confirming what they already suspect?"

"We gain," Lathe said quietly, "by offering them something besides a draw. Five Novas would be a tremendous prize, and their best chance to get them is to let us lead the way."

Cain stared at him, noticing for the first time lines around his eyes that the Idunine treatments hadn't touched. "You understand what you're saying, don't you?" he said at last. "You're deliberately taking us into a trap."

"I know." Lathe's voice was soft, with none of the overflowing confidence that he seemed to have in front of the Argentians. "It's a borderline crazy thing to do, but the fact that we *know* there'll be a trap may give us the necessary edge. Anyway, I don't see what else we can do."

"Why not just make something up? Tell them we're going back to liberate Earth, for instance."

"Wouldn't work. The collies *have* to know there's a prize worth grabbing or they won't let us off-planet. Besides, it's only fair to let the vets know what they're getting into." The comsquare pushed back his chair and stood up.

"I suppose you're right." Caine stood, too, but put a restraining hand on Lathe's arm. "But there *will* be a way out of this trap, won't there?"

Lathe shrugged. "There's a way out of *any* trap. The real questions are whether we can find it in time and how much it'll cost to use it." A shadow passed across his face. "And whatever that cost is, you can bet it'll be paid in human life." He nodded toward the door. "Let's go."

Even with many of the cars and vans missing—out on reconnaissance patrols in the wake of the Cerbe operation, Caine learned—the garage was crowded. The Star Force vets generally looked to be in their thirties, evidence of consistent Idunine use through the years. Caine's opinion of Radix went up a grudging notch—it was unlikely that the government was voluntarily supplying them with the drug.

Tremayne had taken up a position on top of one of the remaining cars, and as Caine and the blackcollars started toward him held up a hand for silence. "I know you're all wondering what the hell's going on here," he said as the buzz of conversation faded. "I'm going to let the man who sprung you from Cerbe explain it: Blackcollar Comsquare Lathe, late of Plinry." He looked in Lathe's direction and gestured.

A lane began to open through the crowd, but Lathe followed it only to the nearest car, which he then mounted. Caine glanced at Tremayne, wondering if the other would be annoyed at Lathe's failure to join him. But all he saw was intense interest in the Radix leader's face as Lathe began to speak.

Lathe was clearly no orator; his straightforward rendition of the facts was without eloquence or grandeur . . . and yet Caine had rarely seen a crowd that size pay such close attention to a speaker. Even more than with the blackcollar group on Plinry, Caine could sense here a deep appreciation for what five Novas signified in actual strategic terms. Surreptitiously looking around the room, he caught several thoughtful nods and meaningful glances being exchanged between starmen. Not surprisingly, those tactical group members he could see seemed equally intrigued. Miles Cameron and Salli Quinlan, heads almost touching, were engaged in what was probably a discussion of the current Ryqril military strength; a few meters away, Fuess and fellow blackcollar Couturie were staring at Lathe with frowns so intense they were almost scowls. Bakshi's face, in contrast, was a thoughtful mask.

Lathe finished talking, and for a long moment the garage was filled with the silence of mental digestion. Then, across the room, another lane opened in the crowd and a tall, bulky man stepped forward, stopping midway between Lathe and Tremayne. He sent glances at both men, finally turned to the blackcollar. "Comsquare, I'm Commander Garth Nmura, senior Star Force officer here," he said, his voice rich with an accent Caine couldn't place. "I notice you stopped short of actually *ordering* us to assist you. Do you plan to give such an order; and if so, under what authority?"

"I'd prefer voluntary cooperation," Lathe said. "However, if necessary—" he gestured in Caine's direction— "my colleague, Allen Caine, has full military authority under General Kratochvil of Earth. I myself am in direct succession to General Lepkowski of Plinry Sector Command."

Nmura shrugged. "We have only your word for that."

"True. On the other hand, without secure communications, no authorization I could produce would be above suspicion."

"I know," Nmura nodded. "Understand—I'm not just being stubborn. You're asking us to put our lives and the safety of our families on the line, and I can't order that without something besides your unsupported word. For all we know, this could be some crazy entrapment scheme."

"Too subtle for collies," Kwon muttered near Caine's ear. Mordecai, on Caine's other side, grunted agreement.

"Besides which," Nmura continued, glancing back at Tremayne, "I get the impression Radix hasn't quite accepted you, either."

Lathe started to speak, but Tremayne unexpectedly cut in. "Not true, Commander," he said. "Our activity has been minimized at Comsquare Lathe's own request, for valid reasons. But their operation has always had our full support."

Caine looked at the other in surprise; but the sincerity in the Radix leader's voice was fully matched in his face. With an effort Caine kept his own expression neutral, wondering what Tremayne was up to.

Nmura seemed to have doubts, too. Once more he glanced between Lathe and Tremayne before addressing the latter. "Are you saying you've accepted Comsquare Lathe's credentials?"

"His best credentials are that he's a blackcollar comsquare. We accept him on that basis."

"I see," Nmura said slowly. He hesitated, and Caine had the sudden impression of a man trying to find wind direction on a calm day. "The main risks are still there, of course."

A few meters away a hand rose over the crowd. "Garth, can I say something?"

Nmura craned his neck to identify the speaker. "Sure, Rayd, go ahead."

"Well, it seems to me we've been sitting on our duffs long enough," Rayd said. His voice was strong and confident, that of a man used to casual leadership. "We've got a damn good chance here to really hit the Ryqril—and anybody who doesn't believe that should try to remember when blackcollars ever risked their necks on something hopeless." A murmur of approval was beginning to rise all around them, and Rayd raised his voice to compensate. "And I think we ought to remember how many times Radix has stuck their necks out to keep us in Idunine. Let's not give people the impression that the Star Force takes a free ride from *anyone!*"

The calm day was gone, and it was clear which way the wind was blowing. Raising his hand to silence the growing swell, Nmura nodded to Lathe. "It sounds like we have a consensus," he said dryly. "All right; you've got yourself a crew. When do we move?"

"Two or three days," Lathe said. "We'll need to get transport off-planet, and you need to organize into crews and start working out the necessary start-up procedures." He looked at Tremayne. "Can Radix put all these men up here for that long?"

"We'll manage. Jer?" Tremayne located Jeremiah Dan and gestured toward Nmura. "Jer, see the commander about billeting for his men. Lathe, we'll need to talk about the next step."

The meeting was clearly over, and as pockets of conversation began to form around the room, Caine felt Kwon touch his arm. "Let's head back upstairs," the massive blackcollar said. "Lathe can handle things here."

Caine nodded absently, his thoughts elsewhere. From the hostility of a day or two ago Tremayne had become a model of cooperation with surprising speed. Suspicious speed, perhaps. At best it was politics, an effort to appear united in front of the vets. At worst . . . Lathe's earlier prediction about the government's reaction lurked at the base of his mind. It was an unfair thought, he knew—Tremayne had probably done his about-face simply because he now understood the mission's importance.

But if Lathe was right, someone else in Radix also understood things now . . . and if the government chose to go for a draw instead of a win, Mordecai and Kwon were going to start earning their keep the hard way. Shivering slightly, he increased his pace.

CHAPTER 26

"Incredible," Colonel Eakins murmured, staring into his mug and shaking his head slowly. "Sitting out there right under our noses. Do you suppose they're still operational?"

"Probably." Galway felt cold inside; his own mug sat ignored on the desk in front of him. *You'll find out some day,* Lathe had said to him at the Plinry 'port, and from that he'd assumed the blackcollars were on the trail of something big. But not something like *this*. "With all their systems off or on low/standby, all that could go wrong would be fuel or air leakage or slow interior corrosion—and that last will be negligible if they were left unpressurized."

"You seem to know a lot about the subject," Apostoleris commented as he hung up the phone he'd been talking on.

"My father was in the Star Force," Galway explained briefly. "Jensen still holding out?"

Apostoleris nodded. "We'll break him, though."

"Why bother? Your spies have already given you everything he's likely to know. Why not just kill him and get it over with?"

"Dead bait doesn't attract any fish," the other countered. "Or are you forgetting Skyler and Novak?"

"They wouldn't know he was dead until it was too late."

Eakins looked up from his mug. "You keep implying they might actually get that far," he said, sounding a little annoyed. "This is *not* like Cerbe, Galway—we're on top of them this time."

Tired, Galway rubbed his forehead. "I know. I just don't want to underestimate them again."

"We won't." Apostoleris was grimly confident. "You're right about Jensen—I don't think he knows anything useful. But Skyler and Novak have been with Lathe this whole time; they're bound to know more about his plans."

"Your spies in Radix have a better chance of getting that information," Galway insisted.

Apostoleris snorted and shook his head in disgust. "You just don't have the stomach for this, do you?" he said bluntly. "Maybe that's why they got away with all their crap on Plinry. Hey?"

Galway didn't answer. Belatedly, he realized that Apostoleris was taking the blackcollars' operation on an intensely personal level, almost as if he were engaged in a private duel with Lathe. It was a dangerous trap to fall into—the Security prefect could easily lose sight of the war even as he concentrated on winning minor skirmishes. In many ways Apostoleris was behaving like an amateur chess player, equating board strength with number of pieces taken.

Sighing, Galway looked down at his watch. Forty minutes to sunset, the earliest Skyler was likely to move. The blackcollars had their explosives and false IDs, and latest reports indicated Apostoleris's three-level trap was ready. It would work . . . and would surely cost a great deal of human life. Perhaps Apostoleris was right, he thought; perhaps he *didn't* have the stomach for unnecessary death. But then, life on Plinry forced a somewhat more frugal view of one's resources.

Shifting in his chair, Galway picked up his mug and sipped at the cooling drink. Thirty-eight minutes to sunset.

CHAPTER 27

"Ten minutes to sundown," Valentine reported from the front seat of their parked car.

Skyler nodded, willing to take his word for it. The thick overcast was still in place above Millaire, the sun completely invisible behind it. Already the city's streetlights had come on, and Skyler judged it was almost dark enough to move.

"When do we leave?" Novak asked, craning his neck to look back at Skyler.

"Half an hour, I think. We'll take another hour to set the explosives, and by then it'll be dark enough to start." As he spoke, he glanced around, taking a quick survey of the area. No one was visible; he'd picked a commercial-type street in the midst of rush hour to park on an hour ago, and now the block was essentially deserted. Pursing his lips over clenched jaws, he slid his *nunchaku* silently out of its sheath. Taking a deep breath, he swung the sticks in a hard, short arc, striking Valentine at the base of the skull.

Even as the Argentian slumped forward, Novak was twisting around in his seat, his own *nunchaku* coming reflexively to hand. "What—"

Skyler cut him off with a sharp shake of his head, gave him four quick hand signals. Frowning, Novak put his *nunchaku* down and reached under the dashboard, coming up a moment later with two freshly disconnected wires. Taking the portable bug stomper Skyler handed him, he connected the wires to it and flipped it on. The device came to life; a green light flashed briefly as it did so.

"No bugs," Skyler muttered. "They're cockier than I expected."

"Who, the collies?" Novak still looked confused.

"Yeah. I guess they figured their spy had us covered well enough."

Novak glanced at Valentine's crumpled figure and then looked back at Skyler, his eyes demanding explanation.

Skyler sighed. "You heard his slip yourself. Remember earlier, when he suggested a soft penetration? He said we could do the same thing Lathe and O'Hara had done. *How did he know it was O'Hara who hit Cerbe Prison?*"

Novak frowned. "He supposedly got that from Radix contacts—" he began slowly.

"Right. But how would they know which blackcollars were involved? Lathe wouldn't have given that out, and it certainly isn't public knowledge yet. That leaves exactly one source."

Novak shook his head. "This is pretty flimsy evidence to hang a man on."

"I'm not done yet." Skyler dug his new Security ID from his pocket. "What were you going to ask him when he first mentioned this forger of his?"

"When you cut me off? I wanted to know why anybody would bother forging something that could damn you that quickly."

"Good question. *Mine* was why Tremayne had never mentioned these supposed Radix forgers." Skyler slanted the ID toward the fading light. "Beautiful work. I studied it for ten straight minutes earlier and didn't see a single error anywhere."

Novak was gazing thoughtfully at Valentine. "Lathe said he got into the Strip with a simple visual check," he mused. "You'd think the collies would be more thorough if there were false IDs known to be in circulation." Reaching over, he picked up Valentine's right hand. A dragonhead ring glinted there; with some effort Novak got it off. "A hunch," he said, squinting at the ring in the faint glow of his shielded penlight. "If he's a collie spy his ring will be a fake . . .hmm. It's got the Centauri A logo behind the crest." He drew one point of the crest along the steel roof brace, examined both the point and the scratch it made. "*And* it's genuine hullmetal," he said with a sigh, handing the ring and penlight across to Skyler.

"Could be stolen," Skyler offered, but even as he said it he felt uncertainty returning. He'd been a hundred percent sure . . . but the ring dropped that to eighty percent, and he couldn't justify a quick execution with those odds. "I still don't think he should come with us."

"Okay. We leave him for interrogation when we get back?"

"I suppose—" Skyler broke off as something on Valentine's ring caught his eye.

"What is it?" Novak asked.

"Examine the eyes," Skyler said quietly, handing the ring and light back.

"They're just the usual slitted-pupils carved into the metal," the other said. For a long moment he studied the ring in silence; and when he looked up his face was carved from black ice. "The orginal eyes have been removed," he said softly. "These were grafted in afterward. This used to be a comsquare's ring."

"Or a tactor's, or even a secturion's—they may have had to scour the whole TDE for a captured dragonhead that would fit him."

"Deliberate deception." Novak's voice was hard. "That

pretty well settles the issue, I guess. We've been compromised—and we're going to have to modify our plans."

Skyler grimaced. "I know. I've been trying all afternoon to come up with something else that might work."

"Then you haven't been trying. The answer's obvious." Novak explained.

"No." Skyler shook his head. "Out of the question."

Novak snorted impatiently. "You're trying to be noble, but you're just wasting time. It's the only way we're going to clear an escape route all the way out of town, and you know it."

Skyler did; but that didn't make it easier to accept. "I can't allow—"

"Rafe," Novak said quietly, "if Jensen's being tortured in there I want to get him out—or to give him a clean death. He's my friend—please let me take this risk for him."

Skyler sighed. "All right," he said at last. "We'll leave the car here—it's probably known. We can get another vehicle easily enough." Steeling himself, Skyler drew a knife from its forearm sheath. *Execution of a spy is not murder,* he told himself. "Valentine stays too, of course."

He raised the knife, but Novak touched his arm. "I'll do it," the other said grimly. "I consider it his fault Jensen got captured."

A few minutes later, bags of equipment and explosives over their shoulders, the two blackcollars exited from opposite sides of the car and started down the street.

Behind its outer wall and courtyard the ten-story government building stood dark against Millaire's skyline, its only lighted windows those on the first three floors. Gazing at it from the vacant office building across the street, Skyler once more checked the floor plan they'd found among their car's maps. "You know where you're heading?" he asked the shadow beside him.

Novak nodded. "First floor west; control room and secondary support column." His voice was calm, his hands steady as he checked the ties on his shoulder-slung bundle. The bundle worried Skyler; even wrapped in the late Valentine's flexarmor, the high-explosives it contained could be set off prematurely by a direct laser blast. But they hadn't had time to put together anything safer.

"Okay." There was a great deal more to be said, but Skyler could sense Novak didn't want to hear it. Swallowing hard, Skyler contented himself with a brief gripping of the other's shoulder. Then, silently, he led the way back outside.

Their diversionary blasts began right on schedule, sending dull roars one at a time from selected spots a few blocks from the government building. By the third blast the flow of Security men through the wall's mesh gate had begun; by the seventh it had dropped to a trickle.

"Quite a show," Novak murmured through his gas filter as they crouched in an alleyway. "Maybe they really *have* emptied the building."

"Maybe. It's a bunch less to deal with, anyway." Taking a deep breath, Skyler thumbed the safety off the radio detonator they'd rigged up. "Here goes." Flattening himself against the wall beside Novak, he flipped the switch.

The blue-white flash lit up the streets as the sound of the blast echoed through the tall buildings like a mad ricochet. Skyler shot a quick glance around the corner and then was off and running toward the fading red glow where their handmade shaped charge had blown a hole through the wall a quarter of the way around from the gate. Through the ringing in his ears he could hear excited shouts from the guards there. For perhaps a few more seconds, though, they wouldn't realize the script had been changed. . . . Skidding to a halt, Skyler leaned over and thrust his arms and torso through the hole; a tight fit, but he knew he could make it. Novak, arriving half a second behind him, grabbed his legs and pushed, shoving him unceremoniously through onto the ground. Scrambling up into a crouch, Skyler looked around. The courtyard was deserted and, except for a gravel path just inside the wall, basically featureless. Behind him, Novak's bundle came through the hole, followed by Novak himself. "How's it look?" he whispered, slinging the package over his shoulder again.

"No obvious defenses; probably needle mines everywhere except under this path." Skyler pointed toward the building. "That looks like the emergency exit the map showed. Let's go—and stay in my footprints in case there's something stronger than needle mines out there."

Like twin ghosts, they set off across the courtyard . . . and around by the gate, Security slowly began to realize that something had gone wrong.

Jensen became aware only gradually that the latest cycle of questioning was over, bringing with it an end to the debilitating flow of emetics that had been turning his stomach inside out for the past hour. He took a slow breath, forcing his battered digestive system to unknot and trying to ignore the smell of vomit in his nostrils. Characteristically, the collies had turned the lights back on so that he could see what he had done to himself. A wasted refinement; he was too tired to keep his eyes open, anyway.

From in front of him came the sound of a door opening and a light breeze swept over him, inducing a violent shiver. Raising his head against the weakness in his muscles, he saw Prefect Galway enter the interrogation cell and close the door behind him. Stepping over the mess on the floor, he moved to Jensen's right and sat down on a small stool facing the blackcollar. A gunbelt, Jensen noted, was secured to his waist.

For a moment the prefect studied him in silence. "Not easy, is it?" he said at last, his almost conversational tone sounding distant in Jensen's ears. "Pain-block techniques don't work very well against an indirect pain like vomiting."

"They work well enough," Jensen rasped. It's still too early to start gloating."

Galway shook his head. "I don't gloat over pain. If I'd had my way you'd already be dead."

Jensen blinked back the tears of fatigue and tried to read the other's face. But there was no malice there; nothing but grimness and—Jensen thought—a touch of compassion. "Thank you," he said, and meant it.

"Don't bother," Galway retorted. "If I thought you knew anything worthwhile I wouldn't mind them getting it out of you any way they could. But all we're really doing is humiliating you for no justifiable reason. It's a waste of time and ties down far too many men."

"Afraid I'll escape?" Jensen asked. The picture of him breaking out of Security HQ in this condition almost made him smile.

"Actually, yes." Galway drew his laser from its holster, checked the safety, and laid the weapon in his lap. "Skyler and Novak are across the street right now, preparing to launch a rescue attempt."

Jensen's already sore stomach muscles felt knotted up. No—that couldn't be. Galway had to be lying.

The prefect apparently misinterpreted Jensen's expression. "Oh, don't get any false hopes—they can't possibly succeed. We know their penetration plan and one of our spies is with them. The minute they move we'll have them in a pincer maneuver that'll trap them between the outer wall and a squadron of battle-armored troops, away from any possible cover. They won't get close enough for you to hear the noise."

Jensen dropped his eyes to the laser in Galway's lap. "Then why are you here?"

Galway's smile was bitter. "I underestimated you once. I'm not going to do it again. Prefect Apostoleris still doesn't understand how dangerous you are—perhaps because four of his spies have fooled one of you all these years. Whatever the reason, he still expects you to think and act in straight lines. And to behave like normal humans."

"Whereas we're really elfin changelings, of course." A wave of nausea swept over Jensen, and he clenched his teeth until it had passed.

"You're joking, but there's a grain of truth there all the same. The more I see you in action the more I believe your training did something permanent to your minds. Made you . . . different. Monomaniacal, perhaps."

"Why? Because we don't roll over and die for the convenience of the Ryqril?" Jensen shook his head tiredly. "Read your history, Galway. Human beings have never taken kindly to conquest. Guerrilla fighters have always harassed invaders, usually more successfully than their numbers would have indicated."

"Granted—but guerrillas need some measure of popular support and require the morale boost of frequent raids against the enemy. On Plinry you had neither, and yet could put together a devastating attack on a few hours' notice." Galway picked up his laser, ran a thumb thoughtfully along the muzzle. "Did you know my father was a member of the military study group in 2414 that made the blackcollar proposal? He was one of three dissenters, actually—he thought we should expand the Walking Tank program instead."

A short bark escaped Jensen's lips. "*There* was a fiasco. There must be forty separate ways for an antiarmor missile to track a man in a fighting suit, and the Ryqril knew every one of them. There wasn't a single ground battle after Navarre where the Walkers weren't wiped out within the first half hour. Fighting suits are expensive suicide."

"I know. I wish he'd had his way, though. Plinry's had enough grief without the trouble you're about to bring down on her." Galway's eyes fixed on Jensen's with sudden intensity. "Or don't you care what the Ryqril will do to Plinry because of you?"

"You can't lay the blame for Ryqril reprisals on our shoulders," Jensen said. "This is war, and we have a job to do. If you expect to make us tuck tail and slink off by threatening innocent people you aren't even worthy of contempt."

"You misunderstand me," Galway said, his voice quiet again. "I'm not trying to influence your actions. You're hearing this *because* you won't be rejoining your friends; because I—" He paused, then went on, "I suppose because I wanted someone to know that just because I've been loyalty-conditioned doesn't mean I don't care about the people of Plinry. I care a great deal—too much to see them suffer because of a showy mission that can't succeed. That's why I want all of you dead before you can cause any more trouble. The reprisals might be a little lighter."

For a moment Jensen remained silent, pain and fatigue almost forgotten. "You talk the high road well—I'll give you that much. But how much is truth and how much rationalization for something your conditioning forces you to do anyway?"

"I didn't expect you to understand—" Galway broke off suddenly, his gaze focused on infinity. A moment later Jensen heard it too: a faint sound of running footsteps. Scooping up his laser, Galway slid off the stool into a crouching position, extending the weapon toward the door in stiff-armed marksman fashion. Heart pounding, Jensen took a deep breath and drew his last reserves of strength into readiness for one final surge.

The wait was brief. Without warning, the door was abruptly flung open to crash against the wall.

Galway's first shot was a fraction of a second too slow, expending its energy in the doorframe as the black-clad figure charged in. A knife flashed into the invader's hand as Galway corrected his aim; but before the prefect could fire, Jensen threw all his weight against the crucifix frame holding him, pushing forward with one arm and back with the other. The crosspiece rotated only a few degrees, but the motion was enough to catch Galway's eye and reflexively twitch his laser a few centimeters toward Jensen. His second shot was another clean miss as the blackcollar's right leg snapped into Galway's forearm, knocking the laser aside; his knife arced toward the prefect's throat—"

"Don't kill him!" Jensen croaked.

But the blackcollar was already shifting the knife in his hand, turning the hilt so that the blade stuck out to the side as his fist rammed instead into Galway's throat. The prefect toppled with a strangled gasp; even before he hit the ground the blackcollar had turned and sliced the first of Jensen's restraints.

And for the first time Jensen was able to see the Caucasian features behind his goggles. "Skyler?" he gasped.

"Yes," the other confirmed. His knife flashed a half dozen more times and Jensen was free.

"Where's Novak?" he asked, getting shakily to his feet. Only Skyler's quick hand kept him from falling on his face as his legs buckled and sent him slamming back into his chair.

"Take it easy," Skyler told him. "We've got a little time."

"Like hell," Jensen gasped, waiting for the white spots to go away. "This place is one gigantic deathtrap."

"We noticed." Skyler stepped over to the unconscious Galway and began removing his gray-green tunic. "But they've temporarily outsmarted themselves. Their main force was deployed outside the wall waiting for us, and they're still trying to catch up. Aside from the control center area down the hall the building itself is relatively clear of armed guards."

"Sure." Jensen couldn't even count the dirty-gray

wrinklemarks of laser hits and near-misses on the other's flexarmor.

"Well, it is now." Skyler began helping Jensen into Galway's uniform. "I wish we had some flexarmor for you, but the spy they planted on us wasn't your size."

Jensen swallowed, concentrating on getting dressed. A dozen questions swirled through the fog in his brain but only one got out: "Where's Novak?"

"He's—seeing to our escape route."

Something in his voice cut through the haze. "What do you mean? What's he doing?"

Skyler knelt to help Jensen on with Galway's boots. "The control room has to be taken out—they coordinate all Security operations for Millaire and everything around it. But it's behind a thick wall, stronger than our explosives can handle."

"Novak's gone *in?*" A burst of near-panic rose into Jensen's throat; shrugging off Skyler's hand, he forced himself to his feet. This time he stayed up. "Come on, we've got . . . to help him," he gasped. "Have to be guards . . . in there—"

Before the words were out of his mouth the room abruptly rocked slightly as the vibration of an explosion rippled through the floor. "What—?" he began.

Skyler's answer was action. Without a word he hauled Jensen over his shoulder in a modified fireman's carry and made for the door. Glancing quickly both directions down the hall, he headed off to his right—and it was only then that Jensen suddenly realized that the brief vibration of the earlier explosion had been replaced by an ominous rumbling that seemed to come from all around them.

And then the ceiling began to fall in.

For Jensen, still weak and drug-groggy, the sprint down the hall seemed almost an extension of the nightmare preceding it. The world bounced crazily, chunks of it throwing themselves at him, while a roar like a rock crusher filled his ears. Skyler reached the end of the hall, broke sharply left, and skidded to a halt three steps later by a long, featureless wall. Dropping Jensen almost roughly to the shaking floor, he crouched protectively over him. The roar continued; Jensen began to cough violently as the rising cloud of dust found its way into his lungs. Somewhere in the chaos the lights went out, and as his cough turned into dry retching Jensen felt as if he were being buried alive—

And then it was all over. The floor steadied as the roar faded, and Jensen managed to get his cough under control. Through watery eyes, Skyler was a dimly lit figure rising to his feet above him.

Dimly lit?

Jensen turned his head. Barely twenty meters away the litter-strewn hallway ended abruptly in a ragged opening, through which the glow of Millaire's lights was filtering. Listening more carefully, he discovered he could hear faint shouts and occasional screams of pain.

Skyler had his arm and was helping him to his feet. "Novak?" he asked. The question was almost rhetorical; he knew now what had happened.

Skyler nodded anyway as, together, the two men moved carefully toward the opening ahead. "From the floor plans and external design he calculated that the control room was built around the main vertical support for the west end of the building. It was a big risk, but the interrogation rooms were close enough to the central section's main load-bearing wall that he thought we'd be safe."

"He was still in the control room when the blast went off, wasn't he."

Skyler hesitated, then nodded. "We didn't have enough power to just toss in a bomb and run. The explosives had to be carefully placed against the support. There was only a slim chance he'd be able to set them and get out . . . and he would've used his tingler if he'd made it." The big blackcollar paused. "I'm sorry, Jensen. He wouldn't let me take his place."

"You should have left me here."

"He wouldn't have agreed to that, either."

"I know." Jensen stumbled a bit as they topped the rubble at the broken end of the hall, but Skyler's arm around his waist kept him upright. Outside, there was an incredible amount of broken building material littering a courtyard sort of place. A wall forming the outer edge of the courtyard had been breached in at least three places; it was toward one of these that Skyler led him. "What about collie guards?" he asked.

"If Novak timed it as he planned, most of them were

probably in the section that collapsed. Watch your step," he added as Jensen again stumbled. "We need to get out of here before the collies pull whatever's left of their force together. With luck all this junk cleared out the mines for us—if neither of us sprains an ankle we should make it to the car all right."

Jensen nodded. The walk was rapidly draining his last reserves of strength, and he was beginning to feel lightheaded. "Skyler. Galway told me there were four spies in Radix—said they'd fooled a blackcollar here."

"All four, huh?" Skyler said grimly. "Somehow, I'm not surprised."

"I want to kill them."

There was a short pause. "We'll get them—don't worry. That *was* Galway, then," he added, as if wanting to change the subject. "I thought I was seeing things. Did I hear you tell me not to kill him, incidentally?"

Hazy spots were starting to flicker across Jensen's vision. "Yes," he said, his voice fading away into the distance. "It was . . . something I owed . . . Plinry."

The last thing he knew before sliding into the darkness was the feel of Skyler's arm around his waist.

CHAPTER 28

Mordecai found the proper door and paused for a moment outside it, listening. Faint voices were audible; despite the late hour, the room's occupants were still awake. Throwing one last glance down the deserted hallway, he tapped gently on the door.

It opened a few seconds later. "Mordecai!" Fuess said, his expression running through surprise to welcome. "Well; come in."

Mordecai brushed past him, letting the Argentian close the door, and gave the room a fast once-over. Fairly large and nicely furnished, he decided. Against opposite walls were two sets of bunk beds, each with a double-sized military locker at its foot. In the center was an oval table; sitting on opposite sides, playing cards still in their hands, were McKitterick and Couturie.

"Hello." Couturie nodded at Mordecai, laying his cards down and getting to his feet. His dragonhead ring glinted with the movement. "Can I get you a drink?"

Mordecai shook his head. "No. This isn't a social call."

Fuess came around from behind him to stand behind McKitterick. "What can we do for you, then?" he asked.

"Lathe just got a call from a public phone a few klicks outside Millaire. It was Skyler. He had Jensen with him."

They were good, all right. Not a flicker of surprise crossed any of their faces, and Fuess's comment was immediate and enthusiastic. "They got him out? Great! When're they due back?"

"Soon," Mordecai told him. "There were casualties—Novak and Valentine both."

A flicker of uncertainty crossed Fuess's face, quickly vanishing. "Damn stinking quizlers," he growled.

Mordecai shook his head. "Don't blame them for Valentine's death. Skyler had him executed—as a traitor."

"What?" Fuess and Couturie exclaimed together. McKitterick merely looked stunned.

"You heard me. Your friend was a collie spy."

"That's ridiculous!" Couturie snorted. "He was *blackcollar!*"

Mordecai regarded the indignant Argentian. "Did *you* serve with him in the war? Or personally know anyone who did?"

Couturie hesitated at the edge of the trap. "Well . . . no. But I've heard him describe operations that I know took place."

"So what? *I* can describe some operations of the Crimean War back on Earth."

"Are you implying," Fuess said slowly, "that Valentine wasn't a blackcollar at all?"

"Very good. But several years late in coming. Why didn't you ever suspect him before?"

No look passed between them; but almost as if on signal Fuess and Couturie began a nearly imperceptible movement away from their respective sides of the table. For Mordecai it was as good as an admission of guilt: they'd traced his line of questioning to its logical conclusion and were moving to flank him. "You make it sound easy to tell a fraud from a true blackcollar who's suffered neural damage," McKitterick said, his tone halfway between hostile and injured. "I understand your own man Dodds got nailed by those gases—why wasn't *he* killed?"

"Because he wasn't a spy like Valentine was . . . or you three are."

Their lack of facial reaction was simply more proof that they'd anticipated this conclusion. "You're insane," Fuess declared. "Stark raving insane. Where do you get off making an unwarranted accusation like that?"

Mordecai eyed him. "If I were you, I'd think up a better defense than my insanity. I've seen you in action, remember? It takes more than Backlash reflexes to make a blackcollar—a sense of teamwork and respect for authority, for example."

"So I'm not the perfect blackcollar. Is that a crime?"

"And what about us?" McKitterick added quietly. He was still sitting with his legs under the table, and for a moment Mordecai wondered about him. Was he in fact innocent, or had he merely missed the signal to prepare for action? "You've hardly even seen Couturie or me except at tactical group meetings—certainly never in a combat situation. How can you presume to judge us?"

Mordecai's lip twitched in a tight smile. "Cutting yourselves loose from the condemned so soon? The years haven't built up much loyalty, have they."

"Our loyalty is with Radix, where it's always been," Couturie told him. He took a step around the curve of the table as if heading toward Fuess, a move that brought him closer to Mordecai and farther to the blackcollar's side. "And if Fuess *is* a traitor—"

"Wait a second," Fuess objected, panic filtering into his voice. "You're going to take his word—"

Again, there was no visible signal; but halfway through Fuess's sentence they launched their attack. From his chair McKitterick heaved the table toward Mordecai; simultaneously, Fuess and Couturie leaped in to flank the blackcollar. It was as well-coordinated an action as Mordecai had ever seen, and against an average blackcollar it might have had a chance.

But he was Mordecai, and no other fight could ever have prepared them for him. Even as the table came crashing over, the blackcollar took a swift step to his right, moving directly into Fuess's attack and out of range of Couturie's. Fuess was ready; his foot snapped out in a side kick toward Mordecai's knee and his hands flashed in a backfist-reverse punch combination toward head and abdomen. Mordecai didn't even bother to block the attacks, but merely turned and bent the few centimeters necessary to send them flying past his body. His own counterattack was more effective: spinning a hundred eighty degrees, he sent a reverse kick into Fuess's ribcage that threw him a meter backwards to smash into one of the lockers. Mordecai came out of the kick facing the center of the room again; and even as Fuess collapsed to the floor Couturie caught up with him.

He came in low, his right hand flashing claw-fashion toward Mordecai's eyes as his right foot swept horizontally in an effort to kick the blackcollar's legs out from under him. Mordecai whipped his own left hand up to meet the jab, catching Couturie's wrist with his forearm and deflecting the blow over his right shoulder. The foot sweep was equally ineffective; the blackcollar's reflexes enabled him to simply jump over the swinging leg. Catching the wrist he'd deflected, Mordecai twisted it around and back, adding to Couturie's circular momentum. An instant later he had the Argentian's back to him, arm hammerlocked across his shoulder blades . . . and an instant after that smashed his free fist into the back of Couturie's neck with bone-breaking force.

Letting the limp body drop, Mordecai again spun to face the center of the room. Beyond the overturned table McKitterick had finally made it out of his chair and was bringing a compact pistol to bear on the blackcollar. Above the weapon his ashen face was contorted with rage and fear.

With his head and hands unprotected by flexarmor Mordecai's only option was to get out of the line of fire. Twisting to the side, he dropped into a long somersault that took him into the temporary protection of the overturned table. A sound like tearing paper came twice in rapid succession as he moved, the shots splattering into the wall and the tabletop.

With the momentum the somersault had given him, it would have been easiest either to come out the other side or to roll up into a kneeling position. Mordecai did neither, but instead brought himself to a stop and reversed direction, diving out of the shelter on the same side he'd gone in.

The gambit worked. McKitterick was starting forward, his gun pointed over the top of the table. He had just enough time for his expression to mirror knowledge of his fatal error—had nowhere near enough time to shift the gun itself—as Mordecai's *shuriken* flashed across the gap to bury itself into his throat. He toppled backwards to the floor and lay still.

For a moment Mordecai also lay silent, listening for running feet or curious voices. But his straining ears heard only the soft beating of his own heart. Getting to his feet, he confirmed all three Argentians were dead and retrieved his *shuriken* from McKitterick's body. For a moment he considered searching the room, but decided against it and instead stepped to the door.

He paused there, his hand on the knob, surveying the bodies he was leaving behind. He felt no regret, nor any sense that what he had just done was murder. It was, instead, justice.

Leaving the room, he closed the door gently behind him.

CHAPTER 29

The hostility in the conference room hit Caine like a heat wave as he and Lathe crossed to their places at the table. Every eye was on them, every expression icy cold. Caine threw a quick glance at Lathe's face as they sat down, but if the comsquare knew the reason for this unexpected summons he was hiding it well. Across the table, the seats usually occupied by Bakshi's four black-collars were empty.

Tremayne didn't waste any time with preliminaries. "Comsquare Lathe, can you account for the whereabouts of your men between twenty-one o'clock and midnight last night?"

"Not really," Lathe replied, "but there's no need to. *I'm* the one who ordered them killed."

The tension in the room seemed to crack with surprise, then instantly reform into an even denser mass. "Ordered *who* killed?" Caine asked, his stomach tightening.

"Fuess, McKitterick, and Couturie," Tremayne answered coldly. "And I've heard that Valentine didn't return with Skyler and Jensen this morning."

"That's right, he didn't." Lathe's voice was calm, but with an undertone of bitterness. "Neither did Novak. Valentine and the other three were responsible for his death."

"How do you figure *that?*" Miles Cameron snapped.

"They were government spies."

The stunned silence that greeted that statement lasted only a second before a babble of incredulous comments broke out. Through it one voice cut like a knife: "What's your proof?"

Lathe turned to face Faye Picciano. "I have no hard evidence, if that's what you want. If you had the facilities here a biochemist could show that none of them had ever been treated with the Backlash drug. But I *can* give you more indirect evidence."

"Such as?" Faye's voice was cool but, unlike some of the others, she seemed willing to hear him out.

"Such as their loud hatred for the Ryqril and the government. Bakshi here doesn't show that kind of emotional fire; neither do my men. Blackcollars that do can't survive a war of attrition—they burn out far too quickly. But that was the stereotypical blackcollar personality all of you expected—correct me if I'm wrong—so that's the camouflage they wore for you."

Caine tore his gaze from Lathe's face long enough to evaluate the others' expressions. They were still hostile, but here and there slightly creased foreheads indicated Lathe's words had started some of them thinking. For himself, Caine felt like all the props had been knocked out from under him.

"Skyler also brought Valentine's dragonhead ring back," Lathe continued, "and I can show you it's been altered to match his assumed rank of commando, whereas it originally must have belonged to a higher-ranking officer.

And finally, the three that Mordecai killed attacked him first, instead of the other way around."

"Did them a lot of good, didn't it?" Tremayne said, throwing a glare over Caine's shoulder to where Mordecai and Kwon waited quietly by the door. "McKitterick took a throwing star in the throat, Couturie had a broken neck, and Fuess had both lungs collapsed and bone splinters in his heart. I don't even see you limping."

Mordecai remained silent. "The point remains," Lathe said, "that real blackcollars wouldn't have attacked in the first place. They could have cleared themselves easily."

"How?" Cameron growled. "Their word against yours?"

"Use your head, Miles," Bakshi spoke up unexpectedly. "We all went to the same training center on Centauri A. There are a thousand little things about the people and procedures there that any true blackcollar would know."

The attention of the group turned abruptly to Bakshi. "Are you saying Lathe's *right?*" Tremayne asked, clearly surprised.

"I don't know for sure—and any chance of cross-examining them is gone now."

"Very conveniently," Cameron added with heavy sarcasm.

"But," Bakshi continued doggedly, "if Lathe *is* right it would explain all the raids that have gone sour over the years."

"But even if they *weren't* real blackcollars it doesn't necessarily follow that they were spies," Cameron persisted.

"You don't even believe that one yourself," Faye scoffed. "What else would they be?"

"Would I be correct in assuming you brought the four of them into Radix, Cameron?" Lathe put in.

Cameron reddened. "What's that supposed to mean?"

"Only that you're defending them like someone who'll look bad if they're proved phony."

"I'm not. . . . Oh, hell. *Yes,* it was one of my contacts that clued me in to them, and I *was* the one who recommended to Ral that they be brought here to help with strategy and tactics. But that's all." He leveled a finger at Bakshi. "And Serle accepted them as genuine, so how was I to know any different?"

"Why *did* you accept them, Serle?" Faye asked curiously.

"You just said there were questions you could have nailed them with."

Bakshi shrugged. Like Cameron he also looked somewhat embarrassed. "I had no reason to doubt them. They had enough general knowledge of blackcollar tactics and skills that I accepted them at face value. You have to remember that blackcollar teams worked independently within their assigned territories. I couldn't be expected to have known them personally." He nodded at Lathe. "Your squad was put together from remnants the same way, wasn't it—in fact, I understand one of your people suffers from the same neural damage Fuess and the others claimed they had. If you couldn't see through them until now they must have faked the symptoms fairly well."

Lathe nodded his agreement . . . and Caine struggled to keep his expression neutral as all his old questions regarding Dodds came flooding back with sudden new urgency. If Fuess and the others had been able to fool Bakshi for so long, what proof was there that Dodds hadn't been doing the same thing on Plinry? None whatsoever . . . except that Lathe had apparently vouched personally for Dodds.

Caine shook his head minutely to clear it. Surely Lathe was above suspicion—he'd risked his life often enough on the mission to prove that. And yet, he couldn't help but notice that in eliminating the four Argentians Lathe had also rather conveniently silenced his most vocal opposition in the Radix tactical group. It bothered Caine in a way he found impossible to pin down, and he found himself almost hoping Tremayne or Cameron would demand more proof of Lathe's charges. The comsquare's reaction to that might be enlightening.

But with Bakshi and Faye more or less supporting Lathe, the controversy over the killings was cooling down, at least temporarily. Lathe obviously considered the issue closed; all business again, he had pulled out a map and was spreading it on the table. With half an ear Caine listened as the other outlined the plan he and Hawking had worked out to secure space transports from the Brocken military 'port some fifteen kilometers south of Calarand . . . and it became quickly clear that opposition to Lathe's methods hadn't died with Fuess and company.

"You seem confident that this pattern bombardment rigmarole will actually clear a path through the outer defenses before either the tower lasers open up or the Ryqril get some ground forces into the area," Salli Quinlan said, shaking her head. "I'll accept your word on black-collar matters, but you're talking Ryqril spaceports now; and I *know* Ryqril have better security than that."

"True," Lathe agreed, "but that's only the first attack vector. The second comes through here—" he indicated a spot on the map—"led by two double-flexarmored black-collars who'll sweep out a lane through the perimeter mines. Without the usual pattern bombardment there the Ryqril won't have any real warning, so our men should be in among the parked ships before they can react."

"Unless the antiaircraft lasers automatically fire at ground-level incursions," Tremayne said. "I agree with Salli; the whole thing's unworkable." He fixed Lathe with a glare. "Or is this another feint like the big Cerbe operation?"

Lathe shook his head. "No, this one's real. And it *is* unworkable if we were trying to capture the 'port. But as long as all we want to do is get the vets aboard some ships and take off we'll be pretty safe."

"How do you figure *that?*" Tremayne growled.

"Because the Ryqril want the Novas," Faye spoke up, her gaze riveted to Lathe's face. "That's what you're counting on, isn't it?"

"My God!" Jeremiah Dan exclaimed, looking stricken. "She's right, Ral—Fuess and McKitterick were right there when Lathe told us about the ships."

Tremayne gave Lathe a speculative look, then turned to Faye. "What do you mean, that's what he's counting on?"

"It's simple," Faye said, eyes still on Lathe. "Now that the Ryqril know why the blackcollars are here, they've got a choice between raiding us and stopping the operation cold, or letting us go and trying to turn it to their advantage."

Lathe smiled slightly and inclined his head. "Nicely reasoned," he said.

"Thanks." Her voice ignored the compliment. "Then maybe you'll listen when I tell you you've just forced their decision. With his agents dead Apostroleris *has* to stop us now before we get off-planet. He can't just follow us to wherever the Novas are hidden—his ships would have to stay too far back, and by the time he caught up we might have one or more of the ships activated."

"With thirty or more Corsairs available?" Lathe shook his head. "The Ryqril will know we can't possibly get the drive up to full power in less than forty or fifty hours with the number of starmen we have. They could track us by drive trail from here and still get Corsairs there in plenty of time."

"That presupposes the Novas are within forty hours of Argent," Bakshi said.

"They are. Come on now—surely you've all figured out where they're hidden."

There was a short silence. "Somewhere in the Diamond?" Tremayne hazarded.

"Of course." Lathe nodded. "There must be upwards of eighty thousand decently sized asteroids out there. Any one of them could have had five caves carved into it, the Novas put in and sensor shielded—and the Ryqril could search for the next ten years without finding them. No, they'll let us show them the way, all right."

"Well, that's a relief," Cameron growled sarcastically. "And now that Apostoleris has mate in three, why the hell are we still going ahead with this?"

"Because we know something Security doesn't," Lathe said calmly. "One of my people knows a rather exotic shortcut that can have the Novas' weaponry operational in less than four hours. If we can position the ships properly, we should be able to hold off anything the Ryqril have in this system long enough to bring the drives up."

"Why haven't we heard about this miracle cure before?" Tremayne asked suspiciously. "And which one supposedly knows it?"

"Not 'supposedly,' " Lathe corrected mildly. "And you haven't heard about it because the subject hasn't come up until now."

"Who?"

"Jensen, of course. He's our spacecraft expert."

Tremayne frowned sternly at Lathe, and for a long moment Caine thought he was going to demand proof. But Lathe returned the gaze without flinching; and it was the Radix leader who blinked first. "Just remember that if it doesn't work it's your neck, too," he growled. He gestured toward the map of Brocken Base. "And you'd better hope the quizlers see things the same way you do. Otherwise a lot of good men are going to die for nothing—and you and your rads won't escape."

"On the contrary—we'll be at the top of the list," Lathe said calmly. "Or had you forgotten we'll be leading both prongs of the attack?"

Tremayne measured him with his eyes. "All right," he said at last. "When do we attack?"

Lathe's answer was immediate. "Tonight."

The painkiller they'd given Galway was an unfamiliar one, selectively numbing his broken arm and the strained muscles in his neck without fogging up his mental processes. In a way he was sorry; a part of him would have liked to escape from the memories of the past few hours. Waking up to find himself buried under tons of collapsed building . . . he suppressed a shudder at the memory. And yet, it was almost more painful to realize that the blackcollars had once again pulled off the supposedly impossible.

And to know that he himself was responsible for part of the current crisis.

"I'm sure he picked it up," he said again to Colonel Eakins. "He was lucid enough, and blackcollars don't miss clues like that."

"Especially when handed over on a silver platter," Eakins said acidly, leaning back in his chair. He'd looked singularly ill at ease when he'd first sat down there an hour previously, Galway had thought—he'd probably never before been on that side of the Security prefect's desk. Now, after making a couple of dozen phone calls and giving perhaps twice that many orders, he merely looked tired.

"I know." Galway's guilt feelings weren't helped by the knowledge that being in Jensen's interrogation room when the balloon went up had probably saved his life; of those in the control area only Prefect Apostoleris had survived, and he was holding on by a molecular filament back in a Millaire hospital.

Eakins snorted, but then shook his head. "Oh, forget it. If you hadn't said anything they probably would've nailed the other three through association with Valentine anyway. I just hope we can be ready before Lathe makes his next move."

Galway gestured toward the phone with his good arm. "Do you really think you've got enough men to blockade every spaceport on the planet?"

Eakins sighed. "I don't have any choice. Without any ears left in the Radix council we aren't likely to get the Novas' coordinates in time for the Ryqril to get there first."

"Why not just let them go and simply track them?" Galway suggested. "You can make sure that any ship they can grab has long-range transponders aboard. They'd reach the ships first, but once they're there it would only be a matter of hours before the Ryqril could have a wing of Corsairs out to them."

"I thought of that." Eakins was studying the wood-grain pattern of Apostoleris's desk top. "All our experts claim it's feasible, that it'd take nearly two days for them to get the Novas up to fighting strength." He looked up at Galway, his expression tight. "But there's a flaw somewhere we're not seeing. It's too simple an idea for Lathe to have missed it, and yet his operation's going ahead at full speed. Either we've miscalculated or Lathe knows something I don't." He shook his head. "I can't afford to underestimate them again."

The phone rang, and Eakins picked it up. "Security prefect's office; Eakins," he said. A second later his eyes widened. "Yes. Thank you," he said hastily and dropped the handset into its cradle.

"What is it?" Galway asked tensely.

"Ryq on his way," Eakins hissed. The words were still echoing in Galway's ears when the door slammed open and one of the aliens strode in.

Galway had seen Ryqril close up perhaps a dozen times in his life, but there was something about this one that made the experience seem excruciatingly fresh. The Ryq was *big;* his slightly hunched form barely cleared the doorway, and the thump of his footsteps could be felt even through the thick carpet. But even that didn't explain the sheer *presence* the alien radiated, a sense of power and authority Galway had never encountered in a Ryq. Even as he and Eakins scrambled to their feet his eyes flicked over the ornate belt-and-baldric supporting the laser and short sword, searching for a rank or familial pattern he could recognize. But none of the designs were like any he knew.

The Ryq reached the desk and stopped, his black eyes on Eakins. " 'Re'ect A'staeleris?" he said, his gravelly voice distorting the words and adding a deep-pitched tonal fluttering.

Eakins swallowed visibly. "I am Colonel Eakins, Acting Prefect," he said, enunciating carefully. "Prefect Apostoleris has been severely injured."

The Ryq made a gesture with its arm, and Galway winced involuntarily before he realized the alien wasn't going for his sword. Small as it was, his motion drew the Ryq's eyes for a split second. "I an Hrarkh—rarriaer *khassq,*" he ground out, his paw completing its gesture to touch a section of his baldric.

Galway felt cold. *Khassq*-class warriors were the highest stratum of Ryqril society—orders of magnitude above the rear-echelon troops serving on Plinry. How high up this particular Ryq was in the government of Argent or in the war machine arrayed against the Chryselli Galway didn't know, but it didn't really matter. A *khassq* warrior's authority superseded any chain of command.

Obviously, Eakins knew all this even better than Galway did. "What are your commands?" the colonel asked.

"Rithdraw Secaerity rarriaers arornd all landing 'ields," the alien said promptly. "Eneny attack is allared to 'raceed."

Eakins blinked once. "Ah—yes, of course. But—are you aware the enemy has eliminated our top spies?"

"Dae yae qrestion?" Hrarkh's voice had dropped an octave, and Galway felt his mouth go dry. He'd heard that tone only once before from a Ryq; three men had died immediately afterwards.

"I don't question either your order or your authority," Eakins replied hastily. "I question only *our* ability to protect Ryqril interests without information from our spies if we withdraw our defenses."

Hrarkh seemed to relax, achieving the effect without moving any muscle that Galway could detect, and his voice returned to its earlier pitch. "Yaer 'raetection is not needed. Ryqril ha'e contral o' sitaetion."

"Of course," Eakins nodded vigorously. "Our forces will be withdrawn at once."

The Ryq's eyes flicked over Galway once more; then, without another word, he turned and left.

Eakins seated himself carefully in his chair as if trying to hold onto at least a shred of dignity. Galway gave his own pride a vacation and collapsed unashamedly into his own seat. "There are rumors on Plinry that the reason Ryqril always come to humans' offices is that if the Ryq gets mad it's the human's place that he tears apart instead of his own."

"It's no rumor—I've seen it happen." Eakins's face was shiny.

Galway looked at the open doorway. "What the *hell* was that all about?"

Eakins ran a hand across his forehead. "It sounds like they're putting Apostoleris's original plan back into effect."

"That's risky. If Lathe's got something up his sleeve they could lose everything—you just finished convincing me of that."

"That's right," Eakins said slowly. "But maybe they won't have to wait until Lathe reaches the ships to move in."

Galway frowned as he caught the other's drift. "You think the Ryqril have their *own* high-level spy in Radix?"

"I wouldn't be at all surprised."

For a moment the two men looked at each other in silence, and Galway saw his own dislike for the aliens' private spy network mirrored on Eakins's face. But neither said anything; and after a moment Eakins straightened in his chair and reached for the phone. He had, Galway knew, a lot of orders to rescind.

There were a lot of details involved in planning an assault, and it was late afternoon before Lathe could take the time to return to the blackcollars' room. His mind busy with tactical details, he had the door closed behind him before he noticed the three men had company.

Across the room, Lianna Rhodes was conversing in low tones with Caine.

Frowning in mild irritation, the comsquare stepped over to Hawking, who was observing the conversation closely from a chair by the table. "How're Jensen and Skyler doing?" Hawking greeted him quietly.

"Better," Lathe murmured. "Vale says Jensen's suffering mainly dehydration and a fouled-up digestive system, along with some laser and electric burns. Skyler's pretty stiff from all *his* burns, but he'll be okay in a day or two. He'll have to sit out the fighting tonight, though." He nodded slightly toward Lianna. "How long has she been here?"

"About ten minutes," Hawking said, disapproval in his tone. "I didn't want to let her in, but Caine insisted. Apparently he set this up with her right after your meeting earlier with Tremayne's people, before I took over from Kwon."

Lathe glanced at Mordecai, lounging near the door, got a confirming nod. "What're they talking about?"

"I can't get much of what she's saying, but lip-reading Caine's responses, I gather it's an intelligence report of some kind."

Lathe grunted. "Well, she'll have to leave—we haven't got time for Caine to play general." He raised his hand slightly, trying to catch Caine's eye; but even as he did so the two of them got to their feet and started for the door. Lianna nodded at the comsquare as they passed; Caine's expression was several degrees cooler. Mordecai let her out, and as he closed the door behind her Caine turned toward Lathe.

The comsquare got in the first question. "What was that all about?" he asked.

"I asked her to quietly get some information from Cameron and Salli Quinlan for me."

Lathe nodded. "And?"

"Up until three hours ago Brocken 'port was swarming with Security men who were setting up a defense perimeter outside the main fence. Salli's observers say they then just pulled up and left. Scattered reports from other 'ports show the same pattern. One other curious thing: since about noon spotters have seen an unusually high number of Corsairs lifting off, and no one has reported seeing them land."

"Insurance," Hawking murmured from behind Lathe. "The Ryqril are probably scattering them around the Diamond in hopes that one or two might wind up closer to the Novas than the ones that'll be following us from Argent."

"Seems reasonable," Lathe agreed.

"Yes," Caine nodded. "Doesn't it strike you as odd that Security should suddenly offer us an engraved invitation into Brocken?"

"A fair question. Doesn't it strike *you* as odd that they feel the need to send Corsairs to wait for us?"

"Like Hawking said, it's insurance."

"Insurance against Jensen's magic touch with Nova weaponry, perhaps?"

Judging from his expression, it took Caine another couple of heartbeats to catch on. "Are you suggesting there's *still* a spy in that group?" he asked disbelievingly. "Isn't that a little heavy on the overkill, even for someone like Apostoleris?"

Lathe shrugged. "I may be wrong."

"I hope to hell you are—because if you're not, that particular lie just forced Security to weave their noose a little tighter. You *were* lying about Jensen, weren't you?"

"Calm down. It got Tremayne to go along with us, didn't it?"

"Splendid—we can all walk into Security's arms together." Caine paused, his eyes boring into Lathe's. "Lathe, you're going to need one hell of a good trick handy to pull this off."

"I know. I may have one; we'll just have to wait to see if it works."

"Tell me about it."

"I'm sorry, but I can't."

"It involves Dodds, doesn't it?" Caine persisted. "Has he armed his Corsair with heavy weapons from a secret cache or something?"

Lathe shook his head. "I'm sorry. You're just going to have to trust me a little longer."

Caine stared at him, lips tightly compressed. "You've been saying that for a long time now," he said at last. "But I have responsibility for this mission, too, and my patience only stretches so far. If you want my trust you have to give me yours."

"I've risked all of our lives in coming here," Lathe said quietly. "We lost a lot of good men on Plinry, we lost Novak here, and depending on how realistic the collies want to make their defense look, we may lose more tonight. How much more do you want?"

"I've told you—I want to know what happens when we find the Novas."

The room was very still. Lathe could feel the close attention Hawking and Mordecai were paying to the conversation, and he knew they too were wondering what he was planning. "I'm sorry," he repeated, putting a note of finality into his voice. "Now come over here," he added, turning toward the table where Hawking still sat. "We haven't got much time, and we've got a lot of planning yet to do."

"Yes. We certainly do," Caine said softly.

For a moment Lathe wondered about the disgruntlement in the younger man's voice, but he quickly dismissed it. They were heading toward the final hurdle, and there wasn't going to be time for anyone to sulk in his tent.

Whatever hurt feelings Caine had, he'd get over them soon enough.

CHAPTER 30

Though his practical experience was negligible, Caine's theoretical knowledge of warfare was fairly extensive; moreover, from his vantage point on top of one of the transport trucks parked several kilometers away from Brocken he had a grandstand view of the proceedings. Everything he saw pointed to an inescapable conclusion.

The assault was going ridiculously well.

Stretched flat on his belly, Caine lowered his binoculars and hiked his goggles up high enough over his battle hood to rub his eyes, itchy from the salt of perspiration.

Both prongs of Lathe's attack were sweeping virtually unchallenged across the brightly lit 'port field, encountering only sporadic Ryqril resistance. Clearly, Lathe had been right: the aliens wanted them to get off-planet and had cut back their defense lest they discourage the attackers into retreat.

Caine swallowed, and suddenly became very conscious of the laser pistol strapped to his thigh. There could be no further doubt that there was still a spy among them . . . and the thought of what he would soon have to do made his throat ache with tension.

"Caine!" came a whisper from below.

Sliding a meter forward, Caine peered over the edge of the roof. In the dim light a dozen dark figures could just barely be seen moving among the five trucks; directly beneath Caine's position another was looking upward. "Yes?" Caine whispered back.

"Time to go," Mordecai's voice answered.

Gripping the edge, Caine slid his legs over the side, and half a minute later was jammed between Mordecai and Skyler in a commuter-crush of Star Force vets inside the truck. "How's it look?" Skyler asked softly.

"We're creaming them," Caine said. A moment later the truck's doors were closed, and there was a jerk that sent a ripple of motion through the packed crowd as the truck began to roll.

The ride wasn't a long one, and though Caine strained his ears he heard little of interest. Once, far ahead, he heard a faint explosion that probably signaled the opening of the 'port's main gate; minutes later a flatter, gentler crack came. A sharp turn, a few minutes of high-speed driving, and the truck squealed to a halt. Even before the men inside had recovered their balance the doors were flung open and voices were yelling for them to get moving. Caine was near the back; hopping to the ground, he looked around.

They were at the civilian end of the 'port, nestled protectively between two mammoth freighters. Four of their five trucks had already pulled to a halt, their passengers pouring out of the doors and scrambling to the dimly lit loading hatches in the ships. Laser-armed Radix people stood nearby, acting as both guards and traffic directors. Farther away, at either end of the corridor between the ships, more figures could be seen guarding the approaches. Beyond them the landscape seemed to twist and writhe with a surprisingly strong flickering light from the direction of the 'port's buildings. "What's on fire?" he asked Mordecai as the other gestured him toward the nearer ship.

"Nothing important," Skyler said, coming up stiffly on Caine's other side. "Our first truck was loaded with flammable liquid and rigged to spray the stuff to the front and rear. Spadafora parked it between us and the tower and set it off. It puts up a wall of flame about fifty meters long and maybe ten high at the peak. Discourages enemy movement, besides scrambling infrareds."

"Is Spadafora okay?"

"Oh, sure. Tardy's a born pyromaniac—he's set more firescreens than the rest of us put together. He just hitched a ride with the next truck through. Consider it insurance against the Ryqril changing their minds."

The freighter they entered was considerably larger than the one they'd left Plinry in and at least ten years younger. Skyler seemed to know the internal layout, and got the three of them to the bridge without any obviously wrong turns.

Already there was a small crowd present. Besides Lathe, Bakshi, and Tremayne, Commander Nmura and three of his men were there, the latter running a rapid check on the ship's control equipment. Tremayne was seated at the communications console, while Lathe and Bakshi, the latter sporting a laser pistol in addition to his *nunchaku,* had blackcollar communicators out. Finding an unoccupied corner at the rear of the bridge, Caine leaned against the wall and waited, heart thumping loudly in his ribs.

The lift-off came a few minutes later and was so smooth that if Caine hadn't heard the order he might have missed it. For a few seconds the 'port lights and the still-burning firescreen were visible on the visual displays, but Nmura was clearly in a hurry to get out of range of ground antiaircraft defenses, and the landscape beneath them was quickly blurred by speed and altitude into a featureless mass. On other displays the stars grew sharper as the freighter rose above Argent's atmosphere. Casually,

Caine rested his hand on the butt of his laser and forced himself to relax.

"Orbit achieved," one of the starmen reported, his face buried in a sensor hood. "*Chainbreaker II*'s right behind us; no sign of pursuit."

"That won't last long," Nmura said, turning to Lathe. "I need to know where we're going now, Comsquare."

Lathe nodded to Caine. "Okay, Caine. This is it."

"Not quite yet," Caine said. He slid his laser from its holster. "First there's one more government agent to neutralize."

The normal hums of a spaceship bridge where thunderous in the sudden stillness. Lathe spoke first, his eyes on Caine's face as if refusing to acknowledge the laser pointed at his chest. "What the hell are you doing?" he demanded.

Caine ignored the question. "Everyone stay out of my line of fire," he ordered through dry lips. "If you'll consent to being tied up and sedated, Lathe, you'll get a chance to defend yourself at a trial. Otherwise I'll kill you right now. Which will it be?"

"Caine, you'd better have one damn good explanation for this," Skyler warned, his hand hovering near the hilt of one of his knives.

"Lathe's a spy," Caine said. "I don't have proof—yet—but the pointers are all there. How else could everything he pulled always work without a hitch?" He gestured minutely with the laser. "Well, Lathe—you going to let Bakshi and Nmura tie you up?"

"Oh, for—Caine, you've lost your mind. But if it'll make you feel better, all right." Lathe raised his hands shoulder-high—and leaped.

The move was abrupt, without any telegraphing whatsoever—but Caine had expected it, and before Lathe had crossed half of the three-meter gap separating them he dropped to one knee and fired. An instant later he dived to the side as the blackcollar's momentum sent him hurling past to crash into the corner. Sliding to the floor, he lay still.

The silence that returned was a darker thing than had been there seconds earlier. Caine remained crouched on the floor, laser ready, watching the blackcollar for signs of motion. Lathe lay in an almost fetal position on his side, his right arm curled back over his head while his left draped partly over the crinkly-gray rift in his flexarmor that the laser had opened across his chest. Even from a meter away Caine could smell the acrid stink of burnt flesh.

Muscles trembling with reaction, Caine got to his feet, replacing the laser in its holster, and turned to face the horrified stares of the others. "All right," he said, as casually as possible. "I guess we're ready to go now."

Moving like a man in a dream, Skyler detached himself from the group by the control consoles and went over to crouch by Lathe's still form. His hands touched the charred flexarmor, gently probed beneath the battle-hood for the carotid artery. He held the pose a moment before rising with some difficulty to his feet, and Caine decided it was a good thing much of the other's expression was still hidden behind his goggles. "Caine—" he began, his voice deadly.

"He condemned himself," Caine interrupted him. "I claim the same evidence he applied against Fuess and his friends: he attacked first." Deliberately, he turned his back on Skyler and stepped to where Nmura sat, frozen-faced, at the helm. "Commander, I have two sets of space-time coordinates for the Novas. Can this computer handle an orbit calculation from that?"

Nmura nodded, his expression uncertain.

"All right." Carefully, Caine unlocked the mental vault he'd set up an eternity ago and drew out the precious numbers. It felt strange, as if part of him resisted the action. "First position set: standard solar/galactic coordinate system. . . ."

The figures took less than a minute to recite, and within half a minute the computer had done the orbit calculation, extrapolated it thirty-three years forward in time—with all known perturbations taken into account—and displayed both the current location and a choice of three courses from the freighter's own position.

"Yeah, that's somewhere in the Diamond, all right," Caine commented, studying the numbers. "Start off aiming somewhere to one side—we don't want our course extrapolated."

Nmura nodded and reached toward the communications board. "I'll have to give *Chainbreaker II* a preliminary course," he explained.

"Don't bother," a soft voice said from behind them. "No one's going any farther tonight."

There was something in the tone that discouraged hasty movement. Slowly, keeping his hand away from his pistol, Caine turned around. Standing well back from the group, his drawn laser leveled, was Bakshi.

CHAPTER 31

There is a point where the human mind loses its ability to respond emotionally to stress; where successive shocks elicit diminished reactions or none at all . . . and as he gazed at Bakshi's stony expression, Caine sensed their group had reached that point. His shooting of Lathe was still too fresh for any reaction but confused numbness.

"What are you doing, Serle?" Tremayne growled, the question sounding inane in the stillness. Standing to his right and slightly behind him, Caine could clearly see the tightness in the Radix leader's neck and shoulders.

"Skyler, move closer to the others," Bakshi ordered, ignoring Tremayne. "Keep your hands at chest level—remember that my reflexes are as good as yours. And don't block my view of Caine's gun hand."

Peripherally, Caine saw Skyler obey, stepping to within half a meter of Caine's right shoulder before stopping. "Who are *you* planning to kill?" he asked Bakshi sarcastically.

"No one needs to die," Bakshi said in the same soft voice. "There'll be amnesty for everyone who participated in this mission, including Caine and your blackcollars, provided you surrender peacefully. Commander Nmura, inform the other freighter you'll both be landing back at Brocken on this orbit."

"If I refuse?" Nmura said stiffly.

"Staying out here won't do them any good—they don't know where the ships are yet," Bakshi reminded him.

"You traitor." The words came out of Tremayne's mouth with a bitterness Caine hadn't realized a human voice could achieve. "You lousy, *murderous* traitor."

"Send the message, Commander," Bakshi said. His eyes and laser, Caine noted, were firmly fixed somewhere to the left, past the console where Nmura sat. It puzzled him—and it clearly irritated Tremayne.

"*Look* at me, damn you!" the Radix leader snarled suddenly. "Or haven't you got the stomach to face me?"

The barest hint of a smile twitched Bakshi's lips, and he shook his head minutely. "Sorry, Ral, but at the moment you're not any danger to me. Commando Mordecai is a different story."

"Mordecai?" Tremayne glanced to his left.

Caine turned his own head more slowly. The best hand-to-hand fighter that ever lived, Lathe had once called him; but standing motionless in Bakshi's line of fire, a head shorter and twenty-five kilos lighter than the Argentian, he looked merely old. "You overestimate me, Comsquare," he murmured, echoing Caine's thoughts.

"I don't think so. Fuess, McKitterick, and Couturie were no blackcollars, but they were damn good fighters. I have a great deal of respect for anyone who could take them as easily as you did—far too much to take my eyes off you."

"So you knew they were fakes all along," Caine said slowly. "And vice versa, of course. A pity Mordecai didn't kill them more leisurely."

"It wouldn't have helped you," Bakshi said. "They never knew about me. I reported directly to the Ryqril."

"To the Ryqril." Tremayne's voice was quiet, almost calm. But his face was pale, and the one eye Caine could see burned with hatred. "Betraying your own race for a lousy—what's the going rate these days? Still thirty pieces of silver a person?"

Bakshi sighed. "I don't expect you to understand, but I was trying to help."

"Of course. Without traitors we couldn't *possibly* have functioned."

"You couldn't have *survived*," Bakshi snapped, his icy veneer cracking for a second. With a visible effort he regained his control . . . and when he spoke again there was infinite sadness in his voice. "Don't you see," he said softly, almost pleadingly, "that the Ryqril could never have let an effective underground function this close to the Chryselli battle front?"

"So you chose emasculation for us, did you?" Tremayne spat.

"It was that or mass destruction. Apostoleris had the Calarand and Millaire HQs infiltrated from top to bottom. You could have been wiped out in a single night if the Ryqril had ordered it. The outlying Radix cells would have been dealt with even more harshly—whole towns killed, probably, to make sure of getting everyone. Is that what you wanted for Argent, Ral? Really?"

Tremayne exhaled loudly. "There are worse things than dying for a cause you believe in. Living as someone's tame pet, for instance."

"I didn't think you'd understand," Bakshi said, his voice weary. "And get your hand away from your laser. You wouldn't even clear the holster with it."

"No." Tremayne's voice was even. "I'm not accepting Ryqril charity anymore. Let's see if your spineless toadying left you enough guts to gun me down."

"Ral," Bakshi began warningly—

And a chunk of silver light flashed across the room from Caine's right, catching Bakshi's gun arm at the wrist and knocking it to the side.

The impact wasn't all that great; Bakshi kept his grip on the weapon and would have had it back on target in half a second. But for Mordecai half a second was all the time in the world.

His spinning kick sent the laser clattering off the bridge wall with the sharp *crack* of breaking bone. Bakshi countered with an ineffective kick toward Mordecai's stomach and leaped back a meter, landing in combat stance. Mordecai was on him instantly, and for a few seconds the two men stood nose to nose, arms flashing in attack and counter with sudden speed. They broke apart for a moment, and Caine could see a bright line of blood trailing from Bakshi's tightly compressed lips before the Argentian threw himself forward in a final desperate attack. Mordecai stood his ground . . . and with one more flurry of punches it was over.

Tremayne, breaking out of his momentary paralysis, finally yanked out his laser. His eyes seemed uncertain of the proper target, though, flicking between Bakshi's crumpled form and the corner where Lathe had risen to his feet. "You can put that away," Lathe advised him grimly. "It's all over now. Nmura, give the other ship a course and get us moving before the Ryqril realize they've lost the ball."

"Uh . . . yes, sir." Caine glanced around in time to see a thoroughly confused-looking Nmura turn back to his console.

Lathe walked over to Bakshi, trailing flakes of charred flexarmor and the odor of burnt flesh as he did so, and squatted down to check briefly for a pulse. Rising to his feet, he faced Tremayne, the latter still clutching his laser. "It's all over," he repeated. "Unless you have doubts that Bakshi was really a spy, of course."

Slowly, Tremayne slid the pistol into its holster, his eyes glancing at the gash in Lathe's flexarmor. "Just another of your little tricks, huh?" he said bitterly. He shot an angry look back at Caine. "I suppose Caine's laser was specially rigged or something?"

Lathe shook his head. "It was just as deadly as yours—Bakshi wouldn't have been fooled by anything else. I'm wearing a double thickness of flexarmor, with a thin slab of raw meat between to give off the right smell. If Caine had somehow missed and got my head instead I'd be dead now." He had his gloves off now; tiredly, he wiped his forehead.

"We're on our way, Comsquare," Nmura spoke up. "Course heading about ten degrees from target."

"You could have told me," Tremayne growled. "Or didn't you think I could be objective where treason from my own top lieutenant was concerned?"

Lathe gave him a long look. "Your objectivity wasn't in question," he said quietly. "It was your loyalty I wasn't sure of."

Tremayne stiffened, but the explosion Caine had expected didn't come. "I trust you can explain," he said, his tone icy.

"Do you remember the ambush Security laid for us in Calarand, the day I went into Henslowe? The car that stopped us was prepared with four of the heavy-duty mag-lock shackles. *Four*, not three. You and Bakshi were the only ones in the garage that morning, the only ones that knew Caine would be going along. We were in a closed van, so Security's spotters couldn't have counted us, and I'd made sure no one else had been in the garage.

So one of you was a spy, and we had to give that one a chance to hang himself. This is what we came up with."

Slowly, Tremayne nodded. "You're right," he admitted. "Absolutely right. And I never even came close to picking it up." He looked down at Bakshi. "A *blackcollar*. I can still hardly believe it."

Lathe suddenly looked very old. "Neither could I. That's why I waited so long. I wanted to hear why he'd done it, to try and understand him."

"I suppose in his own way he thought he was serving us," Tremayne said. "Hijackings of food and Idunine—that kind of operation always worked. I don't think I ever noticed that before. Probably part of his deal with them."

Lathe stepped across the bridge and stooped to pick up the weapon he'd hit Bakshi's wrist with. For a long moment he stared at the dragonhead's glittering red eyes. Then, almost savagely, he jammed the ring back onto his finger. "His job wasn't to make life easy for you—his *job* was to fight the Ryqril." He glanced at Skyler and Mordecai, nodded toward Bakshi's body, turned his back on it. "Commander, what's our ETA for the Diamond?"

"Both freighters have left orbit," the Security man reported, tapping a key on his console. Displays came to life, showing the ships' locations and projected course. "Do you want me to compute possible destinations, Colonel?"

Eakins shook his head. "They'd be foolish to head for the Novas directly. Wait until they've changed course."

"Yes, sir."

Eakins walked back to the middle of the command center, where Galway waited. "You heard?"

Galway nodded. "Any idea when the Ryqril plan to spring their trap?"

"Not really." Eakins looked back at the displays. "If *I* were the Ryq in charge, though, I would have sprung it before now. Do you suppose something's wrong?"

"I don't know." Galway's neck was beginning to ache again. "Maybe Caine would only give them a course to follow instead of the exact location. Or maybe Lathe simply outsmarted the Ryqril agent."

Eakins gave him a sharp look. "You hope he has, don't

you?" he asked in a low voice. "You'd actually like the Ryqril to lose this, wouldn't you?"

"I don't know," Galway admitted. "If I were suddenly transported to that ship with a laser in my hand I know I'd die trying to stop them. But I'm here, where I can't do anything one way or the other . . . it's hard to explain. Ever since I was prepared, my service to the Ryqril has been tied up with service to the people of Plinry. As Security prefect I maintain order partly because I've been ordered to do so, but also partly because the Ryqril would retaliate if I didn't." He nodded toward the displays. "Every failure to stop Lathe is going to cost Plinry something—even if those Corsairs out there eventually get him. But if he somehow manages to pull this off, he may be able to force them to at least go a little easier on us." He started to shake his head, but winced at the pain. "Am I making any sense?"

Eakins shook his head. "I don't know. I don't think so, really. But you've been pretty badly hurt," he added kindly. "Come on, there are a couple of cots downstairs. We can both do with some sleep, and they can't possibly get anywhere in under thirty hours."

"Yeah." But it seemed so straightforward—or it did until he tried to explain it. Was his love of his world really so hard to understand?

The hell with it. "Yeah," he repeated. "And I think I need another pill, too."

Chainbreaker I had been switched to night mode some hours previously, and as Lathe entered the bridge he was struck by how bright the stars in the display screens seemed by contrast. Some of those "stars," of course, were actually asteroids.

The bridge's single occupant turned at the sound of the opening door. "Hello, Comsquare." He nodded. "What can I do for you?"

"Your officer should have received a coded signal from the other ship within the last hour, and I wanted to make sure it was the proper one. Where is he?"

"Lieutenant Inouye's in the lounge, on break. If you'll watch the bridge, I'll be happy to go get him."

"Please."

Unstrapping his safety harness, the other got up and

left the bridge. Lathe waited a count of five after the door closed, and then set to work.

It took only a few seconds to call up the Novas' most recently updated position figures from the computer. Reaiming the communicator and adjusting it for the proper medium-tight beam took considerably longer, but it couldn't be helped: the message had to reach a large part of the Diamond without being picked up by *Chainbreaker II*, a hundred klicks to their side. But finally everything was ready. Encoding the position figures was a trivial matter of adding a fixed number to each and then rearranging their order, something he could do in his head even as he typed them into the pulse transmitter. Finished, he mentally crossed his fingers and pushed the "transmit" button five times.

He didn't wait for an acknowledgment—there wouldn't be one—but immediately cleared the pulse transmitter memory and computer display, and then reset the communicator to its original setting.

When the starman returned with Lieutenant Inouye they found him hunched over the sensor hood, searching the sky for signs of pursuit.

CHAPTER 32

"There!" Tremayne exclaimed, tapping the display screen with a finger. "That's got to be it."

Caine glanced at the two sets of numbers on the computer screen, noted the minute difference between their own present position and that of the Novas. "I think you're right," he seconded.

"Damn thing's got to be five klicks across," Nmura muttered, squinting at the irregular rock hanging in the middle of the screen. "If they've got any sensor shielding at all it could take us hours to find them."

"We only need to find one," Tremayne said grimly. "If Jensen can get the weapons working on even one we stand a chance."

Caine looked sharply at Lathe. He'd assumed the comsquare had already told Tremayne the truth about Jensen's fictitious magic touch, but it was clear that Lathe had not. "Tremayne—" he began.

"What's the latest on the Corsairs?" Lathe interrupted, giving Caine a warning look. Swallowing, Caine clamped his jaw firmly shut.

"The three coming in from Argent have an ETA of about six hours," the starman at the sensor hood said tightly. "But I can see four more drives coming in from widely different angles."

"Start the search immediately," Tremayne told Nmura. "We're cutting things pretty close already."

For Caine, the next three hours were both the longest and the shortest he'd ever spent in his life. Even with both freighters running complementary patterns over the target asteroid, the search was an exercise in slow frustration—the Novas were too well shielded and their ships too poorly equipped for rapid progress. Compounding the agony was the fact that there was nothing he personally could do to help. He was thus forced to stand by helplessly, watching the rocky surface of the asteroid crawl by on one display screen while the Corsair drive trails grew steadily brighter on the others.

It was to the drive trails that his gaze returned most frequently. The Corsairs were coming in at full power, without making any attempt at sensor shielding. Clearly, Bakshi had passed Lathe's lie on to his superiors and the Ryqril warriors were trying to beat out a deadline that didn't exist. More than once Caine wondered if Lathe had considered the possibility that the Corsairs might launch missiles from maximum range without giving the comsquare a chance to put whatever scheme he had planned into operation.

Lathe. Caine had been following the old blackcollar—had been obeying his orders or otherwise dancing to his tune—practically since his arrival on Plinry. Now, with his forced idleness giving him time to think, Caine realized the man was still largely an enigma to him. He had played a senile fool on his own world for years; then, without missing a beat, he'd become a leader with the full support of his men—men whose lives he was risking on a secret plan he wouldn't even discuss with them. Why did they follow him on such blind faith?

But, then why was Caine doing so?

Caine didn't know . . . and it was looking increasingly like he wouldn't live long enough to find out the answer to that. Or to anything else, for that matter.

"Got something!" the man at the sensor hood snapped suddenly. The helmsman didn't wait for Nmura's order, but threw the ship into emergency deceleration and began a slow reverse thrust. For a moment the air was brittle with tension. Then—"There it is, Hullmetal. . . . I think it's the bow, Commander. Wait—keep going . . . yes . . . yes, there's a second one down there, too."

"Look here," Tremayne pointed at the display screen, excitement in his voice. "You can see the outline of the cave or pit here—" he traced a barely visible curve snaking across the craggy surface—"and here. This could be one, too—I'll bet all five are right here." He looked over at Lathe. "You'd better get Jensen into a suit so he'll be ready to go the minute we find the way in. We haven't got much time."

"Actually—" Lathe glanced toward the displays—"I'm afraid I was a little dishonest with you on that. Jensen really can't do anything special with the Novas."

"What?" Tremayne's voice was soft.

"But as it happens," Lathe continued, "our time limit's no longer critical, either." He gestured toward the screens.

Caine turned to look . . . and froze at what he saw.

"Oh, my *God!*" Tremayne breathed. "Where in hell did *that* come from?"

Even to Caine the answer was obvious. The huge warship bearing down on them was moving at low speed, its drive trail diffuse and virtually invisible except at close range. Without such visual cues even the simplest sensor shielding would have been enough to hide the ship's approach from the freighter's equipment. "They must have been practically on top of us when we got here," he said mechanically. Part of him still refused to give up . . . but the rest knew it was over.

"But how could they have *known?*" Tremayne snarled. His voice showed he, too, knew they were finished.

"Because I sent them the location almost twenty hours ago," Lathe said calmly.

Caine spun to face the blackcollar, his hand falling to his laser butt. "You *what?*"

"Relax," Lathe advised, "and take another look. It's not what you think."

Frowning, Caine looked back at the screen. The warship, nearly Nova-class size itself, was growing clearer by the second as its delicately spined ellipsoid form began to fill the display.

It was Nmura who spotted it. "That's not a Ryqril design," he said, sounding puzzled. "At least not one I've ever seen."

"No reason why it should be," Lathe told him. "It's a Chryselli ship."

"A *Chryselli?*" Nmura gasped. "What in hell is a Chryselli doing *here?*"

And it all clicked together. "Dodds!" Caine whooped. "*That's* where he's been—whistling up some help!"

Lathe stepped to the communications board and made an adjustment. "Comsquare Damon Lathe aboard *Chainbreaker I* to Frank Dodds; come in, please."

Dodds had clearly been waiting; almost instantly the small communications screen came alive with his broadly smiling image. "Dodds to Lathe and *Chainbreaker I,*" his voice boomed from the speaker, sounding as relieved as Caine felt. "Glad you could make it. What's the situation?"

"We've got a number of Corsairs vectoring in on us, but I don't think they've got anything heavier in the system," Lathe said. "Can you hold them off until we get the Novas activated?"

Dodds turned his head and said something inaudible to the alien figures moving around in the background. "My hosts say it should be no problem," he said, turning back to the screen. "But you'd better get moving; we sneaked past some pretty big ships getting in and I want those Novas ready before the Ryqril send for reinforcements."

"Right." Lathe nodded to Nmura. "You heard the man, Commander. Get your teams organized and start checking those ships out. I can handle the bridge for now."

"Yes, sir." Nmura sent Tremayne a questioning look. "There's a lot of nontechnical work your people could help with, if you're willing."

"All right." Tremayne gave Lathe a look that was not quite hostile. "*With* your permission, of course, Comsquare." Turning, he followed Nmura out the door. Leaving Lathe and Caine alone with the bridge crew.

"I see your leadership style hasn't lost its old ramtank-like charm," Dodds said dryly.

"He's just a little disgruntled," Lathe said. "I'm sure he'll feel better when what we've accomplished finally hits him." He stretched tiredly and looked at Caine. "You can leave, too, if you'd like. Mordecai and the others will be down there watching out for possible collie agents, and they could probably use another pair of eyes."

Caine nodded. "Sure." He hesitated. "Before I go, though, I'd like to apologize for certain of the things I've said and thought about both of you these past few weeks. I realize now why you had to keep your plans secret, with Bakshi and the other spies still loose. But I didn't understand at the time."

Lathe waved a hand. "Forget it—you don't get a red-eyed dragon in order to become popular."

"The first time on the battlefield's always pretty rough, Caine," Dodds added. "You look like you survived okay—better than some I've seen."

"Thanks." Caine looked back at Lathe. "For the record, though, I wish you'd told us about the Chryselli ship three hours ago. By then it was too late for the Ryqril to do anything about it, and it would have done my blood pressure a *lot* of good."

"I had my reasons." Lathe shrugged.

"Mainly a promise to me," Dodds murmured unexpectedly.

"Dodds—"

"No, Lathe, it's all right," Dodds assured the blackcollar quietly. "It's bound to come out now anyway. And with these new ships the situation's considerably changed."

Caine looked back and forth between the two men . . . and the last piece of the puzzle fell into place. There was only one man Lathe could have sent to ask for Chryselli aid; only one man from Plinry who knew enough about the aliens to present the request; only one man the Chryselli themselves could conceivably have known, let alone trusted. . . .

Lathe still looked doubtful, but Dodds was studying Caine's face, and his half smile showed he knew Caine had figured it out. Squaring his shoulders, Caine faced the screen and gave Dodds his best salute. "I'm honored to meet you at last, General Lepkowski," he said. "It appears reports of your death have been somewhat premature."

CHAPTER 33

On the ship's blueprints it was the number three officers' lounge; but with its lights out and the protective hull-metal dome retracted it became a fantasy world that was part observation deck, part planetarium, and part private sanctum. The stars seemed to crowd in toward the clear plastic hemisphere, and Caine could imagine the nearest asteroids to be parts of a free-form mobile. In the near distance one of the other Novas was visible, dwarfing the two freighters lying alongside like tender-craft. Half hidden below the dome's rim he could see the Chryselli ship, maintaining its silent vigil against a resumption of the attacks that had already cost the Ryqril a half wing of Corsairs.

Unseen in the starlight, the lounge door slid open and closed. Caine tensed; but as the shadowy figure silently approached he relaxed. "Hello, Lathe," he said into the darkness.

"Hello. I thought I'd find you here." The blackcollar slid into a seat across from Caine.

Caine nodded. He'd spent a lot of time here in the past couple of days—ever since he discovered the *Novak* had such a room, as a matter of fact. It was a good place to think . . . and he had a lot of thinking to do. "What's on your mind?" he asked.

"You. I hear you're not happy with our negotiation position."

Caine sighed. "Oh, I don't know. It's all right as far as it goes, I suppose. It would be nice to open up interstellar travel a little, of course, and I certainly agree that the TDE's economy could use the boosts you're asking for. It just seems to me we could be demanding a hell of a lot more."

"Such as demanding the Ryqril pull entirely out of TDE space?"

Caine felt his face reddening. "Yeah, I suppose I was thinking that," he admitted. "I always envisioned this mission as the stroke that would bring back the pre-war TDE."

"It would have been nice," Lathe agreed. "But I'm afraid the real world doesn't work that way. If we'd demanded anything that drastic they would have had no choice but to hit us with whatever it took to destroy us. That would've gained the Chryselli a brief respite at best and gained *us* nothing at all. But don't mistake a back-door approach for surrender." Lathe's silhouette gestured toward the stars. "With the two ships we're giving the Chryselli the Ryqril war machine is going to be tied up even tighter over there, slowing their response time drastically to events in the TDE. The Novas and the eased restrictions on interstellar travel will meanwhile let us coordinate planetary resistance efforts like we never could before." In the dark Caine sensed, rather than saw, Lathe's smile. "What exactly will come out of a mixture like that I can't predict, but the point is that our end of the deal is a lot better than it looks."

"Maybe." Caine hesitated. "Tell me about Dodds."

Lathe understood. "Not much to tell, really," he said. "New Karachi was under siege, and I was assigned to get Lepkowski to a secondary command post that had been set up. We had to cut through two units of Ryqril assault troops to get through . . . it cost what was left of my squad." Even at a distance of thirty-five years Caine could hear the pain the memory evoked. "And then, half an hour later, the Groundfire attack began. When it ended so did official resistance on Plinry." He fell silent.

"So you took the general and turned him into a blackcollar?" Caine prompted.

"Yes. But not without a great deal of argument. The last shreds of his army were preparing for a final stand, and he wanted to come forward and order them to surrender instead." Lathe sighed. "His silence cost a lot of men their lives. I think probably that's why we never told anyone else his true identity, not even the other blackcollars. The secret had cost both of us a great deal, and we were damned if we were going to take even the slightest risk with it."

"I think I understand," Caine said.

"I doubt it," Lathe returned, not unkindly. "You won't really understand until you've held a command of your own." He paused. "What are you planning to do when we leave here? Go back to Earth?"

That question had occupied a good deal of Caine's thought lately. "I don't know," he confessed. "It's my home, and I can't think of any place I'd rather fight the Ryqril. But. . . ." He trailed off.

"You're not still mad at them for not telling you you're a clone, are you?"

"Oh, no. I don't think so, anyway. It's just that if the government really did crack the top level of the Resistance just before I left, then everyone I ever knew is probably dead or in prison. I'd be completely on my own."

"Nothing wrong with that, is there?"

"Only if I intend to get anything done." Caine smiled tautly. "You're forgetting I was intended to be a one-shot weapon. I was trained for exactly one purpose: to impersonate Alain Rienzi and do whatever damage I could before getting caught. Well, I've done that, and now my programming's run out. No one ever taught me more general skills, like how to organize my own underground or how to plan and carry out missions. Or even how to fade into the general populace while the enemy's hunting me, for that matter."

"You think the Ryqril will be out to get you?"

"I doubt that the leniency concessions you've wangled for Plinry and Argent will apply to me," Caine said dryly. "I also doubt they realize how minor a threat I actually am."

"Well, we can't have them acting on false assumptions, can we?" Lathe said. "Perhaps you'd like to come back to Plinry with us."

For a long moment Caine was sorely tempted. Sanctuary among the blackcollars. . . . "Thanks, but no," he said, almost regretfully. "I'd just be in the way."

"You don't understand—I'm not offering you a place to hide. Lepkowski's going to need trained guerrilla fighters, and Plinry seems the logical place to set up shop, at least for now. We've got the best teachers in the TDE; what we need now is promising students."

"You mean . . . full blackcollar training?"

"As full as we can make it. Understand, though—without the Backlash drug we can't make you into a true blackcollar." Lathe hesitated. "And you should also recognize that you'll be setting yourself up for even more trouble from the Ryqril this way. I understand Galway's already on his way back to Plinry, and he'll be watching us like a hungry fan-dragon."

But the Ryqril were already gunning for him . . . and it occurred to Caine that if the formula for the Backlash drug existed anywhere anymore it was probably on Earth. A worthwile target to go after—possibly even more valuable than five Nova-class ships, in the right hands. And Caine had a pretty good idea whose hands those would be. "All right, you're on," he told Lathe's silhouette. "Just make sure I can get back to Earth after my training—and remember that I'll need a supply of that anti-asthma drug while I'm on Plinry."

"No problem," Lathe said without hesitation. "I've already ordered the lab to mix up a truckload of the stuff for you."

Caine stared at him. "Pretty sure of yourself, aren't you? What if I'd said no?"

"Then I'd be stuck with a truckload of histrophyne," the other said. "But I thought you'd say yes. We're a lot alike, you know, you and I." He stood up and moved toward the door. "Your first class is tomorrow at nine o'clock in the aft ready room; see you there." The door slid open and closed and he was gone.

For a moment Caine gazed after him, feeling the warmth of the other's compliment. A lot like Lathe, was he? High praise indeed—and he was going to do his damnedest to live up to it.

Looking up at the stars; he smiled wryly. The Ryqril didn't know it yet, but they were in big trouble.